WINTERBOURNE

Susan Carroll

WINTERBOURNE

WHEELER
PUBLISHING, INC.
ROCKLAND, MA

★ AN AMERICAN COMPANY ★

Published in Large Print by arrangement with The Ballantine Publishing Group, a division of Random House, Inc., in the United States and Canada.

Wheeler Large Print Book Series.

Set in 16 pt Plantin.

Library of Congress Cataloging-in-Publication Data

Carroll, Susan, 1952–
    Winterbourne / Susan Carroll.
        p. (large print) cm.(Wheeler large print book series)
    ISBN 1-56895-752-1 (hardcover)
    1. Large type books.
I. Title. II. Series
[PS3553.A7654W56   1999]
813'.54—dc21

99-31997
CIP

To my children, Ricky and Serena

Chapter 1

THE WIND BUFFETED the gray stonework like some giant hand seeking to batter down Winterbourne, the one place in all England Lady Melyssan had found shelter. As she struggled up the curving stair to the walkway atop the castle walls, the gusts tugged at her skirts and whistled past her ears, hissing a warning: "Escape. Escape before he returns." He—Lord Jaufre de Macy—the man whom his enemies named *Le Chevalier Noir Sans Mercie— the Dark Knight Without Mercy.*

She trembled in the gathering gloom of twilight and limped to an embrasure in the heavy wall. Down below, the dusty road snaked through the distant village, winding its way to the gates of Castle Winterbourne. The sun had nearly set with no sign of the tall, powerful man astride the black destrier. Lord Jaufre was not coming. She was safe for one more day.

Melyssan swept back the tangled strands of silken brown hair the wind whipped against the pale oval of her face. Aye, she was safe— but for how much longer if she remained at Winterbourne, dreading Lord Jaufre's return? And yet...

Wistfulness clouded her sea-green eyes as she looked again to reassure herself that the road was deserted. A small group of peasants cut across the fields to bear a long white bundle to the ditch. Even at this distance

Melyssan knew it was a corpse enshrouded in a winding sheet.

Crossing herself, she murmured a brief prayer, her heart going out to the tiny figures below. Nearly four years had come and gone since anyone had had a proper burial in England. The pope's interdict had closed the doors of every church in the land. When King John had come last summer to the convent at St. Clare, Melyssan had been emboldened to plead with him, "My liege, is there nothing you can do? Surely what the pope asks is not so... I mean—that is—I have heard Stephen Langton is a very learned man."

She would never have dared to speak thus, except that John Plantagenet had seemed so kind, so pious, bringing his magnificent gift of a golden altar cloth to St. Clare. Melyssan had soon realized her mistake as his face darkened with anger.

"Langton will keep his learning out of England lest he wishes his neck stretched on a gibbet!" the king had shouted. "Rome will not dictate who will be my archbishop, not even if we all rot in hell first."

Shaking, Melyssan had retreated, but then the king's bad mood changed abruptly. His thin lips had twisted into a smile as he'd reached for her hand, his wide-set eyes glistening.

"But what serious counsel to come from the lips of such a lovely lady," he'd purred. "Come to my chamber at midnight, my pretty one, and we will discuss these matters further."

She had fled from the chapel, fled from

the convent all the way home, praying the king would forget he'd ever seen her. But he had not. He had followed her to Wydevale.

And that was when her nightmare had begun.

Melyssan leaned on her staff and drew back from the opening to huddle behind one of the sheltering merlons. Despite her halting step, she moved with a certain grace born of seventeen years coping with a foot malformed from the moment of her birth.

As she clutched the smooth, rounded top of her cane, the band encircling her third finger dug into her flesh, a constant reminder of her dangerous deception. Even in the half-light of dusk the ring gleamed, the wedding ring she had placed there herself to give credence to her lie.

When Lord Jaufre returned, as she knew he soon must, he would likely yank the false symbol from her finger. And then what? The question that haunted her dreams now forced its way into her mind. What would he do when he returned and discovered that she had dared to pass herself off as his wife? Her younger sister, Beatrice, swore that Jaufre had ordered his lovely bride, Yseult, hanged without so much as charging her with a crime. Was that only more of Bea's exaggerations, or could there be some truth in the tale?

The tremor that shot through Melyssan's slender frame was not entirely due to the biting wind. Her hand flew involuntarily to her throat. The braided chain she wore there felt

3

as if it were growing tighter. Would the Dark Knight show her no mercy as well? He had been her champion once in a time long ago, a time before Yseult.

Fingers crept from out of the shadows behind her to rest lightly on her shoulder. Melyssan gasped and twisted around, nearly losing her balance. Features confronted her, not so dissimilar from her own—the same aquiline nose, delicate jawline, golden-brown hair, and green eyes.

"Whitney! You frightened me."

"Did you not hear me approaching?" asked her brother. "I took no pains to conceal my footsteps."

"I—I—'tis only my thoughts were far away."

Whitney joined her behind the protective barrier. He tugged his mantle more closely around a pair of shoulders too narrow, a consequence of the many times he had avoided his practice with sword and quintain. Though he was Melyssan's senior by two years, they were near of a height, and Melyssan often feared the strength of his limbs was no greater than her own.

"I have been looking everywhere for you," Whitney said. "No one would tell me where you had gone. That old badger Sir Dreyfan even had the boldness to say, 'If the lady was wishful of your company, she would have told ye where to find her.'" Her brother imitated the old knight's voice with great bitterness.

Melyssan placed a soothing hand on his arm. "I am sorry, Whitney. I am sure he did not mean to be churlish. He suffers from keen disappointment that Lord Jaufre left him here to command the castle garrison instead of accompanying my lord and his grandfather, the comte, on the mission to Saxony."

Whitney's eyes shifted nervously, as they always did at the mention of Jaufre's name. He continued to scowl, and she thought of remonstrating with Sir Dreyfan, only to dismiss the notion. Her gentle interference would do naught to secure for Whitney the respect he must win for himself.

"What are you doing up here on the walls this late in the evening? I am not sure it is safe for you...." His words trailed off as his gaze lowered to her foot.

"I was looking out at the fields." She stepped away from him and stood in the embrasure, allowing the wind to blow her hair and shield her face from her brother. "A pretty sight, is it not? The harvest is going well."

Whitney reached out and drew her back to his side. He smoothed the curls from her brow. "You were watching the road again, Lyssa. You were looking for *him*."

She did not attempt to deny it, meeting his admonishing gaze with defiance. His fingers gripped her upper arms. "This is madness. When will you permit me to take you away from here? We could be with Enid at Kingsbury Plain within a fortnight."

Melyssan compressed her lips and shook her head. Although Enid was her favorite sister, it had been several years since she had seen her.

"Enid is newly wed, happy at last. I have no wish to embroil her in my problems."

"Then let me take you home or back to the convent. Anywhere miles from here! Each day that you linger only increases your risk of being caught."

"Aye, we must leave soon. Mayhap...next week."

His hands dropped away from her. "I don't understand you. When we first came to Winterbourne, it was only to be a temporary escape from the persecution of the king. Yet you have made one excuse after another to stay. I've seen you becoming more and more involved with Lord Jaufre's affairs until I've become afraid you have run mad and think you truly are his wife."

"Nay, Whitney. I am sane enough." But as her eyes wandered past him to the darkened courtyard below, she acknowledged her own doubts. Although the buildings down in the bailey appeared as indistinguishable looming shapes, a summer spent in this stronghold on the Welsh border enabled her easily to identify them all. The large barns, the stables, the mews that housed my lord's falcons, the herb and flower garden, the great donjon whose dazzling white tower could be seen for miles...she knew the location of each as well as she had known any part of her father's estate. And in many ways, despite the danger she risked of being exposed as an imposter, she

6

felt more at home here at Winterbourne than she ever had under the critical eye of her mother.

"...and I wish I could have such faith in your sanity." She became aware that Whitney was still scolding her. "We should have been gone the second day, not stayed out the summer."

"But after I had my lord's steward driven off—"

"That is another thing I still cannot believe you did, my sweet Lyssa. I was wont to think you were my quiet, gentle sister, and yet you are proving to be more foolhardy than Enid or Beatrice ever were."

"Pevensy was robbing Jaufre—I mean, my lord—blind. And he made Winterbourne not fit for pigs to live in."

"It was not your concern. Do you think Lord Jaufre will thank you for taking over his castle?" Whitney snorted. "If so, I suppose I must bow to your superior knowledge of the man, and we will merrily await his return. After all, you have spent much time in his company and I only met him once."

"I know him little better than you do," she said in a small voice. "I was with him perhaps a half dozen times." As she spoke Melyssan was assailed by a memory of Jaufre's beard abrading her skin as velvet lips pressed against the beating pulse of her neck. She quivered and hoped that the descending night concealed her flushed countenance.

Whitney removed his mantle and placed it around her shoulders. "You puzzle me greatly,

Lyssa. You tell me you fear Lord Jaufre's wrath and yet you will not run away."

Melyssan reached inside her gown and drew forth the heavy ring she wore suspended from her chain. Lord Jaufre's seal. It had been there ever since the day she had discovered her sister Beatrice had stolen it. Bea had been Jaufre's choice for a second wife, but she had betrayed the Dark Knight, jilting him only weeks before the wedding, seeking sanctuary at St. Clare.

Melyssan traced the intricate design of the hawk on the flat surface of the signet ring. How strange that something so small should have had the power to alter her life. If she had never gone to the convent to recover the ring from Beatrice, she would never have fallen under the lecherous eye of the king. She would never have lied and claimed to be secretly wed to Jaufre, using possession of the ring as her proof. "I have been thinking," she said, "that perhaps the just thing to do would be to stay and face Lord Jaufre, try to explain to him."

"The just thing?" Whitney gave an incredulous laugh. "Oh, Lyssa. Your honor threatened by a tyrant king, your freedom, perhaps your very life, threatened by a lord who already has reason enough to loathe our family, thanks to Beatrice, and you talk of being just." He tucked the mantle more closely around her. "I would I had your courage, little sister." His voice grew bitter with self-contempt. "But then if I had, you would not be in this predicament."

"What could you have done against the power of the king?" she protested. "It would have been so easy for him to have you accused of treason. Carry out the vile things he hinted. Jaufre's name was all that could have saved us."

"That is what was so odd, my dear. You in your innocence believe the king did not dishonor you because he thought you a married woman. I know better. That never stopped him before." He frowned. "No, something else is at work here, something between the king and Lord Jaufre that we don't quite understand. You have dissuaded me long enough, Lyssa. Now I am going to do what I should have done months ago and get you away from here."

He swooped her up awkwardly in his arms to carry her to the gateway tower and down the winding stone steps. Melyssan stiffened, gripping her cane. She hated to be carried, hated the pity that the gesture implied; but when she saw the look on his pale face—determination tinged with fear—she held her tongue.

He set her on her feet when they reached the courtyard. Overhead, the clear black sky was lit by a crescent of moon and a scattering of stars, cold, distant, like Jaufre de Macy's eyes the last time she had looked into them.

"Mayhap you are right, Whitney," she said. "We will leave tomorrow."

But as she gave her promise, somehow she sensed that it would never be. She tucked the ring back inside her gown, feeling its weight chain her to Winterbourne even as my lord's falcon was chained to its perch in the mews. She could never escape.

Melyssan writhed amidst a tangle of furs and linen sheets as the fragments of a nightmare pierced her peaceful slumber. It was always the same—hands clawing at her, pulling her off balance. Hands that belonged to bodies without faces...except of late one face was beginning to emerge, a face with dark leering eyes, a cruel sensual mouth. John of England. Her dread sovereign lord, the king. The hands snatched away her walking staff and grabbed hold of her. Struggling helplessly, she was tumbled down into the filthy straw as the king's greedy fingers tore at her breasts like the talons of a hawk, drawing blood.

She screamed and cried out for her brother, the king's mocking laughter echoing in her ears. Whitney was being dragged away, the glow of the hot irons reflected in his terrified eyes. *No...no! Help me! Help me!* The king's mouth smothered her cries with his fetid breath. Her arms flailed helplessly against him.

Then he was there. The tall knight garbed in blue and gold, the falcon crest on his helmet. Jaufre, his ebony hair waving back from the broad plane of his brow, the hard line of his granite-hewn jawline softening as he smiled. But before she could call his name, his features shifted, blurred, until he was no one she recognized. Only another of those faceless forms. The king's weight bore down upon her.

10

"No!" Melyssan sobbed, fighting her way back to wakefulness. She blinked and lay gasping until her mind slowly accepted the fact that King John was no more than the feather pillow sprawled across her chest. With shaking fingers, she flung it aside and sat up. She was alone in Jaufre de Macy's massive timber-framed bed.

She rubbed her eyes to clear away the last vestiges of the dream, then pushed aside the crimson bed curtains. The phantoms had fled with their cruel pushing hands, leaving only the form of her lady-in-waiting, Nelda, slumbering on her straw pallet, and the glow of the fire that had been banked in the hearth. As the rush of cool air assaulted her naked skin, raising goose-flesh, she replaced the curtains and tunneled beneath the furs. She hated the dream, hated the feeling of helplessness it recalled. Though her eyes felt heavy, she stared into the darkness, straining to keep awake. The nightmare lurked in the shadows, waiting for her to drift back into its embrace.

The only way to fight it was to create her own dream—force her mind toward more pleasant imaginings. She had done it ever since she was a child, weaving fantasies in her head. At one time she was Guinevere with Sir Launcelot riding to slay dragons in her honor. Or she was a dazzlingly beautiful lady at the Court of Love, accomplished in composing songs, noted for her graceful movements in the dance....

Tonight she closed her eyes and pretended

that she truly was the mistress of Winter-bourne, eagerly awaiting the return of her lord. As eagerly as Jaufre would ride to return to her. Not Jaufre as he was now, hard, cynical, but the gay young man he had been the first time she had seen him.

Melyssan snuggled deeper into the soft nest of furs. The memory of that day remained clear in her mind, even though she had been but a child of nine years. The baron de Scoville, her father's liege lord, had held a great tournament in honor of the knighting of his eldest son. As a rare treat, she and her sisters were permitted to accompany their parents on the short journey, although much against her mother's wishes.

"Take Enid and Beatrice if you must," Dame Alice had said. "But not Melyssan. Do you wish all the great lords and ladies of the land to be gawking at her foot?" Her mother had rolled her eyes and launched into her familiar plaint. "I am a God-fearing woman. What sin was mine that one of my children should be so accursed? Better that she had died instead of Nancy."

"Yes, yes, but she did not," Sir William had replied wearily, "and since she is to be walled up alive in a convent one day, what is the harm in her having a little amusement now?" Her father had reached down to give her a careless pat on the head. "Poor little cripple-foot."

And so she was permitted to go, although with strict orders to stay as much out of sight and do as little walking as possible. Perhaps what happened to her was God's punishment for disobeying her mother....

She and Beatrice slipped away from their nurse and made their way to the field, where the draped stands and the lists had been erected. Ladies and knights bedecked in silk tunics and surcoats trimmed with ermine and sable moved among the tents, laughing, some even dancing to the tunes of a wandering minstrel. Squires bustled about harnessing up their masters' sleek chargers. Bea, although only seven, soon attracted a crowd of young pages. She was already a little beauty with her long blond hair and cerulean-blue eyes. The boys outdid themselves in their efforts to show off for her and surpass each other in wit.

One plump, freckled lad, noting Melyssan's awkward gait, sang out, "Why, she walks like a crane, a pettigrew." He flapped imaginary wings and imitated that bird's exaggerated manner of placing one foot before the other.

The others roared with laughter. "Mistress Pettigrew. Mistress Pettigrew," the boys chanted. Even Bea put a hand to her mouth and collapsed into a fit of giggling.

Tears stung Melyssan's eyes until, unable to bear the torment any longer, she swung her cane at the freckled boy. He promptly grabbed it and yanked it away from her.

"Give that back!" she cried shrilly, flinging herself at him.

The boys tossed her cane from one to the

other, easily keeping it out of her reach as they pushed her among them, holding her up so that she teetered like a helpless doll. Her tears flowed freely, blinding her, as she stumbled forward onto her face.

Deep sobs racking her, she placed her palms flat against the earth and tried to push herself up. She flinched as something went whirling past her. The freckled page landed in the dirt, wailing and holding his ear.

"Mannerless whelps," growled a deep voice. "Is this how you treat a lady? And you expect one day that you will become knights? I will see the lot of you cowards whipped. Now be off and out of my sight."

The boys scattered, even the freckled lad scrambling to his feet and fleeing as if he had just seen the devil. Melyssan felt herself lifted and set upon her feet. The cane was pressed back into her shaking hand. A man's fingertips, rough with calluses, smoothed back her hair and brushed the moisture and dirt from her cheeks.

When she dared to look up, her breath caught in her throat. Bending over her was Sir Launcelot, stepped straight out of her dreams. His hair was blue-black as a starless midnight. Thick-fringed lashes framed a pair of twinkling brown eyes that warmed her like fire.

"Are you hurt, my lady?" he asked in that richly timbred voice that was like balm to her wounded feelings.

She shook her head, too stunned by the mere proximity of such a godlike being to

14

make reply. She could only stare at him as he straightened her tunic. His eye fell inevitably upon her foot, the special leather boot disguising little of its strange shape. She began to cry anew, and one tear dropped from her cheek to fall upon his hand.

"Nay, my lady, you must not weep," he said. "Would you let such pearls as these fall upon the insensible ground?" He raised his hand to where the drop had fallen and kissed it. Then, to her astonishment, he dropped to one knee before her, his smooth-shaven face now at a level with her own.

"Permit me to make myself known to you, my lady. One Jaufre de Macy, a humble knight who had sighted you from afar and been so moved by your beauty, I am come to seek your favor."

Her surprise at these words brought her hiccuping sobs to a halt. She peered suspiciously at him. "You—you are teasing me?"

"Nay, my lady, and to prove it, I will not rise from this spot until you give me leave."

She looked into his deep brown eyes but could find not a trace of mockery, only kindness. A rustling movement nearby told her that Beatrice stood watching. When Melyssan glanced at her, she saw that her younger sister was gaping at her with newfound respect.

Flicking back one long tress over her shoulder, she arched her neck proudly. "You may rise, my lord."

But still he knelt. "First, I would beg my favor of thee, fair one."

Graciously she inclined her head. "What is it, my lord?"

"Some small token that I might carry with me into the tournament today so that my vanquished opponents will come to pay homage to the beauty of my lady...?"

"Melyssan," she whispered, and then, "I could give you my veil." With trembling fingers, she tugged the head covering free from her gilt circlet and handed the gossamer silk to Sir Jaufre. He rose to his feet and gravely accepted the token.

"God grant you victory today, Sir Launcelot," she said solemnly.

Smiling, he carried her small hand to his lips and brushed it with a gentle kiss. Then he chucked her under the chin and strode away to mount his horse....

Melyssan burrowed her head into the pillow as the memory faded. The little girl was gone, as was the courtly young man who had knelt at her feet and banished her tears. He had never been able to keep his pledge of having the other knights bow down to her. Long before the tournament began, Melyssan had been hustled away by her nurse. Scolded for losing her veil, she was sent to bed supperless, though later her older sister, Enid, had contrived to smuggle some cheese to her. And Jaufre's heart had been captured by Lady Yseult of the fair skin and indigo eyes.

Melyssan groaned softly and rolled onto her back. Often she had dreamed of how things might have been different, if only she had been older that day, if only Lady Yseult had not been present at the tournament to bewitch Lord Jaufre. If only...

Melyssan glanced down toward her foot and sighed. She played this game of wistful imaginings too often. It took away the sting of truth for a moment but only made facing the facts doubly hard.

For the reality was Jaufre had married Yseult, and by the next time she saw him, Yseult was dead. Melyssan's shining young knight had turned into a harsh, bitter man who would not be moved by the tears of a child in distress any more than he would by those of a woman.

He had ridden north early last summer to pay court to her sister Beatrice, much to the surprise and delight of her parents. It was a matter of wonder that such a great lord, heir to large estates in Normandy and England, earl of Winterbourne in his own right, should seek the daughter of a humble knight to be his second wife....

Dame Alice turned the manor house inside out preparing for Lord Jaufre's coming. It was with the greatest reluctance that she made Melyssan's presence known to him at all. Shyly, Melyssan stepped forward to greet him. Eight years had not dimmed her remembrance of him, but she saw no trace of recognition on the earl's countenance.

His face had grown lean and hard, the lower portion covered with a trim black beard. Lines etched deep into his forehead and around the eyes. Those merry brown eyes

17

that once had warmed her were now as cold and empty as a hearth where the fire has died.

Lord Jaufre spent most of his visit with her father, arranging the details of the marriage contract. Melyssan thought him almost unaware of her existence, although at times she caught him staring at her, his expression unreadable. Few words passed between them until the evening she and Beatrice lingered overlong in the garden.

The warm June twilight was heady with the fragrance of roses just beginning to blossom, mingled with the scent of rosemary, sage, sweet fennel. Melyssan sank onto a wooden bench, weary from trying to reconcile Beatrice to her forthcoming marriage with Lord Jaufre. In truth, her heart was not in the task.

"I won't marry him, Lyssa. He's old, nearly thirty-five, and I hate dark men," Bea stormed. "Enid chose her own husband. Why shouldn't I?"

Melyssan sighed. "Our sister was a very wealthy widow. Providing she did not offend the king, she was free to marry again as she pleased. It is different for you. I am sure that in time—"

"No! He's a horrid, cold-hearted man. I loathe him. He had Lady Yseult hanged. I want to marry Aubrey." Bea sniffed. "You don't understand what 'tis like to be in love, Lyssa. Someone like you could never understand." Her sister ran out of the garden before she could say another word.

Mayhap Bea is right, Melyssan thought as she stood up, placing her staff directly in front of her. She leaned on it with both hands, stretching the stiffness out of her limbs. Mayhap I don't understand. I know nothing of love, nor am I likely ever to find out.

The time was rapidly approaching when she would be expected to join the order of sisters at St. Clare's. She should have entered the convent long ago, but surprisingly, her mother had found one excuse after another to detain her at home. Melyssan had not objected. She was troubled to find she did not view the prospect of dedicating her life to God with the joy expected of her. How could she take such vows when of late her peace was constantly troubled by strange longings, longings to which she could not put a name?

Footsteps behind her put an end to her disturbing reverie, but before she could turn around, she heard Jaufre's deep voice disconcertingly close behind her.

"Ah, there you are, my betrothed. I find you alone at last."

Melyssan opened her mouth to correct his error, but his arms encircled her from behind, his hands cupping her breasts. She gasped as she felt the heat of his fingers even through the layers of her kirtle and chemise. Starting from the sensitive area behind her ear, his lips caressed a path to the base of her neck.

The words she had been about to utter died in her throat, and her cane clattered to the ground as she brought her own hands up to cover his. She felt peculiarly weak, unable to pry his fingers away and instead found that she pressed him more tightly against her. Her mind whirled from the warm sensation of his mouth gliding along her flesh. She turned slightly in his arms until she faced him. Melyssan felt him start as he recognized her, but still he did not let go. His lips parted and he brought them nearer, ever nearer. She opened her eyes wide, measuring the depth of his gaze.

Then he jerked back, releasing her so suddenly she staggered. He had to grip her by the elbow to prevent her from falling.

"I'm sorry," he said gruffly. "The veil concealed your hair. I thought you were Beatrice."

Melyssan did not reply. She knew she should be covered with confusion, furious at him for making such a stupid error. Yet she was incapable of remonstrating. She felt most unlike her usual calm self, as if Jaufre's touch had awakened her from a dream, stirring feelings she had not known she possessed. Never had she felt so...so alive.

"I...I am not Beatrice," she said foolishly. She had never envied her beautiful younger sister, but at that moment she thought she would have given her soul to have changed places with her.

"A ridiculous mistake on my part. I most humbly beg my lady's pardon." Lord Jaufre bent to retrieve her staff. As he straightened and placed it in her hand, it was a strange playing out of an earlier scene. A sad half smile crossed Jaufre's face, and a trace of warmth crept into his brown eyes, tempered with an expression of deep hidden pain that had not been there before. What had Yseult and the world done to her Launcelot, Melyssan wondered unhappily, in those eight years since he had carried her veil to the tournament?

"Do not distress yourself," she said, lightly touching his hand. "I understand."

He drew back immediately, as if her fingertips had seared him. A cold mask settled over his features.

"How good of you to be so understanding, my lady," he replied sneeringly. "But you should take care. Such generous *understanding* might be misconstrued as an invitation for more 'errors.'"

He made a mocking bow and left her feeling hurt by his cynical dismissal and embarrassed by her own eager response to his embrace....

The memory of it still brought a heated blush to her cheeks even now as she pressed herself against the linen sheets, sheets where Jaufre had once lain. Whitney was right: she must get away from Winterbourne. Even worse than the nightmare, Jaufre had begun to haunt her waking moments as well. It was becoming more and more difficult to lose herself in the old daydreams, where the young Jaufre humbly knelt at her feet, pledging his devotion. More and more she saw him standing very close to her, his eyes hard, dangerous, his hands...

Melyssan crossed her arms over her breasts, shifting restlessly. The springs of interlaced ropes creaked as sleep eluded her. She tried to close her eyes, ready now to banish all thought and will herself back into the oblivion of a deep, dreamless slumber.

But she was disturbed by the sound of the heavy oak door to her chamber scraping against the rushes. A low voice whispered her name. "Lady Melyssan? My lady?"

Her eyes opened at once, and she could detect a soft glow of light through a slit in the bed curtains. Cautiously she parted them and peeked out without revealing herself.

An eerie figure robed in black stood just inside the doorway. The tallow candle gripped in his hand illuminated his long melancholy face.

"Father Andrew?" Melyssan called softly in astonishment.

Her brother's thin chaplain held a finger to his lips and motioned toward the sleeping Nelda. Then he beckoned Melyssan to join him and glided out of the room.

Mystified, and more than a little alarmed, Melyssan scrambled into her chemise and woolen gown. Slipping her feet into a pair of soft leather pattens, she groped for her cane, then inched cautiously past Nelda. She stepped out into the adjoining oriel, pulling the heavy door closed behind her.

The wall torch had long ago burned itself out, and the only light came from the priest's candlestick.

"Forgive me for disturbing your rest, my

lady," he whispered. "But it is a matter of some importance and secrecy."

"W-what is it?" Melyssan asked. "Has something happened to Whitney?"

"No, my lady. Your brother knows naught of this. The stranger that just arrived asked only for you."

"Stranger," she repeated, a chill prickling up her spine. What sort of stranger would risk travel by night and then seek her out in such a clandestine manner?

"I don't think..." she began, shrinking back.

"I was told to give you this." The priest held out a small scrap of linen. With unsteady fingers, she accepted it. He moved the candle closer so that she could examine the cloth. Tiny threads of gold and green embroidered a square of pristine white, stitches that she had set there herself not so long ago, a gift to a bride on her wedding day.

"Where is the lady that gave you this?" she demanded.

"Below in the cellars."

"Take me to her at once."

On the ground-level floor of the donjon, the flambeau still burned, periodically sending out small showers of sparks. The dank cold air enfolded Melyssan, causing her to regret she had not taken the time to go back for her mantle. But the strangeness of her visitor's arrival and the urgency in the priest's voice drew her on.

They approached that part of the castle

where the very edge of the river flowed past the massive iron portcullis of the west gateway. She could hear water lapping against the stone. Winterbourne had been built to control passage along the river and to take advantage of it as a source of transportation. Supplies could thus be floated directly inside the donjon itself.

One of the guards caught sight of Melyssan and came forward blustering. "Beg pardon, my lady. But I never would have let 'em in. It was that priest there insistin'. Who but the devil's servants, says I, dare take to the road at night? I says—"

"Thank you, Master Galvan," Melyssan interrupted him. "You may return to your post."

He continued his protestations, but she stepped around him. She could see two adults and a tiny child huddled near the great casks where the wine was stored. When the guard was out of hearing range, Melyssan took the small end of candle from Father Andrew.

"Thank you, Father. I will tend to matters from here."

The priest nodded. "When you need me, I will be in the chapel...praying."

So he already knew what was amiss, Melyssan thought as she watched his quiet retreat. Well, it was time someone told her.

As she approached the strangers whose hoods and caps hid their faces from her sight, one of them ran forward, clutching a bundle in her arms.

"Oh, my lady!" cried a female voice familiar

to Melyssan. She flung back her hood, revealing a young face more kindly than beautiful, with a round, receding chin, broad, flat nose, and normally placid gray eyes now widened with fear.

"Gunnor," Melyssan exclaimed. "So it is you." She had not seen Dame Alice's former lady-in-waiting since Gunnor's wedding day.

The other figure now stepped forward, leading the child by the hand. Beneath the grime and his broad-brimmed straw hat, Melyssan recognized Gunnor's husband.

"Sir Hugh," she murmured. The bundle stirred in Gunnor's arms. "And these are your little ones?" Melyssan asked, considerably bemused by their ragged appearance.

Lady Gunnor clutched at her sleeve, her reply lost in a bout of weeping. Sir Hugh swallowed, his huge Adam's apple bobbing up and down his long, scrawny neck. "We—we regret this intrusion, my lady. We were obliged to flee from my estate at Penhurst and—and Winterbourne was the closest...We knew not where else to go."

"Aye, the king's men are ev-everywhere," Gunnor managed to choke out.

At the mention of the king, Melyssan froze. "King John?" she asked in a whisper.

Sir Hugh's scraggly beard stood on end as he attempted a feeble smile. "Gunnor exaggerates a little. It is not so bad as all that. If we could only get to Ireland. I have cousins there."

Melyssan's head spun with mingled dread

and confusion. But she noticed the child, a small boy of about three, shivering, and bit back the host of questions crowding upon her tongue.

"Let me take you up to the solar, and I will have a fire lit," she said.

Gunnor's moist eyes rolled fearfully. "Can you trust your people here? If we should be betrayed—" Her voice broke again.

"Is the king trying to arrest you?" Melyssan asked, no longer able to restrain herself. "What does he say you have done?"

Gunnor broke out into a wild laugh. "'Tis nothing that we have done. But my brother, Adelard...my holy brother has undone us all." She buried her face against her baby's blanket, leaving Sir Hugh to take up the explanation.

"Adelard has run mad," he said. "He joined the order of Cistercian monks at Swineshead. The king offered to secure his election as abbot, and what must the fellow do but denounce John before the whole court. He said that since John is excommunicate, he can appoint no one. Adelard even refused to speak directly to the king for fear of contamination."

Melyssan closed her eyes, picturing the scene in her mind. She could not help but admire the monk's courage. She well knew what it took to defend one's honor in the face of a king. The old sensation of panic crept over her, feelings of being pressed on all sides, by the king's hot, leering gaze, by the accusation in Dame Alice's eye as she berated her daughter for inciting the king's lust, by her father's

26

indifference, and most of all by Whitney's white-faced fear as John had complimented him on his handsome eyes—all the while prodding the poker into the fire.

"...and after Adelard fled to safety in Scotland, the king accused me." Sir Hugh's whining voice snapped Melyssan back to the present. "The king accused all of us of treason, of conspiring to smuggle Stephen Langton into England against his wishes. He demanded our children as hostages to insure our good behavior. We refused." The knight concluded his story with a helpless wave of his hand. "And...well, here we are."

Gunnor raised her head and regarded Melyssan piteously. "Dare you help us, shelter us for a day until we can gather up our strength to continue our journey to Ireland?"

"Of course I will help," Melyssan said. "How could you even doubt it?"

Gunnor shifted the baby nervously to her other arm. "'Tis well known your husband is the king's man. He might not like it an he returns to find you helping accused traitors escape."

"I am sure Jaufre..." Melyssan began, and then stopped. She was sure of nothing where Jaufre was concerned. "In any event, it matters naught," she continued. "Lord Jaufre...er, my husband is across the Channel traveling somewhere in Saxony."

Lady Gunnor and Sir Hugh exchanged an uneasy glance. Sir Hugh cleared his throat. "Then you have not heard?"

"Heard what?" Melyssan asked, her pulse beginning to beat unaccountably faster. Somehow she already knew what Sir Hugh was about to say.

"When we left London, the entire court was buzzing with the news. My lady, your husband landed at Dover last week. He will arrive here any day now."

Chapter 2

ONE MONTH EARLIER, even as Melyssan imagined herself to be safe, Jaufre de Macy, earl of Winterbourne, stretched his aching limbs out on his bed at the Château Le Vis and wondered how soon his grandfather would be well enough to cross the Channel over to England.

Jaufre longed for Winterbourne almost as much as he longed to get some sleep, if it would please the lady Finette to allow him to do so. He rolled over onto his side, his broad dark-haired chest matted with sweat, every muscle in his body aching from the day's hard ride into Normandy. Finette only pressed her damp body closer to his back. Her long fingernails scored a path along his powerful thigh, inching toward the glistening shaft between his legs.

He caught her wrist and shoved the hand back at her. "Twice is enough. I am weary and would sleep."

"But, Jaufre..." she whined, nuzzling his ear.

"Have done, Finette," he growled, and brushed her away as if she were an annoying gadfly. He pulled the satin sheet tightly around him, isolating his body from hers.

Finette sighed. "Very well. Until tomorrow, then, my sweet." She bent over and pecked him on the cheek.

Jaufre winced, waiting impatiently for her to leave him so that he could at last close his stinging eyelids and drift off into peaceful oblivion. When she snuggled happily down on the pillow next to his own, he propped himself into a sitting position and glared at her. "What the devil do you think you are doing?"

The lady brushed a thick mass of chestnut hair out of her face before replying, "I am going to sleep. What else?"

"Not here you are not." Jaufre caught her by the elbow and hauled her up beside him.

Finette gave a throaty laugh and attempted to entwine her arms around his neck. "And why not? I thought that in the morning we could—"

"No! I will have to attend upon my grandfather. He did not look well when he retired from your table this evening."

"So? You are not a physician. And I have seen to the old man's comfort. I gave up my own chamber for his use. Of course I thought I would be sleeping elsewhere." Her wide red lips curved into a pretty pout. She tried to kiss him, but Jaufre pried himself free and pushed her away.

"Out!"

Finette gasped and drew herself to a kneeling position on the bed. Even in the dying firelight, Jaufre could see her large breasts swaying with her indignation. "You forget whom you are addressing. I am a noblewoman, not some peasant girl you have carted off for a romp in the fields."

"I do not share my bed with any woman, noble or otherwise." He fingered the long white scar running from the base of his neck down to the region of his heart. A legacy from his beautiful departed Yseult and a permanent warning of the dangers of sleeping too soundly with a woman nearby.

"Come, Finette," he said softly. "The mating is done and we are both satisfied. I bid you good night."

"Remember whose castle this is, sirrah. When you are under my roof, you do not give me commands. I sleep where I choose." Finette tossed her head and flung herself back down onto the feather mattress. Jaufre regarded her for a moment and then raised one foot against her exposed rump and shoved. She tumbled out of bed in a welter of sheets, furs, and pillow.

Legs and arms flailing, she struggled to her feet, plucking the straw rushes from her hair, her eyes spitting fury. "English pig! I will scream to bring the rafters down. You—you take advantage of a lonely widow, despoil my honor, rape me!"

"If we are going to speak of rape, it was you who came in here and straddled yourself over top of me when all I wanted was a good night's rest." Jaufre got out of bed and draped the discarded sheet around his midsection. While Finette continued to rail at him, he went to a large chest lodged near the hearth and opened it.

"I will demand satisfaction for this insult. Do not think that I will not."

"Here is your satisfaction." Jaufre pulled a silver brooch from the chest and flung it at her. It landed near her feet, the brilliant gemstones winking through the darkness.

Finette glanced down at it and paused a moment, licking her lips. "You—you dog. Do you take me for a whore to be paid thus?" She snatched up her chemise and gown and yanked the garments over her head. "'Tis you who will pay for this night—with your blood."

"Ah, yes, I forgot. I have heard it said you prefer to be paid in coin when your honor is offended," Jaufre drawled. "I am afraid I have better use for my money. You will have to be content with the brooch."

"Auggh!" Finette heaved her pillow at him, but he caught it easily and dropped it onto the bed. "Now I see why your wife tried to kill you. When she scarred that chest of yours, she scarred your heart as well."

"You are mistaken, my lady," he said icily. "I have no heart."

She sucked in a deep breath, and her fingers curled as if she were about to spring at him. Jaufre tensed for the attack, but she apparently thought better of it. Still muttering curses, she tossed her head and whirled to leave. The dignity of her exit was marred when she dipped down at the last moment to retrieve the brooch before she quit the chamber. As he had known she would.

Jaufre's lips curved into a cynical smile. Was there any woman—or man, for that matter—who would not sell his honor a dozen times over for less than he had offered Finette? Reaching into the chest, he caught up a handful of silver coins and allowed the cold metal pieces to trickle between his fingers.

He'd seen greed win out time and again. Even with Richard Coeur de Lion, with whom Jaufre had traveled as a boy on the Crusades. Had the mighty Lion's Heart died striking down the enemies of Christ? Nay, Jaufre's idol had been pierced through with an arrow while shrieking for his share of a treasure trove that had not even existed.

And then there had been Yseult, his beautiful Yseult, and young Godric, her lover.... Jaufre could think of the lad in no other way since that night he had caught Godric ensnared deep in Yseult's plots against his life.

Slamming the lid down on the chest, Jaufre closed his mind to memories that only consumed him with their bitterness. He threw himself back on the bed and shut his eyes. But now that he was alone, sleep eluded him. Damn Finette with her overheated thighs and equally overheated temper. After all her nonsense, he was wide awake.

Sitting up again, he wondered if he would find such a thing as a candle in Finette's miserly household. Groping along the wall, he found a half-melted piece of tallow stuck in one of the wall sconces. He lit the wick in the dying fire, crinkling his nose at the stinking smell of burning animal fat. Carefully propping the candle, he slipped on his woolen drawers and turned to the chest where his real treasure lay, some dozen beautifully illuminated manuscripts he had collected over the years: *The Romance of Rollo*, Bede's *History of the English Nation*, *The Life of Alfred*, *King Alisaunder the Great*, *The Roman da la Rose*...Lovingly he fingered the pages as he lifted each volume in turn. He'd read them so often, he could recite many passages by heart.

Crushed beneath Tacitus' *Germanicus*, he found an aged document he had half forgotten. Snorting with amusement, he unrolled the wrinkled parchment. *This is the Charter of Henry I by means of which the barons sought their liberties.* Pledges from Jaufre's great-grandfather's day, long ago forgotten. Jaufre recalled how impressed he'd been as a young man when he'd first discovered the charter hidden amongst the family records. Rights...liberties. Such stirring words. Such stirring nonsense!

Scornfully, he tossed the parchment back in the chest. The only other object remaining in the trunk was a small wooden jewel box containing a lock of his mother's hair, the crest from his father's helmet, and a child's silken veil.

Jaufre removed the veil from its hiding place after looking over his shoulder at the dark outline of the door, half dreading that someone might enter and catch him at such foolishness. He crumpled the small garment in his fist.

"I should fling it into the fire," he muttered, and wondered why he had not done so long ago. He had never saved any other lady's favor from a tournament, not even Yseult's. What ridiculous sort of sentimentality caused him to cling to this relic of his past?

But instead of consigning the fabric to the flames, he smoothed it, a half smile touching his lips. Ah, but the little girl had radiated such innocence as she had offered him the veil. As simple and naive as had been the knight who had accepted it. "God grant you victory, Sir Launcelot," she had said even after he had told her his name, her young face shining with dreams and ideals of chivalry that at that time he had shared with her.

The only difference was, the lady Melyssan had kept her dreams. Jaufre knew that the minute he had seen her again. Even while arranging his marriage to her pert bratling of a sister, he was conscious of Melyssan's quiet presence lingering in the shadows. Although she had grown taller, her frame was slender, delicate as he remembered it, her glossy brown hair retaining those baby-fine strands of gold, her sea-green eyes that look of childlike trust....

She was never obtrusive during the days he spent at Sir William's manor, yet he saw her everywhere, fetching the towels for his morning wash from the locked linen cupboard, sending a page with extra logs for the fire in his chamber, commanding the cook to prepare an extra brace of partridge because "Lord Jaufre has been hunting and will be famished."

He was not long at Wydevale before he realized it was she who ran the manor house. While Beatrice flirted with the other knights and Dame Alice embroidered or prayed, Melyssan saw to the comfort of her father's guests. Unhampered by her halting step, she held gentle sway over the small household, performing such humble tasks as strewing fresh rushes upon the floor herself when necessary. He even came across her one afternoon mending her father's drawers while humming a little tune. Half envying her air of cheerful serenity, her mind obviously at peace, he backed out of the room hoping to escape undetected. But she glanced up and smiled.

"Good day, Lord Jaufre. I trust you slept well last night."

"Yes. Yes, thank you," he said, trying not to stare. For once her hair was not bound up in tight coils over her ears or hidden within the folds of a veil. The silken waves flowed over her shoulders in charming disarray. Tendrils damp from perspiration clung to the soft curve of cheeks flushed a rosy hue from the warmth of the afternoon.

Suddenly she tugged at the neckline of her cambric gown as if it irritated the expanse of creamy flesh beneath. Moistening the outline

35

of full, tempting lips with the tip of her tongue, she concentrated on rethreading her needle, and Jaufre shuddered, startled by a familiar stirring in his loins.

She caught the movement and looked back at him with large candid eyes. "Is there aught I can do for you, my lord? Anything that you desire?"

Jaufre felt the redness surging up his neck. "I—I—no, nothing at all."

He stumbled from the room, out of the house to the yard, where he splashed large handfuls of cold water over his face. What was he thinking of? She was still as untouched as a child and destined for the nunnery besides. What sort of savage had he allowed himself to become?

He avoided her after that, pressing Sir William to move forward the date of his marriage to Beatrice, despite the sullen looks he received from his bride-to-be. The girl was young, malleable, not too clever—everything he wanted in his second wife. A strong wench to bear his sons, a woman who would be pleased enough with a steady supply of new gowns and trinkets, a simple creature incapable of entangling him in a silken web of lies and deceit.

At least she seemed so when her parents were present—demure, her mouth drawn down into a sulky little pucker. He'd almost felt sorry for forcing her into a marriage she did not want. But that was before he overheard her at mealtime boasting to some whey-faced youth,

"Even though I detest Lord Jaufre, I do pity the man. He adores me. Why, I have even had him kneel at my feet just to kiss the hem of my gown."

Suppressing his anger, Jaufre shoved in another mouthful of the tasteless stew from his trencher and resolved then and there to show Beatrice that he would be the master if he decided to go through with this wedding. As soon as he found her alone, he would teach her that he meant to kiss more than her skirts.

His opportunity came at dusk when he saw her standing in the garden. Gliding up behind her, he encircled her breasts and pressed kisses along her neck. Her reaction was not the frightened gasp he had expected. Instead she sighed, leaning against him, her warm, slender fingers caressing his own. He was beginning to forget he had begun this only to teach her a lesson when she turned her head to face him. And he found himself gazing down into eyes not an insipid blue, but a vivid green. Melyssan.

In that startling second, he was honest enough to wonder if he had indeed made an error. Had he not sensed somehow before he ever touched her that she was not Beatrice? And yet he had allowed some demon to drive him on. He could not check his desire this time with the illusion that Melyssan was still a child. The evidence of his hands molding her soft curves told him otherwise. Inexorably he drew her nearer, wanting just one taste of those soft, trembling pink lips. If only she had closed her eyes, those haunting, sea-shaded eyes.

But she didn't. She came to him unresisting, her eyes wide with wonder, as if she expected something beautiful, instead of the kiss he was about to bestow, a caress to ease his own selfish passion. He shoved her away, ashamed of himself for tampering with such innocence. Leaving her alone in the garden, looking hurt and bewildered, he consoled himself with the thought she was no more confused than he was himself.

If he wanted Melyssan, it would be an easy matter to go to Sir William and ask for her hand instead. Melyssan had taken no vows thus far, and he knew that even promises to the church could be broken if the earl of Winterbourne demanded it. Yet the girl already had an aura of holiness about her, while he...he was on more intimate terms with the patrons of hell than those of heaven.

So he remained silent, even after Beatrice had released him from any sense of obligation by running away to seek sanctuary at St. Clare. He rode off without speaking to Sir William about Melyssan, without even saying good-bye to her....

Jaufre's remembrance dimmed as a draft caused the candle to flicker, reminding him he still knelt on the floor half-naked, clutching the child's veil. Shivering, he folded the cloth and returned it to the chest. Well, mayhap he would keep the thing after all, as a token of more innocent days, a memento of the one wise decision he had ever made in his life.

For wisdom it was not to have wed Melyssan. Those eyes of hers, how they would have tormented him with their sweet gravity, twin mirrors reflecting the dark corners of his soul he had kept so well hidden all these years. And he, with his black-hearted cynicism, before long he would have eroded all her shining ideals, destroyed her faith in God and man until she became no different from all the other shallow women he knew.

He had just slammed down the lid on the chest when he heard the hammering on the bedchamber door. Had it been going on for some time, getting progressively louder, and he'd just become aware of it? Why did no one call his name—why this insistent thump, thump, thump?

A wariness that had more than once saved his life stole over him and sent him scrambling for his sword. The summons came thundering again. It would not be long before the pounding fist discovered the door was unbarred.

Jaufre's hand closed over the hilt of his sword, and he blew out the candle, every muscle tensed, waiting. Finette's temper may have driven her to more extreme measures than he thought. If she went whining about being insulted to her cleric, a drunkard clothing himself in priest's robes, she might have persuaded him to come down here. The fat Father Hubert fancied himself something of a swordsman.

The knock came one final time, weaker than before. And then, at last, a muffled call: "Jaufre, it's Tristan. Open, for God's sake."

Jaufre relaxed, his tension turning into irritation as he recognized the voice of Sir Tristan Mallory, a knight bachelor of his grandfather's household. Wrenching open the door, Jaufre shaded his eyes against the light from the flaming torch Tristan carried.

"What the hell! Why did you not identify yourself at once, man, instead of raising enough racket to make me think the entire castle guard was out there?"

"Sorry," Tristan whispered. He stepped into the room without saying anything more.

"What the devil's amiss?" Jaufre's eyes flicked over the younger man, and he noted that his boyhood friend's square jaw was tightly clenched. It suddenly occurred to him that Tristan had not immediately called out because he was incapable of doing so. The knight swallowed hard, and moisture welled in his eyes.

"What is it?" Jaufre asked more quietly.

"I—I'm sorry," Tristan choked out. "Jaufre, it's the comte. You—you have to go to him. I summoned a physician from the town, but he says...he says 'tis too late." He reached out to place his hand on Jaufre's shoulder, but the earl drew back instinctively, rejecting the gesture as he rejected the compassion he saw etched on Tristan's face.

"My grandfather? You've brought in some

blasted leech to disturb his rest? I swear by all the saints—"

"Jaufre...Jaufre, he's dying."

"No, you lie!" With great effort, Jaufre lowered his voice. "That is, you are mistaken. Damn that fool physician."

Tristan tried to speak again, but Jaufre gestured him to silence as he tore around the room, shoving aside the bedclothes, the chests, until he found his woolen shirt and yanked it on. As he pulled the fur-lined surcoat over his tunic, he kept his back to Tristan, not wanting to see the sorrowful conviction in his friend's eyes. He remembered his grandfather's face as he had risen from the table at supper, pale, worn with exhaustion, the lines of age standing out in sharp relief.

No, Jaufre had seen him look that way a dozen times or more within the past year. It meant nothing. Tristan had been misled.

Pushing past the knight, he strode from the room, not waiting for Tristan to keep pace with him. He did not know what ailed Raoul de Macy, but when he reached his grandfather's side, together they would fight as they had always done, cheating death one more time.

When Jaufre entered the great hall, he saw that word of the comte's condition had reached other ears as well. Finette, Father Hubert, and some of the comte's knights hovered by the circular stair leading to the tower bedchamber. Just like a flock of black-winged corbies awaiting the final throes of a mighty lion.

Finette's shrill voice carried above the other murmurs. "A plague upon the old fool. Why did he decide he has to die here—in my bed?"

"Devil take your bed." The priest yawned. "Why did he have to bother me with his confession in the middle of the night?"

"None of you need be *bothered*," Jaufre shouted as he crossed the hall. "Clear out, the lot of you scavengers. No one is dying here."

Most of the men fell back at his approach, some of them averting their gaze, shamefaced. But Finette blocked his path, smiling maliciously. "I'm sorry to have to contradict you, my lord. But the physician here thinks otherwise."

Jaufre shoved her out of his way, his eyes raking the assembled company until he found a sallow-faced little man whose bony hands trembled as he confronted Jaufre's piercing gaze. "My—my regrets, Your Lordship. There is nothing more I can do. Monsieur le Comte has fallen sick of a most feverish carbuncle."

"A carbuncle, you ass!" Jaufre said. "If I find you've done some harm to my lord with your quack notions, I will make your whole body one open running sore."

The scrawny man slunk behind the huge bulk of Hubert Le Vis. Jaufre turned away in disgust and mounted the first of the stone steps to the chamber above. He felt Father Hubert's hamlike hand catch his arm.

"I'd wait a while before going up there," he said, wagging the heavy jowls that had earned him the nickname *Le Gros*. "I've heard his

42

confession and given him the last rites. It will not be long."

Confession. Last rites. Jaufre struck away the priest's hand. By the blood of Christ, these knaves had all but dug the old comte's grave and flung him into it whilst he still lived.

"He has got some strange notion. Going to make you swear an oath. Why not stay down here until he's drawn his last. Save yourself a great deal of trouble." Father Hubert's beady eye disappeared into layers of flesh as he gave Jaufre a sly wink.

Jaufre's fingers knotted into a tight fist. "Why, you—"

Tristan stepped in between them. "Go on, Jaufre," he urged. "I will see to dispersing these—these persons."

"You do that," Jaufre said, glaring past him at Father Hubert. "Make sure no one comes up to disturb him again lest they have their fat stomachs lined with my steel."

Jaufre whirled and took the rest of the steps two at a time. Behind him, he heard *Le Gros* rumble, "I only tried to warn the man," and then Tristan's indistinguishable reply along with receding footsteps.

All was unearthly quiet outside the door to the chamber where his grandfather lay. Try as he might, Jaufre could not stop his hand from shaking as he reached for the handle, dreading what might await him inside.

The chamber was dark except for one light left burning in an iron candelabrum. Those jackals had even permitted the fire to go out. Jaufre's conscience smote him. The comte hadn't wanted to stop at the Château Le Vis. It was Jaufre who had insisted they break their journey, hoping a comfortable bed might restore the old man. But while he rutted with Finette, his grandfather must have lain here suffering, so poorly attended.

"Jaufre? Is that you?" The comte's voice came to him, muted behind the thick bed curtains.

"Yes, my lord."

Jaufre stepped forward and parted the heavy damask hangings. The gaunt form of Raoul de Macy lay in the shadows, motionless but for his labored breathing. "What folly is this?" Jaufre forced himself to speak with a false heartiness. "This place reeks of incense. Why did you not give Hubert's fat backside the flat end of your sword when he came troubling you with his absurd unction and paternosters?"

"I—I sent for him." The comte gave a weak chuckle that ended in a spasm of coughing. "Better such a fat dolt than no confessor at all. Best I could find here. Château Le Vis is not the place I would have chosen to die."

His words sent a chill to Jaufre's heart; his grandfather had never spoken thus before. "'Tis this room," Jaufre muttered. "This cold darkness is enough to put anyone in mind of dying."

He threw back all the bed curtains and moved the candle closer, preparing to relight the fire. But he nearly toppled the candelabrum when the tiny flame illuminated the comte's face, white as the snowy waves of hair that lay tumbled upon the pillow, his skin stretched taut against hollow cheeks. His eyes, once so remarkable for their unusual coloring, the brilliant hue of polished silver, were now as hazy as the morning mist. Arms that only that afternoon had reined in a restive mount now lay limp at his sides.

"How could this be?" Jaufre cried. "I never imagined that— Why did you not send for me sooner?"

"Sharp pain came. Then I found I—could not move. Had to have...priest first, in case I died in state of bad grace."

Jaufre began piling logs onto the hearth with frantic energy, as if somehow the fire could bring back the spark of life he saw fading before his very eyes.

"Leave that," said the comte. "Not cold."

"You must be. It's freezing in here. It will only take—"

"Leave it."

The comte drew a sharp intake of breath that sent Jaufre flying to his side. He saw the old man's eyes dilate in agony, and he seized one withered hand and wrung it helplessly, willing his own strength to somehow pass into those weakened limbs.

"Damn Finette," he said. "If she knew what a woman is supposed to know, what any peasant's wife would know about healing...Never mind. We—we will find another physician. A better one."

The comte's pain-racked features suddenly

45

relaxed. "No. No help for it and little time. Sit by me."

"You're exhausted. You need to sleep. I should never have allowed you to undertake that mission for the king to Saxony. 'Twas too much."

For a moment something gleamed in the old man's eye. "Was important. England needs alliance with the emperor if we're ever going to retake Normandy. Besides, you forget yourself, m'boy. Where I go...my choice. Not yours."

"Then do not choose to die. Fight!"

A half smile tugged at the corner of his grandfather's thin, bloodless lips. "I've seen seventy-six years, Jaufre. Old enough to know when to lay down my sword." He closed his eyes.

Jaufre pulled up a wooden stool, settling himself beside the bed, wrestling with his anger, his longing to smash his fist against the wooden frame and rage at the comte. *Fight, damn you, fight! I want you to live.* He'd seen war and disease carry off his father, mother, uncle, brothers. If he lost his grandfather, he would truly be alone, the last of the de Macys.

When the comte spoke again, his voice was barely a whisper, and Jaufre had to lean forward in order to hear him.

"I needed confession for my sins...one deed weighs heavy. Never been forgiven."

Jaufre feared the old man's mind had begun to wander. "Hush, my lord. The priest is gone. You have been absolved."

"No, not the priest. You forgive." The comte's chin trembled as he turned his head a fraction, struggling to focus on Jaufre's face. "She was evil. Nearly killed you. I—I loved you beyond all, even own sons. I hanged Yseult. You...never forgave. You hated me."

A great constriction knotted in Jaufre's chest, suffocating him. "Nay, Grandfather, do not say that. I was a fool. 'Tis you who must pardon me."

"And Godric...young Godric."

"Stop, my lord. There is no need to speak of this now. 'Tis all long past, forgotten."

"Forgot?" Raoul de Macy's brow wrinkled with a slight frown. "Yes, I did forget. The sword. Jaufre. Fetch my sword."

"What?" Jaufre asked, still disturbed by the painful memories evoked by the comte's fragmented speech. But he realized his grandfather's thoughts had abruptly taken a new direction.

"Fetch my sword. In yon corner. Hurry."

Although he thought his grandfather confused, Jaufre hastened to obey lest the old man grow agitated. When he removed the heavy broadsword from its scabbard, he was assailed by other images from the past, a long-ago summer's day. This same battered weapon, the sun striking off the shining blade as it was held aloft in Raoul de Macy's powerful bronzed hands. Then the sword arcing through the air, the tip coming to thud down upon Jaufre's own shoulders, first one, then the other, and the comte's deep voice charging him, "Be thou a good knight."

"Jaufre, Jaufre. Bring the sword." The feeble whisper from the bed called him back to the present. Jaufre carried the sword over and would have laid it beside the comte so that his fingers could rest one more time on the carved silver hilt, but his grandfather said, "No, yours now. You hold it, swear by it—to retake Clairemont."

It had been eight years since the comte's beloved Château Clairemont had fallen to the French, along with the rest of Normandy. Most Englishmen had given up the idea of recovering their continental possessions and turned with renewed vigor to managing their English estates. Jaufre agreed with them, but his grandfather did not. The Norman blood had always flowed in Raoul de Macy's veins, stronger than his Saxon heritage.

"My lord, do not trouble your mind with such things," Jaufre soothed him, adding what he no longer believed himself. "We will take your Norman lands back from the French soon, very soon."

"Swear it. By the sword. One of my blood...again be lord of Clairemont."

Jaufre hesitated, nervously fingering the weapon's jeweled hilt. A knight's oath was a sacred thing, not to be given lightly. If he failed to keep his promise, he would be guilty of perjury, damned.

But a tear trickling from the corner of his grandfather's eye swept all such doubt aside.

He raised the sword, gripping the hilt with both hands.

"By the blood of Christ, I do so swear."

As soon as the words were spoken, Jaufre felt as if a great burden descended upon his shoulders. But he forgot the strange impression as he watched the comte's eyes flutter closed, the furrows on his brow smoothing as he issued a great sigh.

Jaufre flung the sword aside. "Grandfather?"

"Now I can sleep," murmured the comte. "Will—will you stay?"

"Yes, my lord," Jaufre said hoarsely, and sank back down on the stool, feeling drained, defeated. Reaching out, he enfolded cold, emaciated fingers within the warmth of his own grasp. Gently, he traced the crescent shape on his grandfather's wrist, a birthmark peculiar to the de Macy family. Jaufre's father had had it, as had his older brother, Malcolm. Mayhap one day a son of his would also bear the mark, a great-grandson the comte would never...

Jaufre swallowed hard and stared unblinking at the canopy overhead. The comte was quiet now. Even his breathing seemed to come more slowly. During the long night, he spoke once as if in his sleep. "No regrets. Only...would like to feel...sun on my face one last time."

Never certain when his own weariness overtook him, Jaufre's head rolled forward onto his chest, and when he next opened his eyes, the light of dawn was filtering through the arrow slits that formed the château's only windows. He straightened up, rubbing the back of his stiff neck, trying to get his bearings. His fingers curled around something that felt like ice. His grandfather's hand. As Jaufre remembered where he was, a heavy weight pressed down upon his heart. His eyes traveled slowly up the still form of the Comte de Clairemont le Fleur, up to where the sunlight bathed his face, the proud features now smoothed into a peaceful mask of death.

Jaufre wondered dully if his grandfather had still been alive when the sun rose, felt its rays touch him one last time, as he had desired. He would never know.

Sliding off the stool, he knelt in homage to the man who had been everything to him, father, brother, seigneur. Although he fought against the aching sensation of loss, the pain would come. Starting at the pit of his stomach and working its way up, it burned his throat with the tears he could not shed.

Raising the comte's cold hand to his lips, he kissed the gold signet ring, ancient symbol of the lords of Clairemont. Then he slowly stood and folded his grandfather's arms across his chest. He began to draw the sheet up around him, then stopped, unable to bring himself to cover that familiar face; even now it looked as if the old man but slept.

Stumbling from the room, Jaufre discovered Tristan where he had been keeping his vigil just outside the door. His friend's red-rimmed eyes bored into Jaufre's, but there was no need for words. Jaufre touched him on the shoulder, indicating he was now to go in to the comte.

Without waiting for any further response, Jaufre raced down the curving stone stair. He needed to get outside, to be alone. The castle was closing in on him.

In the château's courtyard, the household bustled with its normal morning activity. The guard gathered around a trough, washing sleep from their faces while pages trotted forward with slices of fresh wheaten bread to break their fast. Jaufre paused a moment to stare. Nothing changed. Another death, and the world marched on exactly as before.

Cloying lavender perfume filled his nostrils, and Finette pressed forward to stand beside him, munching on a roll dripping with honey. Before she could speak, one of the guard hastened over.

"Your pardon, my lord, my lady, but there is a strange boy at the gates. A peasant, or so I believe. He demands to see Lord Jaufre."

"Demands!" Finette said after swallowing the large bite she had stuffed in her mouth. "Set the dogs on the insolent beggar. They will hasten him on his way."

"That is hardly necessary." Jaufre fumbled in his purse for a coin and tossed it to the guard. "Give him this."

As he walked away, he noted with contempt that Finette intercepted the money and whispered something to the guard, but he felt too weary to rebuke her or give more than a passing thought as to why a beggar should ask for him by name.

Finette followed him, the silken train of her gown rustling through the dirt. "So the old man's dead at last. Well, I hope you do not think to bury him here. You can damn well cart him back to England. You must have some room left in the ditches."

The next instant she cried out as Jaufre spun around and caught her shoulders in an iron grip. He felt almost grateful to Finette. It was so much easier to deal with anger than grief.

"Never fear. I would not bury my dog in this stinking hole. I will take the comte where he belongs, back to Clairemont."

Finette gave a near hysterical laugh. "Clairemont? And do you think the French constable will simply open the gates and let you march right in to hold your touching little rites?"

"He will open the gates," Jaufre said, releasing her. "By God, he will. Or I will open them for him."

Jaufre's threat proved unnecessary. The constable at Clairemont willingly flung wide the castle gates by gracious permission of His Most Sovereign Majesty, Philip Augustus of France. Although the comte had ever been his enemy, the French king sent his condolences at the death of the right brave knight Raoul de Macy and begged that as soon as his grief was somewhat assuaged, Lord Jaufre would do him the honor of paying a visit to the court in Paris.

After Jaufre had the old comte entombed at Clairemont's chapel in a magnificent porphyry sarcophagus with all the pomp and respect due his high rank, the earl considered King Philip's invitation despite strong objections from Tristan.

"I do not trust the man." Tristan scowled. "Can you forget how he conspired to keep King Richard a captive of the emperor?"

Jaufre shrugged. "Philip would have little to gain by imprisoning me. No one is going to raise one hundred and fifty thousand marks for my release."

Paying final respects to his grandfather's tomb, Jaufre ordered his knights to pack their gear and be ready to ride to Paris. He girded on the comte's sword, which still felt strange strapped to his side, being heavier and far more ornate than his own weapon. But it felt no stranger than the thick seal ring he now slipped onto his right hand. Engraved on its flat surface were two swans, their long necks entwined, the badge of the lords of Clairemont.

Tristan shifted awkwardly as he watched Jaufre put it on. "I removed it from the comte's finger the morning after he died. Before he sent me to fetch you that night, he instructed me to see that you received it when he was gone. He—he bade me make certain you did not lose his seal as you did your own."

Tristan's eyes locked with Jaufre's, and

then they both burst out laughing, the first easing of their solemn mood for many days. The remark Tristan repeated was so typical of the old comte. When Jaufre had mislaid his own signet ring during his stay at Sir William's manor, his grandfather had groused at him unmercifully for his carelessness.

In somewhat lighter spirits than when they had arrived, Lord Jaufre's entourage rode away from Clairemont to Paris. As his black stallion cantered through the double gates of the city wall and over the drawbridge that spanned the green waters of the Seine, the earl saw at once that the reports he had heard were true. Philip Augustus was rebuilding Paris. Church spires warred for precedence with the cone-capped towers of what had once been an old hunting lodge and was now the mighty fortress known as the Louvre. Burghers shoved their way through the throngs of students, peasants, and artisans making their way to Les Halles, the brightly painted buildings housing the new marketplace.

And still the air rang with the boatmen's shouts as they unloaded more sand and limestone from their leather-sailed boats onto the quays. Jaufre's ears were assailed with the steady chink of workmen's tools and the creak and clank of the hoisting machines as the construction continued. A man of vision, this Philip Augustus, he thought. A man of ruthless ambition. So what did he want of the earl of Winterbourne?

As they crossed the Petit Pont, Jaufre drew

alongside Tristan to gauge his reaction to Paris's new splendors. He was amused to note the younger man's eyes darting from side to side as if he expected an ambush to be launched at them from every side street. The look on his face bordered on panic when they arrived at the old island palace and Jaufre was summoned to a private audience with Philip Augustus.

Jaufre returned from the meeting to find Tristan in the great hall pacing before the fire. Deeply aware of the jealous glances cast his way from the French nobles who lingered hoping to have but one word with their king, Jaufre crossed the room to his friend's side.

Tristan halted his nervous footsteps and scanned the earl's face. Keeping his features blank, Jaufre held out his hands to the fire, maintaining a maddening silence.

"Well, my lord?"

"Well what?" Jaufre asked, quirking an eyebrow at the knight's agitated countenance.

"What happened? Was he threatening?"

"Oh, nay. Quite the reverse. Charming, manners like figured silk, so smooth and fancy you wonder what it's going to cost you. He took me out on the walkway around the tower and pointed out how far they have come with the work on the new cathedral. Too much effort to be spent on a church, I thought. Now if it were a new fortress—"

"He did not invite you to Paris to show you Notre Dame," Tristan said impatiently. "What else did he speak of?"

"Well, he expressed his sympathy again and—" Teasingly, Jaufre broke off as he bowed, returning the nod he received in passing from the chevalier de Grenville and Baron Fecamp, worthy opponents from his tournament days.

Tristan seized hold of his friend's sleeve. "Damn it, Jaufre. What does Philip want?"

Jaufre grinned but decided he had goaded Tristan enough. Prying his friend's fingers loose from his black tunic, he replied, "In his own subtle fashion, His Majesty wished to remind me there might be more than one way back to Clairemont."

"And what the devil does that mean?"

"It means that our dear King John is not the only monarch with invasion plans."

Despite the heat thrown out by the massive hearth, Tristan turned pale. "You—you think Philip means to invade England?"

"If the time were right," Jaufre said, remembering the covetous gleam in the French king's eye when he had talked about his island neighbor. "And when that time comes, he has invited me to throw over my allegiance to John and cast in my lot with him—for the return of Clairemont, of course."

He waited for an indignant outburst from Tristan at the mere suggestion of such a thing. He was surprised when the knight frowned and lapsed into a thoughtful silence.

At last Tristan said, "Much as I hate to admit it, the French king has shown himself more skilled at warfare than John. Philip's proposal may well be the only way for you to fulfill the pledge to the old comte."

"Surely you jest. Set aside my fealty to King John! Risk losing Winterbourne! And for what? Clairemont is not worth a tenth of my English holdings."

"To your grandfather, Clairemont was worth all of England," Tristan reproached him. "What will you do, my lord? Simply forget your promise?"

"I'll do as I see fit," Jaufre replied flatly. "And I do not need fools like you constantly reminding me of that damned oath."

Tristan compressed his lips and turned his back on Jaufre. Jaufre raised his hand, wanting to reach out to assure Tristan that his irritation was not with his friend but with the predicament in which he found himself. But the knight was already striding away.

Jaufre dropped his arm to his side and swore softly. He had had much time to regret the pledge given to his dying grandfather. By the wounds of Christ, it would have been easier to keep a promise to find the Holy Grail. King John was no Richard the Lion-Hearted. While Normandy fell to the French, castle by castle, 'twas rumored that John lolled abed with his young queen. Even with the support of his barony, it would be a miracle if John Softsword, with his lack of military prowess, could reconquer the lost territory. And the barons did not support John. Most of them were not interested in wasting men and money in a futile attempt to win back continental possessions they had learned to do without. In vain had Jaufre labored to convince his grandfather to be satisfied with his English estates. He had failed, and now he was pledged to carry on with this madness himself.

Yet Jaufre knew that he could never accept Philip's offer to betray John. Even as he had sworn an oath to his grandfather, he had also sworn an oath of loyalty to the king of England. Other men might devise excuses to break their word, but not the lords of Clairemont; their motto was "My honor, my life." To a de Macy, honor and life were one and the same. No matter how great his reluctance, he had no choice but to try and retake Clairemont with his sword, even if it seemed a certainty he would die in the attempt.

A commotion at one end of the hall disrupted Jaufre's gloom-filled train of thought. He looked up expecting to see that Philip Augustus had descended to greet his nobles at last, but the disturbance came from a new arrival to court. Head held high, the lady Finette made her entrance, resplendent in a yellow damask gown and pillbox cap scalloped to resemble a coronet. Jaufre's lips curved in a sardonic smile. Her red velvet mantle was pinned into place with the jeweled brooch he had flung at her.

After their last encounter, he fully expected her to sweep haughtily past him. He was therefore surprised when she ignored the inviting stares she was receiving from most of the Frenchmen and walked straight to where he stood.

"My lord Jaufre." Her dark eyes glinted at him over the rim of her fan. "How fortunate that I find you still in Paris. I feared you might already have embarked for England, and that would have been a great pity."

"How so, my lady? Are you still out for my blood or only eager to earn yourself a necklace to match the brooch?"

An angry red surged into Finette's cheeks, but she kept the smile fixed on her lips. The expression reminded Jaufre of a sleek greyhound he'd once had, how the animal would look when it managed to capture one of the tiny wrens flitting into the garden.

"'Tis most unchivalrous of you to address me thus, especially when I have come so far to bring you urgent news from England. I am afraid you must brace yourself for more unpleasantness."

Finette's smile broadened as she turned and snapped her fingers. A short figure emerged from the shadows of the arched entryway. Cautiously he approached Lord Jaufre, pausing midway to doff his cap, thus exposing a familiar balding pate.

"Pevensy. What the devil!" Jaufre said, taking a menacing step forward, which caused the little man to falter.

"You do know this fellow, then," Finette purred. "He came to my château looking for you, but I was not sure whether to put faith in his claims or not."

"Know him? 'Tis my steward from Winterbourne. Come here at once, varlet."

" 'Twas not my fault, my lord," Pevensy began to whine. "I have been grievously wronged. All summer I have awaited your return from Brunswick so that you might redress—"

"Redress be damned. What are you doing so far from your duties?" A horrible thought struck Jaufre, and he seized Pevensy by the front of his tunic. "Winterbourne. Something has happened at Winterbourne. Quickly. Tell me. Has it been overrun by the Welsh?"

"N-nay, my lord. By a woman."

"What!"

"S-she—she drove me from the gates of Winterbourne," Pevensy sputtered. "But I swear I did nothing wrong."

Jaufre gave him a quick shake. "Who? *Who?*"

"Y-your lady wife, my lord."

Stunned, Jaufre loosened his grip.

"Why, Jaufre," Finette mocked him. "How secretive you have been. Faith! Are you ashamed of your new bride?"

"Damn you. You know I have no wife!" Jaufre caught hold of Pevensy again and this time lifted him so that his toes barely touched the ground. "You had best come across with the truth, you lying miscreant, before I flay you alive."

Pevensy went white from his neck to the top of his bald head. "I—I swear, my lord. The lady...she did say she was your wife. Everyone at Winterbourne believes her."

Finette bubbled over with merriment. "An imposter! Lord Jaufre's mighty fortress has been taken single-handed by some clever harlot."

Her shrill voice carried and captured the attention of half the room. To his annoyance, Jaufre saw that many of the French barons were drawing closer, their faces twitching with curiosity. With great effort, he lowered his own voice. "You are telling me you turned Winterbourne over to some whore?"

"No. No. 'Twas a lady. Sir William's daughter," Pevensy cried. "She had your falcon's seal, my lord, and was escorted by the king's own men."

The chevalier de Grenville's voice rang out. "By heaven, it seems English castles are easily taken. Perhaps we should arm our ladies and send them across the Channel." His comment was followed by a chorus of booming male laughter.

Jaufre felt his face flush a deep red. He gave Pevensy a rough shove that nearly sent him toppling to the floor. "Get out of my sight, you whoreson knave, before I plant my foot up your arse."

The laughter ran louder as Pevensy scuttled for the door, still sniveling. Finette doubled over with mirth. "Months this thieving wench has had, queening it as the countess of Winterbourne. When you return, my lord, you will be lucky to find a cellar left to hold your salt."

She took hold of Jaufre's arm, clearly enjoying every minute of his discomfiture.

"Poor Jaufre. This creature at Winterbourne must be a madwoman, doubtlessly possessed of a demon. Shall I send Father Hubert back to England with you to perform an exorcism?"

Jaufre shook free of Finette as he strove to control his anger, lest he be tempted to wipe the smirks off these French faces. He strode away without replying and did not check his step until he was well clear of the great hall.

Sir William's daughter, that dolt Pevensy had said. Who would have thought that simpering little Beatrice would have been cunning enough to play him such a trick? But now that he thought about it, he could see how she had brought the thing about.

He pictured again in his mind the day he had lost his seal ring at Wydevale. Standing in the apple orchard, he had suffered a bee sting in the webbing between his fingers. Noting his hand beginning to swell, he had stripped off his ring before it could become painfully tight. Then she had come up, annoying him by wanting to squeeze his hand and recite some curing incantation she had learned from her old nurse. In the process of struggling to avoid her nonsense, he had dropped the ring, unnoticed, into the grass. Later, when he had returned to the spot, all efforts to find it had been in vain.

Obviously Beatrice had retrieved it, saving it until a time when she could put it to good use. Using his seal, she had somehow convinced King John of her claim to be his wife and installed herself at Winterbourne.

All summer. Jaufre's hands clenched. The conniving wench had had nigh an entire summer to wring whatever she could out of his estates. She probably had some lover waiting in the background, and perhaps they planned to murder him when he returned, or simply flee together. Yseult and Godric's tale played out all over again.

Except this time, he was no infatuated young fool. And no matter what hole Beatrice chose to hide in, even if it was within the sacred confines of the convent, he would find her and haul her out by the scruff of her neck.

"And then, my lady wife," he whispered fiercely, "you will regret you ever slipped on my ring and planned your 'wedding day'—regret the day you were ever born."

Chapter 3

CHICKENS SQUAWKED, SCATTERING out from beneath the hooves of the dun-colored palfrey that galloped into the courtyard at Winterbourne. The young rider garbed in the de Macy livery of blue tunic and gold hose waved his cap in acknowledgment of the greetings from soldiers manning the walls.

"Halloo, young Arric," Sir Dreyfan called down to the page. "What distance away is Lord Jaufre?"

"Not more than a league, sir," Arric piped up, squinting against the rays of the late afternoon sun. "The master sent me on ahead to tell you he brings a guest with him from France. He bids you make all ready for their comfort."

"I will inform his lady."

His lady. The words caused Melyssan to draw back from the crosslet through which she had watched the messenger's arrival. She pressed her cool hands against cheeks gone pale. The dreaded day had arrived at last. Lord Jaufre was coming home. Intermixed with her fear was a strange fluttery sense of anticipation.

Her fingers closed over the handle of her cane, and she made her way slowly across the solar, avoiding the only pieces of furniture contained within the private withdrawing room: a heavy oak trestle table and a high-backed chair. Along one wall was a mural depicting a scene from the Norman invasion of 1066. Melyssan trailed her hand over one of the soldiers standing on shore awaiting the onslaught of the conqueror's army.

"Did your knees knock together, little Saxon," she whispered, "as badly as mine want to do?"

Someone seized her arm, and she spun around to confront Whitney, his face as pale as her own. "Melyssan, here you are. What are you doing?"

"I suppose I am going down to prepare for the arrival of my lord and his guest. The chambers in the north tower will want new rushes, and then there must be food."

"Are you planning to bake the meats for your own funeral? We must flee from here. There's still time."

"But I can't leave Sir Hugh and Lady Gunnor."

"Then bring them with us, for Christ's sake."

"No," Melyssan said, pulling away from him. "'Tis not safe for them. They must wait until tonight when Sir Hugh's cousin comes with the boat."

"That is what you told me when they arrived two days ago, and so far no cousin has ever showed. We can all escape right now through the water gateway below the castle. There is a supply boat that—"

"We would never get that far in the daylight before we were overtaken. And Lady Gunnor's children! If there were a struggle, they might be harmed."

"What about the harm to us if we stay?" Perspiration beaded Whitney's brow. "I'm not arguing anymore. I will take you out of here even if I have to carry you."

He took a step toward her, but she backed off and held her staff before her as if to ward him away.

"For the love of God, Lyssa, please," Whitney begged. "What am I to do if the Dark Knight should draw his sword upon me? You know I cannot..."

Stark terror crept into his soft green eyes, the same terror Melyssan had seen on her gentle brother's face a hundred times before when threatened with the clash of arms. She reached out to touch his cheek.

"Oh, Whitney, you go. By yourself, you could get away."

"But I cannot leave you."

"I—I will be all right. At the most, Lord Jaufre will imprison me. And you could ride home to Wydevale for help."

Whitney seized on the suggestion with pathetic eagerness. "Yes, I could, couldn't I? I could get Father to intervene with Lord Jaufre."

"I will be safe until then." She gave him an overbright smile, hoping to hide her disbelief in her own words. "But you must hurry."

They both became aware of a clamor of voices and a scurrying of feet at the bottom of the stairway leading to the solar. Knights, men-at-arms, servants, all scrambled to the courtyard to shout a welcome to their returning lord.

"Lyssa!" Whitney said in an agonized whisper. He caught her up in his arms and planted a kiss on her cheek. Then he turned and was gone, leaving Melyssan with a strange sinking feeling.

She was truly alone now—alone to face Jaufre's fury. Outside the narrow window, she heard a guard up on the parapet walk cry, "I can just make out the horses. They're coming over the crest of the hill."

Squaring her shoulders, she descended to the great hall and then down the covered stair leading to the bailey. She could scarcely see over the throng of heads to the main gate. The doughty figure of an elderly knight elbowed his way through the milling crowd of grooms, chambermaids, and clerks.

Sir Dreyfan's deep voice boomed, "My lady. What do ye back here? The earl will wonder what has become of ye." His smile beaming through his thick, grizzled beard, he offered her his arm with a grand flourish. She could not look at him as she accepted it. The gruff old knight had been so protective of her, so courteous since that long-ago summer day she had first arrived at Winterbourne. How his broad, honest face would harden with contempt when Lord Jaufre exposed her lies!

With an almost boyish spring in his step, he led her forward. Kitchen wenches, stableboys, soldiers, her ladies-in-waiting, all fell back, their faces shining with a joy and excitement she wished she could share. Sir Dreyfan escorted her to the very front of the assembled household and a few steps beyond, so that she stood out, a solitary figure, the first one Jaufre would see when he came through the gate.

Oh, Jaufre, she thought. Could it be true, all those things Beatrice said about you? "He hanged his wife, Lyssa." Bea's voice echoed in Melyssan's head. "No one even knew what Yseult had done to displease him. He just hanged her."

The clear high notes of a trumpet sounded, followed by a thundering of horses' hooves.

The guards standing up on the castle walls began to cheer. Melyssan closed her eyes tight, wishing desperately she was a little girl again and it was young Sir Jaufre outside the ramparts, only come to claim her veil. She felt a light touch on her shoulder as someone stepped into place beside her. Her eyes fluttered open, and she choked back a glad outcry.

Whitney. Fear still etched his features, but now it was mingled with shame as he hung his head. Blinking away her tears, she squeezed his hand, and he looked up to give her a rueful smile. Together they turned, hearing the creak of the pulleys as the iron portcullis slowly inched its way upward.

On the other side, the restive horses of Jaufre's knights shifted and brushed against one another, pawing the ground as if they, too, were eager to return to Winterbourne. Tristan barked a command to the excited pages to keep better hold of the bridles on the baggage mules and then snapped at the squire, Ross, to have a care what he was about: in another minute he would be dropping the earl's banner into the dirt. Maneuvering his way to Jaufre's side, Tristan stole a glance at the earl's stony profile and reflected he had never seen Jaufre so grim when returning to Winterbourne. Father Hubert didn't help matters with his constant needling about the bold hussy passing herself off as Jaufre's wife.

Le Gros swilled a large mouthful of wine from his leather flask. Wiping a spray of red droplets from his lips, he said, "Well, my lord. At least the bitch didn't turn away any more of your people. Good thing. You might not have been able to get back inside your own castle."

Jaufre said nothing, but Tristan noticed the slight tic at the corner of his mouth. The knight wished to heaven the stupid priest had some notion of when to hold his tongue. Jaufre was most dangerous when he went quiet like that, his eyes as hard as slate.

Tristan heartily regretted that Father Hubert had not been left on the other side of the Channel. He put little credence in Lady Finette's explanation that the priest had ecclesiastical affairs to conduct, but broaching the subject to Jaufre had been useless. The earl didn't care if the devil rode with him so long as he got back to Winterbourne to punish the woman pretending to be his lady. But *Le Gros*'s presence worried Tristan. There was always a dagger or a sword strapped where the priest's rosary beads should have been, and the pack of servants who accompanied him looked more fit for hanging than praying.

Tristan had tried to caution Jaufre before they set out. "'Tis rumored that *Le Gros* is not above pilfering from his host. It would not surprise me if Finette has not foisted this fellow on to you out of spite, hoping he will cause you some mischief. Everyone at Winterbourne knows you house your silver in the cupboard behind the mural. If *Le Gros* were to have opportunity..."

"If it worries you so, hide the money in

the chapel," Jaufre quipped. "That is one place you will never find the good father."

And that had been all the satisfaction Tristan got from warning Jaufre. He would have to keep an eye on *Le Gros* himself, Tristan thought, and then returned his attention to the business at hand as the great spiked bars were raised high enough at last to clear the entranceway to the castle.

Jaufre dug his heels into his stallion's glossy black sides and surged forward over the drawbridge, the pleasure he had anticipated from returning home vanished completely. Instead of this frustrated anger, his heart should have swelled with pride at the sight of his castle's gleaming white square towers and conical roofs set against the backdrop of the rolling Welsh hills. The fortress was his own, purchased by years of hard campaigning, winning prizes in tournaments, ransoming captured knights. Where was she, the scheming witch who had dared plunder Winterbourne in his absence?

As he traveled through the gate, he raised two fingers and nodded, perfunctorily acknowledging the salute of his castle guard. He wondered what sly laughter would spread amongst them when they discovered the truth about his so-called wife. Perhaps they knew already if Beatrice had taken flight.

But no. Standing next to Sir Dreyfan in a place of honor was a lady. Jaufre's heart filled with a kind of savage joy. So the wench had been too feeble-witted to run when she had the chance. Perhaps she hoped to throw herself upon his mercy. She would soon learn there was a reason for his byname.

As he cantered farther into the courtyard, the woman shifted position, and then he saw what her skirts had concealed. She leaned upon a staff.

Jaufre reined in sharply, nearly wheeling his horse around and spooking Tristan's skittish mount. But the Dark Knight was only vaguely aware of his friend's struggles to calm his animal.

No! No, it couldn't be. *She* could not possibly have anything to do with this deceit. Not—not Melyssan. He slapped the reins down, moving forward until he halted only a few paces away. There was no question of it now. It was Melyssan, her slender figure garbed in an unadorned kirtle of forest green, her brown hair bound demurely in a linen fillet with a stiff barbette passing from ear to ear under her chin. Her only ornament was a braided gold chain worn around her neck, and from the end of it dangled *his ring*.

Jaufre bit his lips tightly together to keep from roaring aloud. It was as if he could feel Yseult's dagger twisting through his flesh all over again. Damn Melyssan. Damn her to hell. The only woman he had brought himself to trust, to respect, since Yseult, and she proved a greater liar than all of them.

He swallowed hard, the extent of his rage and disappointment astonishing him. Tossing his reins down to a waiting page, Jaufre flung himself out of the saddle. He covered the ground between himself and Melyssan in three furious strides.

Sir Dreyfan clapped him on the back in boisterous greeting, then tried to express his sorrow at the tidings of the old comte's death.

"Later," Jaufre hissed, never taking his eyes from Melyssan. He planted himself in front of her, glad that she kept her head bent toward the ground. He didn't want to see those large round eyes that would remind him of the innocent little maid who had once thought him Sir Launcelot. Where had she gone? The way of all women, grown up to be a calculating, greedy bitch.

Then she did look up, and it infuriated him further to see no change in her serenely beautiful face, no trace of guilt. Sorrow, perhaps, and fear reflected from those luminous green eyes, but that was all. Soft pink lips trembled and then parted.

"W-welcome home, my lord Jaufre," she whispered.

Plague take her! What right did she have to stand there looking like a wistful young angel when her heart was so full of treachery? Jaufre drew back his hand, wanting to strike away that false expression, force her to glare at him with hatred, show herself for what she truly was.

Melyssan flinched and then steadied herself to accept the blow. But Jaufre lowered his hand, an icy calm encrusting his heart. No, he wouldn't make it that easy for her. He would dole her punishment out with poison-sweet slowness, racking her with uncertainty as to what he meant to do next. So the lady liked to play pretend, did she? Then he would join her in the game. Instead of flaying her body, he would flay her nerves, until she collapsed quivering at his feet. And then for his final vengeance...By the time this night ended, she would be ready to crawl the length and breadth of England, begging people to believe that she was not his wife.

Melyssan watched the emotions on Jaufre's face shift and change like sands on a shore raked by the tides of an angry sea. Sternness had given way to shocked recognition, to be replaced by the crimson flush of rage. But none of those expressions was as alarming as the devilish light that now danced in his night-dark eyes. The slow smile that spread across his face sent a chill up her spine.

"Melyssan, my sweet wife," he purred. "How I've missed you."

She gaped at him in wordless astonishment. Before she could resist, he seized her in his arms, grinding her body against the hardness of his chest until she thought her bones would snap. He claimed her mouth with a ruthless intensity that both stirred and frightened her, the rough satin of his beard abrading her chin, his warm, moist lips punishing and searing her with a heat that left her breathless.

When he finally released her, what little self-control she'd had shattered, leaving her quaking from head to toe. The delighted approval of the crowd roared in her ears until she thought she would swoon into an undignified heap. But Jaufre's arm, as unyielding as a band of iron, slipped around her waist, manacling her to his side.

"Dismount. Dismount, my friends," he called to the other horsemen. "Come forward and pay your respects to my lady wife."

"My lord, please..." She tried to protest, but her voice came out in a pathetic croak. As in a dream, the figures in the courtyard flitted before her eyes, leaving her with fragmented impressions of a bulky priest who nearly crushed the small page handing him out of the saddle; a knight who regarded her through kind eyes not entirely devoid of pity; her pale-faced brother stumbling forward until he blocked Lord Jaufre's path.

"M-my lord, what mean you by my sister?" Whitney stammered, his shaking fingers tugging clumsily at the hilt of his sword. "I—I do not understand."

"Ah, my esteemed brother-in-law," Jaufre drawled, giving Whitney such a buffet on the shoulder that the young man nearly lost his footing. "Whitford, is it not?"

Knocked off balance by the words as much as the blow, her brother replied, "N-no, Whitney."

"Of course. Whitney. The young scholar. I remember now." Without releasing Melyssan, Jaufre turned to face his knights. "A man of much learning, gentlemen. Schooled in both Latin and Greek. Despite his youth, I'll wager he has read more books than you have, Father Hubert."

"Humph, nothing to boast of," said the priest, rubbing his stiff backside. "'Cause I never read any."

Jaufre laughed, and Whitney flushed under the derisive stares he was receiving from most of the men.

Melyssan's protective instincts prompted her to try to wriggle free from Jaufre's embrace so that she could run to Whitney's side and somehow regain control over this bewildering turn of events. But her struggles were as ineffectual as those of a tiny linnet attempting to escape the powerful clutch of a mighty falcon.

"Be still, my little wife," Jaufre murmured in her ear, his breath hot upon her neck. "Would you pull away knowing how long I have desired to get my hands upon you?"

The words struck her like the double-edged steel of a sword, and she froze, allowing him to drag her wherever he chose. He stopped in front of the burly priest.

"This is Father Hubert, my sweet Melyssan, come all the way from Normandy to greet my bride and confer his blessing upon you."

"G-God give you good day, Father," Melyssan said, dipping into a weak-kneed curtsy and thinking she surely needed someone willing to pray for her.

"Your wife." Father Hubert scowled. "I thought you said—" Suddenly understanding lit his florid countenance. "Oh. Aye, your wife." He gave Jaufre a huge wink, then turned to Melyssan and bent forward. "Blessings upon you, my daughter," he said as thick wet lips reeking of sour wine smacked a kiss against the corner of her mouth.

Dismayed, Melyssan jerked back and stared into tiny snake-like eyes leering at her through puffs of flesh.

"That will do, *Le Gros.*" Jaufre elbowed the priest aside. "You have blessed my wife quite enough."

"How could I forget?" Father Hubert snickered. "All the world knows what a jealous husband you can be."

The lazy smile Jaufre wore faded, and his fingers dug painfully into Melyssan's side. The kind-looking knight drew in a sharp breath as his eyes flicked anxiously from the priest to Lord Jaufre.

What had there been in Father Hubert's teasing words to produce such a strong reaction? Melyssan wondered. Had it anything to do with the lady Yseult? She felt Jaufre's fingers loosening one by one as he forced himself to relax, and at last the tense moment passed.

"I am not all that ungenerous," Jaufre said dryly. "What about you, Sir Tristan? You have a bold heart. Would you not like to kiss my bride?"

Melyssan flushed with embarrassment as Jaufre propelled her toward the knight. Sir Tristan frowned at Jaufre, but he bowed stiffly over her hand and placed a chaste kiss upon the fingertips.

"Not so bold-hearted after all," Jaufre mocked. "Well, then, away, my friends, under my roof to rest your weary bones. Father Hubert, the hospitality of Winterbourne is yours to command."

He made the priest an exaggerated bow and then, glancing down at Melyssan, continued, "Let us celebrate my homecoming. Tonight, my dear little wife, we shall eat, drink..." Smiling wickedly, he pressed Melyssan even closer against the length of his hard-muscled thigh. "And be merry."

As dusk fell, servants hurried to light the flambeau in the great hall and set up the long trestle tables and benches for Lord Jaufre's feast. Above them in the solar, the earl prepared to lead the procession of knights and ladies-in-waiting down to supper. He paused once to glance at Melyssan, her profile illuminated by the flickering wall torch. Her delicate features were so pinched with apprehension, he almost repented of the course he intended to follow. From the look of her, she had not been squandering his money upon her garb. Even for the feast, she was still clothed in her plain green gown, although she had released her hair from its headdress to flow down her back, a simple gilt circlet banding her forehead. Yet what more ornament did a woman need when she possessed such a glorious cascade of shimmering nutmeg tresses?

The answer came to taunt him: his stolen

ring that she yet dared flaunt before his eyes. The sight of it glittering on the chain around her neck immediately dispelled any softness, any weakening of his angry resolve.

Melyssan felt Jaufre's eyes rake over her, assessing the outline of her breasts, the slender curve of her hips beneath her gown. Heat crept into her cheeks, and she fidgeted with her braided chain only to note the Dark Knight's eyes rivet on her hand.

What was amiss? Her fingers faltered as she suddenly realized. Oh, Holy Mother, the ring! She had forgotten she was still wearing his stolen ring.

"M-my lord," she said. "You—you must allow me to explain. I—"

"No time for chat now, my sweetheart." He chucked her under the chin. "Father Hubert is famished, I swear, he'll soon be eating the ties off Sir Tristan's cap. Come, it is time to go down."

And thus he cut her off again in the same manner as he did every time she tried to tell him how she came to be at Winterbourne, pretending to be his wife.

Below the horn sounded, announcing that all was ready. Jaufre linked his arm through hers and led her down the circular stair, slowing his pace to a degree that annoyed her. Gripping her cane, she hastened her step, meaning to show him she needed no such extraordinary consideration. But Father Hubert chose that particular moment to tread upon the train of her gown, and she found herself about to pitch headlong down the steps. Jaufre threw himself in front of her, and she tumbled into his arms. Her hands clutched at his blue velvet surcoat, its softness so at odds with the virile male body sheathed beneath. He held her against him longer than was necessary, his fingers sliding up her arm to linger alongside the swell of her breast.

"Such eagerness, sweetheart," he said. "You must go more slowly. You will get what you have coming to you soon enough." When her startled eyes flew to his face, he smiled mockingly. "I mean your dinner, of course."

She pushed away from him, her heart thudding as she smoothed out her skirts, trying to pull together the shreds of her dignity. As they entered the great hall, her skin still tingled from the impression of his hands upon her body.

The men-at-arms and household staff already settled at their tables stood respectfully to attention as Jaufre led Melyssan to the head table. At the bottom of the third table, she saw Sir Hugh and Lady Gunnor in their guise of humble pilgrims, blending in with a troupe of traveling minstrels. Faces were wreathed in smiles as the earl seated Melyssan in the high-backed carved chair and caught up her hand, tenderly brushing it with his lips. To everyone present, he must appear the doting husband, overjoyed to be reunited with his new bride. Only she could see the dangerous glint lurking in those hooded brown eyes.

No more of this taunting! She would force Jaufre to acknowledge she was not his wife, and then he could mete out punishment to her in honest fashion and make an end to this subtle torture. Her jaw set with determination, she half rose from her chair, catching Whitney's eye as he moved forward to take his place at the table.

As though he guessed her intention, he shook his head vigorously, calling to mind the counsel he had whispered to her earlier. "Do not anger Lord Jaufre. Continue to pretend you are his wife, if that's what he desires, until we can find some way to escape."

Even though Whitney was placed with the knights of lower rank below the salt and too far away to speak to her, the same message now flashed across his haggard features. As she sank back into her chair, she saw her brother heave a sigh of relief.

But how far would you have me go, Whitney? she thought. How far to appease His Lordship? She ran her finger over lips still bruised from the punishing fury of Jaufre's kiss. And how much more did the Dark Knight intend to demand?

Try as she might, she could not keep herself from staring at the earl as he stood and gave the signal for the servingmen to enter. Beneath the velvet surcoat, a tunic of blue satin strained across the powerful set of his broad shoulders. A silver belt cinched his narrow waist, raising his tunic enough to expose muscular calves encased in white hose. His thick black beard was newly trimmed and his blue-black mane swept back from his forehead to rest in perfect waves along the nape of his neck.

As he seated himself beside her in his canopied chair, she thought there surely remained within the depths of this noble-looking lord some notion of chivalry. He would not, could not, be planning anything to her dishonor.

Jaufre gave her that slow smile she was coming to dread and with one finger traced lazy circles along her forearm. The butlers and servingmen filed from behind the screens and paraded the length of the hall to the high table. They presented dish after dish of venison, mutton, roast boar, stews, minces, pies, all without gaining Lord Jaufre's attention. He feigned not to see them as he leaned on one elbow, gazing at Melyssan like a star-struck youth, until ripples of amusement spread along the lower tables. Melyssan's cheeks burned as Nelda giggled and Jaufre affected to come to with a start, waving the servants on to place their burdens on the carving table.

Father Hubert knocked the linen table-cloth askew as he scrambled to open his *nef*, the ornamental box placed before each guest that contained their silverplate.

Jaufre coughed discreetly. "Perhaps you would care to favor us with the benediction, Father?"

"What—oh, of course." Wiping the drool from his mouth as he took one last glance at the pages hurrying to slice the meat, *Le Gros* heaved himself to his feet.

"Oh, God, thank you for this food we are about to receive," he said in one great rush before Melyssan could even fold her hands together. "And—and we hope to hell there will always be plenty more of it. Amen."

A wave of laughter rocked the hall, until Melyssan thought that she and the shocked Father Andrew were the only ones who did not join in the merriment. She scarce knew what to think of Father Hubert. He made her uncomfortable when he chanced to look her way, his wide mouth stretching into a lascivious grin as if—as if he lusted for something more than his dinner. She averted her eyes to the table, ashamed of herself for allowing her imagination such free rein. Dame Alice had schooled her daughters to respect all men in holy orders. Father Hubert was likely only more convivial than the somber Father Andrew.

After *Le Gros* plunked back down onto his seat, Jaufre indicated that the pages could begin serving. Because she was the dinner partner who would share his trencher, he inquired of Melyssan what she desired for the first course. She gave a tiny shrug, leaving the choice up to him. He selected a portion of the roast boar and proceeded to cut off spoon-size chunks of meat and lift them from the trencher onto her manchet. The pink juices melted into the thick slice of wheaten bread that served as her plate. She removed a silver spoon from her *nef*, which was shaped like a tiny ship, and then proceeded to pick at her meat, the strong aroma of spiced pork doing little to tempt her appetite.

Jaufre ate heartily, keeping her within his gaze the whole time. His regard waxed bolder as he studied her flushed face, the arch of her neck, even while he continued to tear off portions of the meat, placing them between his lips and chewing with deliberate slowness. Licking the tips of his fingers one by one, he eyed her suggestively, mentally stripping away her kirtle and chemise until Melyssan felt naked before him. She gagged on the one bite she had managed to swallow and groped for the golden chalice she shared with Jaufre.

A moment later she began to choke. She had taken a huge gulp before she realized it was mead and not the watered-down wine she was accustomed to. Jaufre pounded her on the back as she came up sputtering for air. Her temper began to fray as, through streaming eyes, she caught a flash of his grin. Clenching her hands together in her lap, she resisted the urge to dump the rest of the vessel's honey-colored liquid over his head. She collapsed back in her chair, longing for an end to this torturous ordeal.

"Tired, my dear?" Jaufre leaned so close that his whiskers nearly grazed her chin. "Perhaps, if you are not hungry, we can retire early. I am sure our guests would not mind."

Melyssan sat bolt upright. "I am starved," she gasped, and began spooning the pork into her mouth without tasting it.

Conversation at the high table followed its customary bent, grumblings against King John's latest tyrannies.

"As if it were not enough, he wrung nearly every last cent out of the lady Blythe while she was his ward," Sir Dreyfan said heatedly. "Now the king has debased her by forcing her to marry some wool merchant who lined the royal coffers with a fat bribe."

Tristan lowered his spoon, frowning. "What more can be expected of a man who locks women and children away in a dungeon to die?"

"Not that old heart-rending tale again about Matilda de Briouse and her brat," groaned Father Hubert. "Served the proud bitch right, I say." He belched and drained his wine cup for the second time, although Father Andrew, who sat to his left, had not yet tasted a drop.

"Well, I suppose 'tis true her husband most grievously offended the king," Sir Dreyfan said.

"Grievously offended! And for this an innocent woman and her son were killed!" Melyssan cried out, then shrank back as the eyes of all the men turned upon her. She had not meant to take part in the conversation, but the story of Lady Matilda had upset her most strangely ever since her father had first told her of it.

When Matilda's husband fled the king's anger, John seized the lady and her son, shutting them up in a narrow cell until they slowly died of starvation. It was said the young man perished first, and, driven to the extremes of agony by her hunger, his mother had gnawed on the dead boy's shoulder.

The horrible tale had preyed upon Melyssan's mind for weeks, giving her nightmares. Even after all this time, hearing the woman spoken of caused her to shudder. Jaufre insinuated his arm along the back of her chair, allowing his fingertips to rest upon her shoulder.

"Come, my friends, I pray you find some other topic. You distress my bride with this talk of women dying."

But Father Hubert refused to let the matter rest. Thumping his palm on the table, he called for more wine and said, "The amusing part of the whole story is that John swore he would never harm the lady Matilda and her son. And he didn't. When he shut the pair up, he said he wasn't harming them, but he wasn't helping them, either." *Le Gros* burst into guffaws, spraying the linen cloth with his spittle. "Didn't harm...but didn't help, either."

Despite the fact that no one shared in his mirth, he slapped his huge thigh and began to wolf down his manchet, ignoring the polite custom that dictated the wheat bread be saved for the almoner to distribute among the poor. Crumbs fell from his mouth as he continued, "Now what I heard tell is that Lady de Briouse didn't know how to stop her tongue from running. When the king first demanded she dispatch her son to London as hostage, she told John's officer she had no intention of sending any of her children to a king who murdered his own nephew."

Tristan eyed the priest disdainfully. "In

which case the lady never said anything that the rest of us have not thought."

"If you've been thinking such things, you had best keep it to yourself," Jaufre warned Tristan. As he spoke he inched his hand up Melyssan's shoulder until he was able to stroke the base of her neck. "Young Arthur may have died under mysterious circumstances, but he was guilty of rebellion against his uncle and sovereign lord."

The idle caress from Jaufre's callused fingers produced a strange quickening in Melyssan's blood. She squirmed in her seat and finally pushed Jaufre's arm away. "It was only rebellion if you thought John had better right to the throne than Arthur. The people in Wales believed that Arthur was the true king. They believed he was Arthur the..."

Her words trailed off at the sound of Jaufre's rich baritone laughter. "Arthur the Pendragon born again? Come back with his sword Excalibur to lead his people in founding another Camelot?"

"Aye!" Her face burning, she raised her chin in defiance of the earl's patronizing scorn.

"Oh, Melyssan, I thought by now you would have outgrown such fairy tales." Jaufre chuckled. "To imagine John's nephew was the Pendragon reborn! You may as well believe that I am Sir Launcelot."

She shrank back as if he had dealt her a slap to the face. So he *did* remember the time he had met her at the tournament. How cruel he had become since then—that he should now seek to taunt her with her childhood dreams, mock her most cherished memory of him.

"Nay, my lord," said Tristan. "Forbear teasing your lady over events of which she cannot be expected to know the truth. She must have been no more than a toddling babe at the time of Arthur's rebellion."

"My old nurse was from Brittany, where the young prince was born," Melyssan said, staring unhappily down at her manchet, grown soggy with her uneaten dinner. "She explained everything to me."

"Did she also explain to you that such ideas about Arthur can be construed as treason?" The sharp edge in Jaufre's voice caused her to look up and find his brows snapped together in annoyance. "Now, talk of something else."

His command boomed down the length of the table, and after a brief silence, Sir Dreyfan started up a discussion of how good the hunting had been this summer, despite some Welsh bandits who had been poaching in Lord Jaufre's wood. Everyone seemed to forget the conversation regarding Arthur except Melyssan. She sat, twisting her linen napkin into knots as Jaufre's words returned to haunt her. *Arthur was a rebel against his sovereign lord, the king. Treason,* Jaufre had said. Did that mean the earl was unswervingly loyal to John, no matter what injustices the king might be guilty of? She shivered. Perhaps when he learned the king desired her, the Dark Knight would offer her to John with his compliments.

And Sir Hugh and Lady Gunnor...Melyssan's eyes strayed to the end of the hall, where the couple ate their dinner unremarked by most of the other guests. She prayed the Irish cousin would come tonight and she could get Lady Gunnor and her family away before Jaufre became aware that he sheltered so-called traitors at Winterbourne.

As the second course was served, Jaufre found that his own appetite had diminished. He studied Melyssan's pale face, wondering what she was thinking. She'd turned very pensive since the talk about Arthur, and her eyes kept darting toward the troubadours and pilgrims who sat near the screens.

Pilgrims. Jaufre's hand froze in the act of lifting his cup to his lips. When he had paused in the great hall earlier to greet some of his men-at-arms, one of the guards—Master Galvan it was—had whined something about how he'd tried to do his job, but the lady would insist upon admitting beggarly pilgrims in the dead of night.

Who journeyed by dead of night? No honest folk, surely. First thing on the morrow, he would examine these holy travelers whose presence made Melyssan so uneasy. He did not know what mischief she plotted with these strangers, but he would have none of it at Winterbourne. Bad enough it had been for him to permit all this loose talk of John's tyranny. There were too many knaves abroad these days ready to carry tales to the king. One such had already reported Jaufre's visit to the French court, arousing John's suspicions against his earl. Jaufre hoped to placate the king, not annoy him further. He would need John's support if he ever hoped to recapture Clairemont.

The banquet began to pall on Jaufre, and he pressed his knee against Melyssan's leg under the table, but she had become so quiet and withdrawn that she no longer responded to his baiting. She barely noticed when the pages served the last course of fruits, nuts, cheese, wafers, and spiced wine.

Then the pastry cook entered, his chest puffed out, as he supervised two young boys carrying a towering subtlety molded into the shape of a castle, the cunningly wrought battlements and turrets garnished with nuts and almond paste.

As they set the sweet confection before the earl, he started in recognition. By God, 'twas the Château Clairemont—to the last detail of the drawbridge and miniature watchmen constructed of sugar. The walnut Jaufre had been about to crack for Melyssan crushed between his fingers into a handful of tiny fragments. The last thing he wanted was another reminder of the burden placed upon him by his grandfather.

"I hope it pleases Your Lordship," the cook simpered, and bowed. "'Tis done in honor of your succession to the titles of the late comte, may God rest his soul."

"Thank you," Jaufre said, trying to summon forth a gracious smile.

Le Gros half stood, the rolls of his stomach

resting on the table as he squinted at the pastry as if he'd just noticed it. "C-Clairemont," he slurred, the effects of the wine he'd consumed evident in his florid countenance. "I—I'll be damned."

He smiled slyly at Jaufre. "Well, my lord, thash one way to re—redeem the pledge to the old comte." The priest waved his hand with a wild flourish. "Grandfather, I 'ave retaken the pashtry." Erupting into a fit of giggling, he dove across the table and broke off one of the turrets, spilling out the honey-sweet raisins that were stuffed inside.

As *Le Gros* dropped the hunk of pastry into his trencher, Jaufre's fingers clenched around the side of the table until his knuckles were white. Struggling to control his temper, he reminded himself that Father Hubert was his guest. It would be a waste of time and dignity to try and teach the pig better manners.

"Take that thing away," Jaufre snapped to the downcast pastry cook. "We have already eaten our fill."

When the subtlety was removed from his sight, Jaufre sat back down, drumming his fingers on the table. The sound of *Le Gros* sucking his fingers as he gorged himself on the pastry rasped at nerves already raw since his discovery of Melyssan's deception.

"Let us have some entertainment, my lord," Tristan interposed hastily.

"It appears we are already having it," Jaufre growled, his stare withering the grins off the faces of some of the younger knights who found *Le Gros*'s crudity amusing. "What say you, my lady? Are you of a mind for a little diversion?"

"What—whatever you wish, my lord."

Her meek demeanor only served to fan the flames of Jaufre's smoldering anger. Well, he would soon see how complacent she remained. "I think I should like to hear a tale...a traveler's tale. I see that we have some pilgrims amongst us this evening. Come forward, good people, and regale us with the wonders of holy shrines you have seen on your journey."

Her reaction was all that he desired. Shocked out of her lethargy, her face drained of color and her sea-shaded eyes dilated with fear.

"N-no," Melyssan stammered, her heart hammering against her rib cage. Sir Hugh and Lady Gunnor cowered on their bench, and she knew the simple couple lacked the wit and imagination to make up stories of their supposed pilgrimage. If they came before Jaufre, they were certain to expose themselves.

"See, my lord," she said desperately. "We have also jongleurs present. I should prefer some music."

For once Melyssan felt grateful to Father Hubert, for he loudly seconded her request. "A song. A song!" he bawled out, banging his cup against the table. "Lesh have a song." But her gratitude soon turned to dismay when the priest winked at her and added, "Lesh have a song from y'r lady, Lord Joffey. Bet she can warble a pretty tune."

91

"Oh, no," Melyssan protested, knowing full well her limitations. Enid had always been the musical one in their family. "I am sure one of the minstrels will be eager to oblige."

"Ah, but my guests long to hear your sweet voice, my dear," Jaufre said. His eyes glittered with mischief as he began to pull back her chair.

The other knights chorused their agreement, but Melyssan hung her head in mortification and gripped the sides of her seat.

"Surely you would not refuse us, my dear, when you are such a skilled performer." The barb behind his words only strengthened her resolve not to be made any more his fool than she already was. Stubbornly she shook her head, then gasped when she felt Jaufre's hand gliding over her knee. When his fingers began creeping up the inside of her thigh, she scrambled to get to her feet, glaring down at the earl's triumphant smile.

"Ah, my lady has changed her mind." He snapped his fingers. "Jongleur, if you would be so good as to accompany her."

One of the minstrels rushed forward with his lute, and Melyssan shook out her skirts, fuming over how neatly Jaufre had trapped her again. Still, if it kept his mind off Sir Hugh and Lady Gunnor...

The silence that settled over the great hall was enough to suffocate her. Clutching her trembling hands behind her back, she cleared her throat, her mind going terrifyingly blank. Then slowly she recalled the words to a song her nurse had taught her. It had come from the court of the old queen, Eleanor of Aquitaine, written by one of her protégés, Bernard de Ventadour.

When the flowers appear beside the green leaf,
When I see the weather bright and serene...

She sang in a wooden little voice, which had become inaudible by the time she reached the end. However, Sir Dreyfan came to her aid and swelled the last two verses with his booming bass.

And I must sing as all my days are full of joy and song
And I think of nothing else.

Smiling weakly at the gallant old knight, she plopped back down in her chair, her knees shaking in time with the polite smattering of applause.

Le Gros scowled, his nose nearly sunk inside his wine cup. "Thash a May song. Whash she singing a May song for when winter is coming?"

"Spring has always been my favorite time of year," she said quietly. "I have my fill of winter as soon as the first snow flies."

"And how long does it take y' to get y'r fill of the earl of Winterbourne?" asked *Le Gros*. "I bet it takes more'n one snow then. Thash quite a wench y' have there, Joffey. Don't go ahanging her as quick as y' did the lash one."

93

His coarse laughter echoed strangely in the great hall as a deathly silence fell over its occupants. All heads turned to Lord Jaufre, who had gone very still. Yet Melyssan saw no spark of anger in his deep brown eyes—rather, they were like granite.

The tension crackled in the air like damp pine logs tossed onto a dying fire. Everyone was aware of it except *Le Gros*, who hugged his trencher, scooping up some more of the pastry he had plunked on top of his meat. "Lesh have some dancing. Tell those rogues to play shumthing, Joffey."

The earl of Winterbourne snapped his fingers for a page to present him with ewer and basin to wash his hands. Then he rose slowly to his feet. "Come, Melyssan. 'Tis time to retire."

As he drew her up beside him and wrapped his arm around her waist, Melyssan's pulse leapt; she dreaded being alone with Jaufre as much as she was relieved to be escaping *Le Gros*.

But they had not moved two paces away from the table when *Le Gros* called out, "Leaving show soon, Joffey? Oh, thash right. Y'r lady wouldn't 'ave mush luck trippin' a meashure. But I'll wager that little crippled leg dances pretty enough when y' get down between 'er thighs."

Melyssan felt the muscle in Jaufre's arm jerk as if something had snapped deep inside. He whirled around and came at *Le Gros* from behind. Seizing him by the neck, the earl forced the thick skull downward, until *Le Gros*'s face smashed into his trencher. Jaufre's face contorted with fury, the cords standing out on his bronzed neck, as he jammed the head down harder despite Hubert's flailing efforts to get free.

Melyssan bit on her knuckle. Dear God, Jaufre was going to kill the man! *Le Gros*'s servants apparently thought so, too, for many of them had leapt from their seats and were moving forward, groping for their daggers. Jaufre's men-at-arms jumped up, more than ready to meet them with drawn sword. Some of the women screamed.

Tristan kicked his stool aside as he flung himself at Jaufre, attempting to pry the Dark Knight's fingers from *Le Gros*'s neck.

"Stop it, Jaufre! Do you hear me? *Stop it!* We'll have a full-scale battle here in a minute."

Either Tristan's words or the sight of his agitated face penetrated Jaufre's consciousness. Abruptly he released *Le Gros*, who sagged in his seat, his head lolling back as he gasped for air. Melyssan did also, realizing for the first time that she had been holding her breath.

"Keep your swords sheathed," Tristan ordered Jaufre's knights while he placed himself between the priest and the earl.

Le Gros's lackeys hesitated, waiting to take their cue from their master. Twisting his neck around, Hubert attempted to focus on Jaufre. His tongue shot out, and he licked almond paste and congealed gravy from his double chin. Then his eyes rolled back into their sockets, and he crashed to the floor in a drunken stupor.

Sighs of relief intermingled with the sonorous sounds of Hubert's snoring. Tristan bent down beside the priest, but Jaufre yanked him back.

"Leave him where he is 'til morning. The hounds will keep him warm." Without waiting for reply, Jaufre spun around, looking for Melyssan, his jaw working with the rage he had been forced to check.

When his eyes locked with hers, Melyssan could feel the heat of his anger scorch her like a red-hot brand. As he strode to her side, she backed away until she bumped into the wall. She knew her hour of reckoning had come.

Placing his arm behind her knees, he swooped her up high into his arms. Giddy from the helpless sensation of being borne aloft like a feather in a storm, Melyssan was dimly aware of Whitney's feeble protest. Jaufre carried her from the room and up the circular stair.

"P-put me down," she said, stiffening her spine. "I can walk."

"I do not doubt that you can, my sweet. But you must excuse a bridegroom's eagerness."

No one had ever looked less like an ardent groom than Jaufre with his thunderous countenance. Ramming her staff between them, she pushed feebly against the unyielding hardness of his chest. Her struggles became more frantic when she realized they stood just outside the bedchamber door.

"Take care, my little wife, lest I drop you."

"I am not your wife. I'm not," she cried, pounding on his back with clenched fist. "Now let me go."

"Not my wife?" he mimicked. "Then what does that make you? Surely not a liar? A scheming harlot?"

Melyssan flinched before the harsh insults.

"No, you musn't stop now, Melyssan. You've played your part to such perfection thus far. Now I mean to give you the chance to conclude your performance. Here—"

He kicked open the door with a resounding crash. "In my bed."

Chapter 4

JAUFRE TOSSED MELYSSAN onto the fur-covered mattress, the lean hardness of his body a crushing weight as he flung himself down on top of her. Her fingers gripped the handle of her staff, but she could not bring herself to use it as a weapon against him.

Instead she placed both hands against his shoulders, feeling tense muscle ripple beneath the satin cloth as she struggled to hold him back.

"Jaufre, please..."

"Please what, sweetheart?" he whispered hoarsely. "Make love to you? Aye, I will."

Love! How could he put such a name to this, this... The thought was swept away as he seized her by the nape of the neck, his mouth taking savage possession of hers, bruising, scorching her with the fury of his desire. And she, God help her, felt her own pent-up tension break free, nearly overwhelming her with the urge to return his kiss with a ruthless passion to match his own.

What more would the Dark Knight need to confirm his belief she was a harlot? Desperately she yanked her head away, turning her face into the sable coverlet as she panted. "Please, listen! I knew not what else to do. The king wanted me."

"As I do." His beard caressed the slender column of her neck as he pressed moist velvet lips against the sensitive hollow behind her ear, his hot breath fanning the tendrils of her hair.

"The king followed me to Wydevale. He— he made vile hints of what he'd do to my brother if I didn't..."

The words caught in her throat as Jaufre teased her earlobe between his teeth, tugging gently. He rolled off her and edged her skirt above her knee, skimming warm, rough fingers along her leg. Melyssan gasped and clamped her hand on her gown to keep him from lifting it any higher. "Please! I didn't know what else to do. I was so afraid. I—I remembered I had your ring, and 'twas then I told the king that I—"

She got no further, for Jaufre's fingers gouged into her thigh. "Yes, my ring! I'd almost forgotten." Propping himself up onto one elbow, he released her and seized the chain around her neck, jerking on it. She cried out as the links bit deeply into her flesh before the chain snapped free in Jaufre's hand. He thrust the signet ring forward until the falcon engraving was inches from her nose.

"While you're offering excuses, mayhap you'd like to explain how you came by this."

She shook her head helplessly. "I—I..."

In truth, she was not sure how Beatrice had gained possession of the ring. She only knew her sister had used the seal to forge a letter. That was how she had tricked her father's knights into taking her to St. Clare—under the pretense that it was instructions from her future husband. When Melyssan realized what had happened, she had followed Bea to the convent to reclaim the ring, meaning to return it to Jaufre one day.

Only she'd never envisioned it happening like this.

"Well?" Jaufre prompted when she remained silent.

In spite of Bea's deceit, Melyssan could not bring herself to betray her sister as a thief. "I—I found it."

Jaufre's dark eyes blazed, and for a brief moment, she thought he meant to lash the chain across her face. Instead he stood up and stalked over to one of the chests he had brought back from France.

"*She found it,*" he muttered through clenched teeth, knocking open the lid of his chest and throwing the ring inside.

Melyssan sat up, crossing her arms protectively in front of her, praying that Jaufre's rage was abating, praying he would become more reasonable.

"I am sorry, my lord. I never meant to anger you."

"I'll wager you didn't." He slammed the chest closed.

"I only took your name for a little while, only as a temporary escape from the king."

"Temporary?" His eyes raked her with contempt. "You've been at Winterbourne all summer, living off my estate. You even had the effrontery to get rid of Pevensy so you could continue your thieving with no interference."

"Pevensy?" Something flared inside Melyssan at the mere mention of that name. "Aye, now, if you wish to talk of thieves! I caught him selling off the oats while your horses went hungry, stealing crops from the peasants until they'd scarce strength enough left to till the fields—"

"Be silent! You'd best seek to defend yourself, not accuse my steward."

Heedless of the livid red mottling Jaufre's cheeks, Melyssan went on, "And the hall. Rushes stank like a pigsty. There was a dead bird left to taint the well, maggots in the meat. How could you leave such a knave in charge of Winterbourne?"

"Enough!" He'd had to listen to his grandfather upbraid him when he'd given Pevensy the post—he'd be damned before he'd endure such a tirade from Melyssan. By the feet of

Christ, the wench forgot herself and acted as if she *were* his wife!

"I didn't carry you up to my bed to be regaled with more of your tales." Had she not lied from the beginning, pretending to be his lady, making him look a fool? He'd believe nothing she had to say.

Tugging on his silver belt, he dropped it to the floor and then slipped the surcoat off his shoulders. She sat frozen, watching as he slid his tunic over his head. But when he began to untruss the points that held up his hose, she suddenly came to life and began scrambling for the door.

He seized her around the waist and dragged her back to the bed, wincing as the palm of her hand slapped him full in the face. Pinioning her wrists together, he began undoing the girdle that encircled her waist. He'd never taken a woman by force before, never had to. But this one, he tried to tell himself, this one deserved to be bent to his will.

She tossed her head back and forth, writhing as he began to pull the gown up over her. "Stop it. Stop it!" she cried. "Let me go. I hate you."

"You're not the first woman to tell me that." He sneered. "Though most of them wait to be satisfied before saying so."

Melyssan choked back the sob that threatened to rise in her throat. This could not be happening. Not even in her worst imaginings had she ever pictured Jaufre as he was now, his eyes hard, merciless, as he prepared to use his body to punish her, all honor, all gentleness, vanished. Despair washed over her as he ripped off her gown, leaving her clad only in her chemise.

Boldly he explored her body, his hands ravaging her with their heat even through the thin linen garment. He captured one breast, kneading it with his thumb, and much to her shame she felt the nipple grow taut with aroused longing. Her struggles ceased. It was hopeless, hopeless that she could prevent him having his way when a small secret part of her whispered she should surrender.

She went limp, making no resistance as he cupped her face between his hands, his kiss brushing her lips, coaxing them apart, then gradually deepening, drowning her in a sea of fire. She followed him into his own dark world, a void of swirling passionate emotions, but none of them love...none of them love.

Tears pooled in the corners of her eyes, spilling over, scalding down her cheeks. Jaufre's demanding mouth suddenly stilled, and then he drew slowly away from her, staring at the moisture that had trickled over his fingers. Staring as if struck dumb with astonishment, as if he knew not whence the droplets had come. When he reached out to her again, his arm trembled as he used the back of his hand to dry her cheeks, his brow knit into a frown as if he searched his mind for some memory that eluded him. He pulled his hand back to his body, clenching it as he rolled away, turning his back to her.

"Damn," he said hoarsely. "Damn it all to hell." He found her cane and hurled it across the room, the wooden staff striking the wall with a sharp crack. Leaping to his feet, he snatched up his discarded clothes. Without looking around, he stormed out of the bedchamber, the door crashing behind him with such force, the very walls seemed to shake on their foundations.

Melyssan lay still, too stunned by Jaufre's actions to move. Then her body began shaking as if with the chills that follow the onslaught of a burning fever. She hugged one of the pillows tight against her chest, feeling swallowed up by the great empty bed that seemed cold, barren now that he'd gone.

What had stopped him, driven him away, when he'd had her so completely at his mercy, even her own body betraying her to his desires? She lifted one hand to her cheek, where traces of her tears lingered, lingered with the impression of bronzed fingers brushing aside the dampness.

"Would you let such pearls as these fall upon the insensible ground?" The deep male voice echoed from the recesses of her mind, confusing the image of Jaufre, angry, bitter as he was, with her remembrance of a beardless knight whose youthful eyes shone with compassion as he...

Swept aside her tears. She sat bolt upright as the images blurred, became one man. Her heart raced with the realization that for one brief moment before he'd torn himself from her side, it had been Sir Jaufre de Macy who had regarded her through the eyes of the earl of Winterbourne, the Jaufre who could not hurt her, the Jaufre who yet might know how to love. He still lived, the Launcelot of her childhood dreams, buried within the battle-scarred chest of the Dark Knight.

But as she sank back down onto the feather mattress, her excitement over the discovery faded. Yes, he was still there. But would she ever find him again?

The lower floor of the donjon was dank and cold as it had been the first night Sir Hugh and Lady Gunnor had arrived at Winterbourne. Even though she wore only her chemise beneath her thick mantle, Melyssan remained oblivious to the chill, her heart much lighter than it had been the last time Father Andrew had summoned her from her bed.

Shifting her sleeping babe up over her shoulder, Gunnor embraced Melyssan, tears glistening in her eyes. "Never, never will I forget your kindness, my lady. If ever there comes a time when I can repay you, even if it should mean my life—"

"Nay, Gunnor, talk not of such things. 'Twas little enough I could do." Melyssan planted a kiss on the lady's round, dimpled cheek. "I only pray we meet again in happier times."

She hugged Gunnor one more time, then drew away, saying, "Now you must hurry. I vow your cousin waxes impatient."

She glanced down at the darkened waterway, where Sir Hugh had just lifted his son to a tall man seated in a small wherry. The knight mounted the stone steps made slick by the lapping water and held out his hand to help his wife down. With a misty-eyed smile, Gunnor carefully descended to the lightly rocking boat.

Sir Hugh turned to Melyssan. "Thank you again, Lady Melyssan. I hope that our stay here has caused no discord between you and the earl."

Truthfully Melyssan could assure him it had not, since Jaufre as yet remained in ignorance of the true identity of his guests and she hoped that he would remain so. Sir Hugh saluted her hand with his lips, then leapt down to join his family.

Huddling in the warm folds of her mantle, she watched until the boat was rowed under the arched gateway and became naught but a dim shadow on the river beyond.

Master Galvan hustled to lower the iron portcullis, grumbling to himself, "Pilgrimages in the middle of the night. Pilgrimages to the devil, I say. Good riddance!"

Although she would not have expressed it the same way, Melyssan shared the guard's relief. She limped back to where Father Andrew stood, holding the candle, waiting to guide her back to her room.

"Well, we did it, Father." She smiled. "Sir Hugh and his lady are safely away from Winterbourne."

"Aye," the priest agreed, his gaunt face still lined with anxiety. "But I would feel better if we had got you safely away as well."

"I will be all right," Melyssan said, for the first believing it herself, that she had weathered the worst of Jaufre's stormy temper and come through the experience untouched.

No, she deceived herself if she thought that. Although she was a maiden still, Jaufre's kiss, his fierce embrace, had touched her, shattered her calm forever, awakening in her a longing to know what it was like to be loved by a man. One man...the lord of Winterbourne.

She became aware that the old priest regarded her through troubled eyes almost as if she'd spoken aloud, as if Jaufre's caress had left some visible mark on her countenance. A telltale blush mounted her cheeks, and she said, "You must not worry about me, Father."

"I have worried about you ever since that day I perjured myself before the king, telling him 'twas I who married you and Lord Jaufre. Now I fear I may not have helped save your honor after all. When—when His Lordship carried you from the great hall..."

"Nay, Father, 'tis not as it seemed. Although Lord Jaufre was exceedingly wroth with me, I swear to you I am unharmed."

"I am glad to hear that, my daughter," the priest said as if he still reserved some doubt. "Even so, I wish you were far away from this place."

"As I surely will be soon. On my way to St.

Clare." She felt even less joy than usual at the thought of the convent. "In any case, I would not have gone without Whitney. How fared he after I left the hall?"

Father Andrew frowned. "He took no physical hurt. But his own meekness, his inability to defend you, gave him much spiritual pain. He went off with some of my lord's knights and I fear drank himself into the same condition as Father..." The priest's lips tightened as he corrected himself. "I mean Hubert Le Vis."

"My poor gentle Whitney." Melyssan sighed. "If only he were not an only son, if only he had your choice, Father."

"The priesthood was not meant to be an escape from the problems of this world," Father Andrew said sternly. "Any more than a convent is. Now come, child. 'Tis time you returned to your bed."

He walked on ahead, illuminating the treacherous curved steps. Melyssan followed, pondering what the priest had said. Were his remarks meant for her as well as Whitney? Yet it was not as if she willingly sought to hide herself at St. Clare. In her wickedness, she'd begun to think she would offer up her soul for another future, a future such as other women enjoyed—the shelter of a warm home, a strong husband, babes.

All those things that Jaufre's wife would have when he married again. And if he ever chose to give his heart as well, that lady would be more blessed than all the saints.

Of course when Jaufre took a bride, it would be a maiden like her sister Beatrice, lithesome, beautiful, able to walk straight, graceful beside him, dance on their wedding day.

Her shoulders sagged at the thought until she felt leaden with weariness, drained by the day's events that had so unsettled her existence at Winterbourne. She parted from Father Andrew in the great hall, assuring him that the wall torches were adequate lighting for her to find her way back. Shuffling across the rush-strewn floor, her eyes were drawn to the spot where Father Hubert had collapsed, and she half expected to find him nestled amongst the many servants asleep on their pallets. But the huge bulk of the man was gone, and she assumed that in spite of Jaufre's command, Tristan had moved the priest to a more comfortable resting place.

All was silent, even the guards making their rounds in another part of the castle. Therefore when she approached the door to the solar, the scraping noise, slight as it was, carried to her ears. She paused, wondering if one of the greyhounds had somehow gotten itself shut up inside the room. Strange, though, that the animal did not howl and bark until it was released.

Leaning against the door, she opened it a crack and peered inside. Much to her amazement, a tallow candle burned, throwing out a small circle of light from its position on the table. The scratching issued not from just inside the threshold, but over by the

Conquest mural. Swinging the door open wider, she confronted the broad buttocks of Hubert Le Vis as he bent down to squint at something, wiping away the perspiration glistening on his rotund face with a linen napkin.

Her gasp of surprise startled him, and he twisted his head around. Spotting her in the doorway, he scrambled to his feet with astonishing swiftness for a man of his size and one moreover who had been presumed dead drunk only hours earlier.

"Why, if it isn't Lord Jaufre's...lady." After his initial shock at seeing her had faded, he leered at her, moving closer. "What draws you from your bed at this hour?"

A twinge of apprehension nipped at her, and she paused uncertainly in the doorway. "I thought I heard some sort of scratching in here."

Father Hubert mopped at his brow again. "Oh, that. Yes, I heard it, too. Rats behind the wainscoting, I think."

"Rats! 'Tis impossible. That's a solid stone wall." She ventured a timid step inside the room, trying to see the painting, but Father Hubert blocked her path. He reeked of wine, his red-veined eyes staring at her with an odd intensity, his mouth going slack. The hair prickled along her arm at having him so near, but she tried to repress her shivers. Despite his peasantlike manners, the man was, after all, a priest.

"Surely a lusty wench like you can find better ways to spend her nights other than rat catching." He chuckled, his coarse fingers brushing her neck as he lifted one of her tresses, inspecting the golden-brown wave.

She snatched the strands away, stumbling back, her uneasiness at being alone with him growing stronger every minute. But she forgot her disquiet when she spotted a sword and a small pile of wood chips on the floor beyond him. "What is— Oh, no. The mural!"

Stooping down, she stretched her fingers out to the Saxon warrior she had touched only that morning. Now the figure was mutilated beyond recognition along with several other of King Harold's soldiers. Why would anyone want to deface such a magnificent painting? It was almost as if the vandal expected to find something behind…She froze as she remembered how she'd once heard her father speak of ambries, spaces many noblemen carved out in the walls of their castle to hide their valuables. But she'd never thought of there being such a thing at Winterbourne. Lifting her staff, she rapped on the mural panel. It was hollow.

"Some thief must have been trying to get at Lord Jaufre's treasure," she said, straightening up. "Did you see anyone, Father?" She stopped as an unwelcome realization crowded into her mind.

"No one at all," he said with a chilling smile.

"I—I had best summon the guard."

Striving to suppress her growing panic, she hobbled toward the solar entrance, but *Le Gros*'s thick hand shot past her, slamming the door shut as he leaned his weight against it.

"A pretty performance, my dear." His porcine features split into an evil grin. "Such wide-eyed innocence. But I've a notion you've known about the cupboard for some time, clever girl that you are. Now why don't you be a good child and show Father Hubert how to open it, and perhaps I'll share with you."

"Let me out of here," she said, outrage and fear making her voice shrill. "Open this door at once, or I'll scream!"

Her threat was useless as large, grimy fingers clamped down over her jaw, *Le Gros*'s other arm coming around her waist and lifting her off her feet.

"Think again, my lovely little bitch. You'd better be more—God damn you!" he hissed as she sank her teeth into him. With a guttural cry of pain, he dropped her.

Frantically, she crawled toward the door, but *Le Gros* was upon her again. He seized the top of her mantle, yanking it upward so that her head snapped back, the metal clasp cutting deep into her throat, choking her. She clawed at the joining until it released, sending her flying forward, her forehead grazing the oaken door.

Tossing the mantle aside, he grabbed for her. Her breath came in ragged little gasps as she found the strength to thwack her staff against his shinbone. But as she drew back to strike again, he wrenched the staff from her grasp. His fingers gnarled in her hair, dragging her away from the door as she screamed only to be silenced by his meaty fist cracking into her jaw. The room spun sickeningly as he flung her to the floor, crushing her beneath the flaccid layers of his obese frame.

She opened her mouth to cry out again, but this time it was his thick wet lips that cut off the sound. A tongue fetid with the taste of stale wine and rotting teeth thrust deep into her throat, gagging her. Suffocating, she flailed about wildly until she caught hold of the chair leg and tried to topple it onto him, but it crashed harmlessly to the floor.

The noise did have the effect of causing *Le Gros* to raise his head, allowing her to breathe. Her stomach heaved, and she wheezed pathetically, terror having robbed her of her voice.

His reptilian eyes burned with something akin to madness as he panted, "Should've been reasonable, my lady. So you want to betray me? Then I must wring your pretty little neck. But first I'll have a sample of what Lord Jaufre's been feasting on."

Shifting his weight, he hooked his fingers around the neckline of her chemise, and the sound of rending material assailed her ears as he tore it down the middle, exposing her breasts to his lustful gaze.

New sensations of horror shot through her body, reviving her flagging strength. She clawed at his eyes, scratching the flabby pockets of skin as he ripped the garment the rest of the way, leaving her completely naked beneath him.

Grunting with rage, he caught her arms and pinioned them over her head. With his free hand, he administered a series of open-palmed slaps to her face until her senses reeled and she was dizzy with pain.

"N-no," she sobbed. "Oh, God help me. Jaufre...Jaufre!"

He smothered her cries by stuffing the sweat-soaked napkin into her mouth, taunting as he did so, "Do y'think he'd care who has a piece of you, bitch? After what you've done to him? Wonder is he 'asn't already snapped your neck at the end of a rope like he did his first whore. Nay, wench. He's likely to thank me for this."

Le Gros's hand closed over her breast, dirt-encrusted nails scraping the tender flesh, pinching the nipple until her throat went raw from the anguish she could not release by screaming.

She forced her tear-filled eyes to remain open even though *Le Gros*'s puffy jowls and drooling lips swam before her. She had to wake up. It was the only way to make the nightmare go away, make the king vanish like the dreadful phantom he was.

But it was not the king bearing down upon her. It was *Le Gros*, and the knee he slammed between her legs, prying her thighs apart, was agonizingly real. There would be no waking up this time, no sweet fantasy of Jaufre to keep the night demons locked away where they belonged.

Oh, Holy Mother, she prayed. Let me die. Just let me die before he...

Her eyelids fluttered as she willed herself

into oblivion; the last sight misting before her was Jaufre's face. She imagined he cried her name, yet she heard nothing but a muffled growl as darkness claimed her.

The next she knew, her body felt strangely free, as if a great burden had been torn away, leaving her floating in a spinning black emptiness. And cold, so cold. She managed to open her eyes and was dazzled by blinding light. Was this what it was like to die?

The roaring in her ears slowly disappeared until she could hear other sounds, muted at first, then louder, inhuman shrieks and curses spawned from the depths of hell.

"Goddamned bastard...should've killed you."

The light resolved itself into a single candle flame, and Melyssan rolled her head toward the voice, the pain that knifed through her head telling her that she was still very much alive. Her vision clouded and then cleared, so that she saw figures moving as if through a fog. Jaufre, his face twisted with demonic fury, towering over a shapeless brown form...pudgy, thick-knuckled hands lunging for Jaufre's throat...Jaufre's fist plunging into Father Hubert's stomach...the priest doubling over...Jaufre's booted foot, flashing, taking *Le Gros* full in the face.

Jaufre was going to kill him. Tristan must stop him before it was...The confused thought slipped away as she closed her eyes, trying to remember where she was. No, she'd left the banquet hours ago. She was in—she opened her eyes—in the solar. And Jaufre had appeared from nowhere, attacking Father Hubert again, because, because the priest had...

Her hand fell on something, thin fabric shredded, tattered remnants clinging to her bare skin. Because the priest had raped her. Waves of nausea swept over her with the return of anguished memory.

"Get up, you whoreson dog." The toe of the Dark Knight's boot slammed into *Le Gros*'s rib cage, punctuating every word. "I said, get up!" Father Hubert groaned and was still.

Melyssan saw her arms and legs move as if they belonged to someone else, dragging her up until she crouched on the floor, violent tremors racking her body. Suddenly Jaufre hovered over her, tucking her mantle around her. But it didn't warm her. Nothing, nothing would ever draw the chill from her bones. She glanced up and found in his brown eyes a reflection of her own torment. Hands bruised from the savage blows inflicted upon *Le Gros* now gently stroked the tangled curls back from her face.

"No!" She wrenched her head away, forcing the words through swollen lips. "Don't touch. Don't look at me. I'm vile, dirty. He—"

"He didn't," Jaufre whispered fiercely. "I stopped him, tore him away. Melyssan, please believe me."

Her eyes roved fearfully around the shadowed corners of the room. "Is he gone?" she quavered.

"He's over there." At her terrified start,

he clutched her shoulders. "Don't be afraid. He's unconscious, perhaps even dead. He won't hurt you again, I swear it."

But as if Jaufre's oath had been an incantation, *Le Gros* loomed up behind the earl, like a malevolent gargoyle springing to life from stone, red eyes blazing, red mouth foaming with blood.

The blade of his sword glinted as it hissed through the air, arcing toward Jaufre's neck. Melyssan's strangled cry alerted the Dark Knight, giving him precious seconds to dive for the floor, taking her with him. The sharp edge whizzed inches from the top of his head and clanged loudly against the wall. In one fluid motion, Jaufre was on his feet, assuming a defensive stance between Melyssan and *Le Gros* while he drew forth his dagger. The short blade looked absurdly inadequate beside the priest's length of gleaming steel, the sting of a wasp against the fang of a wolf.

Le Gros spat out a mouthful of blood and teeth and began to circle Jaufre, demented laughter shaking his bulky form. "You tried twice. Kill me over a whore. Now my turn." He made a wild lunge, which Jaufre barely sidestepped.

"Melyssan," Jaufre said. "The door. Crawl to the door."

She heard him, but she could not make her paralyzed limbs obey. She watched as *Le Gros* flew at Jaufre again and again, the wildness of his swings and his lack of agility the only things that saved the earl. Jaufre danced

116

around him, his body tensed to spring if he ever found his opening. One instant of bad timing and *Le Gros*'s weapon would hew deep into the earl's flesh. If Jaufre should tire, stumble...

She had to help him. Had to. Fighting off the numbness terror had imposed upon her, she crept forward, the straw rushes abrading her hands and knees. A few yards away she saw her staff. If she could reach it, trip Father Hubert with it or strike him, distract him for but a moment, allowing Jaufre his chance...

There, the staff was now only a foot away. She cowered back as heavy feet trampled dangerously near her arm. *Le Gros* spared her not so much as a glance, his eyes now glazed with a lust to kill. As he launched himself at Jaufre, she summoned up one last effort, throwing herself at the walking stick. Her fingers closed over the tip as Hubert's sword ripped the side of Jaufre's tunic, the blade coming to rest with a dull thud against the table. The blow reverberated the length of the wood, toppling over the candle and sending it rolling toward the edge. Jaufre swooped on it to prevent the flaming wax from dropping into the straw. The room plunged into darkness.

Melyssan could no longer identify the shapes of the two men, but she could hear, sounds all the more terrifying because she could not see who made them. The clatter of steel, a scuffling of feet, then a deep groan, someone falling, crashing to the floor near her. Nearly crazed by her blindness, she longed for the courage to reach out but dreaded what she might find.

"Jau-Jaufre?" she called softly, her heart thundering in the deathly stillness. She received no reply except for heavy breathing and boots rustling through the straw, moving inexorably to where she crouched, the thin staff her only shield.

Chapter 5

MELYSSAN HELD HER breath, trying to still the movement of quaking limbs, but the footsteps continued to advance upon her as if guided by unerring instinct. Hands slick with perspiration closed on the end of the staff and she drew it back, poised to strike.

At that instant the door crashed open, flooding the room with torchlight, illuminating the face of the man bending over her. Raven strands tumbled down into mahogany eyes. *Jaufre.*

The staff fell from her nerveless fingers as she staggered into his strong arms, which closed tightly around her, banding her to his hard-muscled chest. Through labored breaths, he murmured her name, burying his lips against her hair.

Dry sobs convulsed her frail shoulders. "I thought he killed you."

"Jaufre! What the devil!" Tristan's voice broke

into her consciousness. He stood frozen in the doorway, sword drawn. *"Le Gros,"* he croaked. "Sweet Mother of Christ!"

Tristan stared down at the floor, and then she saw what riveted his gaze. Large feet sprawled apart, jutting out from a mound of black wool in which the hilt of the dagger poised like a jeweled ornament. A red stain pooled over the huge expanse of chest.

Jaufre felt Melyssan shudder, and he pressed her face against his tunic, blocking out *Le Gros*'s white, puffy face contorted into a grimace of death.

"Tristan," he said, snapping the knight out of his shocked trance. "No questions. Dispose of that carcass. Keep this quiet until I talk to you."

Folding the mantle more tightly around her, he swept Melyssan off her feet, cradling her against his chest. "Now I must look after my wife."

"Your wife," Tristan repeated, giving him an odd look. "Oh. Aye, my—my lord."

But the strangeness of what he'd just said barely registered with Jaufre as he raced up the curving stair, clutching her tight against him, his only thought that he must get her warm. The hand that gripped the neckline of his woolen shirt was clammy, and the only sound issuing from her was ragged little gasps.

He'd rebuild the fire, wrap her up in the furs, and beyond that he didn't know. He didn't know how he would deal with the shattered look in those sea-green eyes, didn't know

119

how he could soothe the pale forehead pinched with tormented thoughts he could only guess at.

Up in his chamber, he eased her onto the bed and tried to pull the coverlet over her, thinking if she would just go to sleep, then perhaps in the morning...

But she sat up, shoving the furs away. Underneath the mantle, she hugged herself across her breasts and rubbed her arms. "I have to wash," she whispered.

"What?" he asked, not understanding. "'Tis not morning yet, Melyssan. You need to rest, forget—"

"No! I need water. Need to wash away the feel of *him*."

He could not reason with her and, in the end, sent a page to fetch a pail from the cistern. When Jaufre brought the leather bucket inside the room, he thought the icy water was the last thing she needed, but she snatched the receptacle away from him with the eagerness of one dying of thirst.

Turning her back to him, she stood near the fire he had kindled in the hearth, dropping what remained of her torn chemise. She slipped the cloak back so that it hung just from her neck, baring ivory shoulders along with glimpses of the creamy swell of her hips and firm, high breasts as she began splashing the frigid water over herself.

Ashamed to find himself staring, Jaufre averted his eyes toward the door, confused thoughts tangling a web in his mind. By God's blood, he'd killed a priest tonight. There would likely be hell to pay when his deed was discovered by the church, by the king. And yet the very idea of *Le Gros* set his blood to boiling all over again. He relived with vicious satisfaction the moment he'd snuffed the candle and pinned Hubert's wrist to the table, guiding his dagger through the dark with feral accuracy, thrusting it through the layers of soft, blubbering flesh into that maggot-ridden lump that passed for a heart.

He had killed men before in battle, but never with such a degree of hatred. The intensity of his loathing surprised him. He'd viewed Hubert as a buffoon, an irritating clown, at most. Yet earlier this evening, when *Le Gros* insulted Melyssan, when he'd caught the bastard trying to rape her, he'd fallen upon the fat knave as if he'd had the chance to rid the world of the devil himself.

And all over a woman Jaufre had termed a lying wench, a scheming harlot. Yet it was no harlot's reactions to a man's lust that now drove her to scour herself as if her skin were infected with a leprosy. He stole a peek at her and saw her abrading the tender flesh of her forearm with a violence that left it raw.

Unable to restrain himself, he rushed to her side. "Melyssan, what are you doing? Stop it."

Quickly she draped the mantle around herself again, but not before he saw the livid red splotches marring the pearl-colored skin. She continued to scrape at her hands, crying out with a little catch in her voice, "It won't come off. I can still feel it. It—won't—come—off."

He grabbed the linen towel away from her, and when she struggled to get it back, he seized her by the wrists and hauled her away from the water bucket.

For a moment she held herself rigid, glaring at him, her eyes a mirror of helpless rage, shame, and despair. Then she collapsed, the tears flowing free at last, as she muffled her sobs against his chest.

His previous anger and mistrust of her were for the moment swept aside as he sat down on the stool by the hearth, pulling her onto his lap, cradling her in the protective circle of his arms, wanting only to comfort her, restore the serenity that was as natural a part of her as the flowing nutmeg hair he caressed.

Her arms tightened around his neck, her hot tears trickling down his throat as she pressed her face against his shoulder, weeping as stormily as a little girl.

"Why—why did he do it? Why?" The words came brokenly between her sobs. "He took—holy—vows. He was a priest—a priest!"

Jaufre did not know what answer to give as he stifled his own cynical opinion that priests were no different from other men in their lusts, and very likely worse, having to keep up a front of holiness and celibacy. Awkwardly, he patted her on the back, his hand tense with frustration that he, who could put the heart back into war-weary soldiers with but a look, was so inept at mending the broken spirit of one sensitive girl.

To his relief, she quieted at last, her arms relaxing their hold on him as she nestled her head beneath his chin. She still shuddered from time to time, the movement of her warm breasts penetrating his senses even through the layers of clothing. He became self-conscious of the fact that she was naked beneath the mantle and shifted restlessly on the stool.

"Melyssan," he said, "'Tis time you were abed."

But when he attempted to lay her down upon the feather mattress, she clung to him, fear once more clouding her red-rimmed eyes.

"Do not leave me," she said. "He—he will come back if I am alone."

"Nay, little one. He cannot. He is dead." Gently he traced the outline of the bruise *Le Gros*'s brutality had left on her babe-soft cheek.

She grasped his hand and hung on with desperation. "In my dreams. He'll come back for me in my dreams the same as the king always does."

Vaguely he remembered her telling him something about King John desiring her, using that as her reason for posing as his wife. But he hadn't believed her then, would have rejected any excuse she had to offer. Now he began to wonder. She was a skilled mummer indeed if she could feign that great a look of terror.

He found he was not proof against the plea

in those misty, sea-shaded eyes. "Very well, I'll stay," he said, stretching out reluctantly on the bed. "You—you sleep now. I'll allow no nightmares to escape past my guard this night."

She gave him a tremulous smile and settled down beside him. He held his body rigid, aloof, but it was useless. She snuggled close to him like a lost soul in a storm seeking the shelter of a mighty fortress. She begged that he leave the bed curtains open, the candles burning, so that he had no choice but to stare at her face, so young and vulnerable as her swollen lids drifted closed, resting gold-fringed lashes against the blue shadows beneath her eyes. Her pink lips parted, issuing warm, sleep-blurred breaths. Beneath the coverlet, he could feel the soft contours of her body molding against his hip and thigh.

"Sweet Jesu," he muttered as he was assailed by a burning sensation in his groin, the same burning sensation that had driven him to walk the castle walls after he had left her earlier, hoping the frigid night air would douse the fire of his frustrated passion. He had been affected then as he was now by her air of innocence, her childlike trust. When he had dragged her away from the feast, he had been determined to punish her, but her tears had checked his angry lust, tears that reminded him of the little girl who had once thought him Sir Launcelot.

So what was she now—a little girl with a

woman's body tempting him with every artless gesture she made? Or a clever schemer using all the wiles known to womankind to pluck at the chords of his compassion, playing him for a greater fool than he'd ever been before?

Was she like Yseult had been that afternoon she'd claimed Godric had raped her, pretending to be distraught? Or was Melyssan truly as she appeared, a maiden whose virginity had been spared, but whose very soul had been violated by the priest's betrayal?

He was not sure, uncertain of anything except that he wanted her, wanted her with a desire more exacting than he had known before, when his passion had been fueled only by anger. Tentatively he touched the pale hollow of her throat, but when she stirred in her sleep, he snatched his hand away in disgust.

Faugh! He was no better than that stinking whoreson *Le Gros*. If she had not wept before when he had tossed her down onto the bed, it would have been he who had ravished her and not the drunken priest, the memory of his own touch driving her near to madness, abrading her flesh to be cleansed of him.

After what she had been through, how could he allow images to flit through his mind of her warm, supple body writhing beneath his— and she all the while sleeping beside him with the peace of the angels on her face? 'Twould be best if he left her again.

But when he tried to ease himself back off the bed, a tiny whimper of protest escaped her.

Even in the depths of slumber, a furrow knit her brow.

Christ, he'd promised her to stay, promised to fend off all the bad dreams. He pictured her waking after her nightmare phantoms had once more stalked their cruel path through her mind, waking to cower alone in the empty bed, cowering as when she'd first believed *Le Gros* had succeeded in raping her. The devastated look in her eyes had pierced him more keenly than any swordpoint that ever scored his flesh. No, he could not risk leaving her alone again.

Resigning himself to his torment, he settled next to her, his mouth twisting into a wry smile at the irony of his situation. He, who had not endured a woman sleeping in his bed since the death of Yseult, now had to spend the long hours until dawn embracing Melyssan's naked beauty without so much as a kiss for his reward. Forcing his eyes closed, he eventually drifted off into a night of fitful dozing, a night of the sweetest torture he'd ever known.

The light prickling along her eyelids was too strong to come from the candles. Melyssan opened her eyes to see the morning sun filtering through the bedchamber window, one of the few embrasures in the castle that was wider than the arrow slits and fitted with a mosaic of stained glass. Without quite knowing what she was reaching out for, her hands trailed across the feather mattress only to find a

126

hollow, an empty space, where Jaufre should have been.

Hearing a movement by the foot of the bed, Melyssan bolted into a sitting position, clutching the fur coverlet in front of her. But it was only Nelda laying out a fresh chemise and gown.

"Good morrow, my lady." The curly-headed girl gave her a cheerful smile. Then, as if she noticed the way Melyssan's eyes searched the room, she said, "His Lordship's gone down this hour and more. He bade me leave you sleep as long as you desired."

"Oh." Melyssan leaned back against her pillow, feeling strangely deserted. Something jabbed against her neck, and she realized she still had her cloak hooked around her shoulders. She remembered how she had worn it to bed last night, the woolen folds keeping her back warm beneath the coverlet while the hard length of Jaufre's body... The heat of a blush crept into her cheeks.

Nelda bustled around the room, whistling softly despite the fact that it was a thing Melyssan oft gently reminded her no lady should do. She filled a basin with warm water for her mistress's bath and then stooped to pick up the remains of the tattered chemise from in front of the hearth.

She rolled her eyes at Melyssan and giggled. "My lord must have been very glad indeed to be home again!"

Melyssan compressed her lips into a tight line. "Burn it!"

"My—my lady? I crave your pardon, but did you say—?"

"I said 'burn it'!"

"But perhaps I could mend it."

"Toss it into the fire," Melyssan said sharply, her nails digging into the bedclothes. "Now."

Bewilderment etching her pretty face, Nelda turned slowly and obeyed. The flames leaped up to consume the torn linen, transforming it into a blackened rag whose ashes were carried up the chimney by the draft. Only then did Melyssan relax and rise to bathe and dress herself.

Her body was stiff and bore the mark of more than one bruise inflicted by *Le Gros*'s rough hands. Although a part of her was still raw and aching from the experience, recollections of Jaufre's tenderness, the strength of his arms around her, his wordless comfort, overshadowed the other, more bitter memory.

Donning a kirtle of cornflower blue with wide flowing sleeves, and fastening the household keys and a kerchief onto her belt, she started when she saw her staff propped next to the bed.

"Oh, the earl brought that up earlier," Nelda explained. "He said you had forgotten it."

Although Melyssan could manage to walk without the cane, her movements came easier and more graceful with its support. She caressed the smooth wood, touched that Jaufre should have remembered to go back to the solar and find it for her, but her fingers froze around the handle with Nelda's next words.

"And he also said I was not to discuss what happened last night with you, but you must hear of it soon, and I shall burst if I can't tell you. What do you think? Someone murdered that fat Norman priest."

"Murdered?" Melyssan said, not wanting to speak of it, yet puzzled by Nelda's version of the incident, so different from what she to her sorrow knew to be true.

"Aye, skewered his heart with a dagger like a chicken on a spit." Nelda nodded her head, obviously relishing every detail. "That pack of ruffians he brought with him were causing quite a stir about it this morning, but Lord Jaufre already sent them on their way. Made them take Father Hubert's body with them, he did. All the way back to France. Said he didn't want any such carrion rotting in our English ditches. Now who do you suppose would have killed the priest, my lady? One of our people?"

"I have no idea," Melyssan snapped, wanting to put an end to Nelda's stream of excited chatter. "If Lord Jaufre said you were not to discuss the matter, you'd best obey him."

She hastened to quit the chamber lest Nelda see her agitation. So as yet no one knew the shameful truth of what had occurred in the solar. She was grateful, for it would make it easier for her to face the household this morning; but she wondered how long the facts behind Father Hubert's death could remain a secret.

Her steps faltered when she reached the circular stair that descended to the solar. She dreaded passing through that room, but there was no other way down to the great hall. Fortifying herself with a deep breath, she planted one foot after the other, forcing herself onward although her heart pounded as if she expected to find Father Hubert bent over the mural to begin her terrible ordeal all over again.

But when she reached the room, she found that the sun had swept away all the sinister shadows like cobwebs whisked before a broom. Even the rushes had been changed, concealing any trace of blood that might linger on the wooden floor. The only reminders that anything out of the ordinary had taken place were the scarred faces of the soldiers on the Conquest painting and a few drops of hardened wax on the table.

Although the room was back in order, she had to force herself to relax, only to jump again with fright when she heard the rustle of straw behind her. She whirled around, eyes dilating as she drew up her staff in a defensive posture.

"Melyssan." Father Andrew's mild features regarded her with surprise. "I missed you this morning when you did not come for prayers. Are you ill, my child? You look so pale."

"No. No, nothing is wrong." She lowered her staff and backed away to stare unseeing out the croslet, anything to avoid looking at him. Father Andrew's spare frame was so different from that of *Le Gros*, but the black wool was the same, the same kind of cloth that had scraped against her bare skin last night. She bit down hard on her trembling lip.

The old priest was silent for a moment, and then he asked, "You have heard, then, about the death of Father Hubert?"

She nodded.

"A terrible thing. He was not a man I admired, but still it was a terrible thing. I have been waiting all morning, half supposing Lord Jaufre would approach me for absolution, for it must have been he who did the killing."

Melyssan ran her fingers along the narrow opening, feeling loose stone crumble away. Outside she could hear the wind howling, see it tugging at the maids' skirts as they crossed the yard. "Why do you assume that?" she asked at last.

"Because of what happened at the banquet yesterday and simply the nature of the earl. He's a dark, vengeful man."

It disturbed her to hear Father Andrew, whose opinion she respected, pronounce such harsh judgment upon Jaufre. Facing the priest, she said, "If Lord Jaufre killed Father Hubert, I am sure he had good reason."

Father Andrew pursed his lips. "No, a petty matter, so I understand. Father Hubert was caught pilfering, and I have heard that Lord Jaufre is an unforgiving man who values his silver above life itself."

"Then you have heard wrong," she blurted out. "Because Lord Jaufre fought for his life and mine. Father Hubert tried to kill my lord after—after Jaufre caught him trying to rape me." Her voice trailed off to a whisper.

She heard Father Andrew sharply draw in his breath. "My poor child." He reached one thin, blue-veined hand out to cover hers.

She jerked away. "I don't ask for your pity, only that you should not condemn Lord Jaufre."

"You should not worry about him. He must make his own peace. My concern now is for the pain I see on your face. Come down to the chapel and pray with me, Melyssan."

"I don't feel much like praying," she said, not wanting to be alone in the chapel with Father Andrew, staring at his frock, which reminded her so much of that other hated one. She raised her chin to stare into the priest's pale blue eyes, hardening herself against the compassion and gentle understanding she saw reflected there.

"The chapel will be a lonely place if you cease your morning visits. So few come there anymore." He fetched a wistful sigh, which carried her mind back to the days she had first known Father Andrew.

He had come to be the chaplain at Wydevale just as the pope pronounced the interdict upon England. She remembered hearing him in the chapel every morning at the time mass would have been said. He knelt at the altar before the shrouded crucifix, weeping softly like a man whose entire reason for living had been swept away. It was then she had begun the practice of praying with him each day, praying that King John would capitulate or the pope would relent and lift the terrible ban that men were beginning to take for granted, remove the curse from the English church before her people forgot there was a God.

The memory raised feelings of guilt at having refused his request. Doggedly she scuffed her toe in the rushes and said, "What does it matter if I visit the chapel or not? If the Church can ordain men like Hubert Le Vis…well, then we didn't really need any interdict to make sure we all go to the devil."

She was surprised when, instead of being offended, a slight smile touched Father Andrew's lips.

"I am sorry," he said. "Don't think that I mock you with my smile. 'Tis only your remark reminds me of words I once said myself. 'Twas the morning I found the bishop I served abed with two stout peasant wenches. I was a very young priest then and the trouble was I mistook the man for God. When I discovered he was not, I defrocked myself and went storming out of the cathedral."

Although Father Andrew chuckled, Melyssan thought she could still see the traces of his youthful pain tighten the lines on his face. Watching the sunlight from the croslet glint down upon his silver-gray hair, she tried to picture him as such an angry young man.

"And why did you go back?" she asked in spite of herself.

"A strange thing happened. You will hardly believe it." He hung his head. "I took myself off to an inn and was ruining my stomach with large amounts of very bad ale. A man came and sat down to join me—a plain honest fellow, a hayward by way of occupation—and like any sad drunk I found myself pouring out my whole wretched tale."

"And then what?" she prompted impatiently when he paused.

"Well, Will Hayward was not impressed by my sorrows. 'Saints be praised, Father,' he says. 'Now hasn't ye ever heard tell of the twelve apostles?' I assured him rather haughtily that I had. 'Then ye know all about that Judas Escaro. He was a downright bad 'un, but it didn't make the good Lord lose his faith in the other eleven. Ye can't let one knave ruin yer trust in all men. Now ye hightail it back to that cathedral and get about the work God planned for ye, lest I send ye on yer way with the toe of me boot.'"

She shared in his laughter at the conclusion of the story and felt some of the depression that had settled over her heart lifting.

"Well, I've taken up enough of your time with my long-winded tales. I'm sure you have many more important things to attend to." He excused himself and headed for the door.

After a moment's hesitation, she called after him, "Wait, Father." He glanced back at her, his bushy gray brows lifted in inquiry.

She swallowed hard. "If you like, I—I will come and bear you company while you pray."

He smiled. "I would like that very much." He waited until she crossed the room to offer her his arm. "I fear I will need a great deal of help this morning. I want you to stop me from praying for Hubert Le Vis."

"S-stop you?" she faltered.

"Yes." A strange glint sparkled in the pale blue eyes. "Stop me from praying to the good Lord that he roast Hubert's fat buttocks over the hottest flames in hell."

The falconer extended his arm, holding out the large, charcoal-winged peregrine for Lord Jaufre's inspection. The hawk remained still except for occasionally tilting a head concealed by a small hood.

"And we acquired this beauty whilst you were gone, my lord. Good Irish stock. We almost have him trained to the point we can unsew the eyes."

Lord Jaufre made a vague reply, his gaze more on the towering stone donjon than the bird. Where was Melyssan? Had she awakened yet? It seemed like hours since he had stolen from her bed, pausing only long enough to tuck the covers up around her face, pale with sleep and the shock of what had happened last night.

"Perhaps today Your Lordship would care to walk around with the bird, get him used to perching upon your wrist."

"What?" Jaufre asked, the sharp note in his voice startling the hawk. A woman had just emerged from the covered stairway—and yes, when the wind whipped back her mantle, he could see she walked with a cane.

The falconer stroked the peregrine's ruffled

feathers. "I said, my lord, perhaps you would like to begin to get this beauty accustomed to the sound of your voice, the feel of your touch."

"Yes, I sometimes think that I would," Jaufre murmured, never taking his eyes from Melyssan's distant figure until she disappeared around the corner of the donjon. Then he realized with a start that the falconer was offering him the hawk. "N-no. Unhood him and place him back in the mews. I will look at him again, mayhap tomorrow."

He strode away in pursuit of Melyssan. She had not gone far, having paused by the washing trough near the kitchen. She bent over, trying to see her reflection in the water as she restored the strands of hair escaping from the net at the back of her head. As Jaufre came up behind her, he saw her efforts were futile, since the wind kept rippling the surface of the water.

He cleared his throat to announce his presence, but the way her shoulders tensed revealed she was already aware of him. " 'Twould be easier if you consulted your mirror."

She continued to stare down into the trough, trailing her fingers through the part of the water where the image of his own face wavered. "Mayhap it would, but I have not got a mirror."

"What! No mirror? I thought 'twas the first thing every mother pressed into her daughter's hand, teaching her at a tender age the art of admiring herself."

"My mother never thought I had much to admire," she said as she turned around. The bruise on her cheek had already dulled to a yellow shade, and although deep shadows ringed her eyes, they were once more as the sea becalmed. An uncomfortable silence stretched out between them, and she pulled her mantle more snugly around her shoulders, putting him in mind of last night, when it had been the only thing she wore.

Quickly he averted his eyes, lest his imagination wax too hot. "Did you sleep well?" he asked. The instant the words were spoken he could have driven his fist into his mouth.

"Y-yes," she whispered.

When he glanced back, he saw two bright spots of color glowing in her cheeks. He dreaded that she would turn his own fool question around on him, but fortunately she did not. His face would have flushed as red as hers if he had been obliged to describe his agonized slumber in polite terms.

He crossed his arms in front of his chest, feeling as awkward as a page slipping up to the ladies' bower to leave flowers for the lord's daughter. Whatever intimacy had existed between himself and Melyssan in his bedchamber was now whipped away by the morning wind.

"I need to talk to you in private," he said. "Is it too cold for you out here?"

She shook her head. "There is a bench in the garden behind the kitchen."

It was on the tip of his tongue to tell her he

remembered it well, he'd lived at Winterbourne much longer than she, but he swallowed the comment, aware that his irritation was more with himself for feeling so stiff and clumsy. He indicated his agreement with her suggestion and refrained from taking her elbow to steady her. Such gestures were one of the few things he'd ever seen raise the light of anger in those otherwise gentle eyes.

Most of the flowers in the small garden had already died on the vine—heliotropes, roses, irises, all withered brown, not to bloom again until the spring. There was a strong scent of apple in the air as Melyssan seated herself on the wooden bench beneath the tree, the ground around her feet littered with rotten fruit.

Jaufre chose to stand, not wishing to add to his sense of confusion by the feel of her body brushing up against his side.

"I fear I may distress you, my lady," he said. "But I must broach the matter of Hubert Le Vis's death."

The color began to drain from her cheeks, but she replied in a steady voice, "I can understand that, considering I have heard some strange accounts of it this morning."

"Mostly put about by myself. As far as the world is concerned, I caught Father Hubert breaking into my silver cupboard. We fought and I killed him. I saw no reason to risk your reputation by having people believe you had actually been—been..."

"Despoiled?" Her lips curved into a bitter

smile. "Thank you for such consideration, my lord."

"I am sorry if my words give you pain, Melyssan. But you must know 'tis the way of the world to hold the woman responsible for such attacks upon her person."

She flinched. "And is that what you believe, my lord? That I invited Father Hubert to try and rape me?"

He began to pace, kicking aside the soft brown apples. "Don't be absurd. If I thought that, I would not be trying to shield you. I place the blame solely where it belongs—with that dead bastard they carted out of here."

But his voice lacked conviction because of something Tristan had said earlier that morning, stirring in Jaufre feelings of his own guilt.

"What possessed *Le Gros* to think he could ravish a lady under the protection of your roof?" Tristan had scowled.

"Too drunk. Too stupid. Take your pick." Jaufre had shrugged.

But Tristan had been satisfied with neither explanation. "Nay, part of the blame is yours, Jaufre. The wild way you talked to me on the way back from Normandy about what you would do to that harlot back at Winterbourne. *Le Gros* must have overheard you, probably thought you would not care. And you never even knew anything about the woman you called a whore. I'll wager you still don't."

Although he had silenced Tristan and tried to dismiss his words, the knight's criticism stung all the more because Jaufre feared there might be some truth in the accusation. The supposition was not a pleasant one, and he turned the wrath he felt at himself back against Melyssan. He had never invited the wench to come to Winterbourne. If she'd stayed at Wydevale where she belonged, *Le Gros* never could have touched her.

He stopped his pacing and planted himself in front of her. "I think the time has finally come, my lady, when you had best tender your excuses to me of why you did pretend to be my wife."

Melyssan gasped. "Why, yesterday, I tried and tried to tell you."

"Now I am of a humor to listen, so proceed. And, mind you, I am a fair judge of when someone is lying to me, so take care you speak nothing but the truth."

She set her mouth into a mutinous line, angry and dismayed by Jaufre's manner of questioning her. Muscular calves spread wide apart, hands resting on lean hips, his face darkened with a scowl, Jaufre looked no more of a humor to hear her explanation than he had upon his arrival at Winterbourne. He made her feel like a criminal brought before the king's justice—and Jaufre was her executioner.

She could almost laugh at herself when she remembered how she had descended to the courtyard, her heart fluttering with the thought of seeing him again. Alternating between shyness and anticipation, she had slowed and then scurried, her mind colored with remembrance of Jaufre cradling her in his arms, the tenderness of his caress as he laid her down upon the bed, his chest her pillow, the heat of his body restoring her to a warmth she thought she'd never feel again. He'd been so kind, so gentle, almost as if he genuinely cared that she'd been hurt, almost as if he cared....

That she'd cherished such notions was now a source of embarrassment to her as she faced her inquisitor. This Lord Jaufre with his stony brown eyes was enough to make her believe the man who had rescued her from Hubert Le Vis did not exist. She'd been daydreaming again, imagining an ebony-haired champion who was not real. The tall lord who towered over her now looked more like Father Andrew's description of the earl, *a dark, vengeful man.*

"Well?" Jaufre said, the sharpness of his voice making her jump. "I do not have the rest of the day to await your reply, Melyssan."

She sighed and with great patience began to recount her tale. She told it simply, leaving out much of the terror she had experienced at the thought of surrendering herself to the king, how much it had gone against her notions of honor to use his stolen ring, to tell such lies.

"And somehow the king believed my story about a secret marriage, and he arranged an escort to bring me to Winterbourne. He must have a great deal of respect for you, my lord."

Jaufre's lips curled. "Well, for my grandfather he had, since the old comte was one of the few to support John's pathetic attempts to retake

Normandy. As for myself, that remains to be seen."

"But—but he made you the earl of Winterbourne."

"Aye, he did." Jaufre laughed derisively. "'Tis amazing what you can purchase for the sum of a thousand pounds."

Melyssan's mouth dropped as Jaufre thus smashed another of her cherished illusions. "You bought your title?"

"What did you think—that I'd won it by some heroic deed of arms?"

She ducked her head and said in a small voice, "But even at Wydevale, we heard the tales of your valor in the Norman wars, how you risked your life to bring food to the soldiers starving at the siege of Gaillard."

"Valor does not fill a man's coffers or bring him advancement. Now enough about me. Get on with your tale."

"There's not much more to tell. After the trouble with Pevensy, I just stayed on and tried to help look after Winterbourne. I felt I owed you that much for the use of your name."

"Such a sense of duty. I trust it's strong enough to make you accede gracefully to my next request, for I must insist that you keep on being my wife."

Melyssan's heart skipped a beat. She was sure she had not heard him correctly. He could not...could not possibly be asking her to marry him. Despite herself, a foolish hope fluttered to life, only to be crushed by his next words.

"Of course, it would only be until I can find a bride to replace your bratling of a sister."

"Of course," she echoed bitterly, her hands resting on the staff, a reminder of her folly. How should she have dared think that Lord Jaufre would wed a crippled girl, risk having children that might be as accursed as their mother! Nonetheless she rose to her feet with quiet dignity.

"Lord Jaufre, I know that I have wronged you, but I think it a harsh punishment that you should force me to become your mistress." Then, as he raised one mocking eyebrow, she soon realized she'd made another humiliating mistake.

"We both know by now that I have no taste for forcing women, so there's no need for you to try to summon up any more tears. Nay, my only intention was that you should continue in your role as chatelaine of the castle, everywhere except in my bed."

Melyssan rubbed her throat in an attempt to rid herself of the lump rising there. "Can— can you not just let me go?"

"No, I can't!" When she regarded him with surprise, he added more calmly, "I am in enough difficulties. I shall probably be called to account for the death of Hubert Le Vis, and the king's suspicions have already been aroused against me since my trip to Paris. I don't need to further incur his displeasure by having him think I conspired to deprive him of a plaything he desired."

"Then why not just hand me over to him?"

"Nay, I might as well have let *Le Gros* have you last night as give you up to John now." Jaufre gave her an annoying pat on the shoulder. "I will continue to protect you from the king if you do as I say. In time we'll find some pretext for an annulment, and no one need ever be the wiser about your deception. Who knows? Mayhap we are distantly related."

"I hope the connection is very distant," she muttered.

He laughed and turned to walk away, seeming to take her lack of further protest as her consent to stay on at Winterbourne. But he halted at the corner of the low wooden kitchen building and looked back at her.

"There was one other thing that has been bothering me, Melyssan. How came you to be out of your bed at such a late hour last night?"

The question came so soft and sudden, she was not prepared. Before she could will it down, the flush of guilt spread over her cheeks. "I—I heard Father Hubert down in the solar scratching at the mural and I went to see what was wrong."

"You have remarkably keen hearing, my lady, to detect such a slight noise when you were on the floor above. Now I was passing right next the door, and the thickness nearly muffled the sounds of your struggle with *Le Gros*. It was only by chance that I entered the room in time to help you."

"Sometimes I just sense things," she said,

staring down at his boots. "And I often walk at night. My—my leg gets stiff."

"I see." But the bland tone of his voice did not tell her exactly how much.

"Another strange event took place last night," he continued. "Those pilgrims that were at our feast just vanished. Do you not find that odd?"

She gave a tiny shrug of her shoulders, her mouth having gone so dry she could not speak. Jaufre gently pressed her, "What think you of that? Did you share any speech with these travelers whilst they were at Winterbourne, obtain any inkling of why they would risk the perils of the night to be on their way so suddenly?"

"Nay," she cried with too quick a denial. "Not at all. I have never been on a pilgrimage, so I know nothing of such things."

To her great relief, he let the subject drop. But before he strode out of sight, he gave her an odd penetrating look, and she knew with frightening certainty he had not believed a word she'd said.

Chapter 6

THE CLANG OF metal striking metal disrupted the quiet of the still morning air. Lord Jaufre drummed his fingers upon the hilt of his broadsword as he watched the progress of his squires paired off with sword and shield to practice the skills that would one day earn them their spurs.

But the young men whacking away at each other with such enthusiasm blurred as his vision scanned farther afield, across the bailey to the lone figure of a woman. She hugged the folds of her cloak tightly against her delicate frame, appearing to shudder as much from the blows she saw delivered as the biting cold.

"It's been a fortnight now," Tristan remarked softly as he brushed against Jaufre's elbow. "How much longer are you going to make that girl stay here?"

"As long as it pleases me."

"'Tis not fair. She did not pose as your wife out of any motives of treachery or malice. Do you not believe what she said about the king?"

"Aye," Jaufre said. "I believe most of what she told me. That still does not mean I can permit her to walk away completely unchastised when her actions made me look such a fool."

Tristan wiped the back of one hand against his sweat-begrimed forehead, set beneath a steel cap. "The punishment is excessive. Teasing her, forcing her to keep up this pretense!"

"What harm has it done? Have I laid so much as a hand upon her?"

"I know not. Have you?" Tristan shot him a penetrating glance.

"No, I have not," Jaufre said, careful to keep the note of regret out of his voice.

"At least not yet. But I've seen the way you look at her, tense as a catapult that's wound too tight."

"Who appointed you her guardian?" Jaufre snapped, striding away from Tristan. Melyssan had limped too close to the spot where her brother was taking quite a drubbing from the beefy young squire he was matched against. Instinctively Jaufre moved in that direction, but Sir Dreyfan was already guiding her back to a safe distance.

Tristan followed hard on Jaufre's heels. "I only think you should send her away before you do something you might be sorry for. She is the sweetest, most gentle—"

"Peace!" Jaufre said, his eyes locking with Tristan's. "I can see she has quite won your heart. Mayhap if you're not too lovesick, you will return to your task of training my squires. At the moment, your charges look more as if they are having a game of hot cockles than any serious sword exercise." With the tip of his sword, he indicated where one dark-haired lad, having lost his footing on the frost-slick ground, now proceeded to tackle his opponent.

"Oh, aye, my lord. By your command, my lord."

Tristan swept Jaufre a mocking bow. Snatching up his shield, he strode onto the field and thwacked the young wrestler on the buttocks with the flat of his sword. "Arric!" he bellowed to his page. "Bring up the horses. We'll start the runs against the quintain."

Jaufre sheathed his sword, glaring at his

friend's retreating back. Plague take Tristan, haranguing him about the girl at such a time. As if he didn't have enough on his mind. Every time he glanced up, there was another messenger clamoring for admittance at the infernal gates.

Messengers from Philip of France reaffirming his offer to return Clairemont if Jaufre would help make war on John of England. Messengers from John of England demanding that Jaufre renew his oath of allegiance to him. He had freely pardoned the earl for the death of Hubert Le Vis. As he reminded Jaufre in his letters, both the Church and France were England's enemies, so Jaufre had done his king a service by killing the Norman priest. Despite this expression of gratitude, John assessed exorbitant death duties against the earl for his inheritance of the comte's English manors and his castle in the north, Ashlar. Grudgingly, Jaufre paid, monies that would have been better spent improving the fortifications at Winterbourne.

John's latest complaint was the continued absence from court of Jaufre and his lovely new bride. He had strongly begun to hint that if the earl and his countess did not present themselves soon, the king would be obliged to heed those many voices whispering against the Dark Knight, whispering that Ashlar and Winterbourne would be better placed in the hands of some more loyal baron.

On top of these worries, Jaufre didn't need

Tristan pricking his conscience over Melyssan. After all, he was protecting the girl from John, wasn't he, at the risk of drawing the king's wrath down upon his own head? It was Jaufre who suffered most from his mad decision to keep her, putting constant temptation in his path when he had resolved to maintain an honorable distance from her.

No easy task. Even now as he gazed at her, the sunlight burnished gold in the silken nutmeg hair flowing loose about her shoulders. The breeze occasionally tugged the cloak from her closed fingers and flapped it back to allow glimpses of her supple figure, reminding him all too well of the velvet body beneath, creamy skin as translucent as pearls.

He felt the blood rush to his loins and ran one finger inside the neckline of his chain mail hauberk, which suddenly struck him as being rather warm, despite the chill in the air nipping him with the promise of an early winter.

Well, he'd desired women before and survived. He would never become besotted again as he'd done with Yseult. No, not even over this lass with the wistful sea-shaded eyes who so disturbed his senses.

He did have to accord Melyssan a certain grudging respect. How many ladies would have accepted his dictums without dissolving into tears, to be wife and yet no wife, her fate uncertain for as long as he commanded? She bore it all so patiently, devoting herself to the many tasks required of the lady of

Winterbourne, seeing to everyone's needs before her own.

It was typical of her that she would stand out here in the cold to keep an anxious eye on that nithling brother of hers while Whitney joined in the practice according to Jaufre's orders. If the youth persisted in remaining at Winterbourne, clinging to his sister's skirts, Jaufre thought, then, by God, he'd be treated no differently from the other squires and learn to play a man's part.

The earl kicked his toe against what remained of the brown grass made brittle by the coating of white frost. Melyssan had not spared him so much as a glance this morning. Her concern was all for her milksop brother as he mounted a roan destrier, preparing to take his turn riding at the wooden dummy the pages attached to the crosspiece at the other end of the courtyard.

Jaufre could not remember any woman ever showing such anxiety on his behalf. Oh, aye, Yseult had cried her pretty blue eyes out the day he told her he was riding to relieve the siege at Gaillard, but by then she and Godric must already have been arranging their tryst in Jaufre's own bed.

And when caught, how his fair-skinned Yseult had wept again, swearing it was all Godric's doing and none of her own. Like a fool, he'd believed her and given her another chance—another chance to kill him. Jaufre stroked the tip of the scar at his throat.

Melyssan clasped her hand to her mouth as

Whitney careened clumsily toward the quintain. Was this show of dismay but a performance to attract attention to herself? He wished he could decide.

Mayhap Tristan was right. Mayhap she was just as innocent and unselfish as Jaufre himself had once imagined her to be. He wanted to accord her the benefit of the doubt, but he knew women and their cunning deceits all too well. And there was still the unresolved matter of those pilgrims....

Having organized the quintain practice, Tristan returned to stand beside him. "There," he said. "I hope you are at least satisfied with the horsemanship of our lads."

"Tolerable." Jaufre was loath to admit he had been staring at Melyssan and not the riders.

"Tolerable! There's not one out there whose skill in the saddle would put you to shame. Except," Tristan amended, "I do wish I could teach young Whitney to keep his weight more forward in the saddle when he charges."

They watched Whitney make a thundering run at the quintain, only to drop his lance. He yanked on the reins and veered aside barely in time to avoid crashing into the crosspiece.

"You might begin by telling him that as far as we know," Jaufre drawled, "no one has ever been killed by a wooden dummy."

The earl crossed his arms over his chest in disgust as the young man rode back to try again. But the page Arric swiped someone's horse and galloped in ahead of Whitney despite the hoots of the men. The boy hit the dummy square between the eyes with the tip of his lance.

"'Tis time that lad was made a squire." Jaufre nodded his approval to the excited boy who whooped and shook his fist in the air.

Whitney now steeled himself to begin his second run. The young man approached the quintain more cautiously this time, slowing to a sedate trot at the end. He missed the head, catching his lance on the edge of the dummy's shield, which sent the wooden man veering around to thump Whitney on the back, nearly unhorsing him.

It vexed Jaufre to note how Melyssan applauded the feeble performance, waving her kerchief by way of encouragement. "For the love of St. George," he growled. "My grandmother could have done better."

Although Tristan smiled, he said, "Be not so impatient with Whitney. He tries."

"He is a weakling. Soft-hearted and soft-headed. He reminds me too much of—" Jaufre sucked in his breath as the painful realization caught him unaware.

"Of who?"

"Godric!" Jaufre grabbed up his helmet and plunked the heavy kettle-shaped piece of steel over his head. His vision was now restricted to a narrow slit, so he did not see Tristan's reaction to his comparison. "'Tis time I put some heart into those lads," he growled.

He marched out onto the field, his shield and sword held aloft by outstretched arms, issuing a challenge. The squires recognized the invitation and forgot the quintain. Horses were consigned to the care of pages amidst joyous war cries while the young men scrambled for their swords, shields, and helmets.

With a little shiver, Melyssan realized Jaufre meant to take them all on—some half-dozen stalwart men, not including her own brother, who reluctantly eased his helmet over disordered brown locks.

She had taken great care to keep her eyes averted from the earl this morning, although she was very much aware of his presence as he stood idly watching the squires. Now she decided she might be pardoned for staring, since the earl had made himself the center of attention.

The sun glinted off the helmet that concealed his features, the gold plumes of his crest ruffled by the breeze. The squires were mostly strapping fellows in their late teens, but next to Jaufre's tall, hard-muscled physique, they dwindled in significance. The earl's royal-blue tunic bore his falcon emblem emblazoned across his broad chest. Slits in the garment's sides revealed the taut cords of his powerful thighs, which moved with catlike grace as he tensed, waiting for his squires to marshal their attack.

"Surely 'tis no contest," Melyssan breathed. "He cannot possibly hold off all of them."

Sir Dreyfan, who stood next to her, chuckled. "Wait and see, my lady."

The bolder of the squires closed in for the

attack. Jaufre wheeled, preventing any of them from coming at his flank, his sword slashing with a speed and accuracy that left Melyssan dizzy trying to follow its movement. In short order, one squire was crawling across the field to retrieve the weapon knocked from his grasp and two more retreated, nursing bruised ribs.

Sir Dreyfan's peppery beard bristled with pride. "There has never yet been a warrior to equal my lord, save perhaps William Le Marshal and the great Lion's Heart himself."

"Oh?" Melyssan said, feigning indifference although her heart had begun to pound unaccountably faster. For once she was fascinated by a sport whose violence she normally abhorred. The tireless strength in Jaufre's arms astonished her as he repelled yet two more attackers. In spite of herself, she remembered how effortlessly he had swooped her off her feet the night he'd carried her from the great hall, how he'd soothed her to sleep, her naked breasts and thighs absorbing the heat of his virile male body even through the layers of his wool shirt and tunic.

Melyssan quickly ducked her head lest Sir Dreyfan see the blush coursing into her cheeks from such remembrance. Where had Jaufre slept since then? She had no idea and dared not ask. As she had lain fighting wakefulness night after night in his bed, the old magic of dreaming of her young Launcelot did not work anymore. Instead she'd tossed and turned, envisioning the earl as he was now, lean, hard, with dangerous glints in his dark eyes. Then she felt ashamed, almost as if she betrayed a memory she'd long held sacred.

Why should she torment herself over a man who had forgotten her very existence? All too well had Jaufre kept his promise of not forcing his attentions upon her. She'd lived in dread for days that he would confront her, demanding to know more about Sir Hugh and Lady Gunnor; but even that seemed to have been dismissed from his mind as having little importance. Although he still kept her trapped at Winterbourne like a sparrow beating its wings against the bars of a cage, he treated her with an offhand courtesy as though he took her presence for granted, like any other officer of his household staff. Watching him as he now fought his way across the field, Melyssan reflected that he could probably trip over her and keep right on going.

Jaufre grunted as the largest of his squires caught him in the ribs, but he recovered and sent the brawny youth stumbling over backward with a well-placed blow to the thigh. Although the sweat streamed down his cheeks, making the helmet as stuffy as a bake oven, he was enjoying the exercise, ridding himself of his sexual and political frustrations with the same strokes. He caught a flash of Melyssan through his eye slit and was annoyed to see her staring down at the ground.

Raising his weapon aloft, he looked for fresh opponents, but he had crossed swords with all the men save one. Whitney hung back, his sword held halfheartedly in the ready position as if he hoped to escape unnoticed—the exact same tactic Godric had always used whenever there was a melee. Jaufre clenched his teeth and charged at Whitney, delivering a hard *thunk!* against his shield that sent the young man staggering.

To the earl's annoyance, Whitney scarce made use of his sword at all, relying mostly on the shield to deflect Jaufre's blows. The Dark Knight crashed his weapon down again and again, determined to rouse some aggressive response from the weak-kneed man before him.

"Fight, damn you!" Jaufre roared, but Whitney seemed to have given up. He cowered back, almost losing his grip on the shield.

Hearing such a clatter, Melyssan stole a glance and found Jaufre bearing down hard upon her brother. Whitney's shield was not doing him much service, allowing Jaufre to rain a volley of direct hits upon his helmet.

Stifling her cry, she tried to hurry to his rescue, but Sir Dreyfan caught her by the arm. "Please, my lady. Ye must remember to stay back."

"But he's slaying my brother." She struggled against the old knight's large, restraining hands.

"Nay, lass, 'tis all in sport. His Lordship is only using blunted weapons."

Only blunted weapons. Sir Dreyfan might well have said the Dark Knight was only using a cudgel the way his heavy sword clattered down upon Whitney's head. After one particularly savage buffet, her brother dropped both sword and shield and sank to his knees, pitching forward onto his belly. Sir Dreyfan released Melyssan, and she hobbled across the field, half falling, half sobbing, in her haste to reach Whitney.

Lord Jaufre looked down at his handiwork, his expression masked by his armor. Melyssan flung herself down beside Whitney, then reeled back in horror. Although it was Whitney's back she touched, what stared up at her was the front of his helmet.

"Dear God," she choked. "You twisted his head around."

To her outraged astonishment, a deep chuckle rumbled inside Jaufre's steel kettle. "'Tis not the head that's turned around, only the helmet."

The earl removed his own head covering and tossed it to a page, while swiping at the perspiration glistening in his dark beard.

As if to lend credence to Jaufre's words, a low moan echoed from the back of Whitney's helmet. Sir Dreyfan moved in and rolled Whitney over, testing his limbs. "Easy, lad. No bones broken. Only the wind knocked out of ye."

"Only the wind!" Melyssan said. "He's half-dead. Take that thing off him before he suffocates."

Dreyfan tugged at the metal headgear, but it wouldn't budge. "Take care," Tristan said as he rushed to kneel beside them. "'Tis crushed here on this side. You might rip his face. Arric, go get the blacksmith."

As the page tore off in the direction of the barn, Melyssan felt Jaufre step behind her. "Do not fret, my dear. Your valiant brother isn't the first man this has ever happened to. He will live to fight another day."

The earl's bronzed fingers rested on her shoulder, but she wrenched herself from his grasp and said, "No thanks to you." She captured one of Whitney's groping hands. The fingers curled pathetically around hers as he issued another muffled groan.

"I was only trying to teach the lad his sword was meant for something more than a place to store holy relics in the hilt."

"You pounded him into the ground as if he were a—a tent stake." She sniffed and glowered up at Jaufre.

"Well, to be sure." He stroked his beard, the thoughtful gesture belied by the unholy glint in his mahogany eyes. "There were times I did wonder if I was not fighting the wooden dummy by mistake."

The chortle of mirth from the other men who had gathered around only added more fuel to her indignation. Seething inwardly, Melyssan continued to caress Whitney's hand until the burly figure of the blacksmith arrived, hefting a large iron hammer and chisel in his fist.

Melyssan was pushed aside as Sir Dreyfan dragged Whitney's body to position his head on a large rock. He and Tristan held her brother down as the smithy commenced the delicate task of trying to batter the helmet back into shape without crushing Whitney's skull. Melyssan cringed with every chink of the hammer while the cause of her brother's torment looked on with folded arms, his face alight with sardonic amusement.

"Don't be too concerned if you can't get the helmet turned around," Jaufre said. "I'll wager Master Whitney fights just as well with it on backward."

"Oh, go to the devil, Jaufre," Tristan snapped as another whimper escaped from the young man.

Shrugging, Jaufre sauntered over to Melyssan, where he tried to flick the tears off her cheeks, but she slapped his hand.

"Don't touch me, you great oaf. How could you so strike down a defenseless boy?"

Jaufre's brows drew together in annoyance. Perhaps he had gotten a little rough, but she had no call to speak to him as if he were some sort of a monster, attacking unarmed children.

"When I was the age of that 'defenseless boy,' I'd already been knighted two years and acclaimed the champion of at least twenty tournaments."

"Truly?" she said, her green eyes flashing. "I believe I may swoon, I am so impressed."

"You should," he said, feeling red heat sting his cheeks at being made to sound like such a braggart. "Though most men could do as well. At least those not coddled by their sister. Your brother will never win his spurs at this rate."

"If that means changing into a great hulking brute like you, I'll see the damned spurs flung to the bottom of the well first."

Jaufre threw his hands into the air and grimaced at his squires. "Women!"

Their answering snickers caused Melyssan to ball her hands into tight fists until her nails gouged her palms. And to think she'd dared to imagine that in the heart of Jaufre de Macy existed some fragment of chivalry, some part of the gentle knight who had rescued her as a child. Bah, what a fool's dream.

She tensed as the helmet was eased upward, revealing Whitney's white, bruised features. With trembling hands, he felt his chin, nose, and teeth as if checking that they were still intact. Rolling to his knees, he retched into the grass for several seconds.

"Never let it be said the lad has no stomach," Jaufre said. "He's leaving half of it scattered over the bailey."

"Oh, let up on him, Jaufre." Tristan scowled.

Melyssan crossed over to Whitney and gave his shoulder a sympathetic squeeze, her heart wrung by the sight of his peaked, humiliated face. But her ungrateful brother shoved her hand away.

"Stop, Lyssa," he whispered. "You're only making everything worse."

Tucking his helmet under his arm, Jaufre approached and bent down to peer at Whitney. "All better now? Come on. I'll give you another chance, but I'll fight with my left hand this time."

Whitney's only reply was a sullen shake of his head. He struggled to his feet and walked away. Melyssan tried to hold him back, fearing that if he left now, he would never be able to face these men again. But he yanked free and kept on going, causing her to stumble back and stub her bent foot on the blacksmith's discarded hammer.

"Another time, mayhap when you've more the belly for it," Jaufre called after Whitney.

Melyssan grimaced with pain as she wriggled her throbbing toe, fury and frustration churning inside her at Jaufre for his insensitivity and at her brother for his meekness.

"Well, lads," said the earl, "despite the mighty buffets I sustained from Sir Whitney, I believe I'm still up to a little more exercise." Something in the jaunty way he donned his helmet and stooped to pick up his shield snapped Melyssan's remaining hold on her temper.

"I'll give you mighty buffets," she cried. Dropping her staff and using both hands, she strained to lift the heavy iron hammer. As Jaufre was straightening up, she banged the smithy's tool down on his helmet near the region of his ear. The force of the blow reverberated up her arms, causing her to fly backward, tripping over the hem of her cloak so that she landed on her bottom with a hard thud.

Jaufre sank to one knee and then, with a muttered curse, staggered up and ripped off the helmet. Bells were ringing in his ear louder than the chimes at Westminster the day of the king's coronation. He struck his palm vigorously against his temple to stop the insistent clanging.

Sweeping the crowd of laughing men, his furious gaze wiped the mirth from their faces, except for Tristan, who continued to smirk, and Sir Dreyfan, who slapped his thighs and guffawed until tears streamed down onto his beard. By the feet of Christ, who had dared to—

Then he saw her sprawled upon the ground, skirts shoved up past her knees to where her garters were tied around shapely thighs. Disheveled strands of golden-brown hair fell across storm-washed green eyes as her dainty hands contended with the unwieldy hammer. The way she looked up at him, baring small white teeth, put him in mind of a ferocious kitten.

"Why, you little witch," he hissed, although he was having great difficulty keeping up the appearance of being furious.

Melyssan trembled with savage exhilaration. It was the first time in her life she'd ever permitted her temper such free rein. But when she saw the Dark Knight advancing, her jaw dropped open in dismay. Dear God, what lunacy had come over her? Feeling much like a foolish mouse who has just tweaked a lion's tail, she attempted to escape, but the hammer rolled between her legs, pinning the folds of her kirtle to the ground so that all she could do was scoot helplessly backward.

Jaufre straddled over her, his face screwed into an expression of angry menace as he lifted the hammer with one hand, tossing it aside effortlessly. Seizing both her arms, he hauled her to her feet and rammed her against his chest until she could feel the hard links of chain beneath his tunic. Her heart leapt into her throat, but she compelled herself to raise defiant eyes to his, biting the inside of her lip to keep it from quivering. Even though his mouth was set into a tight line, she had the fleeting impression it cost him an effort to look so fierce. Beneath Jaufre's thick-fringed black lashes glittered devilish lights she remembered all too well.

"So, little vixen," he said with a mock growl. "You're not as tame as I thought. Well, I know how to deal with that."

Banding her squirming wrists to her back with one large hand, he brought his other arm up behind her shoulders. Her startled gasp was smothered beneath the burning sensation of his lips crashing down upon hers. Struggling against the hard embrace and his demanding mouth became even more futile as fire coursed through her veins, robbing her of what little resistance she possessed, until she melted to him, the iron strength of his arms all that prevented her shaking limbs from collapsing beneath her.

Suddenly she realized how much she had hungered for his touch all these long endless days at Winterbourne. Remnants of her anger, her frustration, her growing passion, all swirled inside of her, sweeping away her natural shyness, until she pressed her lips back against his, returning the kiss with equal fervor. It was Jaufre who ended the embrace, slowly drawing back, his lips lingering as if they parted from hers with the greatest reluctance. While her giddy world gradually ceased revolving, she felt the rise of his chest as he drew in a shuddering breath. His face drained of color as if he had received a great shock.

Sir Dreyfan's voice boomed out. "By St. Michael, the lord looks more befuddled now than when she hit him with the hammer."

Befuddled? Jaufre thought as the knight's comment penetrated his consciousness. No, more like stunned. What had happened? The kiss has begun as a game, to tease her for daring to strike him. He had expected her to squirm and kick in indignation, not mold the soft curves of her body to his in a way that felt too right while her lips captured him with their sweetness, arousing a passion that seemed so much stronger than the mere physical ache in his groin, as if his very soul...

Soul! The word jolted him into releasing her as if she'd burned him. What the devil was he thinking of? He had no soul. That was claptrap put about by romantic minstrels and priests afraid of dying.

He backed away, unnerved by the trembling pink mouth that invited him to kiss her again. And God, how he wanted to! The sharpness of his longing cut through his delusions. He had not kept her at Winterbourne to protect her from the king, or to punish her, either. He had kept her there for himself, because...

Scenting danger as cannily as a wolf being stalked by a hunter, the Dark Knight hardened his jaw, determined to shatter the glow he saw in Melyssan's vulnerable sea-shaded eyes, fearful of what such a look betokened.

"No, not nearly so tame as I thought," he said harshly, "but in future, madam wife, you'd best learn to control yourself and not behave so wantonly in front of my men."

His cruel words had the desired effect. One hand flew to her cheek as if he'd struck her, her eyes brimming with confusion and hurt. He gave her no chance to reply but whirled around, blundering into the squires, who had gone silent, their faces clearly showing their puzzlement over his abrupt change of mood.

"Stop gawking! The show is over. Get back to your practice. Arric, bring me a horse."

They all scattered, even Dreyfan daring no more than an inquiring lift of his brows. As Arric led forward the black stallion, Jaufre pushed the boy aside and flung himself onto the animal's back. He was dimly aware that Tristan had crossed over to Melyssan's side, but he dared not risk looking at her again. He didn't know what madness was stealing over him, but he would rid himself of it, if he had to ride halfway to hell.

Chapter 7

Melyssan's cheeks flamed as Sir Tristan picked up her staff from where she had dropped it. Mumbling her thanks, she accepted the walking stick but shrank from the sympathy she saw reflected in the knight's kind gray eyes.

"Mayhap it would be better, my lady, if you did not come down to where the men are practicing with their weapons," he said gently. "*Some* tend to get a little rough."

"So it would seem." Her gaze traveled involuntarily to where Jaufre's black stallion disappeared through the iron gate. Bitter envy and resentment surged through her. How pleasant it must be to leap on one's horse and just ride away from a humiliating situation. She touched a finger to lips yet tender from the heated embrace; anger and embarrassment churned inside her, mingled with a small twinge of fear at her own boldness.

How much of her feelings for Jaufre had she permitted to show in those few unguarded moments? Enough for the earl to have regarded her with scorn, sneering his disapproval over her "wantonness." She had dared to offer him only a small part of her affections, and even that he had rejected.

Her chin trembled. It was so unfair. He had begun the kiss. She had first tasted of desire from his lips. What right had he then to despise her for returning his passion? How could he kiss her with such scorching intensity and yet mean nothing by it?

"Lady Melyssan." The sound of Tristan's voice jolted her into realizing that he stood watching her with troubled eyes. He took one of her hands between his own and patted it awkwardly. "Please...be not distressed, my lady. You must not take the earl's teasing to heart. He was ever one for tormenting the ladies.

"Though I swear you are the first one who ever paid him back in full measure." The ghost of a smile flitted across his face. "I believe he's not taken such a knock as that to his pate for a good many years."

"I am astonished that he has not," she replied, "if he treats all ladies so unchivalrously."

"None has had your courage, or—if you will forgive me—has been as sensitive as you. I hate seeing you thus upset. Sometimes Jaufre carries his jests too far, but you have nothing to fear from the earl. Despite his hard ways, he is a man of honor. I promise you he meant nothing by that kiss."

Melyssan pulled her hand away, little comforted by Tristan's well-meant assurances. She forced herself to smile. "You mistake my feelings, Sir Tristan. The only part of the earl's boorish behavior that disturbs me is his treatment of my brother. Whitney has done naught to offend my lord. I cannot understand why Jaufre should hate him."

"Nay, my lady, he does not hate the lad. 'Tis

only that Whitney bears an unfortunate resemblance to Godric."

"Godric? Who is Godric?"

Tristan looked rather flustered and very much as if he wished he had not spoken. "Well, the lady Yseult—after she— We—we do not speak much of Godric anymore. Jaufre killed him in a duel. 'Twas all a long time ago."

The knight avoided her eyes and began pacing across the field. "Now, by the rood, where did I set down my shield? You had best go back to the donjon, my lady. 'Tis too cold for you to keep standing there."

Since Tristan obviously intended to say no more, Melyssan followed his advice. Raising the hem of her cloak so it did not trail across the damp grass, she walked away, pondering the information Tristan had allowed to slip, information about Jaufre that even the lowest menials at Winterbourne took care never to discuss. Those mystery-shrouded events of the earl's past that had taken a gallant young knight and carved him into a man of granite, a man who could flood her entire being with the heat of his kiss and the next moment all but stone her as a harlot.

Now she had another shadowy figure to wonder about along with that of Lady Yseult. Yseult and Godric. The pairing of those names and remembering the comment Hubert Le Vis had made about Jaufre being a jealous husband provided her with some clue as to what might have happened. Melyssan had seen for herself that Jaufre was not one to wait for explanations. If he had thought himself wronged, the earl's retribution would have been sure, swift, and violent. And both Yseult and Godric were dead.

The Dark Knight Without Mercy. Melyssan shivered and suddenly felt afraid for her brother. If Whitney did indeed remind Jaufre of a man he had hated enough to kill, then perhaps it was no longer safe for her brother to remain at Winterbourne. The earl did not insist that Whitney stay. It had been her brother's own choice, trying to protect her in whatever small way he could. She would have to try to persuade Whitney that he must go now and leave her alone to sort out this tangle with Jaufre. Surely the earl would release her soon. Perhaps even today Jaufre would order her to be gone because of his evident disgust for her.

She had no opportunity for speech with her brother, for after the morning's humiliation Whitney refused to talk with anyone. In desperation, Melyssan sent Father Andrew to deal with the young man. Part of her whispered that she worried for naught. Part of her could not believe that Jaufre would ever harm anyone in a spirit of cruel, unreasoning vengeance.

But the appearance of the earl the next time she saw him was not calculated to soothe her apprehensions. Lord Jaufre had decided to go hawking that afternoon, and Tristan had invited Melyssan and her lady Nelda to join in the sport. Melyssan would have refused, preferring to avoid Jaufre and the sight of the birds cruelly rending their prey. But she had not been outside the walls of Winterbourne since the day of her arrival. The mighty white stone fortress, once so sheltering, seemed more and more like a trap, where she had lost not only her freedom, but stood in danger of losing her heart as well.

When the great portcullis creaked upward, she restrained herself from kicking her pony's sides and galloping away from Tristan and Nelda, away across the open fields until there was nothing in her mind but the joy of the animal moving beneath her, the wind tearing her hair free from the wimple that confined it. But even had she given in to the mad desire, her pony appeared content to move at no more than a brisk trot. Her mount and Nelda's had been selected for their stolidity and not for speed. The last thing one desired around temperamental hawks was a skittish horse.

When they joined up with Lord Jaufre and his party of grooms, austringers, and spaniels just outside the village, Melyssan saw that even the earl had exchanged his formidable black stallion for a quiet roan gelding. Jaufre sat in the midst of a group of knights, unhooding his hawk for their inspection. These were tenants from outlying manors, Tristan explained, who had come to pay their respects and render their yearly accounting to Jaufre's clerks as Michaelmas was fast approaching, the saint's day when the annual audit of the earl's property would be taken.

When Jaufre saw her coming, he edged his mount forward with such a dark scowl upon his brow, Melyssan was tempted to turn and gallop back toward the safety of the castle. The earl was garbed in a black cloak that billowed behind him and a sable-colored surcoat trimmed with silver so that it was as if his plumage matched that of the large, fierce hawk that perched on his gloved wrist. The charcoal-winged peregrine spanned the length of the Dark Knight's arm, its beak at a level with his shoulder. As Jaufre moved closer, Melyssan felt as if she were being studied by two pairs of cold, unmoving eyes, the man's and the bird's, measured as if for prey, measured and then dismissed as not worth the bother.

"Where the devil have you been?" Jaufre growled at Tristan. "I thought you meant to go hawking, not—" He eyed Melyssan and Nelda with distaste. "Not skirt chasing."

"I invited the ladies to join in our sport. I am sure the other *gentlemen* will not mind."

"Well, then 'tis your responsibility to keep them out of the way." Without sparing her so much as another glance, Jaufre wheeled his horse around and rode off. Despite the encouraging smile she received from Tristan, Melyssan found that her pleasure in the ride was already gone. Unwilling to let Jaufre see how much his cold reception had daunted her, she slapped down on her reins and continued doggedly.

In summer, they would have had to skirt the fields for fear of damaging the crops, but now fences were pulled back to allow the sheep to graze on the stubble that was all that remained after the harvest. In the distance loomed the outline of the Welsh hills, gray as the sky above that threatened rain before the day was out.

Nelda fell in readily with Jaufre's knights, her dark curls bouncing as she laughed and flirted. But Melyssan did not converse easily with strangers, and she found herself riding alone. The others maintained an unhurried canter to allow the grooms, who were on foot leading the hounds, and the austringers, who were carrying the smaller hawks on their square frames, to keep pace with them.

Discovering that her pony had more spirit than she supposed, Melyssan drew ahead of the rest, her eyes on the forestland, a sinister patch of blackness on the horizon. Suddenly she was aware of galloping hoofs close behind her, and then Jaufre's horse shot past her. He plunged the large gelding in front of the pony, coming to a dead stop so that Melyssan was obliged to rein so sharply her mount nearly reared back on its haunches. The hawk on Jaufre's opposite hand twitched its long wings, the clawed talons tugging against the leather jesses that held its legs secure. He paused a moment to soothe the bird, his hand stroking its head near the hooked beak that could easily rip the fingers from a man. Melyssan shuddered to watch him.

Then he glared at her. "'Tis not a race,

my lady. Or mayhap you were running away. How far did you expect to get on that pony?"

"I was not running away," she said. "I—I simply did not realize how far I had outstripped the others."

"I suggest you pay more attention. We are on the border of a hostile land. The possibility of encountering a party of Welsh raiders exists even in the light of day."

She bit her lip. "I know that. I am sorry. I will turn back and rejoin the others."

"You need not bother. They are catching up. Just ride more slowly."

She did as he bade her, although discomfited to have him trotting beside her looking as put out as if he had been saddled with a troublesome child. He rode so close at times his knee nearly brushed against her thigh. The silence between them stretched out to such uncomfortable length, Melyssan sought words to break the awkwardness. When she saw Jaufre glance toward the distant towers of Winterbourne, a perceptible softening in his granite features, she said, "Aye, you have a right to look so proud, my lord. 'Tis a most magnificent castle."

He started as if surprised she should guess his thoughts, then shrugged, trying to appear indifferent. "'Tis well enough."

"Well enough! Camelot itself cannot have been more beautiful."

He snorted. "Certainly not as costly. I would prefer less beauty and stronger walls, more flanking towers. I only hope if we are ever under siege, Winterbourne proves to have been worth my thousand pounds."

Melyssan hung her head, determined to attempt no further conversation. Why must he always value everything in terms of silver?

After a time, he peered down at her. "Still sulking over what happened this morning?"

She gasped and swallowed the urge to tell him it was not she whose face looked more thunderous than the clouds gathering overhead. "No," she said, "but I have been wondering whether you were ready to let me leave Winterbourne."

"Leave! By God, you are in a great hurry all of a sudden. You seemed content with the situation not so long ago. What a deal of fuss you are making over one kiss."

"I?" she croaked, unconsciously giving the pony a kick that sent him surging forward. As she struggled to bring him back under control, she stared up at Jaufre. The hawk on his wrist emitted a strident cry as if mocking her.

"Nay, my lord, I only thought that as you were so displeased with my behavior, it would content you that I should be gone."

"I would not say I was displeased, my lady, only startled," Jaufre said. "After all, you creep as quietly about my castle as a nun, and you dress..." He curled his lip as he glanced at her drab brown kirtle and wimple. "You dress as if you were my widow. 'Tis no wonder I was not prepared to have you kiss me in such a way as would have put the most experienced courtesan to the blush."

To her annoyance, blushing was exactly what Melyssan discovered she was doing. "How dare you! You instigated that kiss. 'Tis not my wont to behave thus. I—I was not myself."

"You think you were not," continued her merciless tormentor. "All this time you spent praying in my chapel, you never dreamed you had this other wicked side to your nature, did you? I am surprised that pale priest never warned you against yourself."

Melyssan nudged her pony forward, but Jaufre dug his heels into the gelding and kept up with her. "I heard a sermon once regarding women. Vessels of sin. Of male and female, 'tis the woman who is most lascivious. You need to keep up your guard against your own evil, my lady."

"How astonishing you should have remembered that sermon all these years," she said through clenched teeth. "For you must have heard it the day you were baptized, since I'm sure that's the last time you were ever in a church."

Jaufre gave a short bark of laughter, which frightened the hawk. It shifted its wings in angry protest. "Well, be not ruffled," said the earl, although Melyssan was not sure if he addressed her or the bird. "You have nothing to worry about. Fortunately I have enough self-control for the both of us."

Before she could think of a proper retort, he reined in his horse and gave the signal for the party to halt. Reluctantly, Melyssan did likewise.

"Get those hounds up here," Jaufre shouted. "They should be able to flush a hare out from under the hawthorn, and at least we will provide some sport for the goshawk."

He moved off looking as if he had not a care in the world except finding some hapless rabbit for his birds to rip apart. Melyssan's shoulders slumped. How could she be thinking that she was in love with such a man, a man who scorned and ridiculed her, a man who mocked every belief and ideal that she held sacred? It was ridiculous. And yet as he rode away, something deep inside her yearned after him, making her want even now to cry out his name and call him back to her side.

Aware of her regard, Jaufre was annoyed by his desire to prance his horse and blustered to the beaters to start the dogs through the bushes at the edge of the forest. Hadn't he made enough of a fool of himself earlier, vaunting his skill on the practice field, showing off like a squire at his first tournament? That was bad enough without now flexing his muscles and preening like a peacock before his hen.

And a plain little brown hen at that. Jaufre glowered at Melyssan, determined to find some flaw in that perfect oval of a face that peered out from the folds of the wimple. Not a striking beauty by any means. She had not Yseult's high cheekbones, nor Finette's pouting red lips. But damn those green eyes of hers that always put him in mind of the sun sparkling upon the sea. Even now they chipped away at the layers of stone he had masoned around his heart.

He had ridden all morning as if the devil were after him to escape the memory of those eyes. And he'd flattered himself that he had had some measure of success, only to feel thrown off balance all over again when she but looked at him. Jaufre watched as Tristan took charge of one of the goshawks and presented the bird to Melyssan for her use, but she vigorously shook her head.

The earl shifted in the saddle, the great bird on his arm stretching its talons in such a way that Jaufre was grateful for the protection of the leather glove. So if Melyssan had no desire to participate in the sport, why had she come out? Simply to throw herself in his way?

With great consideration, Melyssan now suggested to Tristan that her lady would like to try the bird, then smiled with artless pleasure at the way Nelda crowded forward for her first lesson in hawking.

Jaufre worried the ends of his mustache with his teeth. In his experience women did not usually take much account of the wishes of others of their sex. Nor did they usually relinquish male attention to another female. Yet Melyssan appeared quite content to efface herself while the men gathered around offering all manner of foolish advice as Nelda held out her wrist for the little hawk to perch there.

A bark and a splash announced that one of the spaniels had blundered into the pond on the other side of the trees. A small coot collided with a branch as it flew out of the forest to escape the intruder. As the gray duck spiraled upward, Tristan deftly unhooded the goshawk and then cautioned Nelda, "Now wait—wait. You must select just the right moment to release the bird. If you send her too soon, 'twill be too easy a kill. If you hold back too long, you could lose your own bird. And if—"

"And if you continue this lecture," Jaufre growled, "the coot will be gone. Release that damn bird now."

Nelda jumped at the sound of Jaufre's harsh voice, then awkwardly jerked up her wrist, flinging the bird free into the air. With a flutter of wings, the little hawk flapped off in pursuit of its prey, playfully following every dodge and turn of the coot now flying for its life. The chase went far afield, obliging Jaufre and the others to turn their horses and gallop after the birds.

The earl, however, paid scant attention to the age-old drama of hunter and hunted unfolding in the sky above him. As he rode, his eyes were upon Melyssan in spite of himself, grudgingly admiring her seat, the capable way she handled the reins. It was as if to make up for her awkwardness on foot, nature had gifted her with the ability to be a superb horsewoman, straddling her mount with an easy grace that made even the simple pony appear a spirited creature, she and the horse moving as if they were one.

Her pleasure in the ride was apparent, a rose-colored glow tinging each cheek, green lights dancing in her eyes, although she avoided looking up to check the progress of the hawk. Who had taught her that trick, Jaufre mused, of bundling up her cascade of golden-brown hair from his sight, hiding the undulating curves of her supple young body within the folds of that shapeless brown sack she called a gown? She was more tempting thus concealed than if she had displayed herself half-naked before him. In fact, if he permitted his mind to speculate much further on all her hidden charms, riding was soon going to become a very uncomfortable exercise.

Disappointed shouts from the men and the way Melyssan's face lightened with relief told him the hawk had missed its catch. One of the austringers prepared his lure, a piece of meat attached to some duck feathers. Walking forward, he whirled it around his head, imitating with startling precision the cry of the bird.

"Oh, look. He's coming back," Nelda cried. She clapped her hands in delight as the goshawk homed lazily in on the lure and came to rest on the falconer's gloved hand, where it was fed a small bit of meat and placed back on the wooden frame.

Melyssan heaved a sigh, glad that the chase was over. The slight sound drew the earl's attention to her at once. Guiding his mount closer, he asked, "What, not enjoying the sport, my lady? Can it be you already wish for us to make an end?"

"I would not dream of depriving you of your pleasure," she said. "I am sure you will not be content to leave until you find something for *it* to destroy." She eyed Jaufre's fierce-looking hawk with repugnance.

"Him." Jaufre smiled, giving a slight lift of his dark brows. "It's a him. Alas, only the king may own the larger female hawks, for which I envy His Majesty. The males are not nearly as predatory as their sisters." A hard glint came into the lord's eyes as he stroked the bird. "No," he murmured. "If you want real killing power, give me a female every time."

Before Melyssan had time to speculate on the double meaning implied in Jaufre's words, the falconer cried out, " 'Ware, my lord. There goes a beauty of a mallard."

Jaufre looked up and caught his breath. Slowly he began to undo the leather leash that held his falcon.

"Hurry, my lord," urged the falconer. "The duck is getting too far, and that peregrine has as yet not made—"

"Quiet, you fool," Jaufre said tersely. "Do you think I don't know when to set my bird on?"

The hawk craned its neck upward but otherwise moved not a feather, and yet Melyssan imagined that it knew it was about to be released for the attack. She could sense the tension emanating from both the man and the falcon, two sets of hard stares never leaving the unsuspecting mallard.

"Now," Jaufre whispered, and flung his

arm upward. The hawk's powerful wings beat the air in two wide circles before soaring after the duck, sure and straight like an arrow released from a bow. A shaft of sunlight broke through the gray clouds, touching the peregrine's black feathers and casting a dark, winged shadow upon the dried brown grass below.

As they followed the pursuit on horseback, Melyssan saw the pulse begin to throb in the hollow of Jaufre's bared throat as he leaned forward in the stirrups, his face tipped up toward the sky. The wind swept back the waves of his ebony hair as his piercing dark eyes narrowed to slits. His full, sensual lips parted, half-hidden by the black satin of his beard as the broad expanse of his chest rose and fell with short, rapid breaths. She felt a shiver trickle up her spine as she recognized in the man the same savage beauty as in the falcon gliding above, some part of Jaufre that, like the hawk, would remain forever wild and untamed.

The falcon flew directly above its prey and then plummeted like a rock, binding to the mallard in one swift motion so that there was not even a cry, only the flutter of wings before both birds disappeared in the brush at the edge of the forest.

Melyssan's stomach churned, and she tried not to think of sharp claws digging into a softly feathered breast. Jaufre drew in the reins, relaxing back into his saddle to compliment the falconer on his training of the bird. The austringer moved ahead, cautiously approaching the spot where the hawk had gone down. But the next instant, the falcon looped back up from the underbrush and took to the sky.

The master falconer himself ran forward and seized the lure. Whirling it around his head, he called to the hawk in its own tongue. But each stroke of the bird's wings carried it farther away.

"What the devil!" Jaufre said, urging his horse forward. The entire party began riding after the peregrine. By this time, the falconer was running, each swing of the lure becoming a little more frantic than the last. The great black bird was now but a silhouette on the horizon until the gray clouds shifted, swallowing both the pale sun and the hawk from sight.

The falconer stopped, his shoulders slumping as the lure arced around his body in one last, slow circle, clunking to a standstill against his leg. He wiped the sweat from his brow and turned to face the earl, who reined to a halt beside him.

Melyssan felt a surge of pity for the man as she saw the livid red stinging Jaufre's face.

"You told me that bird was trained," Jaufre bellowed.

"I—I was certain he was, m-my lord."

"Then how came I to lose one of the most promising hunters I ever set eyes on?"

The man shuffled his feet, staring down at the ground. "I—I don't know. 'Tis not uncommon to lose a bird. I flew him myself several times, but—"

"But you are trying to tell me I don't know how to hunt with my own birds? Is that it?"

Although the falconer flinched, he rolled his eyes in such a way as to suggest that was exactly what he would have liked to tell the earl if he dared. Melyssan's hands tightened on the reins as she wished she could take Jaufre aside and give him a gentle shake, scold him into controlling his temper and being more reasonable.

But the falconer's hide was saved by a diversion from another source.

"Oh, look," Nelda gasped, pointing toward the forest. The earl started to command her silence when he raised his head and saw it, too. Two men garbed in the blue-and-gold livery of Lord Jaufre's guard emerged from the woods. One was leading a large skittish horse over which a dead buck was slung. The other soldier was mounted. Behind him he dragged a peasant, hands bound in front of him, secured to the horse's pommel by a rope and halter tied around his neck.

Melyssan's hand flew to her own throat. If the man chanced to stumble, his thin neck would surely snap. But somehow the prisoner managed to keep his footing.

Jaufre's dark brows knit together. He brought his horse around to meet the arriving guard, his anger at the falconer for the moment forgotten. The mounted soldier, a burly red-faced individual with a bulbous nose, called out, "Greetings, my lord. We finally caught the Welsh bastard who's been poaching your deer."

183

With a toothy grin, the guard hauled forward the prisoner as if he had been a recalcitrant hound. Melyssan choked back her cry as she got a better look at the unfortunate captive. Despite his height, the delicate face set beneath the fringe of unruly black hair was that of a lad not more than fifteen years old. The oversized green tunic he wore hung on a frame all lanky arms and legs.

"You saw this man kill that stag?" Jaufre asked after a cursory glance at the prisoner.

"Found him bending over it, we did, my lord, preparing to strip the carcass bold as you please."

The earl stared at the deer. It was a large creature with at least twelve points to its antlers. "Well, sirrah," he snapped without looking at the boy. "Are you so ignorant you do not know the penalty for killing my deer is death?"

The boy stubbornly regarded the nose of Jaufre's horse. The guard jerked the lad's head up until he gurgled, standing on his toes to avoid being strangled. "Answer His Lordship, you Welsh scum, whilst you're still able to speak."

"Oh, pray, stop," Melyssan cried. "If the boy is Welsh, perhaps he simply doesn't understand French."

"Naw, milady. This young buzzard understands right enough."

But Tristan came to her support. "Lady Melyssan could well be right, Jaufre. I know a smattering of Welsh. Let me try to pose your—"

"There is no need to address me in any of your barbarous English dialects," the boy interrupted. His aquiline nose and cleft chin were set into an expression of such hauteur, Melyssan would have found it amusing under other circumstances. "I speak French far better than any of you do."

Tristan's jaw dropped. "Then why the devil didn't you answer, boy?"

Ignoring Tristan, the boy addressed himself to Jaufre. "I have already told these varlets that I will not speak of this matter until I am formally charged by you, my lord."

"If you have aught to say of your innocence, you'd best spit it out now," said the earl.

The lad's thin lips twisted into a sneer. "Nay, my lord, it may suit the all-mighty and powerful Jaufre de Macy to forget his dignity by holding crude court before a rabble in the field, but I will answer charges nowhere but in the formal court of your hallmoot."

One of the knights behind Melyssan muttered, "Of all the impudent sauce."

Jaufre flushed. "I have already wasted as much time on this matter as my *crude* disposition will tolerate. Take this dignified peasant away and see how well he upholds his pride at the end of a rope."

"Aye, my lord," the guard replied, and began to haul the boy off.

"No! Stop." At Melyssan's ringing cry, both the guard and Jaufre stared at her as if she had run mad. The earl was the first to recover, shooting Melyssan a scorching glance

185

before hissing to the guard, "You heard my command. Get on with it."

Melyssan brought her pony up beside Jaufre and tried to catch his arm. "Nay, my lord. You have not taken time to reflect. Look at him. 'Tis only a boy, trying to hide his fear behind brave words. I beg you..."

Jaufre jerked his sleeve away from her, his horse bumping the pony's shoulder as he did so.

"You know in your heart he is right," she continued vehemently. "He's had no proper trial, no court of justice."

"I am the justice on my lands," the earl said. "Sergeant, if you delay any longer, you may prepare a rope for yourself as well."

"A-aye, my lord."

The guard tried to ride off, but Melyssan wheeled her pony in front of him, blocking his path. As the man groaned, looking helplessly at Lord Jaufre, Melyssan slipped off of her mount. Limping awkwardly because she did not have her staff, she nonetheless managed to reach the boy before the guard could gather his wits. Seizing hold of the rope, she clung to it so the tall soldier could not move his horse forward without dragging her off balance as well. The boy regarded her warily, terror and suspicion lurking in the depths of the most unusual silver eyes Melyssan had ever seen.

Although the high treble voice came out in a croak, he still managed to say, "Pray do not put yourself to any trouble on my account, my lady."

"Melyssan, I'm warning you," Jaufre said. "Let go of that rope and get back on your horse."

She winced as the rough hemp abraded her tender palms, but still she held on. "Jaufre, please, just look at him, really look at him one time. He's only a poor frightened boy."

"Nay, I am not afraid to die." The boy glared. "Not even at the hands of your terrible Dark Knight Without Mercy. Get back on your horse, madam."

Desperation welled inside of Melyssan. She could see the red weals the cruel rope had already made on the lad's stiff neck, could imagine how the guard would pull on it in a few moments, how the boy would be dragged upward, his long white fingers clawing as his tortured lungs fought for air.

"Melyssan..." Tristan stepped behind her, his low voice close to her ear. "Please. You are doing no good with this. You must not interfere with the earl's justice, especially not in front of his tenants."

Justice! How could Tristan so term this ruthless whim of Jaufre's? As the knight pried her fingers from the rope, she longed to box the ears of this foolish, haughty youth, but even more so Jaufre. The earl, at least, was old enough to know better than to let his temper interfere with his judgment. She whirled around and caught hold of his horse's bridle.

"My lord, surely there is some lesser punishment you can inflict for this crime."

Jaufre stared past her. "The law decrees death."

"You must have pity," she said, her voice breaking. "I will go down on my knees to you if that is what you require—"

"What I require is that you hold your tongue. Get on that pony and gallop back to Winterbourne as fast as it will take you."

A sob constricted in her chest and she stepped back, gazing up at him through a haze of angry tears. "How cruel you can be. And all because of a fit of pique over that damned hawk getting away from you. You cannot wring its neck, but the boy will serve just as well."

She heard several indrawn breaths from the other knights, and most of them averted their gaze, looking very much as if they wished themselves elsewhere. Jaufre compressed his lips and yanked on his reins as he prepared to ride away. A half-hysterical laugh escaped her.

"Go ahead and hang him, then!" she screamed. "God forbid you should fail to live up to your name. The Dark Knight Without Mercy. And God forbid you should trouble yourself to listen to this boy's explanation any more than I'm sure you ever listened to Yseult before you hanged her."

The instant the words were out, she wished them unsaid. The wild accusation was borne of her despair for the young boy's life, and for Jaufre that he should so lessen his nobility with such heedless cruelty.

Jaufre's neck went rigid, and when he turned back to her his face was drained, his eyes glazed over until they glittered like dark stones beneath the rushing surface of a turbulent stream. An ominous silence settled over the group except for the occasional snort and restless pawing of the horses.

Before she realized what he meant to do, Jaufre trotted his mount forward and bent over. One sinewy arm seized her roughly about the waist and hauled her off her feet to a sitting position in front of him. Too stunned to protest, she clutched her arms around his neck to prevent herself from falling off. Jaufre reached his hands around her to steady the gelding, who had been as startled by the sudden action as she was.

"Hold that prisoner until I return," he said. "If you will excuse me a moment, gentlemen. I want a word in private with my wife."

With that, he turned the horse and galloped off in the direction of the forest. Melyssan lurched against his powerful chest and clung to him, fearful of being thrown from her precarious perch. For the first time, she became aware of the distant rumble of thunder overhead. They had ridden well out of hearing of the others before Jaufre pulled the reins in on the gelding under a copse of trees.

Fear gripped her as cold and icy as the stray drop of rain that splashed against her face and trickled down her neck. She tried to draw back, but there was no place to go. Every way she moved, she was crushed close against the hardness of his thighs, his chest, his arms. The autumn wind caught up a handful of brittle red-gold leaves and swirled them past her head, swirled them like the maelstrom of fury and pain she saw seething in Jaufre's eyes.

"Jaufre, I'm sorry. I didn't mean to speak of Yseult," she whispered.

"Didn't you? Oh, I'll wager you've been dying to hear about my first wife for some time now. A woman like you, who so cherishes her explanations."

He began pulling free one of the arms she still entwined around his neck for balance. "Give me your hand."

"W-what are you going to do?"

"You needn't worry. I'm not going to cut it off. If I was seeking retribution, I'd be more likely to rip out your tongue. Nay, I simply want you to feel what listening to explanations has done for me."

Pulling loose the ruby brooch that drew in the neckline of his tunic, he forced her hand inside his woolen shirt and pressed her fingers against the warm bare flesh. She trembled as she touched hair-roughened skin and then gasped as her hand came into contact with the thick, raised tissue of a scar that seemed to continue endlessly down the length of Jaufre's chest.

"Feel that?" he snarled. "That was Yseult's final word to me after I spent hours listening to her, listening to her explain after I caught her in bed with Godric."

Melyssan felt the angry thudding of his heart beneath her fingertips as he gave a self-mocking laugh. "There are not many men who would pause to ask questions if they found their wife sprawled under the body of another man. Oh, but I let her sob her heart out to me. Tell me all about how Godric had raped her, how he was plotting to poison me for my money, and how she was almost too terrified to speak. And I believed every last damned lying word."

Melyssan tried to beg him to stop, but her throat was too constricted to speak. The intensity of his painful memories was carved in every strained line of his face, in the muscle that twitched along his jawline. But having once started, it was as if he could not stop.

"And then after Godric was dead, after I killed him, I drew her into my arms for comfort, and somehow I was able to sleep—sleep, when I never thought I'd be able to do so again. I thought I'd spend the rest of my life seeing Godric lying there in that pool of blood. Little did I realize my loving bride was determined to spare me such torment.

"God knows what instinct caused me to wake. But wake I did, in time to save my throat. As it was, she nearly ripped my heart out with her dagger. And that was the last I ever saw of my beautiful Yseult, her face so distorted with her blood lust she looked like a succubus spawned from hell."

Jaufre concluded his tale in dull, wooden tones. "While I lay unconscious, my grandfather had her hanged. Probably as well, for who knows? I might have listened to her explanations again, damn bloody fool that I was. Damn besotted young fool."

191

"No more," Melyssan said, her warm tears now mingling with the slow drops of rain that fell upon Jaufre's chest. She stroked the scar as if somehow the gesture could draw out the pain from his heart. "Do not berate yourself so bitterly. You did nothing wrong. You loved, trusted. 'Twas she who betrayed you."

"Love." He jerked her hand away, his voice hardening once more. "Don't make me sick. I never loved her. 'Twas a madness, an infatuation. Blindly following the dictates of my heart instead of my head.

"'Tis a mistake I've never made since." He caught Melyssan by the arm and gave her a rough shake. "So you remember that the next time you are tempted to appeal to my mercy."

Jaufre hauled in on the reins, pulling up the head of his horse, who had used the interval to crop at some dried grass. He turned the animal around and galloped back toward his waiting knights.

Melyssan's head collided with his shoulder as she entwined her arms around his neck, making no attempt to shield her face from the pelting rain. At St. Clare, the good sisters had taught her much of medicine, but she knew of no herbs that could heal the bitterness in Jaufre's heart. She sickened with despair at her own helplessness, helpless to save the boy about to lose his life, helpless to restore that part of the man that was already lost.

When they rode back into the circle of restive horses, Jaufre lowered her to the ground, where Tristan hastened to help her remount her pony.

"Are you going to stand here all day getting soaked?" Jaufre shouted to his people. "Head back for Winterbourne at once."

They all moved to obey except Tristan, who waited for Melyssan. She lingered, ignoring the folds of her wimple clinging wet to her cheeks and her gown weighted down by the rain. Haunted by the thin captive trembling with cold at the end of the rope, she could not tear herself away.

The guard started to ride off, preparing to carry out his grim commission, when the earl said, "Wait." Edging his horse closer, he peered down at the boy. "Tip his face up."

Although his mouth opened in bewilderment, the guard obeyed, yanking on the rope in such a way that the lad was obliged to face Jaufre. The black hair was plastered to the boy's forehead, sending trickles of water down his narrow cheeks, but he met the earl's regard with sullen defiance.

Jaufre tugged at his beard in frowning concentration. The boy's strange silver-hued eyes momentarily lost some of their fierceness, and his lips parted in a look that was almost eager, expectant.

Dear God, help him, Melyssan offered up in silent prayer. Help both of them.

It seemed to her they spent hours in that meadow, heedless of the sheets of rain pouring down. At last, Jaufre shook his head and said, "Whip him for trespass and send him on his way. Warn him never to set foot on my lands again."

"Aye, my lord," the guard agreed, scratching his thick skull in bewilderment.

Without another word, the earl turned and rode away.

Melyssan choked back a sob of relief, but as she looked down at the boy she wondered if he understood that he had been spared, despite his boast of how well he spoke French. He continued to stare in the direction where the earl's horse had disappeared. Melyssan shivered as her wet clothes layered to her back like a second skin, but she was more chilled by the boy's face before her...a young face suddenly aged with hate.

Chapter 8

THUNDER REVERBERATED OFF the thick walls of the gray stone solar, rumbling as if the sky made war on Winterbourne. Jaufre sprawled in his chair, his fingers crooked around a pewter goblet. He left the wine untasted as he stared through the croslet at the black night pierced by jagged spears of lightning, pierced like the darkness of his life with flashes of illumination, revealing to him some hidden truth if he could but catch the light long enough to see....

He raked his nails back through his hair,

attempting to shake off the strange thoughts that had taken possession of him since he had returned from the hawking. What madness had beguiled him into releasing that boy? He knew full well the dangers of his position as a marcher lord. Any sign of weakness, and the wild, rebellious Welshmen would swoop out of the hills to overrun Winterbourne. The king trusted him to keep order on these lands, not encourage his enemies to think they could defy the law with impunity.

Yet there had been something disturbing about the boy that Jaufre could not define. Those peculiar silver eyes of his, his manner of speaking French. Obviously no Welsh peasant, so whence had he come? Bah! Jaufre scowled, and his fingers clenched the goblet's stem. Why did he deceive himself? It was nothing about the lad that had softened his heart: it was Melyssan. She clouded his judgment with her honeyed beauty, her gold-fringed green eyes misting with tears, begging, accusing, until he had become unsure of his own verdict.

He prided himself on the justice he dispensed on his fiefs. Hard he was, yes, the Dark Knight Without Mercy, but just, always just. Or so he had thought. He was no longer certain of anything. Perhaps over the years he had come to mistake ruthlessness for stern impartiality.

Nay, he must not allow her softness to steal over him, wreak havoc with his senses, weaken him. Jaufre propped his elbows on the table and lowered his head, splaying his fingers against throbbing temples.

It was surely a weakness for a man not to stand by his first conviction. He hoped he never had cause to regret having spared the boy. Already he repented of his outburst about his first marriage. What charms had Melyssan used to so loosen his tongue until he'd told her almost everything about Yseult and Godric, revealing to her the secret pain he had kept locked inside himself for so many years? The confession left him feeling exposed, raw, like a wound with the healing scab ripped away.

No matter how he fought it, Melyssan was bewitching him in a way not even Yseult had done. He thought he had kept her at Winterbourne only to punish her, to make her serve him for the use of his name, but he'd forced her to stay because he desired her beyond all reason. Today even in the midst of his fury, when she had sat perched in front of him upon his horse, he had been painfully aware of the full curve of her hips pressed against his thighs, the soft swell of her small firm breasts moving against his chest, the feel of her slender warm fingers tracing the scar on his flesh....

He wanted nothing so much as to bury himself inside her gentle sweetness, losing all his anger, anguish, and pent-up longing in one great, shuddering release. Jaufre mopped at the perspiration beading on his brow. Sweet Jesu, what was he thinking? She had repaid her debt to him many times over. If he took her, he might end by owing her a price he could never pay.

The earl pushed back from the table and heaved himself to his feet. Then let her go from Winterbourne. Go to the nunnery where she belonged. He would tell her tonight she was free and thus free himself before it was too late. Then he could find a woman to wed who would give him his heir, someone like Finette, who would be satisfied with his wealth and his titles and never expect more. Never haunt him with sea-green eyes probing too deeply into old wounds, seeking out that vulnerable part of him he thought had died long ago.

By this time tomorrow, Melyssan could be far away from Winterbourne. A cold emptiness washed over him, but he shook off the feeling. He strode from the solar, his footsteps never faltering until he came to the heavy oak door leading to his bedchamber. To his annoyance, his stomach knotted as if he were some guilty lad gone to confront his confessor.

Irritated by his nervousness, he flung the door open with unnecessary force. Melyssan sat on a low stool before the hearth while Nelda leaned over, combing the damp tendrils of her mistress's newly washed hair. At the sound of the wood crashing against the stone wall, the lady-in-waiting gasped and dropped the comb. Melyssan twisted around with a start, her robe of blue wool slipping off one shoulder.

Jaufre towered in the doorway, the flickering light from the hearth illuminating only the thick boots and powerful outline of his thighs. His face was obscured by the shadows from the darkened outer room, but Melyssan could feel the tension emanating from every muscle in his body. She trembled as a surge of fear mingled inside her with a strange quivering anticipation.

Jaufre entered the chamber and closed the door behind him. He stepped forward until the firelight revealed his face to her. It was blank, masked by his heavy black beard and bushy eyebrows. Only the mahogany eyes were alive, darting restlessly around the room before settling on her naked shoulder until his stare became almost a physical thing, warming her flesh far more than the burning logs.

Hastily she pulled up the rough wool and held it pinned against her neck. The defensive gesture snapped Jaufre out of his trance.

"Get out," he snapped to Nelda. "I would be alone with your mistress."

Nelda ducked into a respectful curtsy and with a nervous giggle skittered out of the chamber. Conscious of the fire crackling behind her in the stillness of the room, the pounding of her own heart, Melyssan bent to retrieve the comb Nelda had dropped, delaying to regain her composure. Why had he come? Was he still angry at her interference over the lad? But he had let the boy go. Surely that augured well, suggested that some change had come over Jaufre, some return of the gentleness she had once known in him.

"What is your will, my lord?" She straightened

and, trying to appear calm, began to feather the damp ends of her hair before the dancing flames.

He cleared his throat. "To talk," he said, and then immediately fell silent. He spun around and paced to the stained-glass window, now only a mosaic of odd dark shapes without the sun to give it life. Even from where he stood, he could breathe in the scent of rosemary the heat coaxed from her drying curls. The fire played upon the glints of gold in her long, flowing hair as the comb fanned out nutmeg strands only to allow them to fall and nestle back against the ivory hollow of her throat. His fingers tingled from the urge to sweep aside that mass of tawny waves and press his lips against the warm, slender column of her neck.

"Melyssan. I—I want you gone from here."

Her hand froze in midstroke. She raised her head to face him, but he refused to meet her gaze.

"I mean," he stumbled on, "'tis time we put an end to this mummery. I am letting you go."

The comb fell unheeded onto her lap and her lips parted, but no words would come. In that instant she admitted to herself what she had always known deep in her heart. She loved him, always had, always would. Only that afternoon she had begged him to allow her to leave, but now his pronouncement passed over her like a sentence of death.

"By the blood of Christ," he said. "Why must you make even this so difficult? You are free, damn it. Don't you understand? Free of any further obligation to me.

"My men will escort you safely to the convent. 'Twill be done in secret so that you will be safe even from the king. Most likely he will forget you in time."

As easily as you will, Jaufre? She choked back the question before uttering it aloud. She had thought to steel herself against any further wounds from him, but once more, with the skill of a master warrior, he had found the blow capable of bringing her to her knees.

"When did you want me gone?" she whispered.

"Could you be ready tomorrow?"

"Of course, if you wish it." Moisture pricked at her eyelids and she leaned forward, cursing the fact that she must always dissolve so easily into a bout of tears. She pulled her hair around her, hoping to conceal her face from Jaufre.

He swore softly. "I should have sent you away that first day I returned."

"Then why didn't you?" she asked with a brittle laugh. "Are you so fond of wanton women you decided to keep..." Her words trailed off as her voice thickened.

Jaufre crossed his arms over the region of his heart. He knew he should stay as he was, keeping distance between them, but the firelight formed an aureole with the wisps of her fine hair, and the fragrance of her perfume hung in the air. A strange notion stole over him, the notion that he was trapped, a creature lost in the shadows...and there ahead of him, radiating around Melyssan's gentle beauty, was a circle of light and warmth. He could be free of the chilling blackness, if only he could reach out and touch her. Drawn by a force he scarce understood, he approached and reached inside the shimmering veil until he found her chin and raised her head.

"Melyssan," he murmured. He gazed into aqua eyes glistening with tears and rimmed by deep blue shadows that spoke of the grief he had brought to her. " 'Twas an ill-mannered jest of mine to call you wanton. I never believed such a thing of you. I don't know why I...I only know that it is best you leave. I do not want to hurt you."

Using his knuckles, he gently traced a path along her cheekbone up to her temple, down and back, down and back. Melyssan closed her eyes, desperately wanting to clutch at his hand and keep him from ever withdrawing it, to make this moment last forever so the dreaded time of parting would never come. After tomorrow she would never know his touch, never hear his voice, never know what it would have been like to truly belong to him. Suddenly nothing mattered but the warmth of his fingers, as with each caressing stroke they trailed farther down her face. Eagerly she waited for him to drift down along her jaw-line, down her neck, lower...

Her lips parted in unknowing invitation. The stroking suddenly ceased.

"Nay, you must go." He spoke as if to himself. "Go away before I..."

Her eyes flickered open, and she saw that he had backed off, putting the open mouth of the hearth between them. His dark brown eyes glowed with a strange hunger.

He does want me, she thought, a fierce joy flooding through her. He wore the look on his face she had imagined a hundred times, the yearning of a man for a woman. But his features contorted in agony, and she sensed he was using all his will to fight against his desire. Why?

Leaning against the coarse stone of the fireplace, she struggled to her feet. As she did so, Jaufre's gaze dropped to the ground—and then she thought she understood.

The robe had fallen back, exposing her twisted foot. In her mind, it waxed more grotesque placed in comparison with Jaufre's own straight limb. He shuddered and seemed incapable of tearing his eyes away.

Bitterness edged her voice. "That is why you are sending me away. You've learned to pity me the same as the rest of them."

He shook his head slowly, and then she realized it was not the foot that riveted him. Jaufre's eyes followed the curve of her calf, up the rounded, silky texture of her thigh, disappearing into dark regions yet concealed by the robe. He clenched his teeth.

"You are wrong. I pity you not. But I wish to God you had some pity for me."

"I would happily take pity upon you, my lord. Command me what you will." She moved closer, allowing the robe to slip down her shoulders, knowing that she was goading him. But she didn't care. Some sweet madness seemed to have taken possession of her.

"Stop it," he snapped. "I have no wish to dishonor you."

"And if I think it no shame?"

"Then I have confused you with my damned cynicism." He edged past her. "I never believed in the angels until I met you. But you are one of them, and I can't...I won't destroy you."

In a panic, she saw that he was going, robbing her of her last chance of ever being loved by him. She hobbled after him, placing herself between him and the door.

"I'm not any kind of a saint," she cried. "Look at me. I—am—a—woman."

She tugged at the robe until it billowed to a sea of blue at her feet. She stood before him proudly, exposing skin rosy-tinted from the blood drumming through her veins. Jaufre turned pale and raised his arm as if to ward her off, but she caught his hand and pulled it toward her.

"Touch me," she pleaded.

He resisted at first, but then, as if mesmerized, he slackened the rigid muscles in his forearm and allowed her to place his hand against the base of her neck. Guiding the unresisting fingers down to the curve of her breast, she felt a tremor shoot through him. Suddenly his arms closed around her, crushing her body against the rough camlet of his tunic. Hard, demanding, his mouth covered hers, and she pressed her lips back against his, exultant, eager to please him.

Swooping her off her feet, he held her cradled high against him and carried her over to the bed. "Melyssan," he said, his voice husky.

Lowering her upon the soft ermine covering, he pressed his weight on top of her, assailing her with fierce kisses on cheeks, her mouth, the side of her neck. When he cupped her breast and clamped his mouth over one pink, swollen nipple, Melyssan knew her first twinge of fear at the storm she had unleashed. She tried to draw his face back up beside her own, but he pulled away. Edging his way to the side of the bed, he pulled off his boots and stripped away his tunic and the shirt beneath, baring the firm muscles of his back, already glistening with perspiration. As he stood up and began to undo the cord to his drawers, Melyssan closed her eyes and tunneled beneath the furs.

Impatiently Jaufre fumbled with the linen undergarment, feeling the blood rush to the painful focus of his swelling groin. Naked now, he turned eagerly back to Melyssan, to find her huddled under the bedclothes. Large, frightened eyes finally risked a peek at him, only to close tightly again.

Berating himself as a savage and a fool, he carefully pried her fingers loose from the fur and eased himself underneath to lie beside her. How could he have forgotten she was a maiden still, in spite of the bold way she had offered herself to him? Even her gesture of disrobing had a kind of innocence about it, displaying a trust in him that he now betrayed—because beneath his desire he was himself afraid...afraid to show any tenderness.

Awkwardly he slid his arm beneath her shoulders and drew her to nestle against his chest. She trembled, and he raised one hand, tentatively this time, to stroke her cheek. Never had a woman come to him like this before, offering everything, demanding nothing but his touch. He had no love to give her, but at least he could try to bring her a pleasure that would equal his own.

Holding back his aching need, he turned slightly on his side and pressed a kiss against her hair. He felt suddenly clumsy, as if it were his first time as well. Moving closer so that her soft nipples just barely grazed his chest, he ran his hand beneath the silken fall of her hair and caressed the nape of her neck, the area behind her ear.

"Don't, please don't be afraid, Melyssan," he whispered, searching for the gentleness he had long ago banished from his heart. He placed his hand beneath her chin, tilting her face upward until he looked down into liquid green eyes.

"Go on, Jaufre," she said tremulously. "Truly I do want you to..."

Her words faltered as he planted featherlike kisses on her eyebrows, her cheeks, her chin, her mouth. With one fingertip, he followed the velvet outline of her lips, coaxing them apart before kissing her again. Melyssan reeled with shock at the first sensation of his tongue dancing teasingly against her own, its rough moisture gliding against the sensitive hollows of her mouth. The cold fear that had been creeping over her faded as the kiss deepened, the insistent pressure of Jaufre's lips and the rhythmic motion of his tongue sending wild currents rushing through her body.

She nearly cried out when he drew his head back, depriving her of the warm sweetness of his lips. But then he began to trail kisses along her neck, down to her shoulders, the crisp mat of his beard abrading her flesh. Kisses that were so soft, yet seemed to brand her everywhere they touched.

He looked up at her, his dark eyes misty with desire. "Melyssan, let me look at you."

Catching hold of the fur, he slipped it down toward the bottom of the bed, revealing their naked bodies lying side by side. Hers white, supple, slender like a young birch, his brown, tough, scarred like a weather-worn oak. Almost reflexively she sought to hide her foot, but he kicked the blanket to the floor.

"No, Melyssan. To me all of you is beautiful. I want to touch all of you." He moved to kneel between her legs, and taking the bent foot between his hands, he caressed it. Then his fingers began to inch their way along her calves. She tried to clamp her knees together, her body tensing in anticipation. But with a teasing smile, Jaufre moved his hands to the outer curve of her thighs and on up to her waist. Stretching himself out beside her once more, he continued his lazy exploration, coming tantalizingly closer to the swell of her breasts until her nipples ached for his touch. At last he enveloped one soft, firm globe, gently stroking until the pink-crested tip stood out hard against his palm.

He buried his face in the valley between her breasts, and where his fingers had lingered before, his mouth now followed, taking her nipple between his teeth and tugging gently, his tongue flickering over the crest as he sucked, starting a fiery blaze that spread downward across her belly to the very core of her being. She tangled her fingers in the thick mane of his ebony hair, and a low moan escaped from her throat, a sound she scarcely recognized as having come from her.

Just when she thought the exquisite torment he wrought upon her could not grow any more intense, his hand skimmed down across her stomach and back to her waist. With each stroke he went lower, until his fingers curled in the light mound of hair, causing her body to tremble with fresh urgency. His mouth captured hers as he insinuated his hand between her thighs, plumbing the soft folds of flesh, finding the pulsating center of her desire. Melyssan gasped, and he had no need to coax her lips apart this time; eagerly her tongue rose to meet his, darting, swirling, as she raised herself into the curve of his insistent caress.

Jaufre groaned. "Melyssan, can't wait— have to..."

The smooth muscles of his bronzed arms stood out in glistening relief as he braced himself above her, his knee gently spreading her legs. As he lowered himself, she felt the velvet-hard mystery of his maleness brush against her. Trembling, she parted her thighs, timidly, like a flowering bud opening to the sun's scorching rays. Slowly, gently, he eased himself inside her until she experienced a searing pain, as if she were being torn asunder.

Biting back a cry, she clutched his shoulders. Jaufre's head snapped up, and he looked at her, brown eyes clouding.

"God, I—I hurt you. Didn't mean to...."

Flinging her arms around his neck, she forced a reassuring smile to her lips. "Please. 'Tis all right. Love me, Jaufre...please just love me." Her shaking hand brushed back a lock from his brow. The pain lessened as she relaxed her muscles, and then she was aware of him inside her, filling her with the heat of his passion. He began to move.

Slowly, cautiously at first lest he hurt her again, Jaufre began a rhythmic stroking, reveling in the warm, moist sheath that enveloped him, the sweet torture of delaying the moment of release. It was his way to close his eyes when he took a woman, concentrating on satisfying his own driving need. But tonight his eyes were open, focused on Melyssan's face; the sight of the delicate pink flush on her cheeks, her sea-colored eyes heavy-lidded with desire, increased his own ecstasy a hundredfold. He bent down to kiss her again and again. With each kiss, he stroked deeper, faster.

Feverishly, Melyssan returned his kisses, her breath coming quick, shallow, as she caught the rhythm from him, small waves of pleasure becoming mighty breakers as she arched against his lean hardness, following him to the top of each new crest. All sound, sight, spun away from her until she felt as if her flesh were dissolving, blending, becoming a part of her lover until they were one being, one heart, one soul.

"Jaufre, Jaufre, I love..."

Her words were swept away as a dam of shuddering sensation burst inside her, flinging her into a whirlpool of incredible rapture. From a great distance, she heard Jaufre's hoarse cry, sensed the spasms that racked his powerful frame. Then her giddy world slowly ceased revolving, leaving her filled with a delicious weariness, ceasing all motion to float peacefully back to consciousness.

Jaufre collapsed, blanketing her with the weight of his warm body, burying his face alongside her neck. She was aware of the sharp rise and fall of his breathing, the racing of his heart in tempo with her own, gradually slowing to its normal steady beat.

She clasped her arms around him, holding his head tightly against her, savoring the joining of their bodies, wanting this moment to go on forever. But she knew it was over. Now he would draw away, leaving her cold with only the memory of his touch to warm her.

Already she felt him stirring, raising his head. The kiss he planted on her forehead was chaste, almost reverent. He rolled off her, and she felt the chill air striking against her skin. The fire had burned itself out, leaving only glowing embers. Melyssan shivered and tried to clear the constriction rising in her throat.

"Are you cold, Melyssan?" He stood up and found the covering to drape over her. But she drew scant comfort from the heavy folds of the fur blanket as she shut her eyes, not wanting to see him begin to dress, readying himself to go.

Then, to her wonderment, she felt him settle beside her again, drawing her close so that her head rested upon the firm flesh of his shoulder. Stifling the joyful sob that threatened to escape her, she snuggled against him, resting her palm against his chest, all cold and fear once more kept at bay by the magic circle of his arms.

"My beautiful..." His chest rumbled as the words came, hoarse, halting. "My...Lyssa."

It was as close to an endearment as he could come, but for Melyssan nothing had ever sounded sweeter. His fingers entwined in her hair and he kissed her, not with the compelling passion of moments before, but softly, lingeringly, a gentle brushing of lips. Her heart full to overflowing, Melyssan's tears spilled over onto the satiny thickness of his beard.

He caressed her cheek, flicking the moisture aside with one callused fingertip. "Oh, God, Lyssa, what have I done? I wish...I should never have allowed this to happen."

Hearing the note of regret in his voice, she jerked her head up, trying to read his expression. But in the darkness all she could make out was the soft glow of his eyes. Fear gripped her heart. He had known so many beautiful women, perfect women, experienced in all the ways to delight a man. And she...Had she been as awkward in lovemaking as she was in her dragging step? She did not delude herself that what had happened between them was as special to him as it had been to her, but that he should be sorry for it...

"Then—then I did not please you?" she asked.

"Yes, yes, of course you did."

Jaufre knew he should say more, offer her more reassurance than his curt reply. But how could he even begin to put into words what he did not understand himself? Even during the days he had been infatuated with Yseult, he had never known the like. A passion so strong he had no control of it, a fulfillment so great that for once he had been sated without the immediate return of his hunger, no restless feeling that there should be something more.

He ran his hands through the lengths of her silken hair, shaken by the way he had surrendered to his desire for her, binding her more closely to him when he knew he must let her go tomorrow.

Unconsciously, his arms tightened about her, forcing her head back down against his shoulder. Although the possessive gesture delighted Melyssan, it did not completely soothe away the doubt he had raised. She wanted to cuddle against him, forgetting that he had all but wished undone the most beautiful event of her life. But she could not.

Nervously twisting her fingers through the dark hairs that curled along his chest, she said in a small voice, "If we made each other happy, then I do not believe what we did was so very wrong, Jaufre."

"It was wrong of me. I robbed you of your innocence, and I do not know how I will ever repay you."

Melyssan stiffened. "Payment. Why must you always talk of payment?"

"Because it is the way of the world, Lyssa. Everybody wants something." He dropped a quick kiss on the top of her head.

"Is that what *she* taught you? Yseult?" Melyssan could have bitten out her tongue. The forbidden name suspended over them like a sword ready to slice down at any second and rend them apart. Although Jaufre did not move a muscle, she could sense his withdrawal.

"Yes, Yseult taught me a great deal," he said. Slowly, he began to shift Melyssan away from him, but she reached out and drew her fingers down the raised white skin that formed his jagged scar. Yseult's legacy.

"'Tis like you never allowed this to heal," she whispered. "And after all this time, although you say you never loved her, she wounds you still."

He caught her hand and held it away from him. "It wasn't Yseult. At least, not only her. It was..."

"What? What was it, Jaufre?" she prodded,

longing to understand the force that had so embittered him, rendered him incapable of receiving her love without counting the cost.

Silence stretched between them, and she thought he would not answer her.

"It was Godric," he replied at last, his grip tightening unconsciously on her hand.

"Yseult's lover? I—I don't understand. I—"

"He was my brother."

Chapter 9

JAUFRE'S WORDS ECHOED inside her head, soft-spoken words that by their very weariness hinted at an agony so great Melyssan could scarce comprehend it.

"Your brother, my lord?" she asked. "You—you killed your own brother?"

She had not meant to sound accusing, but she felt Jaufre flinch. He released the hand he had been crushing with such unconscious strength and rolled away from her. Sitting on the side of the bed, he propped his elbows on his knees and lowered his head into his palms.

"Yes—killed him, or may as well have." Jaufre's voice was muffled as if he spoke more to himself, going over and over the same thoughts with which he must have tortured himself hundreds of times before.

"Never guessed his fear would drive him to

such lengths. So ashamed of plotting against me, so afraid of my grandfather's wrath. Godric threw himself on his own sword."

Melyssan sat up, holding the fur robe across her breasts. Tentatively, she placed one hand against the flat, taut muscles of Jaufre's back. When he did not pull away, she gently stroked the ridge of his spine. "Oh, Jaufre. And you were blamed for his death?"

"I took the blame on myself. Better it should be thought I killed him, or he would not have been buried in consecrated ground." Jaufre lowered his hands and gave a listless shrug. "Not that I set store by such things, but it would have broken the old comte—that one of his grandsons should be so stained with dishonor, discarded like an animal carcass on a refuse heap."

He fell silent, and Melyssan continued her stroking, assailed by the same sensation of helplessness she had experienced that afternoon when Jaufre had first told her about Yseult and Godric. What could she say or do in the face of such pain and bitterness—she, who with her sheltered experience of the world would never have dreamed such betrayal between brothers possible?

She swallowed and said, " 'Twas—'twas very noble of you to shield your brother's good name."

"Noble!" Jaufre wrenched around so suddenly, her caressing fingers grazed against hair-roughened skin. "There was nothing noble about my dealings with Godric. I failed him, Lyssa. Don't you understand? I failed him."

He seized both her wrists and hauled her closer until even in the dark she could see the self-reproach glittering in his night-dark eyes. "He was seven years younger than I, under my protection. He cared naught but for his music, his manuscripts. And I was soft with him. Never pushed him, never taught him to fight as a man should, never taught him a sense of honor."

He released her hands and ran his fingers roughly along her arms until he gripped her shoulders. "And without honor, a man is nothing. Nothing! That is why..." He hesitated. "That is why I was so hard on your brother. He is as Godric was."

"No!" Despite her sorrow for Jaufre, her defensive instincts toward Whitney caused Melyssan to jerk away from the Dark Knight. "No. Don't say that. My brother would never—"

"Betray you? Aye, he would, even as Godric did me. Even love cannot last in the face of cowardice. When a man is weak—"

"Stop. I will not hear any more."

His words were like the remorseless litany of a sorcerer, conjuring up unwelcome images of how Whitney had quailed before King John when her virtue had been threatened, how her brother had nearly abandoned her when Jaufre's return was imminent.

But he came back, she reminded herself fiercely. He came back.

The earl ceased his accusation, but he withdrew to the edge of the bed. As they sat there in silence, Melyssan hugged herself against the chill that settled over the room, feeling as remote from Jaufre as if the warmth and magic of their lovemaking had never taken place.

Folding his arms across his chest, Jaufre tried to tell himself he was right about Whitney, right to force Melyssan to face the truth about her brother lest she be hurt someday as he had been. Yet she was hurting now. Even in the vehemence of her denials he could sense a quality of desperation, and he knew he had imbedded the first seeds of mistrust in her heart. Damn, what was he trying to do to her?

"Lyssa," he whispered, drawing her hard against him. She avoided his kiss by ducking her head, her cold slender arms pressing on his chest, forming a barrier between them. He wanted to tell her to forget what he had said, forget the whole wretched tangle about Yseult, Godric, Whitney...forget everything and turn back to the moment when they had been lost in the wonder of their desire, the desire that he felt building within him again as he clasped her trembling nakedness in his arms.

Her voice came to him, quavering, pleading. "You are wrong about Whitney, Jaufre. I know you have to be. You confuse weakness with being gentle."

"Is there a difference?" he murmured against the silken strands of her hair.

"Aye, my lord."

He tipped her head back and said, "Then

teach me. Teach me the difference, Lyssa."

He swept aside any reply she might have made by covering her mouth with his own. At first her lips strained against his, tight and unyielding. Then they parted, her tongue darting forward to meet his with an urgency that was anything but gentle. Jaufre knew a moment's surprise at the fierce way her arms encircled his neck, so different from the timid embraces she had bestowed upon him earlier.

Then he forgot everything but his need for her. Tumbling down onto the fur-covered mattress, he pulled her with him, his hands and lips feverishly scoring her flesh as if he would absorb all of her into himself.

Melyssan writhed against his lean hardness, trying as frantically as he to recapture the passion they had known before she had raised the specters of Yseult and Godric to haunt them. Clutching the firm muscles of his back, she rose to meet him as he thrust deep inside of her, allowing his driving need to sweep her into a mindless world of fiery sensation, her only awareness the heat of his body inflaming and consuming her as they reached the peak of their mutual desire.

'Twas not like it was the first time, Melyssan reflected with a touch of sadness as she sank back against her pillow. The tenderness, the almost spellbinding rapture, were missing; yet it had been good, for it left her drained of the confusing doubts Jaufre had raised, left her too tired to dread the coming of dawn when she would leave, perhaps never to see him again.

She could tell it had had the same effect upon him, for he collapsed against her, one arm draped possessively across her waist, while his head rested against her breast, his entire body relaxed of all tension. She felt his warm, steady breath against her skin and thought he had fallen asleep.

She was startled when he suddenly said, "You're not leaving tomorrow."

Her heart lurched, hope warring with disbelief. "Wh—what?"

Jaufre raised his head. "I said you're not going. I don't want you to—I mean—do not leave me, Lyssa."

Then out of the darkness came that other word, so soft she scarce heard it.

"Please."

Tears of joy, fear, and uncertainty blurred her vision, but she wound her arms around his neck and pressed her lips against his brow.

"Yes, my lord," she whispered. "I will stay."

"You're not staying!" Whitney said as he slammed down the lid of the chest that contained the meager belongings he had brought with him to Winterbourne. "No matter what it takes, we are riding out of here just as we came in, through the main gate." With shaking fingers, he girded his sword to his belt.

Melyssan bit her lip and stared at the empty dormer room that her brother shared with the young squires and pages. The others were all gone about their daily tasks in a courtyard

218

mud-soaked from yesterday's storm. The large drafty chamber was empty except for Whitney and Father Andrew, who sat on one of the straw pallets stacked up alongside the wall as he silently watched the young man pack. When the priest chanced to look up at her, his face so mournful, knowing, Melyssan could not meet his gaze. Her eyes flicked back to the pale, angry face of her brother.

"There is no need for you to take on so, Whitney," she said. "Lord Jaufre will not try to stop you from leaving."

"Nor you, either. I—I will die before I leave you here with that—that animal. I swear I will." But despite his bluster, beads of sweat gathered on Whitney's brow. "I know you dread going home to face our mother, but Enid has already written to say she would receive you. You were always wont to take her your problems when you were a child—"

"Now I am no longer a child," Melyssan interrupted him. She caught one of his long thin hands between her own. "My dear brother, you do not—nay, you will not understand. I cannot leave Lord Jaufre because I—I love him."

Whitney snatched his hand away, scraping her palm against the facets of his garnet ring. "Love! You dare stand there and tell me you love a man who hates me, who made a fool of me?"

"It takes so little to make a fool of you, Whitney. You are such a willing ally," she snapped, and then immediately repented her outburst. "Nay, I am sorry. I did not mean that.

If you would but let me explain to you about Jaufre, about how I feel—"

Whitney thrust his face forward until his nose was only inches from hers. "There is only one thing I want to know, Melyssan. Do you ride away with me or not?"

She stared into green eyes that reflected her own anger and hurt. "No."

"Fine." Whitney spun away from her and stooped down to hoist the chest onto his shoulder. His body sagged under the weight until she feared his backbone would snap.

"Wait. I will summon one of the grooms to help you."

"I want no help from anyone at this place." He staggered toward the door, pausing to direct a savage glare at her. "Let his servants wait upon you. I'm sure you've earned the right. Be his whore if that is what you wish, but you'll no longer be any sister of mine."

He tromped out of the room, and she could hear his crashing progress as he struggled to drag the chest down the curving stone stairs. Tears stung her eyes. She longed to run after him, but what more could she say?

A rustling from behind alerted her that Father Andrew had risen to his feet and was preparing to glide after her brother. He had been so quiet she had almost forgotten he was a witness to the quarrel. As he passed by her, his black robes brushing against her skirts, he covered his gray head with his cowl so that all she could see of him were the aged white hands fingering the rosary at his waist.

Did he mean to leave her thus without a word of farewell?

Choking back the lump in her throat, she said, "Take care of Whitney, Father. I never meant to hurt him."

"I worry more over the hurt you do yourself, my daughter."

She gave a shaky laugh. "I suppose you mean because I have not come to confess my sins. Of what avail would it be when I cannot say I am sorry?"

She thought of Jaufre's dark brown eyes bathing her with his desire, setting every fiber of her being tingling with want, with love of him. "I could not even promise never to touch him again," she said softly.

Father Andrew's hand tightened around his crucifix. "That is what distresses me more than anything. You have given yourself so completely, risking damnation for a man who is unworthy of you."

"I will not hear anything against Jaufre, not even from you, Father. Can you not see how much I need him, how happy he has made me?"

One withered finger reached out to dab at a tear on her cheek. He held out the glistening drop for her inspection. "I see little of any happiness for you, my lady. Lord Jaufre knows no future, only the darkness of his past; no love, only hate. I care not what honeyed words he whispers in your ear now, he will turn against you one day. Bitterness flows through him like poison, a poison that will spill over and infect even your innocent young life."

"You are as unjust to my lord as Whitney." She turned away, hiding the tremor that crossed her face. "There is no truth in what you say."

"No? Look deep inside yourself, my child. Has not this dark knight already tainted the affection between you and your brother?"

"That is Whitney's doing, not Jaufre's. He…" Her words faltered, and she covered her face with her hands. "You say there will be no happiness for me. Well, I could be happy. I could! If you and Whitney would just leave me be."

His hand touched lightly on her shoulder. "My lady, it pains me as much to say these things as it does you to hear them. 'Tis not too late for you to reconsider. Come away with us, Lady Melyssan, away from this man who will do you naught but harm."

"You'd best go, Father." She raised her head, stiffening her spine. "My brother will grow impatient. He is in great haste to be gone."

She heard the priest's gentle sigh as he withdrew his hand. "Farewell, then, my daughter. I wish I could offer you God's blessing, but I cannot. I will remember you in my prayers."

She nodded but did not turn around until the swish of his robes near the door told her he had gone. With the back of her hand, she wiped the tearstains from her cheeks, wishing she could as easily rid her memory of the priest's warning about Jaufre.

Father Andrew was wrong. He did not know Jaufre as she did. He saw only the Dark Knight striding through Winterbourne, exercising his power with the ruthless efficiency of a warrior. He heard only the legends, whispered secrets of the earl's shadowed past, of which none but she knew the painful truth.

What could the priest or Whitney know of the tender Jaufre who had cleansed away her tears and rocked her to sleep in his protective arms? What did they know of the vulnerable side of Jaufre, still raw and aching from old wounds, the wistfulness that sometimes crept into his dark eyes as the man yet sought for something to believe in?

Perhaps it was a sin to find such pleasure, such peace, from the union of their bodies. Jaufre had not said he loved her. Most likely he never would. But she loved him, and for the moment that was all that mattered. There were a hundred tomorrows for her to be a penitent. She had to hold fast to today, seize whatever happiness she could, accept whatever part of Jaufre's life he was capable of sharing.

Suddenly she was overwhelmed with the need to see him, to feel his arms closing around her, to lose all thought in the heady sensation of his lips on hers.

She nearly stumbled headlong down the stairs in her haste to reach the courtyard. Grooms exercising the horses, milkmaids hastening with their pails to the kitchen, guards preparing to change shift on the castle walls, all blurred before her eyes in the bright sunlight.

She took several cautious steps forward, trying to avoid the huge puddles of water left by the rain. Her staff sank deep in the mire, and as she tugged it free she flew forward, colliding with a large, masculine form. Sinewy arms encircled her waist, lifting her off her feet.

"Take care, my sweet, lest you plunge face first into the muck," Jaufre's deep-timbred voice murmured against her ear. "Or at least defer your mud bath until I have had my morning kiss."

She looked up into a pair of laughing brown eyes. Was it a trick of the sunlight, or did his face look younger, as if some of the creases in his bronzed skin had been smoothed away last night?

"Jaufre," she cried, and buried her hands in his thick mane of hair, so black it seemed to have caught some of the blue of the sky in its glossy strands. She crushed her mouth against his with such force she nearly sent them both tumbling over backward.

Jaufre caught his balance, his arms tightening around her, pressing her body so close to his she could feel the evidence of his aroused desire even through the layers of their clothing. His lips now took command of the kiss, his rough tongue plundering the sensitive hollows of her mouth with a passion that left her breathless. Slowly he released her, lowering her back to the ground so that she slid along the hard-muscled plane of his chest and thighs.

Across the courtyard, the saucy page Arric gave an appreciative whistle before disappearing into the stable. Jaufre drew in a deep breath and then laughed.

"Madam, how often must I caution you about assaulting me in front of my men? I vow you have put me to the blush this time."

Melyssan gave a throaty chuckle, too mesmerized by the teasing smile that so transformed his stern features to make a reply. But the smile vanished abruptly, to be replaced by a look of such tender concern as wreaked even more havoc upon her already racing heart.

"Why have you been weeping?" he asked, caressing her cheek with the warmth of his fingertips.

" 'Twas nothing. I was bidding farewell to my brother."

"If his leaving distresses you so, I will make the whelp stay."

"No!" she protested quickly. "'Tis better that he go."

Jaufre scowled. "No matter what my feelings, I would not harm your brother, my lady."

"I know that, Jaufre. I did not mean— 'Tis only that Whitney cannot cling to my skirts forever. My father will have need of him." She hoped that Jaufre would not see through the weak excuse to her fear that despite his good intentions, a confrontation between her angry brother and the earl was exactly what she dreaded. She tried to take Jaufre's hand and give it a reassuring squeeze. For the first time, she realized he was holding something.

His frown fading, he placed a small carved oaken box into her grasp. Her eyes widening, she regarded him questioningly and found his cheeks tinged red with embarrassment.

"I was saving that to give to you as soon as I saw you this morning. But you were already dressed and gone when I returned to our bedchamber."

As she fumbled with the clasp to open the chest, he added, "'Tis nothing much. My mother gave it to me when I was a stripling, though God knows what she thought I would do with it. Mayhap she meant to encourage me to comb my hair."

As the lid swung open, Melyssan saw herself reflected in the depths of a mirror of polished steel nestled in a frame of crimson velvet. Her wonder at Jaufre's gift was equaled only by her amazement at the woman confronting her. Who was this fey creature with the wild mass of nutmeg curls tumbled around flushed cheeks, sparkling green eyes, and lips bruised a bright pink from the force of a man's kiss?

She held the mirror at arm's length, almost frightened by the strange vision. Jaufre's hands came up to steady her own, which had begun to tremble. "High time this poor looking glass had something more lovely than my grim face peering into it. What think you, my lady?"

"M-my lord, I scarce have words to thank

you," she said. Yet she felt she needed no mirror when Jaufre looked at her as he was now, making her beautiful with his eyes.

No, he had never said he loved her, but this was close, so close to all her dreams of him that the reality of it pierced her heart with a sharp pain. Her fingers clenched down upon the wooden case.

She cared not what Father Andrew said. She would cling to her illusions with all the strength she possessed. As long as Jaufre was near, touching her with the warmth of his hands, of his gaze, nothing could be wrong.

She smiled up at him as he bent to kiss her, her eyes flicking back to his gift. The smile wavered. A distant image behind her flashed across the polished surface of the shining steel, an image of a young man and a black-hooded figure vanishing through the gate.

Sir Tristan Mallory impatiently shoved aside the branch that threatened to tear the cap from his head. He had little liking for these dark, shadowed Welsh forests. Not that the trees grew any thicker here than in the woodland at Ashlar, but at least in the north of England, one need not fear taking an arrow in the back from some crazed Welshman hiding in the bushes.

With new trouble brewing along Wales's borderlands, it was not the time for such dallying pleasures as a day's stag hunting. But the sight of that huge buck brought down a week ago by the peasant lad Jaufre had pardoned had whetted the Dark Knight's appetite to see some sport of his own making.

Tristan scowled, struggling through some rowan bushes into the open space where the hunting party had alighted to break their fast, so early had they set out from Winterbourne.

Damn it. Why did Jaufre pay so little heed to reports of the increased number of rebel uprisings? Tristan had been standing right next to the earl when news had reached Winterbourne of how Sir Kendall's manor house had been burned, his wife and babes slaughtered. The trouble was Tristan could not be sure exactly what penetrated Jaufre's thick skull of late.

The knight's frown deepened as he stepped into the midst of the huntsmen, grooms, and pages. An excited brachet hound nearly tripped him as it tore past his legs, barking at will-o'-the-wisp light patterns the sun cast through the withered autumn leaves. Jaufre perched next to Melyssan on a fallen log, seemingly oblivious to the commotion around him, which was enough to affright any deer within a mile or alert any lurking Welsh rebels within two.

The earl leaned forward, eating out of Melyssan's hand a thick slab of wheat bread and jelly. He chuckled when some of the thick grape jam dribbled down his beard, playfully nipping at Melyssan's fingers as she tried to dab his face with a cloth.

By St. Michael, thought Tristan, the man

is as giddy as a prisoner new released from the dank confines of a dungeon and suddenly comprehending he is free. If 'twere any man but Jaufre, I would swear he was...

He allowed the disturbing thought to trail away as he strode in the couple's direction. It took Jaufre a full minute before he was even aware that Tristan glowered above him, hands on hips.

"Ah, Tristan..." The earl gave him a lazy smile. "Did you find any fumes?"

"No, 'twas not signs of deer that I was looking for."

"That is obvious from the state of your boots, man."

Tristan regarded the substance caking his heel with disgust and scraped his leather-encased foot against the grass. An angry flush crept up his neck at the sound of Jaufre's booming laughter.

"I was looking, an it please you, my lord," Tristan said through gritted teeth, "for any sign you and your lady might end up massacred during this little jaunt in the forest. I appear to be the only one with enough sense to show concern." He gestured scornfully to where Sir Dreyfan played at fetch with one of the hounds.

"Thank you, my friend, but I warrant you I can well take care of my lady." Jaufre wrapped his arm around Melyssan's shoulders, pulling her cloak more tightly around her. A becoming blush mounted to her cheeks under the earl's attentions.

Tristan's lips set into a taut line. As far as

the lady's feelings went, he had no doubts what-soever. She wore her heart in her eyes for all to see, and every pulse of it beat with love for Jaufre de Macy. Damn him, how could he so trifle with her? With much pain, Tristan had watched the changes the years wrought in his friend, the hardness, the cynicism, and the mistrust of all that was good in the world. But through it all Jaufre had maintained his honor, an honor that would never let him despoil an innocent young girl...at least, not until now.

Jaufre glanced up at him again, teasing devils dancing in his dark brown eyes. "Now tell me true, Lyssa. If you met a bear in these woods wearing such a peevish expression as Tristan's, would you not be likely to die of fright?" Jaufre gave an exaggerated shudder. "I promise you I would."

Although she laughed at Jaufre's comment, Melyssan gave Tristan such a kind smile as made him resolve that the earl should do right by this maiden if he, Tristan, had to beat the man insensible first.

"Nay, my lord," she said in her sweet, gentle accents, "there is naught in Sir Tristan's comely face as would frighten any lady."

"Is that so?" Jaufre cupped Melyssan's chin with mock ferocity. "Well, I'd best not find you too admiring of his comely face, or I shall force him to start wearing a mask."

Then he kissed her swiftly, heightening the color in her face to an even brighter hue. She cast Tristan a look, half-embarrassed, half-pleading. He understood her thoughts as well as if she'd spoken them aloud. Please. I am so happy. Do not condemn me.

Tristan whirled on his heel and stalked away, muttering, "If you insist we proceed with this madness, then let's get on with it."

Jaufre's forehead puckered as he watched his friend's retreat. Plague take him! It was not like Tristan to be so surly. What the devil ailed him? Never mind, he told himself at last, drawing Melyssan closer and staring deep into her anxious green eyes. Nay, never mind. He did not want to know. He hadn't given much consideration to anything since he had asked Melyssan to stay with him. He only wanted to feel, to revel in gentle sensations too long denied.

Closing his eyes, Jaufre brushed his lips against her mouth, so tender, so sweet, then across her cheek, so petal-soft, and felt her warm, rapid breaths tickle his beard. Let Tristan keep whatever lectures he harbored shut away in his self-righteous bosom. Jaufre did not want to hear.

Standing up, he lifted Melyssan by the waist and twirled her around, delighting in her laughing pleas for him to stop, and then settled her carefully back in her saddle. How strong he felt when she was in his arms, invincible, as if he could conquer not only Clairemont, but half the world.

One of the huntsmen reported a sighting of some antler rubbings on a birch nearby, and Jaufre led the hunting party in that direction, following the course of the stream as it meandered through the woodland.

In truth, Jaufre cared little whether they found a deer or no. He would have been content to while away the day making love to Melyssan on the moss-covered banks, in less hurry than the brook spilling over the rocks. Aye, content...if he did not constantly fancy Tristan's eyes were boring holes in his back.

He allowed Melyssan to precede him with Sir Dreyfan and held back his own mount until Tristan drew alongside. Something in the knight's stiff-necked manner made Jaufre long to slip a burr under his friend's saddle.

He reached out and snapped off a long twig whose dried leaves of gold and red clung precariously to their stems. Brandishing it like a sword, he rustled it under Tristan's nose.

"Smile, man, before your face freezes that way."

"I see little to smile about, my lord." Tristan slapped the branch out of Jaufre's grasp, sending several of the dried leaves flying in the face of the earl's horse. In spite of Jaufre's lazy grip on the reins, the stallion was too well trained to do more than toss his head.

"Why, whatever is amiss?" Jaufre asked, then snapped his fingers. "Ah, I'll wager I know. You've had an eye to that little chit who waits upon my wife. What's her name? Nellie?"

"Nelda."

"Nelda. And she's been dropping her handkerchief young Arric's way of late." Jaufre fetched a deep sigh. "How fickle these females. Always preferring someone younger. You are growing ancient, my friend. You should think of taking a wife."

For a moment, the earl believed Tristan was going to choke. "So should you!" he shouted, then, as if recalling himself, compressed his lips.

Jaufre grinned. "But I have a wife. I assure you I have never felt so married in my entire life."

"I see. That, I suppose, is why you no longer sleep on the pallet in my chamber."

"Is that what distresses you? I never suspected you were afraid of the dark. Why, you have only to call out, and any of the squires—"

"Will you cease this buffoonery! You know what I am leading to, Jaufre. How soon are you planning to rid yourself of Melyssan? How soon?"

Jaufre's eyes focused on Melyssan's back, her honey-brown hair feathered across the maroon cloak covering her slender shoulders, her colors and delicate frame blending with the fragile beauty of the autumn-scaped woods. But unlike the trees' discarded leaves, he would never allow her to be tossed and buried by the chill storms of winter. Be rid of Melyssan? Why did Tristan even ask him such a thing?

"I only wondered," Tristan continued, "because you summoned to Winterbourne those merchants traveling to display their wares at the fair. I assumed 'twas time to buy the lady her trinkets and send her on her way. You have lain with her for more than a week. 'Tis far longer than any of the others have lasted."

"You dare! You dare to compare *her* to those whores?"

Tristan gave him a stare that was a shade too innocent. "And why shouldn't I? 'Tis what everyone else will do. After all, you surely would not be thinking—heaven forfend—of marrying the girl?"

The line of oak trees spread their gnarled roots closer to the stream bank, and Jaufre was obliged to fall behind or risk plunging into the water. Forced to contain his rising anger until clear of the obstacle, he pulled his horse back alongside Tristan at the first opportunity.

"And why the hell not? Why wouldn't I think to marry her?"

Tristan raised his eyebrows in exaggerated astonishment. "You could have your pick of maidens from noble families, maidens of great beauty...."

"There is none more beautiful. None! None to even compare."

"And women of great accomplishments, skilled in looking after a great lord's household—"

"Melyssan has more learning than the lot of them. I'd entrust her with the care of any of my estates, entrust her with my very—" Jaufre broke off, then added gruffly, "With my very life."

Tristan went on as if he had not heard. "And then a man of your religious piety, of course, must be disturbed by her affliction. That lame foot. Surely a curse of God, that might in turn be visited upon your children."

"What!" Jaufre roared. Any man but Tristan daring to imply such a thing would have been sprawling in the dirt by now, spitting out blood and loosened teeth. As it was, Jaufre leaned over and caught Tristan's bridle, bringing his horse up short.

"Any son of hers, I care not if he were lame in both legs, if he had but half her spirit, my son would wrest Normandy from the French single-handed."

For the first time that morning, Tristan smiled. "Before you get wrought up enough to run me through on behalf of this son of yours, I suggest you and the lady take steps to ensure he will not be a bastard."

"Well, of course there is no son," Jaufre sputtered. "I used that to point out that I—that is, any man would be proud to take Melyssan as his wife."

Tristan pried Jaufre's fingers from his bridle. "Don't tell me. Tell her."

With that, he kicked his horse in the sides and rode to the head of the hunting column, leaving Jaufre fuming and feeling very much as if he'd walked into a velvet-lined trap.

Tristan was getting too clever for his own good. How skillfully he had stirred to life the conscience Jaufre had repressed ever since the night he'd first taken Melyssan. Nay, not taken, he reminded himself fiercely. She had given herself, come to him. He had tried to resist.

But not so very hard, sneered a voice inside him. 'Twas you who begged her stay. Yet he had never constrained her to do so, never forced her to become his mistress. It was her own choice.

But he knew why she had stayed. Even now she glanced back at him, inviting him to ride to her side with that radiant look on her face that both gladdened and terrified him. Terrified him because at times the love glowing in her eyes elicited a response from him that was more than physical.

Damn Tristan! With a few well-chosen barbs, his irritating friend had ruined the enchanted idyll Jaufre had enjoyed with Melyssan. It was all the more annoying because he knew Tristan was right. The knight had only reminded him of what he knew all along must be the outcome of his relationship to Melyssan.

He would have to marry the girl. Honor demanded it. Ask her to make vows, promises that he well knew were so easily broken. And he was afraid he might care too much this time if they were.

What galled him most was the feeling that somehow the decision had been taken out of his hands. At what point had he lost control of his own destiny, been cornered by that same innocence and gentleness that had first attracted him to Melyssan? Perhaps his fate had been sealed that long-ago summer evening when he'd first pulled her into his arms, pretending that he mistook her for her sister.

How would she react when he told her they

were to wed? She would not be human, would not be a woman, if her face did not light up with some sign of triumph. He watched in brooding silence as she brought her pony around and maneuvered into place by his side.

He had no way of knowing the courage it took her to do so. Ever aware of Jaufre, Melyssan had stolen glances at him from time to time while he had talked with Tristan, seen the change come over him, her heart wrenching with fear as she did so.

He did not return her timid smile but instead regarded her with what she had come to think of as his Dark Knight look, mouth set in a grim line, brown eyes half-hooded, forbidding.

"M-my lord is disappointed we have not yet found a deer?" she ventured.

"The morning is young. If you would be a hunter, Melyssan, you must have more patience when you stalk your prey."

"Yes, my lord. I—I do," she said, bewildered by the almost accusing tone in his voice. Had she done something foolish during the course of the hunt to displease him? "I only thought you—you look as if you were disturbed."

"Aye, I am. With matters that have nothing to do with deer hunting."

"Oh." She longed to touch his cheek and ask him to share his trouble, but when Jaufre wore that guarded expression he put such distance between them that he might as well have been riding on the opposite side of the stream.

"If you must know," he said, leveling her

with a hard stare, "I have been thinking 'tis time I took a wife."

Her breath caught in her throat, the words jolting her as if he'd knocked her from the horse. He'd told her once he meant to seek a bride, but it was something she'd allowed herself to forget. The forest around her became a golden blur as she felt the blood draining from her face and a keen whistling past her ears.

The arrow splintered the bark of a mountain ash only inches from her head. Jaufre's hand shot out and clamped down on her upper arm as his mind registered the narrowness of her escape. The next instant something sharp ripped through his thigh, slamming his leg against the saddle. His strangled curse mingled with the shrill cry of his horse as it lunged forward, jostling Melyssan's pony.

"Get down," he said, half shoving, half dragging Melyssan out of the saddle. "Take cover. We are under attack."

Her pale face flashed before his eyes as she clutched at the bridle to save herself from falling. She screamed his name as Dreyfan caught her around the waist and hauled her toward the shelter of the bushes.

"My God. Help him," she sobbed. "He's been wounded."

As he struggled to get his wild-eyed mount under control, it took Jaufre a moment to realize it was himself Melyssan was weeping over. He glanced with a sense of detachment at the blood-flecked feathers and shaft protruding from his upper leg. His fingers closed around the thin rod only to jerk them away as if the crimson staining his palm were fire. Pain spiraled upward along his side like a hundred knife strokes lacerating his flesh. Grinding his teeth, Jaufre hunched over, forcing himself to hold the leg immobile. Sweet Christ, he was pinned to the saddle.

"Jaufre!" He heard Tristan's shout and became aware that his friend was running forward to help him.

The earl shook his head to clear away the black webs rising before his eyes. "No. Get back!" he cried hoarsely, knowing if the arrow were removed now, it would render him useless for the battle to come. Yanking his sword from the scabbard, he drew in a shuddering breath, willing his mind to block out the agony that threatened to rob him of his senses.

Horses and baying hounds bolted around him in confusion as his men sought cover, drawing forth their weapons. His heart pounding, Jaufre scanned bent tree trunks, rustling branches, for some sign of the invisible enemy. His instincts already alerted him that something was wrong. What manner of attack was this? If an ambush, his small band should have been overrun by now. But two arrows fired? It was more like the work of...

His trained eye caught the movement immediately, the dark-hooded figure skulking on the opposite shore, now crawling away in retreat. By St. Michael, 'twas but the work of some cowardly assassin.

Jaufre's lips curled back in a feral snarl as he kicked his horse and whirled around to pursue the whoreson knave who had come so close to killing Melyssan. As the courser's muscles stretched into a gallop, a snapping sound split the air. The arrow imbedded in Jaufre's thigh broke free of the saddle, tearing flesh and sinew. The scream that rose in his gorge erupted in a savage battle cry as the Dark Knight plunged his horse into the narrow stream.

Water splayed out from under the charger's hooves as Jaufre thundered toward the crouching figure, who now abandoned all attempts at concealment and fled into the forest. The earl's throat burned raw with each ragged breath as the white-hot shards that pierced his leg slammed repeatedly against the saddle, the wooden shaft rasping against the marrow of his bone. His horse clambered up the opposite bank, and the green and gold of the woodland misted red before his eyes as he surged forward with the fury of a ravaged beast springing to the defense of its mate.

Although his prey had vanished into the thicket, Jaufre had no difficulty following the enemy's crashing progress as the hooded man tore frantically at the tree limbs barring his escape. The earl's fingers tightened around the hilt of his sword as he galloped after the man, blood pounding in his temples as he closed for the kill.

The man stumbled, fell, clawing wildly at the branches that entangled his cloak. He pulled free of it and rolled over onto his back just as Jaufre checked the speed of his mount.

The cold steel of his weapon sang through the sudden quiet as the Dark Knight arced it back, preparing to deliver the fatal blow. But the blade wavered, froze in midair, as he found himself staring down at a thin white face dominated by large dark-fringed eyes, strange silver-colored eyes glazed with fear and hate.

Chapter 10

JAUFRE HAD NOT succumbed to unconsciousness by the time Tristan and Dreyfan deposited him on the linen-covered mattress in his bedchamber. But Melyssan almost wished that he had as the two knights left her to finish the task of binding Jaufre's wound.

One dark eye fluttered open to glare at her as she pushed aside what remained of Jaufre's blood-soaked woolen hose and drawers, along with the crimson-stained cloth she had used to cleanse the leg.

"What the hell do you think you are going to do with that knife, woman?"

Half-guilty, half-defiant, Melyssan lifted the small blade that had been partly concealed by the folds of her gown. "Please, Jaufre. I told you. I—I felt splinters still lodged in the wound. Sir Dreyfan was not very careful when he—"

"Careful!" Jaufre exploded. "The old fool

plucked that arrow out of me like a scullery wench wriggling the spit out of a pig. He damn near finished what that boy of yours started."

Melyssan bit her lip. "My lord. I have told you three times already how sorry—"

"You're sorry? Not half as sorry as I am that I didn't follow my first instincts and hang the little bastard. What happened today is no more than I deserve for allowing a woman to lead me around by the nose."

Jaufre ground his shoulder back against the mattress as if somehow he could sink deep enough to escape the pain that had turned his face ashen beneath the beard. Gingerly, she settled herself beside him on the bed, the knife feeling slippery against her palm.

Under the direction of the sisters of St. Clare, she had learned to treat many wounds. Once she'd even helped to remove the foot of a huntsman who had injured himself with an axe. But it was different this time, far different when her own heart seemed bound up in that scrap of linen Jaufre pressed against his leg to keep her from touching the torn flesh again.

"The bleeding has stopped," he said. "Let well enough alone."

"'Tis not well enough. Those splinters will fester inside of you until they poison your blood." She tried to remove his fingers from the cloth, but he jerked away, snarling an oath as his other hand clenched deep into the pillow beneath his head.

"Damn you, keep away! I'll have no blood

left to poison if you start carving. I already feel weak as a newborn babe."

"You'll have no leg left if I don't. You may even...Please, Jaufre, I beg you."

He continued to stare belligerently at the knife until understanding dawned on her.

"Oh, I see." She swallowed hard, berating herself for her ridiculous hope that she could have banished the memory of Yseult. "If you are that afraid I am planning to murder you, I will summon Tristan. I am sure he could forestall any blood-thirsty intentions I might have."

When he compressed his lips into a thin white line and made no reply, she eased herself off the bed. But Jaufre's hand closed hard around her wrist.

"Don't be a fool, Lyssa. Oh, hell-kite, if it will make you feel better, hack away." Ripping free the piece of linen, he exposed the jagged line of congealed blood marring the hard-muscled thigh.

Melyssan drew in a deep breath and for a moment wished she could summon Tristan, Dreyfan, one of her ladies, anyone else to inflict this agony upon Jaufre that was so necessary for his recovery. But she'd already seen a sample of the knights' healing capabilities when the arrow had been removed. As to her ladies, it was she who was supposed to be training them. She could not turn coward now.

Taking a moment to steady her hands, she rested her fingers against the coarse-haired skin above Jaufre's knee. As yet the flesh was warm but not overheated, which was a good sign. She could not help remembering how only last night Jaufre had guided her hand along his strong limbs, teaching her how he liked to be caressed, all the while doing such wondrous things to her own body with his bold, exploring fingers.

Her cheeks burned with shame that she should so allow her thoughts to wander. She wondered if Jaufre had noted the way she'd been studying him, for he draped one arm protectively across his manhood. Whether out of a belated sense of modesty or a fear she might somehow let the blade slip, she did not know.

Firmly grasping the knife, she began to probe the wound, her grim task of prying out the splinters made all the more difficult as Jaufre abandoned the silent stoicism he had exhibited earlier, when marching his prisoner out of the woods at swordpoint and riding all the way to Winterbourne unaided. He had not uttered a sound when Dreyfan had so ruthlessly yanked the arrow free of his flesh. But now, with every prick of the knife blade, he spewed forth a string of curses Melyssan had never heard the like of before, in French, in Latin, and in another foreign tongue she was relieved she did not understand.

Interspersed with the swearing were mutters of what he would do to that accursed devil's cub responsible for his injury. At the moment, the boy was lodged in the dungeon below the great hall. Melyssan could still feel remnants of the sick feeling that had curled in her stomach when she had recognized Jaufre's assailant as the lad whose life she'd begged him to spare. She could have wrung the young dog's neck herself when she realized how close he had come to repaying the earl's clemency with death. But surprisingly enough, it had been Jaufre who had interfered when his knights would have sought immediate reprisal upon the boy. The strange light in the Dark Knight's eyes as he regarded his captive had sent a shiver up Melyssan's spine. Even now she feared to speculate upon what dire fate Jaufre might be planning for the young rebel.

"Ow! Christ's wounds," Jaufre hissed, startling her so that she jabbed deeper than she'd intended. He muffled his bellow of rage into the pillow and then panted, "Lady, you are about as gentle as a wild boar rutting for acorns."

Tears of frustration stung Melyssan's eyes as she wiped away some of the blood that was making her fingers slick. He spoke as if she tormented him for her own pleasure.

"If you would but hold still. There is only one splinter remaining. Mayhap I should send for some strong spirits."

"There's not enough mead in this castle to get me drunk enough to endure your poking. Hasten and make an end."

"I was thinking of the drink to fortify me, not you," she mumbled. By the time she had removed the last sliver and cleaned and dressed the wound for the second time, packing it with yarrow leaves, her kirtle clung to her, more damp with perspiration than the shirt Jaufre wore.

He rolled over onto his back. "Praise the Lord, she's done at last." His mouth drew down into a heavy scowl. "Are you sure you removed all the splinters? Beshrew me but I feel as if I still had ten times fifty prickling my flesh."

"I am as sure as you would let me be," Melyssan said as she washed her hands in a basin of water. Returning to Jaufre's side, she felt his brow for any approach of the dreaded fever and was relieved to find his skin damp but cool.

"Try to rest now, my lord. 'Twill be the best thing for you."

"Rest! I do so love a woman with a keen wit." But something of his devil's twinkle returned to the pain-glazed brown eyes before he allowed his lids to flutter closed. He pressed her fingertips to his lips before drifting off into an uneasy sleep.

As restless as he was, he enjoyed more repose than Melyssan did that afternoon and night. Lying nearby on a straw pallet so as not to disturb him, she started awake at every moan and creak coming from the bed above her. Nigh a dozen times she arose, fumbling for her balance in the dark, and groped to touch Jaufre, to assure herself he had not fallen victim to delirium. She could sense the tension in his limbs even as he slept and wondered what agonies he yet suffered.

In the lonely hours before dawn, doubts beset her. Had she done right by her lord? He had lost so much blood. Perhaps her trembling hands had been too clumsy with the knife. Mayhap she had done him more harm than Sir Dreyfan or the boy. Wrapping the blanket tightly around her, she sat on the pallet and hugged her knees to her chest.

What if the leg forever plagued him, forced him to walk with a limp? She could bear the thought of her own affliction, but that her tall and stalwart Jaufre might be so burdened hurt her more than a lifetime of slights and cruel jests.

Her Jaufre. Melyssan's lips curved into a mocking smile that she even dared think such a thing. When only this morning he had said to her...She pressed her head tightly against her knees, but the memory refused to be blocked. He had said, "'Tis time I took a wife."

A wife. Jaufre's long limbs stretched against the mattress as he struggled for a more comfortable position, and Melyssan had a sudden unwelcome image of another lying beside him, some nameless golden-haired beauty, thrusting her sleek, supple body against his broad back.

Melyssan's nails gouged through the thin chemise into her legs as fierce jealousy gnawed at her, the like of which she'd never known before. Hatred surged through her for this noblewoman she'd never met. And Jaufre. She longed to fly at him and pummel his chest with her fists, waking him out of his unthinking slumber wherein he could select a wife as carelessly as he chose a new surcoat.

Hot tears coursed down her cheeks, and she prayed God's forgiveness for indulging in such shameful feelings. What right had she to be jealous of the lawful bride Jaufre would choose? She had offered herself up to him like any common harlot, placed temptation in his path when he would have spared her virtue. It was not fair to upbraid him for what had happened when she had always known what the outcome of her actions must be.

For a brief time, she had been granted a miracle. Jaufre had desired her, made her feel beautiful, made her feel almost...loved. She knew from the beginning it could not last, that she should not expect, should not hope, for anything more.

But she had. She had! Melyssan flung herself back down, stifling her sobs in the pallet. Somewhere in his kisses, in the warm light kindled in his velvet-brown eyes, in the caressing way he called her his Lyssa, hope had been conceived, a hope that she now had to strangle before it drew first breath. She must summon together what remained of her pride and flee from Winterbourne, steel herself to relinquish what had never been hers, bid farewell to the man who had brought love into her life and would just as surely snatch it away again.

Such resolution did little to stem the flood of tears. She wept until she fell asleep from sheer exhaustion. Her eyes felt raw and swollen when she opened them again to find pale sunlight streaming into the room. It took her a few moments to account for the ache in her head and the torpor that weighed down her entire body as if her very spirit had been drained out of her.

Summoning all her will, she forced herself to roll off the pallet. Bracing herself with her hands, she attempted to rise. Her fingers came into contact with something wet and sticky intermingled with the rushes. Snatching back her hand, she stared through sleep-blurred eyes at the red staining her palm.

Fresh blood. Memory jogged her brain like a sharp slap across the face. Jaufre. His wound. Scrambling to her knees, she grabbed at the bed hangings and peered at the mattress.

The great bed was empty.

In the darkness of Winterbourne's dungeon, the boy slammed his head against the damp wall as he tried to shield his eyes from the onslaught of light from the flaming torch. His arms yanked against the fetters that bound both wrists outstretched above his head, pinning him to the rough stonework so that he could not even bend his knees. His hands closed into fists straining toward his face as if he would knuckle away the sleep in a gesture that was so childlike it stirred some strange emotion inside of Jaufre he did not understand.

"Well, 'pears as if the murderin' bastard survived the night, Yer Lordship," Master Galvan said, peering at the prisoner as if he were one of the vermin that skittered through the filthy rushes at his feet.

Jaufre deigned no reply, but it was as if Galvan's addressing him made the boy aware of his presence for the first time. Those odd silver-hued eyes pierced the earl like points of steel, hatred replacing the confusion that had clouded the boy's face. But Jaufre had known hatred before. It was a common enough emotion. Why should this lad's loathing be more disturbing than any other man's?

"His lips are parched," Jaufre said. "Give him a drink. I want him able to speak."

"Aye, my lord." Grudgingly, Master Galvan settled the torch into one of the sconces and fetched a dipperful of water. He held it to the prisoner's lips, pouring the water so roughly down the boy's throat that he choked, half of the liquid slopping over the front of his tunic.

"Don't drown him," Jaufre said.

Leaning heavily on Melyssan's staff, he dragged himself over to a three-legged stool and eased himself down. Shards of pain stabbed the length of his leg as if he'd been shot all over again. Something warm oozed down his thigh, warning him he'd torn the wound open. He ground his teeth together, damning the weakness of his own flesh that would plague him over such a petty matter as this hole in his thigh. As the room spun around, he shook his head to clear it. He had no time for his body to betray him.

Galvan's grumbling finally drew his attention. "Should've been hung at once 'stead of being coddled here at Winterbourne."

When Jaufre shot him an imperious glance, the guard began to whine. "Beg pardon, Yer Lordship. But the scum almost killed you. To say nothing of being a desperate thief as well." Galvan fished inside the opening in his tunic. "Look what we found hiding underneath his shirt ahangin' round his neck."

He handed Jaufre a glittering gold chain from which dangled a medallion. Momentarily the earl forgot the agony of skin stretching away from a tear in his leg as he cupped the finely wrought metal circle in his hands. Numbly, he stared at two swans with their necks intertwined, their sapphire eyes winking at him in the glow of the torchlight. Twisting the chain around his bronzed fingers, he marveled at how the golden links appeared as bright and untarnished as the day he'd first seen the medallion, the day his grandfather had tossed it over Jaufre's head.

And the last time he'd seen it? Jaufre half smiled at the memory of a sixteen-year-old boy experiencing the excitement of his first mistress, a beautiful lady of much sophistication who had taken great delight in tutoring a callow youth in the arts of love.

Amicia. Amicia of Chalon. The most dazzling widow in all of France. Jaufre had been determined to impress her, demonstrate his gratitude for her help on his road to manhood. He could still remember how she'd laughed, although not unkindly, as she'd accepted the medallion.

"Ah, my young friend. You may regret parting with your treasure." A mysterious smile had tugged at the corner of her lips. "But who knows? Someday I may have occasion to send these pretty swans sailing back to you."

The lilting voice of his first lover vanished as harsher accents cut into Jaufre's consciousness, dispelling the memory.

"That's mine," the boy croaked. "Damn you. I didn't steal it. 'Tis my birthright. All the birthright that I have."

As Jaufre looked up from his contemplation of the chain, his eyes locked with the boy's. The shock of having the medallion returned after all these years faded, and Master's Galvan's words registered. The boy. *His* medallion had been hanging around the neck of this strange peasant boy who spoke French so impeccably, and with such a cultured voice. Even the smears of dirt could not disguise those fine-chiseled features: a cleft chin, aquiline nose, and silver eyes that were more suited to a nobleman's face, a nobleman like...

Jaufre's breath caught in his throat. "Unshackle the prisoner. Leave us."

"But—but, my lord," Galvan began to protest.

"Do as you're told."

Galvan jumped as if he'd been cracked with a whip, hastening to obey. If he said anything more, his mutterings were lost in the creak of chains as he freed the captive's hands.

252

The boy sagged to his knees, his hands splayed out to break his fall. By the time Galvan had trudged up the short flight of steps and banged the outer door closed behind him, the boy, though still in the same position, was vigorously rubbing the circulation back into his arms.

"Come here," Jaufre said.

The boy's jawline hardened for a moment, but then he shrugged. His thin legs wobbled as he stood and slowly approached the earl.

Jaufre held out one hand. "Let me see your wrist."

"A trifle belated to express concern over my well-being, is it not, my lord?"

"Damn you! Your wrist!" Jaufre grimaced as he jerked forward on the stool.

The boy sighed and held out his hand.

"Not that one. The right." Jaufre's large hand closed around the pale slender fingers of the boy. Tipping the hand over, he laid the medallion across his leg as he rubbed at the grime on the boy's wrist. He felt the lad's forearm tense, sensed his desire to grab for the chain, but he stood motionless while Jaufre inspected the skin made raw from contact with the manacles.

The mark stood out clearly at the center of the wrist, a small brown crescent shape like the moon when it waned. The boy would have drawn back, but Jaufre's grip tightened as he continued to stare, unable to credit the evidence of his own eyes.

"How came you by this mark?"

" 'Twas there from the time I left my mother's womb." The boy's lips twisted into a grim smile. "I have been scarred from the moment of my birth."

The hand crushed inside of Jaufre's began to tremble, tremble so hard that Jaufre found he could not prevent his own limb from shaking as well.

"What—what is your name, boy?"

"I call myself Roland Fitzmacy."

"Fitzmacy? A strange choice, surely."

"My father never saw fit to leave behind a name for me, so I perforce had to find my own."

The accusing words blasted through the room like the cold draft rushing from above as the dungeon door scraped open. The earl could hear two voices, Master Galvan's and a woman's, arguing. Then the guard fell silent. When Melyssan rounded the curve of the stair, she was alone.

Bracing herself against the wall, she placed one foot carefully after the other upon steps that were more worn here than in any other part of the castle. She cringed as a large rat scuttled past her skirts, and the sticky threads of cobwebs tangled around her fingers. A heavy, dank odor of decay hung in the air, and she half expected to confront the naked bones of some long-forgotten prisoner.

The sight that met her eyes was far stranger. Man and boy confronted each other, frozen immobile as statues except for their interlocked hands, which shook as if under the strain of some mighty contest. Her arrival seemed to break the spell that chained them together.

Jaufre released the lad, shifting himself on the stool so that his cloak covered his leg, but not before Melyssan saw the red patch spreading along his tunic. She all but flung herself the rest of the way down the stairs.

"My lord, what madness is this? When Tristan told me you had come down here, I could scarce believe it. You should be in your bed. You cannot—"

She broke off as the torchlight better revealed Jaufre's face to her. He was pale, with a certain stillness in his eyes she knew instinctively had nothing to do with the pain of his wound.

One eyebrow raised in but a weak imitation of his usual mockery. "Ah, do come in, Lyssa. Come here and meet Roland Fitzmacy, the young gentleman who tried to split your skull with an arrow yesterday."

"Nay, you lie, varlet. Never would I purposefully try to harm a lady." The boy's hands balled into fists as he took a menacing step closer to Jaufre.

Melyssan flung her body in front of the earl as she faced the lad she had come to think of as a bloodthirsty savage. But Jaufre's next words nearly caused her to tumble over onto the earl's lap.

"Rest easy, my lady," he drawled. "Surely there is no need for you to protect me from my own son."

"Your—your son?" She stared at the lad, who propped his hands on his hips, silver-gray eyes defying her disbelief.

"Aye, so it would seem," Jaufre said. "He has the mark, the look of a de Macy about him. And this." The earl dangled the golden medallion before her eyes. "Although I must say, his mother chose a peculiar way of restoring it to me."

"My mother is dead," Roland spat out. "And even if she were alive, she would have restored nothing. She lost interest in me years ago after she had other sons, *legitimate sons* by a man with enough honor to have married her."

"I see." Jaufre lightly touched his injured leg. "Then this tender reunion was all your own idea."

The gesture served to startle Melyssan out of the trance she had fallen into since entering the dungeon. There would be time enough later to sort out this bewildering turn of events. Right now, she had to help Jaufre. But when she tried to examine the new damage he had done to his leg, he pushed her aside, his eyes never wavering from Roland.

"Well, boy?"

Roland's lip jutted out, and he folded his arms across his chest. But his cheeks flushed a bright red, and he lowered his gaze to the ground. "I—I never set out to kill you, if that is what you mean. I heard about you from my mother's chaplain, tales of what a brave and honorable knight my father was. I thought you might care—might have enough sense of responsibility to help me win my spurs."

He scuffed his toe in the straw. "I first tried to see you outside of the Château Le Vis,

256

and you had them set the dogs on me. The next time we met, you were more concerned about that damned stag. I still carry the marks on my back from that encounter. You left me with no other means to draw myself to your attention."

Melyssan heard the sharp intake of Jaufre's breath, but before he could reply to the outrageous speech, Roland astonished her by capturing one of her hands.

"If I frightened you yesterday, my lady, I most humbly crave your pardon. You were never in any danger. I am the finest bowman in all of Normandy."

As he lifted her limp fingers to his lips, a strangled oath issued from Jaufre. The Dark Knight struggled to his feet. Although he braced himself with her staff in one hand, he managed to yank Melyssan to his side with the other.

"I'll have you drawn and quartered yet, you insolent pup. Why the devil didn't you just open your mouth and tell me who you were that day in the field? Your tongue seems to run loose enough upon all other occasions."

A lump bobbed up and down in Roland's thin throat. "I shouldn't have had to tell you. You should have known. You should have recognized me."

"Recognize you? St. Michael, grant me patience! How was I supposed to recognize what I didn't even know existed? Your mother never told me she was with child."

"That makes no difference." Roland's high treble voice rose in volume to match the earl's. "You should have married her after you bedded her. After you wantoned her, 'twas the only honorable course."

"Wantoned? If we are going to speak of lost virginity—" Jaufre halted abruptly, then added more to himself, "But I suppose at that time I cherished the same boyish notions of honor. Must be why Amicia kept quiet about the babe."

In calmer tones, Jaufre addressed Roland again. "Boy, your mother was the daughter of a powerful French baron and a wealthy widow. She had no desire to marry a green youth who was only a younger son. My elder brothers still lived then. I had no prospect of inheritance. 'Twas but a pleasant interlude for both of us, nothing more."

Although Jaufre's fingers on her waist were warm, binding, his casual description of his past *affaire de coeur* struck a chill to Melyssan's heart. A pleasant interlude. Was that how he would think of her when she was gone?

Jaufre's turn of phrase did not set well with his son, either. "Pleasant?" Roland said, his voice ominously quiet. "Aye, pleasant for everyone but me."

"When you are older, when you have had some experience of women yourself, you will understand better how these things happen."

Roland drew himself up to a lofty stance. "I will never stoop to such sordid behavior. For a knight to achieve great deeds, he must remain pure in heart and mind."

Jaufre's face suffused a deep purple. He

258

released Melyssan and turned away, muttering, "Of all the priggish young...I have to get out of here before I kill him with my bare hands." He nearly stumbled as he began climbing the stairs. Halfway up, he bellowed without turning around, "Melyssan!"

The sound of her name set her frozen feet into motion. But before she followed Jaufre out of the dungeon, she took one final look at the boy. She found she could almost forgive him for what he'd done to Jaufre. He looked so small and desolate in that vast empty chamber, blinking up at the torch as if he waited for it to burn out and plunge him into darkness once more.

Jaufre paused on the other side of the heavy oak door to wipe the beads of sweat from his brow. "God's blood, if this isn't the last thing I needed to find out today, that I am sire to some half-lunatic Sir Galahad."

Before Melyssan could say anything, Jaufre's eyes swept her accusingly. "This was most likely Amicia's doing. She probably stuffed the boy's head full of those Camelot legends, that same Arthurian nonsense you are so fond of. If nothing else, this is a lesson to me that a man should be careful where he spills his seed. I want no more bastards."

Self-consciously, Melyssan's hand flew to her stomach. But no, she reassured herself. She had no reason as yet to believe she might be with child. It would not be the first time she had been a few days late.

"What—what will you do with the boy?" she

asked, trying desperately to think of anything but the new fear his words gave her.

"How the devil should I know?" Still using her staff, he hobbled up the inner staircase that led back to the great hall. Walking but a few paces behind him, Melyssan could tell he grew more unsteady with every step he took.

"You must pardon me for appropriating your cane," he said through clenched teeth as they reached the upper archway. "I suppose I will have to have one of my own made."

She tried to draw his arm about her shoulders, fearing soon that her slender weight would not be enough to support him. "You must return to your bed, Jaufre, and let me rebind the wound. 'Tis bleeding again."

"Small wonder, with all the chunks you cut from me. I told you 'twas better to let well enough alone."

Even as he spoke the harsh words and saw her flinch, Jaufre regretted his churlishness, but the burning pain and growing sense of giddiness stifled any attempts he might have made to ask her pardon. He did not want to rip up at Melyssan. If only she could let be. If only she understood the true source of his agitation. But he could not bring himself to add to her distress by telling her of the messenger that had arrived early that morning. He hated to watch the way her face drained of all color, how her sea-green eyes dilated with fear at the mere mention of the king's name.

How would she react if she knew that John had summoned the earl to march with his army against the Welsh, a summons that concluded by declaring that if Jaufre did not come, John would know once and for all that the Dark Knight was his enemy and a traitor to the realm of England?

To send word now of his injury would seem like fabricating a convenient excuse. If he were attainted for treason, what would happen to Melyssan, Tristan, his knights, and all those who followed under his banner? They would be dragged down with him. What of the pledge of his grandfather, which he had not yet tried to fulfill? Jaufre rubbed his thumb over the swans on the signet ring. He had no choice. He had to join the army at Nottingham. But how he would manage it when his head swam with every step he took, he did not know.

"If only you had left those splinters," he said, scarcely aware that he had spoken aloud. "At least I could still walk on the leg without sopping in my own blood."

"Your flesh would have mortified," she cried. "You would have perished."

He shook off her hands, repulsing her attempts to balance him. "I am of little use to anyone the way I am. Better to be dead than crippled."

He pulled away from her, limping across the great hall, not even aware she no longer followed him. The hands that had been reaching out to him dropped back to her sides as she stood there, too stunned to even cry. Such cruel words she could have borne from another man, but not Jaufre! She believed she had won his esteem, and now to hear him voice the same scornful thoughts she had heard since the cradle!

Better dead than crippled. The words pounded through her head as she whirled blindly and fled from the great hall.

Jaufre glanced back in time to obtain a glimpse of the distraught, almost wild look on her face before she disappeared. For the first time, it occurred to him what he had said. But Melyssan could not possibly think he had been speaking of her when he...A fear sharper than any pain from the leg struck through him.

"Melyssan? Lyssa! Come back!" His voice grew hoarse with shouting as he struggled to overtake her. But for once, she was the swifter of the two. Hampered by his awkwardness with the staff and the excruciating agony that now swept over him in waves, he reached the archway at the top of the stairs to find himself alone. Melyssan was nowhere in sight.

"Lyssa!" The cry sounded muffled even to his own ears. He felt hands tugging at him, and Arric's voice drifted to him as if from a great distance.

"Have to stop her...tell her," he mumbled as he felt his legs caving in beneath him. He clutched at the young page, but it was too late. Both he and Arric toppled headlong down the stairs. Something cold and hard struck Jaufre's forehead, and then all was blackness.

Chapter 11

THE LADY ENID thrust her needle into the linen held taut by the tambour and wondered what sort of punishment would be dealt a woman if she shoved her mother out the tower window. Would she be hanged? Drawn and quartered? Burned at the stake? It might be worth the risk. Dame Alice was so reed-thin, Enid wagered that she would fit, even stuffed through the arrow slits of the ladies' bower.

She tucked back a stray tendril that had escaped from the golden braids twisted around her head and glanced across at the older woman, whose jaws worked as swiftly as her fingers winding flax onto the distaff. Time had left some traces of once acclaimed beauty in Dame Alice's angular face, but her voice had never been melodious. Most of Enid's ladies-in-waiting had found some excuse to absent themselves from hearing range of her mother's sharp tongue.

Would that Enid had been as fortunate. The nasal tones droned in her ear with the same monotonous regularity of the katydids in the trees by Kingsbury Castle's moat.

"Never was any woman so plagued by her children. Now here's Beatrice with child and wed to a landless knight as poor as a mendicant friar. Though I suppose I must thank God anyone would have her after the disgraceful way she ran off from Lord Jaufre. And you!"

Dame Alice directed a reproachful glance at Enid. "Your husband not cold in his grave and you marry that—that steward."

"Since my lord Harcourt has been buried a year and more, I trust he is very cold by now," Enid said. "God knows he was frigid enough whilst he lived. And that steward has a name, Mother. 'Tis Robert." She curved her mouth in a slow, sensuous smile, mostly because she derived great pleasure from thinking of her sweet, handsome Rob, but partly because she knew the expression would irritate her mother.

Dame Alice's bloodless lips compressed in a look of disgust. "And then there is Melyssan. Who would ever have thought she would be clever enough to win Lord Jaufre for a husband?" The stiff white wimple that framed Dame Alice's face shook as she tossed her head to express her amazement. "And what a waste. A waste to have such a daughter for a countess, one who can never take her place at court. For even though the earl was taken in enough to marry her, you can be sure once he had his first good look at that foot, he must have shut her away somewhere.

"'Tis the only way I can account for the fact she has never once sent any messengers to me with tidings. Why, with the retainers the earl keeps, she might even have dispatched an entourage to escort me to Winterbourne for a visit. Yet it appears never to have occurred to her."

"Well, I always thought Melyssan a very

clever girl," Enid murmured. When her mother's lips quivered with anger, she added hastily, "Had Whitney naught to say of my sister when he returned home?"

"Him! He has been so closemouthed one might mistake him for a lackwit. And Father Andrew is just as bad. When I made a few pleasant inquiries after my own daughter, he behaved as if I sought to pry into the secrets of the confessional. There is something gravely amiss at Winterbourne, you mind my words." The dame's hawklike eyes glinted with satisfaction. "And whatever the trouble is, you may be sure Melyssan is at the root of it. From the moment of that girl's birth, she has brought nothing but misery. I always said..."

Enid closed her eyes, wishing she could as easily stop up her ears as her mother launched off into another diatribe. The castle was so overrun with guests come to attend the tournament to be held at Kingsbury Plain that this was the first moment Enid had been able to sit down in two days. All the same, she hailed with relief the interruption of the red-haired lady who burst unceremoniously into the chamber.

"Beg pardon, Lady Enid." Dena dropped a quick curtsy and then bent over and whispered in Enid's ear, "There is a passing strange woman in the garden asking for you. A lame beggar woman."

"Why, then tell Cook to give the poor creature some food," Enid replied in low tones.

"Nay, my lady. The woman is amazingly persistent and has such an air about her that…Well, she bade me say that Lyssa begs to be remembered to you."

Lyssa! Enid jabbed the needle into her finger, spattering a few droplets of blood onto the white linen.

"You know who I believe she is?" Dena continued excitedly. "I think 'tis your sis—"

Enid clapped her hand over the girl's mouth while Dame Alice glared at her with suspicion.

"What is that rude wench saying to make you look as if a spirit had crept out of the walls? Pretty behavior you teach your maids, upon my word! Rushing about so boisterously, whispering secrets and suchlike." She stretched out one long, bony arm and poked Dena in the ribs. "If you have aught to say, girl, then out with it."

As Dena pouted and rubbed her side, Enid leapt to her feet, her tambour flying unheeded to the floor. "Ah—'tis only a petty domestic matter, Mother, nothing you should fret yourself about."

Dame Alice started to protest, but for once Enid was able to cut her short. "Nay, pray remain seated, my lady. I will return anon." Lifting the train of her gown, she fled the room with Dena hard after her.

Silencing Dena's stream of breathless questions, Enid raced down the curving stone stair that led to the castle courtyard. In the herb garden near the great stone baking kilns, she caught sight of a small figure whose features were muffled in the folds of a ragged cloak. Drawn by the aroma of fresh wheat bread emanating from the large ovens, many beggars found their way to the castle from the nearby town of Kingsbury Plain. And ever since Lord Harcourt had died, none had been turned aside without something to warm their bellies.

But as to Dena's foolish assertion that this particular pauper could be Enid's youngest sister...Enid halted a few feet away as the figure turned and pulled back her hood. A pale face peered out at her, dark circles rimming sea-shaded eyes. Dear God, 'twas Lyssa.

Melyssan attempted a feeble smile. "Forgive me, Enid," she whispered. "I knew nowhere else to go." Then she collapsed into Enid's outstretched arms.

Swallowed up in the folds of her tall sister's robe, Melyssan leaned against the pillows of Enid's bed. To please Enid, she picked at the contents of the wooden bowl in her lap. The blancmange of chicken and rice boiled in almond milk did little to tempt her appetite. All she desired was to sleep, to sleep and forget....

Enid bustled about the chamber, taking the ointment and towels from the red-haired maid and dismissing the girl. She settled on the edge of the bed near Melyssan's feet.

"I should have cautioned Dena to keep your arrival a secret." Enid frowned. "If our stream ran as fast as that girl's tongue, we would be able to grind enough wheat to feed all of England. Perhaps I shall speak to her as soon as I have attended to your poor feet."

Gently Enid raised the foot that bore most of Melyssan's weight. It was swollen so badly she had to cut away the soft leather pattern whose sole had worn through many miles ago. Both feet were torn and bleeding, and Melyssan winced as her sister began to dab at them with a damp cloth.

"Sweet Jesu, child! How long have you been on the road?"

"I don't know. A fortnight, perhaps as long as a month," Melyssan murmured. "I rode with a merchant and his wife as far as Canterbury."

"At least they must have fed you well, little sister. You were always so thin, but you have rounded out since I saw you last, become quite the woman."

Enid's eyes seemed to linger on Melyssan's midsection, causing her to cross her arms defensively over her stomach. She was fully conscious herself of the changes in her body, the slight swell of her breasts and abdomen. But she could admit her secret dread to no one as yet, not even Enid.

Hastily, she changed the subject and began to speak of her journey. It was so much easier to speak of that than of Jaufre, whose face she tried to block from her mind a hundred times each day. She described how she had hidden in the merchant's wagon and had not been discovered until the caravan was many miles from Winterbourne. The merchant's wife had been so kind, believing Melyssan's tale of wanting to make a pilgrimage to the shrine of St. Thomas à Becket in hopes of attaining a miracle cure for her foot. The good woman even insisted that her husband go miles out of his way to take her to Canterbury.

"When I slipped away from her at the cathedral," Melyssan said, "I left her the gold-braided chain you gave me the Christmas before you left home. I am sorry, Enid. Besides a few coins in my purse, 'twas all I had of value to repay her for her kindness."

"Never mind, sweeting. I have a dozen gold chains to give you." Enid tucked the fur coverlet more snugly around Melyssan's legs. "And then you walked all the way here from Canterbury!"

" 'Twas not so bad," Melyssan whispered. "I was not alone always. I traveled with some strolling tumblers. People were very kind—most of them."

She refrained from troubling Enid with an account of all she had suffered, the bone-shaking weariness, the strange waves of nausea she experienced upon waking every morning, to be followed later by some of the sharpest hunger pangs she had ever known. The feelings of loneliness and desolation. Once, when she had passed by a pond, she had stopped for long moments staring at the dark water. Jaufre's words had echoed in her mind. *Better dead than crippled.* She could not swim. It would have been so easy to consign herself to the peaceful depths of the dark water. Then she had crossed herself and begged God's forgiveness for such wicked thoughts. Doubly wicked, if her growing fears proved true—that more than her own life might be at stake.

There had been those few moments of pure terror as well, a stray dog tearing her cloak, the time she had begged for food at an inn and been forced to watch while the king's soldiers tortured a Jew. They had knocked out his teeth one by one until he revealed where he had hidden his purse.

'Twas rumored the king would do anything these days to acquire more wealth. 'Twas rumored the king was going mad.

Melyssan shivered.

"Are you cold, sweetheart?" Enid asked. "I will have more logs put on the fire."

"You are very good," Melyssan said, putting aside the half-eaten bowl of food.

"Dear Lyssa! Who could be otherwise to you?" Enid flashed her sister a brief smile. "But you make my blood run cold, sweetheart, thinking of all that might have happened to you, wandering about the countryside this way, sleeping out in the open."

"I found shelter most nights." Melyssan managed a weak chuckle. "You've no idea how warm a few pigs braced up against you can feel."

"Faith, I'd rather have a husband to warm my backside."

A husband. Melyssan dropped her eyes to the coverlet and felt the color flooding into her cheeks. Enid moved closer and gently chafed one of Melyssan's cold hands between hers.

"Lyssa, it pains me to distress you so. But—but the time has come for you to tell me something. 'Tis obvious you have run off from your husband." Enid's pretty face hardened. "It does not surprise me. I have worried about you ever since I first heard that you wed the earl."

She drew in a deep breath before continuing. "I want to help you, truly I do. But 'twill not be easy for you to escape your husband, no matter how cruelly the knave treats you. The law will be against you."

"Do not speak of Jaufre that way!" Melyssan raised her chin, defying her sister's scorn, yet dreading it. "He is not my husband, Enid. But I have lain with him, shamelessly seduced him. What think you of that?" She gave a half-hysterical laugh. "And I would do it again, because...because I love him. I love him so much I think I am like to die of it." Her voice trailed away as hot tears trickled down her cheeks, the tears she had refused to shed ever since the day she had fled from Jaufre.

Enid's shocked expression faded as she drew Melyssan's head against her shoulder, stroking her hair. "There, there, my little Lyssa. Hush, babe. Don't cry. 'Tis all right. Enid is here now. Enid will take care of you."

Melyssan clung tightly to her sister, attempting to draw comfort from the words she had heard so many times in her childhood. If only Enid could make all better, as she had done so many times in the past, but what was hurting her now was well beyond her sister's capacity to heal.

"Oh, Enid," she sobbed. "He turned against me, just as Father Andrew warned me he would. In the end, he pitied me the same as all the others. I thought he was different. I thought perhaps he—he cared a little bit. B-but when he said...I knew he didn't...that he never would. But I c-couldn't stop loving him, and I—c-couldn't bear to stay and see the ch-change in him, especially when..."

"When you worry that you might be carrying his child?" Enid asked softly.

Melyssan might have known Enid with her uncanny perception would guess the truth. But it made her situation no easier to hear her fear voiced aloud. Her body shook with fresh spasms of grief.

Enid rocked her to and fro. "Oh, hush, sweetheart. Then, when you are calm, you can tell me everything."

But even after Melyssan's tears had abated somewhat, the tale of her days at Winterbourne was so disjointed, Enid was still greatly confused. She had seen Jaufre de Macy at court often while Lord Harcourt yet lived, had noted the cold, dark eyes, the handsomeness of the man carved from granite. She knew well the earl's reputation as a harsh, ruthless man with the heart of a rock.

Yet Lyssa's wistful remembrances conjured up images that did not fit with what Enid knew of the earl. Who would ever have believed

Lord Jaufre would allow such an outrageous imposture to go unpunished, or that he would risk his life to protect a woman from rape? That he would share his bed with Lyssa and treat her with all the dignity he would have accorded his countess? Or more unheard-of still, that he would allow anyone to persuade him to show mercy to one he deemed a criminal?

As Enid continued to pat Melyssan's quivering shoulders, she wondered if her young sister realized how much out of character Lord Jaufre's behavior was. She wondered if Lyssa understood exactly what she had run away from.

"Now tell me again," she demanded. "What were his exact words?"

"He told me 'twas time for him to take a wife."

"And that—that was all?"

" 'Twas enough." Slowly Melyssan disengaged herself and sat up, mopping the wetness from her cheeks. "I knew what he meant. And then after he was shot, he said...well, I knew then any hopes I cherished were folly and 'twas time I should be gone."

She stole a shy glance at Enid. Her sister was the most generous of women, but surely even she must condemn what could only be construed as wanton behavior. But although Enid's brow puckered, she appeared more abstracted than angry, as if she wrestled with some insoluble problem.

"'Tis the strangest tale I ever heard, Lyssa." She sighed. "And I still do not quite understand why you went to Winterbourne in the first place and began this mad pretense."

"I thought you knew. 'Twas to escape King John. He desired me and made threats if I did not comply. All I could think of was..."

Melyssan got no further, for Enid caught her roughly by the shoulders. Her sister's face blanched as white as the bed linens. "What! You were in peril from the king?"

"Yes, and I should warn you, Enid. I might still be. Since the old comte died, Jaufre does not think—"

"Sweet God in heaven." Enid bit her lip, which had suddenly begun to tremble. The usually serene blue eyes dilated with fear. "Of all the places in England for you to come seeking refuge. Lyssa, I've got to hide you. Don't you know—"

Her words were lost in a thunderous pounding at the door. Enid scrambled off the bed, but before she took another step the door had crashed open, kicked in by a stalwart soldier.

"What means this outrage?" Enid cried. But the soldier was already stepping aside for another to enter.

Melyssan's heart thudded painfully. She dug her nails into the pillow as she watched the small man enter into the room. Wide-set eyes glittered above a black, Mephistophelian beard. The dark gaze swept past Enid's frozen form to pin Melyssan on the bed.

"Ah, so what the red-haired wench said 'tis true," purred John Plantegenet. "What, my lady Countess? Will you make no obeisance to your king?"

The phantom figure of her nightmares

glided closer, becoming more solid, more terrifyingly real, with every step he took. Yet even to save her own life, Melyssan could not move a single muscle.

Enid sank into a deep curtsy. "Pray, excuse my sister, Your Highness. She—she is not well. She has had a most fatiguing journey."

John stroked the sable fur trimming the neckline of his gold-cloth surcoat. "So we would imagine—traveling with such stealth and secrecy." His mesmerizing snakelike eyes snapped to Enid. "And you, my lady, have been most remiss in your duties as hostess by not informing us of the countess's arrival."

"I—I thought it would be of little import to Your Majesty. You gave me to understand your chief reason for visiting Kingsbury is to attend the tournament."

"This woman's movements must always be important to us." Melyssan shrank back as he leveled one jewel-bedecked finger in her direction as though it were a lethal weapon. "Is not she wife to Jaufre de Macy, one of the greatest traitors this realm has ever known?"

Jaufre...traitor. The coupling of that beloved name with one of the most foul words in the language sent a surge of strength through Melyssan's limbs. Quickly she eased herself off the bed, taking care that Enid's robe draped modestly around her. She was doubly glad the garment was overlarge when the king subjected her to a lascivious appraisal, wetting his lips, attempting to bore holes in the robe with his eyes.

Despite the nausea that churned inside her stomach, Melyssan made a stiff curtsy and said in level tones, "Your Majesty is much mistaken. The earl of Winterbourne is ever loyal to England."

"Aye, but what of his king?" John growled. "So you do still possess a tongue, my lady. 'Tis well, for it will take many soft and fair words to convince us of—" His gaze flicked hungrily up and down the length of her body. "Of your devotion to the crown, and why your husband should be spared the fate of all traitors."

The king waved a languid hand in Enid's direction. "You may retire now, my lady. We have much to discuss with my lady Melyssan in private."

Although she was very pale, Enid stepped between Melyssan and the king. "Nay, Your Grace. 'Tis not proper that I should leave my sister unattended in your presence."

"Proper?" The king's lip curled upward into a snarl. "You presume to lecture us on what is proper? Get you hence, woman. We deem it proper you should look after your own husband." His voice softened as his lips tightened into a cruel smile. He fingered the jewel-encrusted dagger sheath affixed to his belt. "Who knows what fate holds in store? Men seem to be so much more shorter-lived than women."

Enid swallowed hard and opened her mouth to speak again, but Melyssan placed a gentle hand upon her shoulder. Although her fingers shook, she maintained the regal posture of a princess as she said, "Do as the king commands,

Enid. I—I am more than ready to stay here and defend my husband against any calumny."

Melyssan's terror was great as the king's soldier accompanied her reluctant sister from the bedchamber, leaving her alone with the king. But unlike the terror that had nigh suffocated her when His Majesty had threatened first her virtue and then her brother, this time her fear sent the blood racing through her veins in a savage way she had never experienced before. For now her fear was for Jaufre. She vowed to draw the king's vengeance down upon her own head rather than see him make one move to harm the man she loved.

She met John's leering eyes boldly, standing her ground without flinching as he came nearer. "How comes Your Majesty to say such vile things about my husband when you must know they are lies?"

"We know nothing of the kind," John said. Chills swept over her as his cold, silky fingers brushed aside the robe so that he could caress the base of her neck. "What we do know is that he would not help us in our war against the Welsh a fortnight ago. He came to Nottingham carried on a litter. Claimed he was too ill to fight."

"'Tis true," she said. "He was wounded with an arrow."

The king's grip tightened. "The infamous wound. Aye, I saw it. I made him undo the bandages. I swear 'twas self-inflicted by the coward so that he could defy his king. He is not the man his grandfather was."

"Jaufre is no coward!" she cried, seizing hold of John's wrist. The way his fingers encircled her throat made it hard for her to breathe.

"They're all cowards. All my barons." John's dark eyes glazed over. "I had to forgo my expedition into Wales. Can't trust any of them. All after my crown. Would have waited until the heat of battle, then thrust a knife in my back."

The king's voice rose with every word, and his fingers gouged harder and harder into her throat. Melyssan fought for air. Dear God, he *was* mad.

But the next instant John blinked and refocused on Melyssan. His hand relaxed and resumed those featherlike caresses, which gave Melyssan the sensation of brushing against cobwebs. She rubbed her throat and took a deep, painful breath to steady herself.

"What were we speaking of?" he murmured. "Ah, now I recollect. We were deciding what proof you would offer to convince us of your husband's loyalty, what reasons to spare Lord Jaufre his head."

He pushed the gown down past her shoulders. "'Tis an ugly thing for a man to be hanged for treason, my dear. The throat knots with pain as the victim writhes in the dance of death. But he is cut down before the thick hemp can quite squeeze the life out of him. Then come the horses pulling on the ropes tied to his legs and arms. Sometimes it takes as long as half an hour before the limbs are ripped off. A strong man like Lord Jaufre might still be alive. Then the executioner, his hands already slick with blood, would have to take a double-edged sword and—"

"Stop it!" Melyssan's hands clenched into fists as she fought the urge to strike out at those black, mocking eyes, rake her nails across the thin, sneering lips. "I—I will offer you whatever proof you desire," she cried, knowing she was lost. She had only one weapon to use in Jaufre's defense.

"We recognized at the first you were a young woman of much good sense." The king chuckled and shoved her back toward the bed.

"Wait." She placed both hands against his chest, the heavy chains and emerald necklets he wore cutting into her palms. "I—I would have your oath that you will not harm my lord if I—if I..."

The king smiled. "Certainly, my dear. We have no sword, but trust this will do as well." He fingered the holy relics he wore around his neck. "I, John, King of England, do solemnly swear I will not command the death of the earl of Winterbourne. By the blood of Christ."

Then, with a throaty growl, he fell upon her, dragging her beneath him onto the bed. Melyssan thought she would suffocate from the cloying smell of his perfumed garments and the shame of what she was about to do. How could she lie here and permit this man to touch her, know her intimately as only Jaufre had?

She could not even scream or fight back as

she had done against *Le Gros*, but instead must remain quiet, submissive, as the king bared one breast and began pinching the nipple as if to test her.

"I see you have ripened well under Lord Jaufre's touch," he whispered roughly against her ear. "My sweet Melyssan. I have thought much about you since I sent you to Winterbourne, bided my time, knowing this day would come."

His lips fastened greedily upon hers, sucking at her mouth until she thought she would be ill. Clenching her eyes tightly closed, she prayed that the king would soon be done.

He nipped sharply along her neck as he began easing the robe up her thigh, his stocky body quivering with laughter. "The sweetest moment of all will come when I tell your husband what you did to save him. There is more than one way of humbling an overproud subject."

Tears pricked the back of Melyssan's eyelids. That was a satisfaction the king would never have. Jaufre would not care.

She steeled herself for the final humiliation as John's hands began moving over her legs. "Let me see what treasures you keep concealed beneath this coarse gown, lady," he gloated. But the fingers that would have yanked away the robe suddenly stilled. With a muffled shriek, he flung himself away from her.

"What—what deviltry is this?"

Bewildered, Melyssan slowly sat up and discovered that his shaking hand gestured toward her bent foot. She regarded her own limbs with a strange detachment, as if seeing them through John's eyes. Scratched and swollen purple from her long days on the road, she had to admit even her good foot appeared as grotesque as the other one.

John backed away from the bed, his sleeve pressed to his lips. Malevolent eyes glared at her over the length of a satin-covered arm. "I thought you but lame. Not—not deformed."

He clutched at his holy relics and shrieked, "De Macy has tricked me. Tricked me! He shall pay for this."

As he whirled to leave, panic surged through Melyssan. She lunged after the king, grabbing hold of his arm. "Nay, Your Grace. I beg you. Remember your promise."

"Let go of me, you bitch." With a vicious backhand, the king sent her sprawling to the floor. "The mark of the devil is upon you."

The salt taste of blood filled Melyssan's mouth, but she struggled to a sitting position. "Please," she said desperately. " 'Twas not Jaufre's trickery, but mine. He is not my husband. You cannot blame him."

John paused by the door, his breath coming in short, rapid gasps, the eyes beginning to cloud.

"I lied to you," she sobbed. "Pretended to be his wife because I couldn't bear for you to touch me. 'Tis I that should be punished."

"Oh, aye, madam, and so you will be. I promise you that." He yanked the door open and screamed, "Guard! Guard! Arrest this woman at once."

Chapter 12

THE POUNDING HOOVES of the sleek black stallion tore up clods of dirt as it thundered along the road toward Wydevale Manor. The horse's dark-bearded rider leaned forward in the saddle, black cape billowing behind him, his reddened eyes glowing like embers from lack of sleep.

Peasants sowing the fields with winter corn paused in their task long enough to cross themselves. One stout lad ripped across the fields screaming for Father Andrew and all the saints to come to the rescue: the devil himself was raging amongst them.

Jaufre de Macy dug his knees into his exhausted mount and rode on, scarcely aware of the turmoil his presence created. Thirty-two days since Melyssan had disappeared. Thirty-two times he'd watched the sun set and plunge him into another night of hell, agonizing over what perils she might be facing, torturing himself over what dire fate had befallen her.

"A woman cannot be standing in the courtyard one moment and just vanish the next as if she were snatched by spirits," he had bellowed at his knights and servants the evening after he'd recovered consciousness and discovered Melyssan missing from Winterbourne.

How was it possible that not one of the dolts had seen her go? How could they just let her slip away? Nay, mocked a harsh voice inside him. How could *you* just let her slip away?

He rubbed at the grit being flung into his eyes and once more was haunted by an image of Melyssan as he'd last seen her, the pain shattering across her delicate features, swirling in the depth of her eyes as she'd turned and fled. So much he needed to tell her. Sweet Christ! Were the last words she was ever to hear from him going to be...

No! Over the next crest was Wydevale Manor. She would be there, safely hidden away in her father's home, no matter what lies Sir William had sent in reply to his urgent inquiries. He'd already spent the morning storming through the sacred cloisters at St. Clare, sending the frightened sisters scurrying before him like a nest of squealing mice until the outraged Mother Abbess had convinced him Melyssan was not amongst them.

Jaufre grimaced, his head still throbbing from the encounter. Why did the old harridan have to whack him with that crucifix in the exact same spot where he'd hit his head before? He reined in his horse and, when the cloud of dust settled, saw the small manor house nestled in the valley below.

He took a gulp from his wine sack to wet his parched throat, allowing his sweating horse to get its second wind, waiting for his entourage to catch up with him. He'd outstripped his knights by some distance, except for Tristan and Roland, who were now the first to reach his side.

The boy rode well, Jaufre admitted grudgingly. Something might be made of him yet if he could resist the urge to fling the insolent whelp back into the dungeons.

Roland took a swig from his leather pouch, wiped his lips, and said, "Well, what now, my lord? Do we terrorize some more nuns?"

Jaufre gave him a dark look that would have quelled anyone else but otherwise ignored the boy as he turned to Tristan. The knight's dirt-streaked face was lined with weariness.

"That's Wydevale." Jaufre gestured toward the distant manor and extended his wine flagon to Tristan.

Tristan nodded grimly. "I trust you mean to exercise more diplomacy down there than you did at the convent."

"A fool's errand," Roland muttered.

Jaufre clenched his jaw. "If her father surrenders Melyssan to me, there will be no trouble. I know she has to be there." When he saw Tristan's skeptical look, he added vehemently, "I should have checked here myself long ago, instead of allowing you to persuade me to waste time placating the king at Nottingham."

"My lord, we had large troops of men out scouring the countryside for your lady. 'Twould have benefited none of us, least of all Melyssan, if you had been arrested for treason."

"I came perilously near it, anyway."

"I admit you and John did not part on the best of terms, but at least he did allow you to depart."

"A paltry fellow, your English king." Roland sniffed. "Now Philip of France—"

"Roland, do you ever know when to hold your tongue?" Tristan snapped.

Jaufre answered for him. "No, he doesn't. Gets that from his mother. A charming woman, Amicia, but Lord, she could talk a man to death."

Roland's face flushed, and he sat up straight in the saddle. "A pity you never succumbed. For my part I wish the lady Melyssan Godspeed in escaping from you. And I warn you now, if she is at Wydevale, I won't let you harass her. She saved my life, and I consider myself her champion."

Jaufre snorted. "The lady would do better defending herself. She's worth ten of you in a fight."

"Damn you. I am the finest bowman in Normandy, and if I chose, I could—"

"Don't threaten me, boy," Jaufre said, the fine threads of his temper beginning to snap. "I never want to see you with a bow in your hands again. If you want to kill me, learn to use a sword and fight me with honor, not like some cowardly peasant."

"I will. Don't you think I won't!"

Tristan edged his horse in between them. "Enough, both of you! I have had about all I can tolerate of—" He broke off, staring past Jaufre into the valley beyond.

"What is it?" Jaufre whirled his mount around eagerly, half hoping for the sight of a slender maiden, her nutmeg hair curling to her waist, the sunlight glowing on her ivory skin. But all he saw was a long line of people wending their way from the manor house to the meadow. It was as if everyone on the estate had turned out for this procession.

"Sweet holy Mother," Roland said, blessing himself. "They are preparing to bury someone in the ditch."

Jaufre's eyes locked with Tristan's. The moisture that welled in his friend's eyes revealed the knight's apprehension as clearly as the whispered prayer that reached Jaufre's ears.

"Peace, gentle lady."

"No!" The denial tore from Jaufre's throat as he spurred his courser and charged down the hill. The horse cleared the small stone fence and galloped across the newly plowed field. Astonished, frightened faces flashed before Jaufre's eyes as he flung himself out of the saddle. The leg that still pained from the arrow wound nearly buckled from beneath him, but he caught his balance and leapt at the dumb-struck servants bearing the corpse. They dropped the body and scattered, one of them shrieking, "Father! 'Tis the devil, just as young Tom tried to warn us."

A woman screamed, "Saints preserve us! He's come for poor Sir Swithbert's soul."

Sir Swithbert! Jaufre stared down at the huge bulk draped in the winding sheet. Far too large to be...A tremor of relief shot through the earl's body, and his hands shook. He raked them back through his sweat-soaked hair.

Dear God. What was the matter with him? He was behaving like a madman.

Damn it. He needed Melyssan, needed her right now. He would shake her until her teeth chattered for giving him such a fright, and then crush her in his arms, demanding her forgiveness, and never let her go until she vowed to be his wife. And then, by St. George, he would never lose her again even if he had to chain her to his side.

Sir William's mild features gradually came into focus. The elderly knight bowed deeply as he greeted Jaufre in flustered tones. "M-my lord. What an unexpected honor! How did you hear of the death of my uncle?"

But Sir William was thrust aside by his son. Whitney's face blanched with rage as he snatched up a pitchfork from one of the hay mows and brandished it at Jaufre.

"My family has borne enough of your insults, de Macy. Get out of here. Now!"

"Aye, so I will, boy. When I have your sister with me." Oblivious to the three sharp prongs leveled at his chest, Jaufre stepped closer. "Where have you hidden her?"

"Clear off, I said," Whitney cried shrilly as he retreated a step, ignoring his father's command that he drop the pitchfork. "Melyssan is not here."

"Then I shall go look for her back at the house," Jaufre said. He turned on his heel and limped toward the manor house as Tristan and the rest of his entourage came riding into the pasture.

"Jaufre, beware!"

Tristan's cry rang out just as Jaufre's own instincts warned him to whirl in time to meet Whitney's stumbling charge. He dodged but was saved more by Whitney himself as the young man deflected his aim at the last second. The pitchfork clattered to the ground as Jaufre dived for Whitney, pinning him beneath his weight.

"Curse you to hell," Whitney said as his thin arms flailed uselessly against the earl's powerful grip. "Haven't you done enough to her? 'Tis your doing that the king has taken her."

"What!" In his shock, Jaufre loosened his hold, but Whitney made no attempt to escape. "What the devil are you talking about?"

Whitney's mouth compressed into a stubborn line as he glared up at Jaufre with those green eyes that reminded him all too painfully of Melyssan, that half-sullen, half-frightened look that reminded him all too damn much of Godric.

"Tell me, you fool, or I swear I'll..." Jaufre lifted one knee and ground it into Whitney's stomach while his hand cracked repeatedly against the young man's face.

"M-my lord!" Sir William said. "I most strongly protest this—"

"Stop it, Jaufre," he heard Tristan hiss in his ear. The next instant, Tristan and one of Sir William's men were dragging him off Whitney while Roland scornfully flung the pitchfork out of reach.

"Let me go. I'll kill him if he doesn't tell me...."

"For God's sake," Tristan said as he hung on to Jaufre, "my lord, it's her brother."

Jaufre wrenched himself free as Whitney staggered to his feet. "Aye, her *brother*." Jaufre spat out the word with loathing. "Well, it seems her brother has betrayed Melyssan to the king."

"Not my betrayal. Yours," Whitney said through swollen lips.

At that moment, Father Andrew pushed his way to Whitney's side, dabbing at his bleeding mouth with a square of linen. Jaufre moved toward Whitney, ignoring the cautioning hand Tristan placed on his arm. "I want some answers, boy. And I want them now. What has the king done with Melyssan?"

Father Andrew shot him a glance full of reproach, the priest's aged blue eyes probing him in such a way as made him squirm inwardly with discomfort. "My lord, there is naught you can do for the lady now but pray."

"Pray! You'd best begin to pray if you don't tell me where she is, and quick."

"She is a prisoner at Kingsbury Castle," Father Andrew replied with calm dignity. "Where she awaits punishment for your sins."

"My sister Enid sent us a messenger with the news. The king knows you never married her." Whitney's voice was choked with bitterness. "Lyssa is charged with being a whore, an adulteress."

Jaufre's hands slowly unclenched as he remembered the terror that had clouded Melyssan's face every time she spoke of the king.

She had first come to Winterbourne seeking shelter from a tyrant. Instead of protecting the lady, he had reviled her for it, forced her to remain his prisoner, robbed her of her innocence, and in the end driven her back to the cruelty she had tried to escape. Was the king even now venting some of the wrath he felt for Jaufre upon that gentle and vulnerable creature?

The earl shuddered. He knew full well how vicious John could be. By God, Lyssa had already suffered too much for what was none of her doing. Well, no more. No more!

His gaze raked the assembled company of men, all of whom had fallen silent. Then Roland's voice piped up. "Well, are we all going to stand here and do nothing to save her? God's teeth!"

"Nay, boy, we'll save her," Jaufre replied, already fingering the hilt of his sword.

Sir William spread his hands wide. "My lord, what is to be done? One dares not go against the king."

"It may not be that hopeless," Tristan said. "But we must proceed with caution, that's certain. Jaufre, I believe the first thing you should do is ride to Kingsbury and request an audience...."

But he was speaking to a cloud of dust. Jaufre had already leapt onto his horse and was racing out of the yard.

Melyssan swayed as the ox cart rumbled through the rocky streets of Kingsbury Plain, indifferent to the ruts that slammed her body against the wooden sides. She was equally insensible of the ropes abrading her wrists and the biting wind that knifed through her thin sackcloth gown. 'Twas as if it were someone else's pain and not her own, as if her soul had already begun its flight to peace during the long week of her imprisonment and only awaited final release.

She had heard the whispers of her gaolers. "Never survive it," they had said. "Too frail. Too weak." She prayed they were right. She was not afraid of death. She would have welcomed it, if only she might have seen Jaufre's face one last time...if only it were not for the child she sensed sheltered so deeply within her womb. But, she tried to tell herself, the babe would be better off never to draw breath in this world. It might be born crippled as she had been, experience all the bitterness she had seen reflected in young Roland's face, the pain of belonging nowhere. Jaufre de Macy wanted no more bastards....

The timber-frame shops and stone-clad houses blurred before her eyes. Ahead loomed the spire of the church and the cloisters of the priory beyond. She became conscious that the market square was thronged with a sea of faces. Some poor man writhed and vomited in the stocks while a foul-smelling meat was burned under his nose.

"Let that teach you to sell bad pork, master butcher." A voice gleefully called out, "Hey, here comes more promising sport."

A chorus of shouts assailed Melyssan's ears as the ox cart jolted to a halt. "Cast-off whore!" "One-legged bitch." It took a moment for her numbed mind to realize the invectives were directed at her. She winced as a rotten apple smacked against her cheek but steadfastly kept her eyes ahead of her, refusing to look at her tormentors.

"Shameless bitch. We'll see how proud ye be when the canon finishes wit' ye. Ye'll not look so saintly then," taunted the voices.

"Aw, hold your tongues, you scum," a deep bass boomed out. "Don't ye know she be our good lady Enid's sister?" The rumblings against Melyssan grew quieter except for one plump dame who squeezed her way up to the cart.

"Ha, my beauty. Where is your lover now? They never tarry long when the sport is all over and done with, do they?"

Melyssan stared down into the toothless face grinning at her.

"He's probably off tossing another wench on his pikestaff while ye take the drubbing."

The hag's jeering remark seared through Melyssan's protective haze like a torturer's fire fork, branding her with visions of Jaufre even now embracing some other beauty in the bed they once had shared. Her lips moved, wanting to deny the woman's mocking words, but no sound came. How often had she foolishly hoped he would come searching for her, riding to her rescue? But he had not even cared enough to discover whether she was safe or no.

Doubtless he was relieved that she was out of his life with so little cost to himself.

Rough hands seized her, hauled her from the cart while the king's soldiers held back the mob. By the steps, Melyssan thrust aside the painful images of Jaufre as she was confronted by other faces that were familiar to her. Her mother glared at her, lips pursed in self-righteous reproach. To her left, Enid was being restrained by her young husband.

"Lyssa," her sister sobbed.

Melyssan raised her chin and managed to smile. "Courage, Enid," she whispered. "Don't weep."

Enid stilled in her husband's arms, her swollen blue eyes opening wide as she stared at her sister. Aye, it was strange, Melyssan reflected. For the first time in their lives, 'twas she who must comfort and impart strength to her older sister. The thought kept her legs steady beneath her as the two guards dragged her up the stone steps of the church's central tower, where the canon awaited her. Garbed in his black cassock, the tall thin priest looked down his protuberant nose at her, sniffing the air as if he found her very existence offensive.

Behind her she heard the clatter of horses' hooves. She whirled around to find people scrambling away from a jewel-caparisoned charger. Flanked by a party of his courtiers, the king leered at her as he rode to the foot of the steps.

Pulling his fur-lined cloak more snugly around his shoulders, he said, "Good morrow, mistress. A chilly day for you to make your penance, but I am sure the blood flowing down your back will keep you warm enough."

The canon cleared his throat. "Then Your Majesty is aware these proceedings cannot take place within the confines of the church." He stroked the side of his nose with one fingertip. "Alas, the interdict."

"No matter," said the king. "You know this woman is guilty of the sin of fornication. I want her humiliation to be as public as possible."

"And let's be quick about it," someone in the mob shouted. "I'll wager the reverend father be in mortal hurry to get back abed with a whore of his own."

"Aye," agreed another voice. "With that nose of his, he can smell a bitch in heat clear in the next shire."

The king joined in the crowd's roar of laughter, while the indignant canon's nostrils flared. When John's fit of mirth had ended, the priest asked, with a touch of asperity in his voice, "And does His Majesty desire the woman to make her parade of penance through the town before or after the whipping?"

At this question, Melyssan's gaze flicked involuntarily to the two stout-armed guards and the thick-corded flails that dangled from their hands. She shuddered, closing her eyes.

"Oh, before," she heard the king say. "She's

not likely to be in much condition to do it after."

Melyssan murmured her own silent prayers as the canon's bored voice began to drone out her penance, adjuring her to give up the evil life she had led from this day hence. She had to fight down the urge to laugh hysterically as a thought struck her. If only she had shown the king her foot the first time he came to Wydevale, he would have left her in peace to become a nun. There would have been no lies, no sins, no Jaufre....

Her eyes fluttered open, and she stared straight at the canon. "I repent of nothing," she said quietly.

She watched the nostrils flare again, one long finger gesturing to the guards to proceed. One of them cut her bonds while the other ripped the rough sackcloth gown, baring her to the waist. She shivered as the cold autumn air raked her exposed skin and the crowd whistled and shouted, urging her to turn around.

Instinctively she sought to cover her breasts, but the canon struck down her arms and forced a lighted taper into her hands. Behind her, she heard a scuffling in the mob as if a fight had broken out, but she tried to blot everything from her mind, recover the same sense of detachment she had known earlier. This wasn't happening to her. She was floating far away, watching some other poor woman endure this shame.

The shrill cry of a horse, followed by screams from the crowd, startled her. Hot wax splashed onto her knuckle, and she gasped, dropping the candle.

The canon gave her a sharp cuff on the ear, which would have knocked her down the steps if one of the guards hadn't caught her. "You stupid..." he began, and then hissed, "What in the name of God—!"

Melyssan clutched her throbbing head and rubbed her ear, but the roaring wouldn't stop. The marketplace spun before her eyes, a reeling tangle of horses' legs and human bodies as men dove and rolled to keep from being crushed.

A black stallion, its heaving sides gleaming with sweat, plunged riderless in the midst of the king and courtiers, spreading panic amongst their horses.

"Treason!" John shrieked while his soldiers grabbed for the stallion's bridle. "Stop that man!"

Melyssan's eyes watered as the canon grabbed her by the hair, as if he feared she might attempt to escape in the confusion.

"What man?" he cried.

"This one!" A dark-bearded figure hurled itself up the steps, black cloak flapping behind him so that he resembled a savage falcon swooping in, claws extended for the kill.

"Jaufre!" Melyssan called out his name at the same moment Jaufre's fist drove into the canon's nose, splintering cartilage. The clergyman dropped to the ground, howling like a lost soul, clamping his hands over his face while the blood spurted between his fingers.

"Turn your heads," Jaufre snarled at the openmouthed monks. "I'll cut the eyes out of the man that dares look at her again." He yanked free the clasp holding his cloak and flung the travel-stained garment around Melyssan. The contact of his leather-gloved fingers, rough against her shoulders, sent currents rushing through her body, jolting her with the realization that this was no strange dream.

"Jaufre," she whispered.

His lips parted in a strange smile as he lightly touched her cheek. He was still smiling when he hurled the first guard that rushed him down the steps. Then another one leapt at him, followed by two more. All three men collapsed on top of him in a struggling heap of fists, elbows, and kicking feet.

Melyssan cried out when she saw Jaufre's head snap back from a well-aimed blow. One burly soldier had his hands pinned, while the others were beating him to death. Without thinking, she flung herself at the guard only to be shoved aside to tumble partway down the steps.

Rolling to her knees, she barely avoided being trampled by the king's horse as John pressed forward, screaming, "Don't kill him. I want that man alive. Bring him to me."

Although one of the guards was doubled over clutching his groin, the other two managed to yank Jaufre to his feet. Melyssan was nigh sick with terror to see the hatred burning in John's dark eyes as he loomed over them, but Jaufre did not spare the king so much as a glance.

Instead he stared at her, the heat of his gaze obvious even through the purple swelling that threatened to close one eye. "Lyssa, you little wretch. Wait until I have you alone...."

Jaufre felt almost giddy, from far more than the blow to his head. A thousand nameless fears tumbled off his shoulders. She was alive, unharmed—a little paler than he liked, with tears trembling on the fringes of her soft brown lashes, but still his beautiful Lyssa, within touching distance if he could make these fools trying to dislocate his arms release him.

But the gravity of their situation soon dispelled his momentary relief as he became aware of Roland forcing his mount forward and waving his sword. "Unhand that man at once!"

Jaufre groaned as he saw one of the soldiers bearing down on Roland, his spear ready to thrust. What folly had ever possessed him to give the boy a weapon? He struggled futilely against his captors, but Roland was saved by the quick action of another of the earl's knights, who deflected the blow in time. Undaunted, the boy maneuvered his horse around, seeking a fresh adversary.

Tristan rode up, looking from Jaufre to Roland with the same distraction as a mother hen who sees her chickens scattering in all directions at once. "Roland! Jaufre! Damn it. When we rode here, we all agreed that...Oh, hell." Expelling an exasperated breath, Tristan drew forth his own sword in preparation for the bloody skirmish to come.

"Treason, treason!" John cried out. "Help! They would murder me."

"Nay, put up your weapons," said Jaufre.

When his captors lessened their vigil to watch the king, he took quick advantage. Wrenching free, he knocked their heads together and seized Melyssan, shoving her toward her sister, who ran forward to pull her to safety. The situation was rapidly getting out of control. He had come to rescue Melyssan, not lead a full-scale rebellion against the king.

Rushing forward, Jaufre caught hold of the bridle of the king's horse. "Tristan, damn it," he called, "keep the men back. Put up your swords. All of you."

The authoritative ring in Jaufre's voice was more effective than the king's hysterical shouts. Knights and soldiers alike hesitated in their advance. Most of the barons who had ridden to Kingsbury with John for the tournament now held back, uneasily waiting to see what would happen next.

John slashed furiously at the earl with his riding whip. "Traitorous dog! We'll see you hanged for this."

Jaufre winced as the whip bit into the arm he had flung up to protect his head. He released John's horse, and although it took all of his self-control, he gritted his teeth and forced himself down on one knee.

"Pardon, Your Majesty, if I have frightened you. 'Tis all a misunderstanding. I have but come for my wife."

"Your wife. Your whore! You make her an excuse to murder your king. Traitor!"

Jaufre leapt to his feet as John wheeled his horse at him. One heavy hoof came crushing down on the toe of his boot, and he swore and backed away. "I am trying to remain loyal, but Your Grace is making it damnably difficult."

"Loyal!" John's face suffused a bright crimson. "You've plotted against me since the day your grandfather died. Sneaking off to see Philip of France, refusing to fight for me in Wales." The king's eyes rolled wildly toward his barons. "This man is a traitor. We demand he be killed at once. Any who hesitate will share his fate."

Jaufre fought down the urge to reach for his sword. Instead he stripped off his gauntlet and waved it aloft. "I will answer these charges. Any man who dares name me traitor come take up my challenge." He threw the leather glove into the dirt.

Even in the crowded marketplace a moment of silence lapsed before a murmur of speculation broke the tension. Most of the knights and barons fixed their gaze pointedly in the opposite direction when the king looked from one to the other, waiting for someone to champion his cause.

"What! Will not one of you defend your king against this man? Are you cowards all?"

Although no one replied, Melyssan noted one stalwart baron begin to fidget with the hilt of his sword. She could bear the suspense no longer. Wrenching away from her sister, she raced toward Jaufre's side, ignoring Enid's anguished pleas for her to return. She swooped down and snatched up Jaufre's gauntlet herself before whirling to face the king.

"Your Majesty has forgotten your promise. You swore to me on your holy relics you would never command the death of the earl of Winterbourne."

The king flushed and his eyes bulged with anger, but before he could reply, Jaufre spun her around, his voice deadly quiet as he asked, "And pray tell me, Lyssa, what did you have to do to make him give you such a promise?"

"I—I..." She flinched under his hard stare.

"Oh, nothing to cause you such dismay, my lord Earl," mocked the king. "We examined the lady for our pleasure, but, unlike you, we have no taste for deformity."

Melyssan heard the intake of Jaufre's breath and moved with lightning speed to grasp his wrist before he could draw his sword. She turned to the king. "Your Majesty, please listen to me. I can attest to the loyalty of Lord Jaufre. Why, he permits no one, not even the lowliest page, to speak ill of you at Winterbourne."

"Aye, but he willingly shelters traitors there, helps them escape my justice." John's beard wagged up and down as he nodded his head. "Aye, de Macy, did you think it would never reach our ears how you helped Sir Hugh of Penhurst and his family escape to Ireland disguised as pilgrims?"

Jaufre had placed his arm protectively

301

around Melyssan's shoulders, and now she felt him start. He quirked an accusing eyebrow in her direction, and she found she was unable to meet his gaze.

"I—I had always meant to explain to you about that, my lord," she whispered. To the king, she said, "Hiding Sir Hugh and Lady Gunnor was my doing, none of Lord Jaufre's. You swore to me—"

"Aye, swore that you would be punished. Where is that wretched priest? Why is our sentence not being carried out?"

"Here, Your Grace." The canon scurried forward, holding a blood-soaked rag to his nose. He was followed by two disheveled guards, who had managed to relocate their whips.

Jaufre thrust Melyssan behind him. She caught a glimpse of Roland and Tristan dismounting, inching protectively closer. "What are the charges against my lady?" the earl asked.

"Forbication," the canon said through his swelling nose. "Libbing with you unwed."

"The fault is mine, not hers. I took her by force, raped her."

"Nay," Melyssan said. "'Tis not true."

"Hold your tongue, Lyssa," Jaufre hissed, then said aloud to the king, "I am fully prepared to make restitution for my offense by marrying the woman."

Melyssan gasped, stung more by Jaufre's careless words than the threat of the lash. She pushed past him, her head arched proudly. "Nay, *the woman* needs no such gallant sacrifice made on her behalf."

"Besides," the king said, yawning and fidgeting with the emeralds on the back of his leather gloves, "such restitution would afford us little amusement."

"Then since 'tis my offense, I will take the punishment for her."

"No!" Melyssan's protest was drowned out by the roar of approval that went up from the crowd. The king nodded his acquiescence, and even the canon's eyes lit up with unholy joy.

"Jaufre, I won't let you be whipped for me." But her words were lost as the earl sprang up the church steps, stripping off his tunic as he went. She tried to follow him, but Enid prevented her.

"Nay, let be, sweetheart. His back is broader than yours."

Desperately Melyssan turned to Tristan, stretching out her hand to the knight. "Tristan, I beg you. Stop him."

Although he grasped her hand warmly, Tristan gave her a rueful smile and shook his head. "This lady is right, Melyssan. You must not interfere. Jaufre can bear this far better than see any harm come to you."

Roland crossed his arms over his thin chest, his mouth turned down in a sulky frown. "I say we should fight them all. 'Tis humiliating for a knight to be whipped like a peasant."

Tristan's lips twitched as his eyes traveled to where Jaufre now peeled off his shirt, exposing the bronzed expanse of his hard-muscled chest while many of the women in the crowd squealed and waved their kerchiefs.

"I don't know," he murmured. "This may be one humiliation which will not turn out exactly as the king expects."

Melyssan, however, did not think the king looked as if he were about to be disappointed. John dismounted and, wetting his lips, made his way up the steps to obtain a closer view. The canon elbowed the guards aside, grabbing one of the flails. "Steb aside, you foods. This pleasure will be mide."

Jaufre braced himself against the church door, glancing over his shoulder long enough to smile at the king. "After all, Your Majesty, if such punishment was good enough for your father, I am sure I shall have no complaints."

John's face contorted with rage at the reminder of how Henry II had endured flogging from the monks at Canterbury in penance for the murder of Thomas Becket. "Get on with it!" the king screamed, but the canon needed no urging.

When the first angry red weals marred the smooth surface of Jaufre's back, Melyssan moaned and buried her face in her hands. But she could still hear the merciless crack of the whip against flesh.

Jaufre's voice raised above the sound. " 'Fore God, you call this a whipping? I've taken harsher blows from my grandmother."

The canon's frustrated shriek rent the air, the thwacks of the whip coming louder and faster. Melyssan could not restrain herself from peeking between her fingers, and she bit her lip at the sight of the first trickle of blood making its way down Jaufre's raw back. His head was thrown back, his lips stretched into a tight parody of a smile. She knew he would never indicate his suffering by so much as a gasp. Nay, not even should the whip flay every inch of skin from his bones.

"Jesu, what a man," Enid said with a sigh. "I could find it in my heart to envy you, Lyssa."

"Enid!" reproached her husband.

"Er...that is, if I did not already have you, my dearest Rob."

Melyssan leaned against Tristan, fighting the sick feeling that churned in her stomach. She felt his arm encircle her waist to steady her. At last the canon lowered the whip, sobbing because he did not have the strength to continue.

Although he wavered a little, Jaufre proceeded to don his shirt with studied nonchalance, oblivious to the wild cheering from the crowd. When he swept the king a deep mocking bow, Melyssan could see the blood seeping through the white linen. Then the earl straightened to his full height so that he towered over the king.

"I trust Your Grace is now satisfied?"

Every muscle in John's face quivered with rage. "I'll not be satisfied until I see you dead." He whirled around, shoving his servants out of the way as he ran to fling himself on his horse. Without looking back, he galloped off toward Kingsbury Castle.

Chapter 13

The logs crackled in the hearth of Enid's bedchamber, the blaze lit by the lady herself before vacating the room to accommodate the earl of Winterbourne. Her ungrateful guest kicked an osier screen forward to block the heat. "What does the wench mean to do?" Jaufre grumbled. "Roast me for the feast this evening?"

He smothered an oath as Tristan helped him don a satin tunic the rich hue of burgundy. At least, he reflected wryly, the color would disguise any further flow of blood. The satisfaction he had taken in goading the king and that self-righteous canon diminished with each little movement. His raw back felt as cracked as the earth when parched by a blistering sun.

A timid knock sounded at the chamber door. Following his curt command to enter, the wooden portal creaked open. Melyssan paused on the threshold, her fingers nervously stroking the handle of a straw basket filled with herbs as she risked a peek at him through gold-fringed lashes. She was garbed in a fresh kirtle many sizes too large for her, the loose neckline affording him a glimpse of the rising swell of her breast. Instantly he felt a familiar tightening in the region between his thighs. Damn her! His initial flush of gratitude in finding her safe dissolved, leaving in its wake a growing anger that she should appear so innocent and enchanting after the hell she had put him through these past weeks.

"Come in, madam," he called, "but leave your basket of devil's herbs outside. Your solicitude comes a trifle late. The lady Enid, who knows *her* duties well, has already been to tend my wounds."

"Oh." Melyssan raised her chin, the shy smile that had graced her lips disappearing. "If Your Lordship has no need of me, then I shan't stay."

She made a stiff curtsy and began to retreat, but Tristan hastened forward to seize her by the hand, drawing her into the room. "Nay, lady. Come sit you down and heed not Jaufre's churlishness. Surely you know his disposition well enough by now to take no offense." Directing an admonishing glance at Jaufre, he coaxed her into taking a seat upon a tapestry-covered stool by the hearth.

Jaufre gritted his teeth. By God, the wench had nearly gotten herself killed, to say nothing of himself and his men. It galled him no end that not only Tristan, but all his knights, every last one of them, were ever ready to champion her against him. Jaufre folded his arms across his chest but rapidly undid them when the gesture scraped the linen shirt over his lacerated flesh.

Tristan looked from Jaufre to Melyssan and then back again. Jaufre deliberately averted his gaze to the high windows cut into the thick limestone walls. What was Tristan waiting for? Did the fool think he meant to swoop Melyssan up and cover her with kisses for running off from him, driving him to the brink of madness? If so, he'd best think again.

The silence stretched between them until Melyssan broke it, saying in a tight little voice, "I am pleased to hear that my sister has— has taken such good care of you."

"Aye, right good care," Jaufre said dryly, remembering Enid's scathing tongue and dire threats of what she would do to him if he did not cherish her little sister. "Lady Enid has inherited the family touch for healing. She cleansed my flesh with wondrous tenderness. I have not known such gentleness since you skewered those splinters from my thigh."

As Melyssan flushed, Jaufre felt a twinge of remorse. What the devil was he trying to do? Goad her into running away from him again? His conscience smote him as he recalled the words that had sent her fleeing from his castle in the first place.

"Enough about me. I would have your account of why you left my protection in such a foolhardy manner. Surely not because of one stupid remark that I made."

"Aye, lady," Tristan said. "If everyone left each time the earl said something stupid, he'd be dwelling in an empty castle."

"And I'd be well rid of some of you!" With great effort, Jaufre lowered his voice. "I never meant to sound ungrateful that day. You did save my life, and I offer you my thanks. The leg scarce troubles me any longer."

She said nothing, only stared past him at the small adjoining chamber where Lady Enid's gowns hung on their pegs. Her green eyes held at once a greater expression of despair and determination than he had ever seen there before. He studied her figure, swallowed up in the voluminous folds of the kirtle, but could detect no sign of what Lady Enid had blurted out in her anger. Melyssan carried his babe within her womb. His babe and Lyssa's. The thought still filled him with wonder. How like Lyssa to say nothing, preparing to bear the shame alone. But there would be no shame attached to this child. He would see to that.

Becoming aware of his scrutiny, Melyssan drew her sheen of honey-brown hair forward to conceal her expression. She seemed to shrink into herself until Jaufre was assailed by a rush of tender protectiveness. He longed to gather her into his arms and murmur into her ear that he would take care of her. They would forget all that had passed. If only she would promise never to leave him again.

But it was Tristan who placed a hand upon her shoulder. "Pray accept my lord's gratitude, Melyssan. God knows it well nigh choked him to death to express it."

Jaufre felt the heat suffuse his cheeks as he snapped at Tristan, "Have you nothing to attend to elsewhere?"

Melyssan clutched at Tristan's sleeve. "No! Pray do not go, Sir Tristan. 'Tis not fitting I should be alone with Lord Jaufre. I—I have brought my family enough dishonor."

"I shall stay for as long as you command, my lady."

"By the blood of Christ, madam," Jaufre thundered, "what am I supposed to be? Some sort of brigand? I made it plain to everyone that I intend to marry you."

She set her mouth into a grim line, shaking her head. Jaufre took a step in her direction, incensed when Tristan moved between them as if Melyssan stood in need of protection from him. He shoved Tristan aside, demanding of her, "What the devil do you mean, 'no'?"

"I mean you—you do not have to marry me."

"I'll be damned if I don't!"

"Very likely," Tristan said.

Other than shooting a withering look at the knight, Jaufre ignored his friend, directing his tirade at Melyssan, who flinched at every word. "First my leg and now my back. Damnation, woman. What next? You are the most costly mistress I have ever had. Only this afternoon I have had to part with a large portion of my estates in the north, to say nothing of five hundred pieces of silver. Silver that I'd saved to improve the fortifications at Winterbourne, make that castle something to be proud of."

"But—but 'tis already beautiful," she faltered.

"Like Camelot?" He sneered. "Well, I don't want a castle fashioned of legends and dreams. My hope was that one day Winterbourne would rival the Château Gailliard in strength, that I might rebuild—"

He clenched his fists with frustration. "But what does it matter now? The money is gone. Gone to bribe the king after you brought his wrath down upon both of us. 'Twould be far cheaper to wed you. Then at least I might have some control—"

"You bribed the king?" she asked, her green eyes opening wide.

"Why else do you think he rode out to London without demanding my head?"

"I—I knew you had talked to him when we all returned to the castle, but I thought...I thought you had persuaded him to believe in your innocence, to pardon you."

"I persuaded him with the color of my money. I bought his goodwill, Lyssa."

"He is a horrid, vindictive man! 'Tis not possible to buy his goodwill."

Jaufre gave a short bark of laughter. "'Tis possible to buy anything, my lady."

"Not anything," she said, struggling to her feet, her eyes brimming with tears. "I am sorry that I should have been the cause of so much trouble for you, my lord. I have no way to repay you. All I can do is refrain from making matters worse. I vow by all that is holy you shall not be suffered to take me as your wife."

With that, she turned and stumbled from the room.

"Suffered!" Jaufre attempted to follow her, only to find his way blocked by Tristan.

"Leave be, Jaufre. You've done enough damage for the present." He rolled his eyes

311

heavenward. "Never did I hear the like before. *'Twould be far cheaper to wed you*. Is this what you tracked her over half of England to tell her? Oh, Lord, what charm! How could a woman resist such tender wooing?"

"I never asked you to stay and listen, much less favor me with your opinion." Jaufre whirled on his heel and stalked back to the bedside to finish dressing. He wound his gold belt around him, cinching it tight and gasping when it settled against one particularly deep gash just above his waist. It was worse when he added the weight of his sword. When had his weapon gotten to be so damned heavy?

Squirming under Tristan's condemning frown, he continued, "At least now you should be satisfied. 'Twas you who insisted I plight my troth with Melyssan. What more do you want from me?"

"I want to know why all this blustering. Would it have cost you so much to let the girl see how much you've yearned after her, how much you need her, how much you—"

"I've said I'll wed her," Jaufre cut in, an odd sensation of panic rising in his chest. "Surely that is enough. Like any wench, Melyssan is merely being contrary. I will speak to her mother. Everything will be settled."

"All but the most important thing." Tristan sighed. "And I dared to hope that Melyssan had banished Yseult's ghost. I see she is very much with us still."

He walked away but paused in the doorway. "Melyssan is stronger than you realize. She has her own notions of honor and will never accept your manner of *settling things*. I very much fear you are going to lose her again."

Jaufre opened his mouth to retort, but before he could say anything Tristan was gone. The earl ran his finger beneath the belt to ease the chafing, ending by ripping it off and flinging the whole thing, sword and all, onto the bed.

Damn it, why did Tristan have to speak of Yseult? She had naught to do with Melyssan— unless one considered how ironic it was that he had been able to pour out his feelings for Yseult. He cringed at the memory of the poetry he had written, the love songs he had composed and sung in her honor, the roses strewn at the feet of his would-be murderess.

And yet for Melyssan, whom he needed in a way he never had any other woman, needed in a way that terrified him to think of, the words never came. The gentle things he wished to say weighed heavy upon his tongue until he could not speak, the music fated to remain locked in his heart, never to find expression.

He frowned. What did he expect? He was no longer an infatuated youth who believed in some dreamlike ideal the troubadours called love. He would only make a fool of himself if he behaved as if he were. He desired Melyssan, and she was carrying his child. Possibly a son. Jaufre's chest swelled with pride. A son to inherit his title, his lands at Winterbourne, and Ashlar. And Clairemont, his conscience prodded.

"Aye, and Clairemont, Grandfather," he murmured. "I've not forgotten. One day your grandson will wear the honors that were yours."

None would stand in the way of this, not the French, not King John, not Melyssan's obstinacy. Jaufre's next son would be born no bastard.

Yet Tristan's prediction worried him. He did not have to be reminded of Melyssan's strength. If she persisted in refusing to marry him, no priest in the land would perform the ceremony. According to the church, if the girl held firm, not even her parents could compel her to take the vows. Most maidens surrendered, however, when the alternatives were starvation, beatings, and imprisonment. Lord Jaufre would not put it beyond Dame Alice to employ any of those methods if Melyssan remained recalcitrant. But that he would never tolerate, any more than he would tolerate losing her.

Jaufre scratched thoughtfully at his beard. Nay, if he was going to win his lady, 'twould not be by force. He must needs have recourse to some more gentle ally.

Melyssan shrank back against the wainscoting of Norwegian fir that ornamented the walls of Kingsbury Castle's great hall. The wood was painted with murals depicting maps of the world, the vastness of which only served to emphasize her feelings of being small and insignificant. The shrill piping of the hautboys mingled with the staccato rhythm of clapping hands as the dancers pranced and swirled under the center archway of the room, celebrating her forthcoming betrothal to Lord Jaufre.

She had told Enid there was naught to celebrate. There would be no betrothal. But her sister had only smiled knowingly, refusing to heed her. As did everyone else. Melyssan bit her lip, twisting a strand of the hair that flowed down past her shoulders. Most of Enid's noble guests had all but forgotten her presence, the ladies more concerned with laughingly sweeping the trains of their velvet gowns from under the feet of the stomping men. And Jaufre? He never once sought her out, as if, having declared his intent to marry her, there was no more to be said on the matter.

She had never seen him as he was tonight, intently playing the role of the practiced courtier. The deep red of the tunic he had selected earlier provided a brilliant foil for the waves of sable hair swept back from his high forehead. Although his movements were a trifle stiff, he showed no sign of discomfort as he bowed to her sister and flashed a dazzling smile. His body swayed through the measures of the carol with the same muscular grace he displayed when wielding his sword.

As he moved through the center, he glanced briefly in Melyssan's direction, then bent forward to whisper something to Enid that caused her to toss back her golden head and laugh. The jeweled circlet slipped from her hair

315

and rolled across the floor, causing much merriment as her young husband retrieved it. Robert and Jaufre tossed the headpiece back and forth, causing Enid to crash into the line of dancers as she tried to catch it. Breathless with mirth, she had to forfeit a kiss to each of the gentlemen before Jaufre placed the circlet back upon her head.

Melyssan suppressed a sudden feeling of bitter envy for her beloved sister. What right had she to feel jealous of Enid's pleasure? It was their world—Enid's, Rob's, Jaufre's. They belonged here in this glittering circle of satin-robed and bejeweled courtiers. She did not.

More strongly than ever, Melyssan resolved she would never wed Jaufre. What use had he for a crippled wife, a wife who belonged cloistered in a nunnery? She winced, remembering his anger earlier that afternoon when he had shouted his tally of what she had cost him. He had every right to be furious. She only wondered why he had even bothered to come searching for her.

Enid placed her hand on Jaufre's arm as they made their way down the line of dancers, disappearing from Melyssan's hungry gaze when a knight blocked her view. The burly fellow wove on his feet, suffering from the effects of the heady spiced wine Enid served her guests. He blundered toward Melyssan as if he did not see her, and she had to scramble out of his way to avoid being trampled. Losing her balance, she flung out her hands to right herself. She clutched at folds of linen only to discover she had yanked Dame Alice's wimple free of her straggly gray hair.

Her mother jerked the material away and slapped Melyssan's arm. "Why can you not be seated somewhere? Must you constantly demonstrate to everyone how clumsy that foot makes you?"

"I—I beg your pardon, Mother," she said, backing away, rubbing her stinging flesh.

Dame Alice's angular chin jutted out. "If I'd had my way, you would not even be here, putting on such a display. You should be up in the chapel, giving thanks to all the saints for your deliverance, my fine lady harlot! Madam Liar." The folds of skin on her mother's scrawny neck flushed redder with every insult she hurled. "You've brought deep disgrace to our family. I tell you now, when the wedding is done, I cleanse my hands of you forever."

"There will be no wedding, Mother. I won't force Lord Jaufre into marriage."

"What foolish talk is this? You ought to go down on your knees and be grateful such a one as the earl will have you." Her mother's lips pursed as she gestured to where Jaufre had begun the lively steps of the branle, linking hands to form part of the large circle. An expression of pain flitted across his countenance, but he managed to grimace a smile at the portly dame next to him.

"He ought to be up in his bed." Dame Alice scowled. "I swear from his performance today, the man is mad, a raving lunatic. But all the same—"

"I will not have him!" Melyssan said, averting her gaze, unable to bear watching Jaufre another minute, so close, yet so much farther away than he had ever been. "I won't have any man who comes to me with a sword at his back. Nay, not another word, Mother." She turned and fled through the archway out of the hall, leaving Dame Alice staring after her, gaping with as much astonishment as if she'd discovered mice could speak.

Melyssan did not pause until she'd reached the oriel outside Enid's bedchamber. The landing that led from the outer stairs of the castle was dark, the moonlight barely penetrating the leaded panes of colored glass fitted into the small window. No one who chanced upon her would see if she gave way to the foolish bout of tears that threatened to overwhelm her at any moment.

She sank down upon a wooden window seat set into the rough masonry blocks of the wall as she fought the urge to stop up her ears. She could still hear the music, echoes of laughter floating up to her from the hall below. Her heart hammered against the gossamer fabric of her chemise as she recalled with astonishment the defiant words she had dared to speak to her mother. But defying Dame Alice had been the easy part. Dealing with Jaufre would be another matter, for she knew well how stubborn the earl could be. She had been wrong to believe he would abandon her to face the world's scorn alone. Beneath his cynical façade, he was a man of honor and, where that honor was concerned, unyielding. But she had her own pride and loved him far too well to allow him to wed her out of pity and a sense of duty, especially when she knew he had far different plans for his life. It was fortunate he knew nothing of the babe nestled inside of her, or she would have no hope of dissuading him from making such a sacrifice.

But did she have the right to keep the child a secret? If a boy, it would be Jaufre's heir. She would be depriving the child of his birthright, depriving Jaufre. ...She slapped her hand against the stonework. Nay; she was weakening, trying to use the babe as an excuse to bind Jaufre any way she could. And the risks involved: they said the children of such a one as she were often as accursed as the mother....

"Lyssa?"

The soft voice startled her. She leapt to her feet, her eyes straining into the darkness. Even though she could not see his face, she knew well the silhouette of the tall man who paused at the top of the stairs. How many times had she caressed the broad expanse of those shoulders, felt those strong arms hold her fast in the long hours before dawn at Winterbourne...and in her dreams.

She turned her face toward the wall, half expecting another angry outburst from him. "Please go away, Jaufre."

"No, I will not. You have already shunned me most of this evening." She heard the timber floorboards creak and stiffened as she sensed him drawing closer. "Why have you left the feast so early, Lyssa?"

Melyssan swallowed the lump that formed in her throat. "I did not think my presence would be missed. I am not much needed when there is—dancing."

She started when his hands came to rest lightly upon her shoulders. His breath stirred against her hair, his lips close to her ear as he murmured, "I needed you. You have not danced with me one time."

She wrenched herself away from him and whirled around. His face loomed above her, shadowed except for the gleam of his eyes. "How can you mock me so? When you know I would give my life to be able to..." Her voice failed her.

Jaufre held wide his arms. "Then give me your life, Lyssa. Place it in my keeping, and I will grant your wish."

She shook her head, moving out of reach. But there was nowhere to go on the small landing. She bumped against the window seat.

"Come dance with me, Lyssa. The music still plays."

His hands encircled her waist, lifting her easily off the ground, his feet beginning to keep time with the haunting melody of the pipe echoing from the chamber below.

"Please, let me go." The tears she had suppressed for so long formed two warm rivulets, streaming down her cheeks. She held herself rigid, pushing against his chest as he spun her around in a slow circle.

He pulled her closer, supporting her with one arm linked firmly around her waist, cradling her head with his large hand, forcing her to seek the security and consolation of his embrace. Her tears soaked into the satin material as he buried his lips in the hollow of her throat.

"Lyssa, Lyssa, forgive me," he whispered. "I never meant to hurt you."

"There is nothing to forgive. ...Please." She tried to ease herself back to the ground, already giddy from the sense of her own weightlessness as Jaufre's body bent and swayed to the lilting refrain.

"Nay, stay here in my arms, Lyssa," he said, murmuring a kiss against her temple. "You ran from me once, from my cruel, heedless words, words never meant for you. You, who are all the beauty and grace I ever look for in this world."

She sobbed, feeling herself weakening, her arms slipping around his neck as she became lost in the slow, sensual motion of the dance.

"Do you know why a man likes to dance?" His voice rumbled out of the darkness, low, seductive. "When he sees a lovely lady, distant, remote, 'tis oft the only way to get near her, feel her brush against him, breathe her sweet perfume. And mayhap the touch of a hand, the chance meeting of the eye, will tell her what he cannot say."

Jaufre slid his hand beneath her hips, pressing her tighter against him as the pipes picked up their tempo. She could feel the taut muscles of his chest, his strong corded thighs undulating against her as her body

321

melted to his. Her heart caught the beat of the music as he swirled her faster and faster, the sweat from his body seeping into the front of her gown, his heat arousing all that he had taught her of desire.

It had been so long....Instinctively, her lips sought his, reveling in the sweet-salt taste of wine mingled with perspiration as their tongues mated, thrusting with the same dizzying rhythm of Jaufre's pulsating body. He staggered to a halt, never breaking the fiery contact of their mouths. Then, somehow, he was carrying her into Enid's bedchamber, pressing her back into the feather pillows.

Vaguely she noted the well-tended fire burning in the hearth of the massive chimney, the fur coverlets turned back over sheets scented with rose petals. A warning sounded in her mind even as Jaufre slipped her gown over her head. What was she doing? She could not let this happen. If she submitted to his loving, allowed herself to become one with him again, she would never have the strength to leave him.

"No, Jaufre, I beg you let me go. We must not."

He inserted one finger inside the neckline of her chemise, stroking a path just above the rise of her breasts that left her quivering. "Surely you will not turn prim upon me now, Lyssa. Not when we are nearly betrothed."

Weakly she tried to stay his hand. "I—I am trying to free you from—from being forced to marry me."

"No one forces me to do anything." His lips brushed along the silky-smooth skin of her collarbone.

"What—what else is it when your sense of honor compels you, your feelings of pity..."

She gasped when he ripped the chemise down to her waist, baring her breasts, the nipples already eagerly erect from the mere warmth of his gaze.

"Since when have I ever felt pity for anyone, Lyssa, least of all you?" His lips curved into a wicked smile. "You know they call me the Dark Knight Without Mercy." As if to prove his words, he teased one pink-crested tip with his finger, the very softness of his touch a gentle torment as she ached for more.

"Please..." she moaned, no longer sure what it was she begged him to do. Her control slipped further away as he eased the chemise down over her hips, leaving her naked beside him.

He stood then by the bedside, and her protests died on her lips as one by one his garments dropped to the floor. The firelight cast a bronzed glow over his bearded face, now heavy-lidded with desire. The muscular contours of his body, the hardened evidence of his growing need, glistened with sweat.

It was not until he lowered himself onto the bed that the light flickered to reveal the angry crisscross of slashes marring the smooth surface of his flesh. How could she have permitted herself to forget?

"No, Jaufre, your back! You cannot," she

cried, pulling up into a sitting position.

His mouth curved into a determined smile. "Aye, lady. I can and will, even had I received ten times the blows. 'Twould be naught compared to the agony of letting another day go by without loving you."

He slipped his arm around her shoulders, guiding her back down onto the bed. Her protests he swept aside with the persuasion of his lips mastering hers in the force of his kiss, now coaxing, now demanding. She could no longer deny the fire coursing along her veins, the flames spreading outward to consume her entire being.

He caressed her with a gentleness greater than she had ever experienced from him before, even in his most tender moments. His hands traced the sensitive hollows of her passion's center with the reverence of one exploring the portals to some holy temple. The lightness of his touch tantalized her until she bit her lip to keep from pleading for the consummation of her desire.

With slow deliberation, as if he would savor every moment, he glided himself inside her, each thrusting movement of his powerful hips seeming calculated to prolong the sweet flame-racked torture, delay the blinding moment of climax. With a low groan, she buried her hands in the thick waves of his hair, drawing his head down beside her, her senses spinning with the musky scent of his maleness, the heady perfume of the roses.

"So right," he said hoarsely, the warmth of his labored breaths tickling the sensitive flesh along her neck. "This is where you belong, my Lyssa."

"A-aye, my lord."

"Then swear it. Swear you'll never leave. Swear—you—are—mine." With each fierce word, his velvet shaft penetrated deeper, faster, as if he now moved to claim all of her with this union of their bodies, wedding her spirit to his with the joining of their flesh.

"I swear it. Forever." The cry tore free from her throat as her world exploded around her, setting her aloft in a storm of fire that flared into white-hot shards of light, then becalmed, leaving her bathed in a warm glow.

And still Jaufre moved inside her, bracing himself on his strong arms as she lay gasping beneath him. She watched him, her heart wrenching with love at the rugged beauty of his male features as, head thrown back, he emitted a guttural cry. A thrill rushed through her almost as potent as Jaufre's lovemaking at the realization she had the power to do this to him, bring him to the same miraculous fulfillment as he did her.

She felt bereft when he drew away from her, dissolving them into two separate beings once more. Her only consolation was that Jaufre settled himself gingerly on his side, drawing so close that his leg interwined with hers. He trailed his fingers over her bare shoulder, a languorous smile upon his lips.

"Ah, Lyssa. What you do to me. How could you be so foolish as to think I would ever let you go?"

"Or that I could go," she whispered, remembering the promise he had wrung from her in the midst of their passion. Right or wrong, she was now pledged to be his as assuredly as if she had taken her marriage vow.

Was it but a trick of her imagination, or was there a certain amount of self-satisfaction in Jaufre's smile? She plucked free some of the velvety pink petals that had somehow become matted in the dark curling hairs of his chest...rose petals, which had been carefully placed in a bed with turned-down sheets, a chamber with a well-lit fire....

She jerked herself up onto one elbow and glared at him accusingly. "Jaufre. You—you planned this whole thing. You seduced me!"

"Nay!" But no matter how wide he stretched those dark brown eyes, he could not quite convey an impression of innocence. "Well, mayhap I did, a little."

When she began to scramble away from him, he sat up and caught hold of her upper arms. "Now, Lyssa," he said, barely suppressing a deep chuckle, "how else could I show you 'twas of no avail, your refusal to wed me? An I mistake not, you enjoyed my little persuasion as much as I."

She felt two hot spots of color settling into her cheeks. "That is not the point. I like not feeling that I have been somehow tricked."

"Is it trickery for a man to woo his bride?" He gave her a gentle shake. "You are so stubborn. You would never believe that I did not wish to wed you out of pity, so I had to offer you proof otherwise."

He sighed in frustration as he saw from the mulish set of her chin that his plans were going awry. His eyes flickered over the soft swell of her stomach, the barely perceptible thickening of her waistline. No. Somehow he sensed this was not the time to tell her he knew about the child.

"Lyssa, 'twas the only way to make you understand. I will have you at any cost."

She stared up at the canopy above them, her eyes blinking back large tears. "'Tis you who do not understand. What I feel for you has no cost. I love you, Jaufre. I have ever since you rescued me from those cruel boys at the tournament. You—you laugh when I say it, but to me you were like Sir Launcelot, everything that was noble, that a knight should be. My dream was always that one day you would come riding back to me, swear that you..." Her voice trailed away as she bowed her head.

Jaufre fidgeted uncomfortably. " 'Twas all a long time ago. A child's fantasy, Lyssa, all this talk of Sir Launcelot and love. Now I come to you as a man to a woman, with an honorable proposal of marriage."

"Aye, honorable!" She choked on the word.

"Lyssa, I want you. I need you for my wife. 'Tis more than most women have from their husbands. Can this not be reason enough for you?"

She raised her head, her sea-shaded eyes

staring into his as if she sought a mirror into his soul. It was all he could do not to look away, her gentle gaze piercing him with an inner pain as if she cleared away the dust from motives hidden in the dark recesses of his heart, motives for wanting her he himself did not as yet dare examine in the bright light of day.

After an eternity, she lowered her eyes. "Aye, Jaufre, I will try to make it enough." Burrowing her face against his chest, she flung her arms around him, pressing her fingers against his naked back.

"Lyssa, my sweet—" His words broke off as she felt a strip of skin tear away.

She recoiled in horror as Jaufre arched back, his lips twisted with pain. He collapsed onto his stomach, mumbling curses into the pillow. For long moments he lay still, gasping for breath until the color gradually returned to his face.

"M-my lord, I am so sorry," she whispered, reaching out to touch him and then drawing back guiltily. "I—I will fetch some of Enid's herbs to numb the pain."

"No!" He caught her hand. "Not necessary. All I need is you beside me. Stay and...all will be well."

Despite her better judgment, she allowed him to dissuade her from doing more than cleansing away the fresh streak of blood that trickled down his back. When she had done, he nuzzled the rough satin of his beard against her shoulder, his arm tightening around her waist as if he feared she might disappear while he slept.

"Lyssa," he murmured. "You look so beautiful, firelight glinting on your hair, your skin....Would that I could make love to you again. When I've rested..."

The furrows disappeared from his brow, the long dark eyelashes rested against his cheeks. She studied his harsh features gentled by repose and placed her fingers against his chest, feeling the strong, steady beat of his heart.

All will be well. So Jaufre had said. She wished she could believe that and chided herself for the lingering doubt that cast a shadow over her happiness. The earl was right. Most women considered themselves lucky if they could tolerate the husband their families selected for them. And she, who had never thought to be wed at all...Why was she such a dreamer as to keep hoping that somewhere in Jaufre's mahogany eyes she would find love?

He had confessed his need for her. She should be satisfied, sweep her misgivings aside. Placing a hand upon her stomach, she reflected that she was glad he knew nothing of her condition. At least she could be sure it was not thought of the babe that drove him on to marry her.

She would tell him the night of their wedding. Would he be pleased? She believed so. He had spoken of his desire for an heir. If only the child would not be born with...No. She blotted that frightening prospect from her mind.

The child would be perfect. And there would be others. She would wait, be patient with Jaufre. Perhaps in time, she could teach him to believe in dreams again, to believe in love. ...They would have all the time in the world now that Jaufre had dealt with the king.

Melyssan closed her eyes tight. Why had she had to think of the king? Perhaps because she could not quite accept that he was gone from their lives. Deep within her was a conviction that all Jaufre had bought them was a little time. No amount of wealth could erase the hatred she had seen blazing in John's soulless eyes. Hatred for Jaufre and herself.

Where the king hated, he had a long and ruthless memory. An image of Matilda de Briouse swam into her mind, and Melyssan shuddered. Matilda and her child, victims of a king's implacable hate, starving to death in that dungeon.

Cupping her hand protectively over the region of her womb, Melyssan snuggled closer to the lean strength coiled in Jaufre's sleeping body. She lay awake for a long time before finally drifting off into a troubled sleep, a sleep in which John's cruel laughter echoed in her ears.

Chapter 14

THE CASTLE BELL clanged incessantly, calling upon all the saints in heaven to ease the painful labor of childbirth for the lady Melyssan. Jaufre scowled as he bent over the papers strewn across the table, trying to concentrate on the plans his architect had submitted for improving Winterbourne's fortifications.

Even here in the solar, the peal of the bell resounded through his brain, a constant reminder that Lyssa lay in the chamber above him, her face waxen with pain as she strained to bring life to his son. Jaufre closed eyes that burned from lack of sleep, pinching the bridge of his nose as he struggled to block from his mind his last sight of her, her slender body racked with agony, before the midwife had commanded him to leave the room. Commanded him! The earl of Winterbourne. And he had departed meekly, slinking away from a situation where he had no control, a female domain where his orders counted for naught. He could not decree an end to Melyssan's pain nor sternly reprimand his son to hasten his entry into this world before his mother's strength gave out.

Sighing, he opened his eyes and once more attempted to focus on the plans: a new outer wall beyond where the moat stood now, more flanking towers reinforced with thicker stone at the bottom, the old square contours to be replaced with circular shapes, convex surfaces to better deflect an arrow....

"M-my lord?" The young page thrust his head inside the door. "The messenger still waits. What shall I—"

"Tell him to go jump in the moat and take that bell with him." Jaufre pushed the papers from him in exasperation, his head throbbing in time with the persistent *dong, dong, dong.* "Nay, send him in, and command those superstitious fools to stop that ringing before they drive me mad."

"Aye, my lord." The page disappeared, to be replaced by a lean gray shadow of a man whose tunic and mantle blended so well with the stone wall that Jaufre had to look twice to ascertain anyone was there. The messenger stepped forward, bowing so deeply that his nose nigh touched his knee, his sallow countenance as apprehensive as an ox about to be led to the slaughter.

"Greetings to you, my lord Earl, from His Most Royal Majesty, King John of England. A thousand thanks for affording me the hospitality of your magnificent castle. The praises of Winterbourne and its master, the Dark Knight, are heard—"

"State your business," Jaufre said, returning his attention to the architect's plans.

"Oh, aye, my lord." The man fumbled with a short baton attached to his belt. "But bless me, what a charming room this is. Such a painting as I've never seen before. What colors! Your artist most truly has brought King Arthur's court to life."

Jaufre tapped his foot impatiently against the table as he followed the messenger's glance to where Arthur and his knights, Gawaine, Percival, Tristan, and Launcelot, jousted on the wall of the solar, blotting out any traces of what had once been William the Conqueror's advancing army. The earl grimaced for the hundredth time at his own whimsy in permitting such legends to grace the walls of his castle. But it had made Melyssan happy. The scarred conquest mural had been a constant reminder to her of the night she'd been attacked by Father Hubert.

Glowering, Jaufre shifted his gaze back to the messenger. "Did the king send you all the way from London merely to admire my murals?"

"N-no, my lord." The man dropped the baton, retrieved it, nearly dropped it again. "I—I beg Your Lordship's pardon. I realize my arrival is most inopportune, considering the condition of your lady. I trust you will hear good report shortly."

Shortly? It had been yesterday afternoon this nightmare had begun. How long did it take a woman to produce a child? Melyssan seemed to be taking forever about the business. How much longer could she endure?

Jaufre leaned forward, slamming the palm of his hand on the table. The messenger jumped back a foot.

"Stop dallying with these pleasantries, man. I grow weary of this waiting. Produce your message or go to the devil."

"A-aye, my lord." The servant's hands shook as he pulled apart the baton, which was hollow inside. From it he produced a scroll, which he handed to Jaufre with another bow.

"Here 'tis. A letter from the king. The king

wrote it. I did not. 'Tis—'tis not from me, but from the king."

"Cease your babbling."

Jaufre snatched the parchment away and then rose, stalking to the croslet to take better advantage of the light from the early afternoon sun. He could smell the sweet scent of new grass that cropped up in the bailey below him, borne aloft by a gentle summer wind. A season of new life, new hope, that banished all thought of death. Yet how many women died in the summer as well as any other time of year while giving birth? 'Twas as common as for a man to fall in battle.

Jaufre's fingers clenched the missive, nearly tearing it in two, and for a moment the words before him blurred. Lyssa, so fragile, warm and gentle as summer itself. Damn! Why was there no word yet?

Shaking his head as if to dispel his forebodings, Jaufre began to read, trying to ignore his growing irritation with the messenger, who hovered nearby, shifting nervously from foot to foot. His annoyance at the servant transformed to anger at the master who had sent him as Jaufre read farther down the page.

Our loyal subject, the most noble Earl of Winterbourne,

To our great distress, we are obliged to refuse the Earl's recent request for license to add further fortification to Winterbourne Castle. Lord Jaufre forgets he is amongst friends here in England and therefore has no

need to prepare for war against his castle.
Rather, he should direct his military
thoughts against his true enemy, Philip of
France.

We deem Winterbourne adequate to hold
against any Welsh uprisings. Beyond that,
Lord Jaufre need not fear.

> *By Grace of God, His Most Sovereign*
> *Majesty, John of England.*

"Adequate!" Jaufre raised his head to glare
at the quaking messenger. "He deems this
adequate. Only look here, sirrah."
He seized the messenger by the front of
his tunic and dragged him over to the croslet.
"Look at the north wall, how weak it sets
upon the edge of the old castle mound. It
could be mined under in a matter of days. And
those old square towers." Jaufre thrust his
pointing finger so close that the servant
blinked. "How is one even supposed to see the
enemy attacking on that side?"
"I—I don't know, my lord."
"And the old water gateway, with no further
outer wall to defend it. Think you Winterbourne
is safe?"
"Ah—ah, 'tis a most noble-looking castle,
my lord."
Jaufre gave him a fierce shake.
"N-no, my lord. Not safe. Ah, St. Michael
bless me. Not safe."
"Bah!" Jaufre released him so abruptly the
man's spiderlike legs all but collapsed beneath

him. Striding over to the table, Jaufre swept his hand across it, sending the plans scattering in all directions, scattering even as his dreams for building Winterbourne into the mightiest fortress in England.

He shoved John's letter back at the messenger. "Here. You know what you can do with this."

The servant nodded bleakly.

Balling his hands into fists, Jaufre stormed toward the door, pausing a moment to look back. "When you return to London, you may tell His Most Sovereign Majesty that—" The earl broke off, his anger momentarily lost in astonishment.

The messenger was tearing off bits of the letter and slowly chewing the parchment with the resignation of a martyr.

"What in the name of St. George are you doing?"

The messenger swallowed, gagged, and then mournfully tore off another piece. "Alas, my lord, this is not the first time I have been required to eat a message I have delivered for the king. Most of the barons—"

"You fool. I only meant for you to rip it up or burn it. I—Oh, God's teeth!" Throwing up his hands in disgust, Jaufre stalked out of the solar. As he took the curving stairs to the great hall two at a time, he reflected it was as well he had been diverted by the servant's folly. He had been about to make a very imprudent reply to John's message.

His fists clenched again at the king's refusal

to allow him to fortify his castle. Obviously John did not want the earl of Winterbourne sheltered behind the walls of a mighty fortress, sheltered beyond his own grasping talons. An uneasy truce had existed between himself and the king ever since his marriage to Melyssan. As preparations moved forward each day for the long-awaited invasion into France, he and John were bound together by a common goal. Sometimes Jaufre dared believe they might succeed in conquering Normandy. It was close to one year since his grandfather had died, and he had not yet kept his pledge. Although he grudged the waste of men and money that would go into the French campaign, he would at least free himself of that accursed oath when the old comte's banner flew over Clairemont again. But when that time came, what would become of his unholy alliance with the king? How could he ensure that Melyssan and their child would remain safe from the tyrant's uncertain temper?

As he entered the dais end of the great hall, the servants were yet clearing away the remains of the midday meal. Most of the food on his trencher remained untouched. It was impossible to eat while Melyssan's chair at his side remained empty, while abovestairs she...

Jaufre halted on the last step. How could it take so damnably long for such a small thing as a babe to be born? Something had to be wrong. Despite himself, he half turned to go back up the stairs. Damn it. There had to be something he could do. Yet he remembered how earlier he had lingered by Melyssan's bedside and reached for her hand.

"Don't touch me," she had said through clenched teeth. For one dumbfounded moment, he thought she had cursed him under her breath as her hands came up to clutch her abdomen. Then she had snapped at him to move back and cease smothering her.

"Well, I'll be hanged if I *smother* her anymore," Jaufre muttered, reluctantly returning to his original course through the great hall. As he passed by, he overheard one of the servants whisper to his fellow, "Lookee, 'ere comes the earl to commence his pacing around the great hall again."

Jaufre glowered at the fellow. Instead of withering under his stare, the impudent creature grinned. "Gor bless Yer Lordship. 'Tis only the first that's so worrisome. By the next time yer lady is in the straw, ye'll be off ahunting somewheres."

Jaufre stepped toward the man. He was seriously considering wringing his scrawy old neck when he was startled by a loud crash from the other end of the hall. Whirling, he saw that two of his young squires had come to blows, sending an iron candelabrum toppling over. If the wax tapers had been lit, the fools would have set the rushes afire. Several of the maidservants scattered away, squealing as the two young men hugged each other like ferocious bears, hurtling to the floor in a tangle of legs and flailing fists.

Jaufre hurried across the hall, mumbling imprecations under his breath. Most heartily did he regret having sent Tristan to replace the aged seneschal whose recent death had left Ashlar in a state of confusion. Because of Melyssan's impending confinement, the earl had hesitated to travel north himself. But without Tristan's sobering presence, his squires were more apt to indulge in unruly confrontations such as this one.

"Hold, both of you, and get to your feet!" Jaufre bellowed, but the young men were too far gone in their anger to heed him. They broke apart, struggling to find room to deliver their blows as fists *whooshed* through the air. One of the combatants was Roland, but that came as no surprise. When a fight broke out, one was always Roland. At least the boy had not gone for his sword this time.

Jaufre lunged forward, grabbing the closest belligerent, the young squire, Arric. As he yanked him back, the priest burst out of the chapel and rushed to intercept Roland.

It was by Melyssan's request Father Andrew had returned as chaplain at Winterbourne. Jaufre conceded that the man, though aged, carried a certain quiet authority. The priest subdued the furious Roland without doing more than laying a hand on his shoulder and staring hard into his eyes. It took Jaufre a moment longer to bring Arric to his senses. The young man came close to gouging the earl with his elbow before he realized who had seized him. Only when he felt the tension slacken from

Arric's shoulders did Jaufre release his grip on the boy.

"What is this, my sons?" asked Father Andrew, his low voice carrying even in the vast cavern that was the great hall. "You behave like peasant lads outside the very door of God's temple, forgetting the respect you owe your Creator and the earl. To treat his great hall as if it were a stableyard—"

"Thank you, Father, but I can preach my own sermons," Jaufre said, staring from Arric's blackened eye to the flushed face of his son. "Would one of you care to favor me with an explanation before I—"

"I can't bear any more of this posturing, my lord," Arric burst out. "Even if he is your son. He is a traitor. He—"

"A traitor? Simply because I speak the truth?" Roland wiped a trickle of blood from his chin, regarding Arric with heated scorn.

"Truth? You lying poltroon! Forever bleating about that knave across the Channel."

"That knave is a great king. You wouldn't catch Philip Augustus crawling on his belly to the pope like your paltry John Softsword—"

Father Andrew sternly intervened. "You forget King John's recent obeisance will put an end to our terrible interdict."

"Your pardon, Father. But for King John to give his crown to the pope! Make England a mere vassal of Rome! Pah, what a weakling! In France, it would not be tolerated."

"If you love the French so much," Arric snarled, "go back over there, you Norman bastard."

"Enough." Jaufre gave Roland a sharp cuff on the ear when the young man took a purposeful step in Arric's direction. His son's eyes flashed silver lightning, his fingers flying to the sword at his belt. But Father Andrew's hand shot out to quickly cover the boy's.

"Have both of you forgotten your original intentions? You had come to pray with me in the chapel for the safe delivery of our lady Melyssan through her ordeal of childbirth."

"They'd best pray for their own safe delivery if I catch them at such mad sport again," Jaufre said. "I'll not have my knights or my squires fighting amongst themselves."

"I will speak to them of their duties," Father Andrew said gently. "But for now, mayhap Your Lordship would care to accompany us to the chapel and—"

"Prayers are your province." Jaufre folded his arms across his chest. "That is what I pay you for...unless you care to say a mass instead," he mocked. "Nay, I forgot. The interdict has not officially been lifted. Your holy master the pope still haggles with the king over what fines John will pay for his insolence in defying Rome. Of course, such monetary considerations are of far more importance to the Church than what few miserable souls may be lost in the meantime."

The priest bowed his head, refusing to be baited, but not before Jaufre noted the tightening of the lips, the spark of anger in the pale blue eyes. Aye, he thought, you loathe me as much I despise you, sir priest. You would have seen Lyssa a nun, dead, anything sooner than become my wife. You've made your feelings plain ever since I permitted you to speak the vows that bound us together, although the words well nigh killed you.

Aloud he said, "Arric, since you have time for such idleness as prayers, you may spend the rest of the day mucking out the stables. Roland will join you after we have had some private speech."

With that he turned on his heel and stalked away, without waiting to see his commands obeyed. Roland shuffled along behind him, but Jaufre did not turn around to face the young man until they were alone in the solar. He seated himself in the highbacked chair while Roland stood stiffly before him, his shoulders squared as if he balanced a block of wood there and dared anyone to knock it off. His resemblance to the old comte was so great, Jaufre found it painful to look upon him. Those silver-gray eyes seemed a reproach to him, a reminder of the promise he had made to Raoul de Macy, a promise unkept.

The earl suppressed an urge to run his hand through his hair. By no gesture or look must he show the sensation of weariness and defeat that came over him when he regarded this son of his. Aye, the boy had trained hard over the past months. He had seen to that, keeping his son under his own eye instead of sending him off to study the skills of a knight while serving another lord, as was the custom.

And Roland had learned quickly. He rode, fought with a sword, and handled the lance with more dexterity than many men who had already won their spurs. But he had not outgrown the reckless lack of self-discipline and the boastful hauteur that brewed trouble wherever he chanced to be.

"Well, boy," Jaufre said at last. "I thought I made it plain I would tolerate no more of you stirring trouble amongst my household."

Roland tipped his head back, a gesture that accented the pugnacious set of his chin. "Take your squires to task, my lord. They are equally to blame. I cannot so much as breathe a word about my old home in France without one of them ready to set upon me."

"Aye, of course, and with no encouragement whatsoever from you. Do not think to cozen me, boy. I hear how your tongue runs apace, bragging of the superior prowess of French knights over the English, singing praise of Philip Augustus."

"'Tis fitting for a man to speak well of his liege lord."

"As long as you remain here at Winterbourne, *I* am your liege lord and I serve John of England. In future, you will remember that or I will whip you myself."

"You may attempt it."

Jaufre swore and half rose from his chair. "One day you will push me too far, boy. You expect special consideration because you are of my blood, but—"

"Special consideration?" Roland laughed bitterly. "I would like only to be treated as well as the other squires. No matter what happens, you always leap to the conclusion I am the one to blame. My punishment is always twice as harsh. Nothing I ever do meets with your approval."

"You asked me to help you win your spurs, boy. Not coddle you like a—" Jaufre halted midsentence as a strange sound penetrated the solar. It was as soft as the mew of a kitten, so soft he was not sure he had heard it until Roland also cocked one ear as if listening to something in the chamber above them.

"'Tis the cry of a babe," said Roland.

Jaufre felt his heartbeat quicken but shook his head. "Nay, it could not be. How could such a small voice carry so far?"

"A lusty pair of lungs. Doubtless those of a male child." Roland swallowed and then choked out, "My felicitations, Your Lordship. It would seem you have finally acquired a son." His face gone quite pale, Roland made Jaufre a stiff bow before sweeping out of the room.

The earl stared after him, unwillingly seized by a pang of sympathy for the young man. For once Roland's customary expression of hauteur had been belied by a look of hurt longing.

Ah, but 'twas too late, Jaufre thought, years too late to forge a bond with this son who resented him. And abovestairs Lyssa awaited him, Lyssa and the child who would one day be his heir.

The sunlight streaming across the bed blurred before Melyssan's eyes as she lay panting, gathering the remains of her strength to keep from plunging into blackness. Her legs trembled violently as her whole body experienced a surge of relief, freed of its great burden. Weak she was, but the pain was gone, and in the distance she could hear her babe screaming loudly enough to bring the castle walls down. She drew in another deep breath, and her head cleared.

The kindly moon-shaped face of the midwife hovered above her, wiping her brow with a damp cloth and pressing a brew of slippery elm bark to her lips. Lyssa sipped and choked on the tea.

"There now, Your Ladyship will do just fine. Nay, don't try to sit up. You must take things slowly. Didn't I promise the eaglestone would bring you safely through?" The woman beamed and touched a chain from which dangled a dark, hollow stone the size of a walnut, which she had placed around Melyssan's neck when labor had begun.

"Aye, thank you," Melyssan whispered, although she placed more faith in the tiny gold crucifix she clutched in her right hand. She released it now for the first time in twenty-three hours, feeling the marks the cross had gouged into her skin.

"My—my babe?" she asked, her eyes going fearfully to the shrieking bundle Nelda cuddled in her arms.

"Ah, that one." The midwife chuckled. "Stronger than ye be at the moment. Ye need have no fears for the babe."

Melyssan struggled to a sitting position despite the old woman's protest. She *did* fear—and it was a dreadful fear that had haunted her all the months she had carried the child in her womb.

"Bring the babe to me."

Although she continued to cluck and fuss, the midwife brought the wailing child to the bedside, laying it gently in the crook of Melyssan's arm. All she could see was dark fuzz adorning the top of a tiny head crimson with fury. With trembling fingers, she began to undo the blankets that swaddled the child.

"My lady," the midwife protested, but Melyssan gestured the woman to silence.

The blankets fell away, and Melyssan studied the little form stretched across her stomach. She caught one red, wrinkled foot and cradled it in the palm of her hand. So small, so cold, so perfect. As was the other one, which she next subjected to the same tender examination. And the arms, thin, wiry as any newborn's, also perfect. Perfect as Jaufre's daughter should be.

"There, you see, Your Ladyship?" said the midwife. "You could not wish for a more hearty, more beautiful little daughter."

"No, I could not," Melyssan said, tears trickling down her cheeks. "Father in heaven,

I thank thee." She trailed her hands over the pink, down-covered skin, pausing to uncurl and count each diminutive finger and then the toes, before at last she was satisfied and pulled the blanket around the child. Drawing the baby close to her breast, she rocked her, cooing soft words of endearment. For the first time since she had drawn breath, Melyssan's daughter ceased her cries and was silent, enabling the mother to better study the round, velvety cheeks, pink lips drawn up like a bow, a petite snub nose. Unfocused blue eyes stared back at her, eyes amazingly alert and as dark-fringed as those of the man who now paused on the room's threshold.

"Jaufre." She leaned forward, surprised by the hesitation in his manner—he, who usually strode into a room with such confidence. Guiltily, she remembered how hours earlier she had driven him from her side. Then her thought had been all for the pain contracting her womb, how to endure it without going mad, how to brace herself for the next wrenching agony.

"My lord, please come in. Do you not wish to see your child?"

He nodded, crossing the room without seeming to see Nelda and the midwife, who curtsied and discreetly retreated outside. As he approached the bed, his gaze swept past the babe and settled on Melyssan, his fingers caressing the tangled strands of her hair.

"Lyssa. You look so—so almost as if you are of another world. Have you...are you well?"

"Aye, my lord." She caught his hand and pressed a kiss along the leathery texture of his knuckles. "Never in my life have I been more so. Look."

She held up the babe, her heart swelling with pride, barely able to restrain herself from crying aloud, *Look! Look at this astonishingly perfect being that came from my womb.*

As Jaufre slipped the child from her grasp, she bit back her protest, overwhelmed by a surge of fierce protectiveness. But his hands were sure and strong as he steadied the babe's head, his lips parting in a broad, flashing smile.

"By my holidame, didst ever see such a sturdy, bright-eyed fellow? We shall name him Raoul, after my grandfather." Jaufre's rich brown eyes turned to her with a warmth such as she'd never seen before. His voice grew husky with emotion. "I have no words, Lyssa, to tell you how happy you've made me."

Her answering smile froze on her lips. "I am pleased you should say so, my lord. But—but I fear there has been some mistake."

"What mistake? A strong, handsome son, all that a man could ask for."

"'Tis a girl, my lord. That—that is your daughter."

She watched the light die in his eyes, like a candle's glow extinguished by a sudden breath of wind. He was silent for a long moment and then said, "A—a daughter. You—you are certain of this?"

"I—I—"

"A stupid question. Of course you are certain." Quickly he handed the babe back to her, withdrawing but a step from the bedside, although his expression put miles between them.

Melyssan snuggled the baby closer against her, feeling the wriggle of her limbs beneath the blanket. She gave a nervous laugh. "A restless child, your daughter. I don't believe Raoul will suit her. What would you have her called?"

"I had not thought." He shrugged. "'Tis of no great import. You decide."

Melyssan bit down on her lower lip. "She—she is perfect, Jaufre. Even both her feet..."

"I am sure she is. You do not need to show me."

She stayed the hand that had begun tugging on the blanket. "And I—I am sure next time we will produce a son just as beautiful." Her luminous green eyes raised to his, pleading.

Much as he loathed himself, he could not give her the reassurance she sought. Damn, he had wanted, needed, a son so badly. Waves of disappointment washed over him. Lyssa looked so pale, the radiant aura that had surrounded her now shattered. He had no desire to see her put through such an ordeal again anytime soon. But the war in France loomed imminent, drawing closer than ever. For the first time in his life, he experienced a stab of fear that he might die in battle, die without leaving a son behind to bear his name.

Nay, there was no way he could respond to

the plea he saw in Melyssan's eyes, begging him to accept this girl in lieu of the son for which he had longed.

"I will leave you now," he said. "I shall send a messenger to bear the—the glad tidings to your family."

Her reply was all but muffled as she buried her face against the babe's blanket. " 'Twill be of small interest to them. My mother will not care, and Whitney has never forgiven me."

"Enid will want to know you are well. She was most concerned even from the day she first told me you were with child. While she treated the wounds on my back, she treated me to a lecture on how frail..." His voice trailed off as he realized from the stricken look on her face that he'd made a mistake.

"You—you knew?" she cried. "You knew I carried your child when you married me?"

"Of course I knew." He looked away, unable to cope with her tear-filled eyes. "You were being obstinate, so I pretended not to. Damn it, what difference does it make now? Let us not rake through those old ashes again." He retreated to the door. "You must excuse me. I slept but little last night. I am completely exhausted."

Before she could say anything more, she found she was alone with her daughter. *He* was exhausted. Weariness tugged her down like the undertow lurking beneath foam-flecked waves. The flow of strength that her joy in the babe had produced vanished as Jaufre's words pounded through her brain.

He knew. He knew. But what difference did it make? Only all the difference in the world. Melyssan was scarce aware when the midwife came to take the babe from her arms, easing her back down upon the pillow. She was too caught up in her misery over Jaufre's revelation.

He had known about the child. Known about it and had done the honorable thing, marrying her and hoping she'd give him a son. But she had failed him. She rolled over onto her side, clenching her fists into the pillows. Now all she had given him was a lifetime to regret.

In the ensuing months, Jaufre found no escape from the child's wails or Melyssan's tragic, dark-rimmed eyes. She had become but a wan shadow of herself, forever flitting from him like a will-o'-the-wisp, she and this new daughter of hers forming a magic circle in which he had no part. He knew he had stirred to life all her old doubts as to his reason for marrying her, yet he could not find the words to reassure her.

Preparations for the war increased each day, pulling him closer to a time of decision. He felt as if he approached a peak in his life, where honor and success might be his or lost forever in the tides of battle. Feelings of doubt beset him, feelings he could share with no one. In some strange way, his marriage to Melyssan had weakened him, made him more vulnerable than he cared to admit. He wanted nothing more than to remain at Winterbourne,

351

by day riding over his lands, by evening lying with his head upon Lyssa's knee, her gentle hands stroking his brow while their children romped before the fire.

The prospect of battle did not thrill him as it had in the days men had first acclaimed him the Dark Knight. Never had he so much to lose. Lyssa and the child they had christened Genevieve were both so fragile. If he died in France, whose strong arm would defend them? The king and his greedy courtiers would descend upon Winterbourne like a pack of ravenous wolves.

The babe's screams acted as a constant reproach to him. One afternoon in early autumn he returned to the castle hot, sweating from a day's exercise of his sword arm, only to hear once more the seemingly perpetual wails coming from the part of the castle garden near the large apple tree. Gritting his teeth, he strode in that direction, heedless of the half-rotted fruit that crunched beneath his boots.

Genevieve's young wet nurse sat dozing on a bench while the child rested in a basket settled at her feet. Dozing! How could the wench possibly sleep with the babe howling like a greyhound with a burr caught in its haunches? The creature must be half-deaf. Jaufre bent over and shook the girl roughly by the shoulder. Her eyes widened in terror as she was startled out of her slumber.

"Awaken, mistress. Is it your intent to starve the bratling? Put her to the breast and quiet this ungodly noise."

The girl leapt to her feet and crossed her arms

protectively over her ample bosom. "I—I pray you, my lord. I but fed the child a half hour since. She could not be hungry."

"Then get her fresh garb. She must be wet."

"Oh, no, my lord. She is well cared for, I promise you."

"Then what the devil is amiss? Why is she forever shrieking?"

The girl made a helpless gesture, a blank expression crossing her simple face. "Why, babes cry, my lord. 'Tis all they can do. I have oft suspected that mayhap they have little demons that torment them, demons so small—"

"Demons!" Jaufre took a menacing step closer until the terrified girl retreated behind the apple tree. "Get you from my sight, you hen-witted fool. If I set eyes on you again, I will show you demons."

The girl's face crumpled. Covering her face with her hands, she fled from the garden. Jaufre's satisfaction in seeing her go was soon dissipated by a wave of panic when he realized he was now alone with a howling infant.

How did one deal with such a small, unreasoning bundle? He risked one peek into the basket and said with all the sternness he could muster, "How now, mistress Genevieve! Cease this unseemly racket. Such behavior will not be tolerated."

Feeling the fool, he glanced around guiltily, dreading he might have been overheard, but the rest of the household seemed to be avoiding this part of the garden where his daughter shrieked. His words had not the least effect on Genevieve. If anything, her howls continued with renewed vigor. Jaufre twitched aside the blanket, unable to suppress a twinge of amusement. He detected no sign of distress in the child. Rather, her round face puckered in an expression of anger, more ferocious than he'd seen on many a redoubtable warrior.

Jaufre clucked his tongue. "I am relieved you have no words as yet, my daughter. I fear what you would say might prove most unladylike. What vexes you so?"

He studied the small body, noting for the first time the swaddling that crisscrossed over her frame and prevented neither arm nor leg from moving so much as an inch.

"By St. George, now I see what ails you, little one." He frowned and scooped the babe out of the basket. "I should curse them myself if they had bound me up like a suckling piglet."

Sitting down upon the bench, he laid the babe across his lap and unwound the bandage until Genevieve was garbed in naught but her tiny shirt and tailclout. Almost immediately upon being freed, her howls stopped and she took a great shuddering breath of relief.

To the earl's delight, she waved her arms through the air and administered several vigorous kicks to his stomach. "What, my lady? Is this how you would repay your rescuer?"

She responded to his voice with a gurgle, and her eyes focused on his face. The tiny lips uptilted in a winsome smile. He caught one of the swinging fists, dwarfing it with his own. The delicate pink fingers curled around his thumb with a grasp not easily broken.

"You are strong for a wench, my lady Genevieve. Genevieve. 'Tis a mouthful of a name for a wee thing like you. Mayhap I shall call you Jenny. What think you of that?"

Jenny cooed, and Jaufre could have sworn she understood. He placed one hand behind her neck and was beginning to lift her back into the basket when he was startled by Melyssan calling his name.

"Jaufre! What are you doing?" She appeared at the entry of the garden, astonishment reflected in her green eyes. He flushed bright red, fearing she might have overheard the nonsense he had been crooning to the child. He thrust Jenny into her arms.

"I was but doing the work that wet nurse you hired seems incapable of," he said, annoyed by the defensive edge he heard creeping into his voice. "I am weary of hearing the child scream from cock's crow to dusk."

Melyssan examined Jenny as if she sought for marks upon her body. He placed his hands upon his hips and glared, hurt and anger warring inside of him. How dare she behave as if she believed he would do some hurt to a helpless infant, let alone his own daughter!

"You have undone her swaddling," she pronounced at last in accusing tones.

"Swaddling? Is that what you call it? I more wondered what crime the child was guilty of that she should be made a prisoner at so tender an age."

Melyssan bent down to retrieve the discarded linen bandage, trying to hide her disappointment. When she had first come upon Jaufre holding the child, she had dared hope he was beginning to accept Genevieve just a little. But how could he make jest of something that was important to the babe's well-being?

She laid Jenny in the basket, preparing to rebind her. The babe's face puckered, dark clouds gathering in her eyes as she drew a shivering breath, the preliminary to an ear-splitting howl.

Jaufre reached down and caught Melyssan by the wrist. His brows snapped together in a frown. "Nay, you shall not truss her up like that again."

"But my lord..." She looked from his determined face to her helpless daughter squirming in the basket. "I must. All babes are swaddled. If they were not, their limbs would not grow strong and straight."

"That is nonsense. I absolutely forbid it. I take no pleasure in listening to her scream."

"Pleasure?" Melyssan wrenched her wrist free. "Then I shall take her where you need never be disturbed. But my daughter shall not grow up to be a cripple."

"She will not, if you leave her alone. I warn you now, if I catch anyone binding her up like that again, I will send them packing from this castle."

"Including me?" she whispered, tears pricking at her eyes. But he was already striding away. The bandage fell from her fingers as she sank to the ground beside the basket. She had heard that implacable note in Jaufre's voice before. He meant what he said.

"What shall we do, Genevieve?" she asked, biting down upon her quivering lip. "He will not heed me. 'Twould seem my fears, my wishes, are unimportant to my lord."

She bent over the basket, gently stroking the babe's petal-soft cheek. Jenny's hands entwined in her hair, tugging on the long nutmeg strands that had lost their luster. She had looked at herself in the mirror only that morning. She was no longer attractive, she told herself, having grown paler, her eyes duller, since her confinement.

"He is weary of me, that is what 'tis. Weary of his honorable marriage." Carefully Melyssan disengaged the babe's fists from her hair, marveling at the child's strength. A strength she was terrified would be lost if Jaufre forbade the swaddling. If Genevieve had been a boy, the earl would never have behaved thus. How could he vent his disappointment upon their innocent daughter?

"Oh, little one. I prayed that if only I was patient, his feelings would change in time. At least he might have learned to love you." A great sob tore free from her throat, her hot tears dropping upon the child's shirt. "But he does not care. He will never care for either one of us."

Chapter 15

THE RED-GOLD BEAUTY of autumn gave way before the first icy breath of winter. December's chilling winds blanketed the ground with a light cover of sparkling snow until Winterbourne's white stone battlements resembled a great palace of ice carved out of the frozen ground.

Melyssan scurried through the great hall, supervising the squires as they decorated for the Christmas Eve feast. The walls were already bedecked with garlands of holly so thick it appeared as if the forest had overrun Winterbourne. She paced the length of the hall, still dissatisfied, calling for the pages to bring forth more ivy, hoping the bright greenery would dispel the sense of foreboding hanging over Winterbourne. It was the season of peace, goodwill toward men, yet only that morning she had seen Jaufre honing the edge of his sword.

She frowned at the chatter of the squires perched above her on their ladders. Roland grumbled to Arric, "What foolishness! I would be better employed practicing with the quintain. Of a certainty, we will be commanded to sail for Normandy any day now."

"Aye," agreed Arric. "How I long to give those Frenchmen a taste of my steel." He executed an imaginary thrust that nearly toppled him from his ladder.

"Hah!" Roland snorted. "You'd best take

care you don't swallow so much of *their* steel that you end up drinking your own blood."

"Roland! Arric!" Melyssan said sharply. "Mind what you are doing and cease all this talk of killing. 'Tis—'tis Christmas, and I will not tolerate it."

"Aye, my lady." Arric sulked, hanging his head.

But Roland clambered down the ladder to prostrate himself on one knee. "My lady, I crave your pardon. I had forgotten you were nearby or never would words have escaped my lips so offensive to a woman's delicate sensibilities."

Despite herself, Melyssan smiled. "You are forgiven, Roland. Do get up. If you truly have more pressing affairs to attend to elsewhere, you may go. I am sure Arric will be pleased to help me hang the mistletoe," she added, forestalling that young man's eager attempt to leap to the ground and follow Roland.

Crestfallen, Arric remounted the ladder. Roland's face split into a triumphant grin before he swept Melyssan a magnificent bow, then raced from the hall as if in fear she would change her mind.

Just as she handed Arric the first boughs of mistletoe, Father Andrew emerged from the chapel. He crossed the hall to where she stood, pursing his lips in disapproval. "I trust you will not bring any of that near the altar, my lady. 'Twould not be fitting. Those pallid berries come from the same kind of tree fashioned into the cross upon which our Lord was crucified."

Melyssan gave the priest an apologetic glance as she stretched to hand Arric another sprig. "I know 'tis pagan to decorate with mistletoe, Father. But I've been told it symbolizes reconciliation, that all past grievances are forgiven. Would that it might have some effect upon all these foolish men and turn their thoughts from battle."

Arric grimaced down at her as he hammered the mistletoe into place. Father Andrew steadied the ladder, which wobbled underneath the stalwart young squire. The frown lines around the priest's mouth relaxed. "Well, I shall pardon you for observing heathen customs this one time. Who is to say? Your mistletoe may bring you luck this evening, may bring about a reconciliation you are not expecting."

Melyssan regarded Father Andrew in surprise. His pale blue eyes twinkled, but he refused to tell her anything more. She was still puzzling over his meaning as she made her way upstairs.

A reconciliation she was not expecting. What could Father Andrew possibly mean? Mentally she reviewed the list of guests who had traveled to spend Christmas at Winterbourne...Lord Oswin, a powerful baron with estates near York...Sir Hugh and Lady Gunnor, newly returned from their exile in Ireland after King John had pardoned Gunnor's brother for offending him during the interdict...

She had no need of reconciliation with any of these. She could only think of one person whose estrangement from her must be obvious to the old priest. Oft she had sensed Father Andrew studying her when she and Jaufre would exit from the hall after supper each evening, her arm placed on top of her husband's with stiff formality. The priest along with everyone else at Winterbourne could have no difficulty in guessing how strained had become her relationship with the earl.

Like all the men, Jaufre was caught up in preparations for the impending war with France, as though nothing else were important to him. She had made a mistake once, blurting out that she prayed each day the cowardly king would change his mind, cancel the invasion. She could not bear to risk losing Jaufre in battle, not even for him to fulfill his oath regarding Clairemont. Then she had wept. Although Jaufre had comforted her, she realized she had closed one more door between them. He retreated behind a wall of silence, keeping whatever he knew of the king's plans to himself.

Ah, if only she and Jaufre could heal the breach between them. If he could forgive her for presenting him with a worthless daughter, she could pardon him for giving her honor when she wanted love. Then they could stand under the mistletoe, exchanging the kiss of peace, a kiss that might deepen into something warmer.

Sighing at the thought, she stepped inside her bedchamber. She was surprised to find Nelda and Jenny's nurse, Canice, peeking at something spread across the bed. When they saw Melyssan, the two women straightened, giggling.

Before she had a chance to question them, she was startled by a rustling sound. She jumped back as something shot toward her. Jenny crawled forward, seizing the hem of Melyssan's gown, her pixieish face beaming beneath her linen coif.

"Ah, by St. Genevieve," Canice wailed. "The child has crept out of her basket again." She bustled forward to swoop up the babe, but Jenny already nestled in her mother's arms, endeavoring to chew upon the gold chain Melyssan wore around her neck.

Melyssan chuckled. "I think you must give over trying to keep Jenny confined to the basket." She regarded her daughter with pride. Was there any other child who at the age of six months could scoot across the floor at such an alarming rate of speed? Despite the earl's unheard-of command that the babe should not be swaddled, Jenny's limbs grew apace, chubby and strong.

"I am sorry, my lady," said Canice. "I try to watch her, truly I do. But whoever heard of a babe performing such feats!"

"Just keep her up off the rushes until she can walk." Melyssan hugged the child before carrying her over to the bed. She nearly laid the babe down upon the shimmering folds of the most lovely gown of blue samite she'd ever beheld.

"What—what—where...?" she stammered.

"Oh, my lady, Lord Jaufre left it here for you,"

Nelda said. "We have been dying, waiting for you to come and find it."

Stunned, Melyssan handed Jenny to Canice. With trembling fingers she raised the gown, touching the silk to her cheek. The long train cascaded to the floor, sparkling as the firelight glinted upon the threads of gold woven through the dark blue silk. Jenny clapped her hands, letting out an "ooooo" of delight.

Nelda sighed. "What a beautiful gown! I would sell my soul for such a one. I only pray that when I marry, my husband will prove as generous."

"A-aye," Melyssan agreed. "I must go and thank my lord at once."

As she hurried from the room, clutching the silken lengths in front of her, her pulse raced with a new hope she could not deny. It was the first sign of favor Jaufre had shown her since Jenny's birth. Did it mean he was no longer as displeased with her?

She found the earl alone in the solar, seated in his carved armchair. Shyly, she stepped forward until she faced him across the oaken table.

"My lord, the gown! How shall I thank you? 'Tis lovely, far too elegant for me. You should not have. I know you have been trying to save every penny for rebuilding Winterbourne."

"As long as the king remains obdurate, it matters naught." Jaufre frowned, scarcely looking up from the letter he was reading. "I would not have you attend the Christmas feast looking like a beggar. 'Tis a man's duty to provide well for his wife."

She lowered the gown, her pleasure in the gift fleeing before the cutting edge of his words. His duty? Aye, she could almost see him marking the entry in his accounts. *Christmas gifts. Forty-three knights: one linen cloak, saddle, and blue tunic each. Wife: one gown with matching belt.* The shining folds of gold-shot fabric suddenly lost some of their luster.

"Well, I thank you, all the same," she whispered.

He did not notice when she backed away from him, preparing to slip out of the room. His attention was all for the letter, his face pale, somber. Then the parchment turned in his hands, and she saw it. The heavy royal seal. She shivered. It was as if she could feel the icy fingers of John Plantagenet once more creeping into their lives.

"Is it—is it more news of the war?" she asked, not wanting to know, yet unable to stop herself.

He glanced up as if surprised to find her still there. "Nothing that need concern you, Lyssa. Do not worry. Leave these matters to me."

"But I only wondered—"

"Tend to the feast, my lady," he said harshly. "And you will have enough to occupy your thoughts."

She nodded, white-lipped, and left the room. As he watched her go, Jaufre cursed himself for his cowardice. *Naught to concern you.* What a liar he was. He crumpled the letter in his fist, the letter commanding him to be in London before the New Year. The king's armada was being readied to set sail.

Why had he not told Melyssan the truth? He had never feared a woman's tears before. He had seen Yseult put on some impassioned displays of weeping, such as would have melted the most hard-hearted warrior. She had only made Jaufre feel uncomfortable. Ah, but Melyssan! He could scarce endure the way her tears trickled down one by one as though her heart were breaking by inches, her pain becoming his own.

It was all the more difficult since he had no more desire to leave her than she a wish to have him go. The thought popped unbidden into his head. Who would be harmed if the oath to retake Clairemont remained unfulfilled? Raoul de Macy was dead.

No! Jaufre rubbed his palm across his forehead. What was he—a knight of honor or some cravenly fat merchant seeking to find ways of remaining by his fire? Damn Melyssan for her beauty, which thus tempted him to break his word.

He would go, follow the king to Normandy, fight...mayhap die. He would tell Melyssan... but not yet. At least they might enjoy this, possibly their last Christmas together. Jaufre turned to the hearth, consigning the king's letter to the flames.

Perhaps Jenny was not the longed-for heir, the future earl of Winterbourne, but Melyssan's

365

head arched with pride as she carried her daughter into the great hall. She determined to be happy, at peace upon this blessed eve of the Christ child's birth, put from her mind all thoughts of war, King John...and Jaufre's coldness.

The large chamber rumbled with the merriment of the earl's tenants, assembled to offer their yearly gifts of bread, hens, and ale, all the while smacking their lips in anticipation of the Christmas dinner to come. The good folk fell back respectfully as Melyssan passed among them, the women curtsying and cooing over Jenny, who regarded them with a complacent smile as if such homage were her due.

"Such a little beauty," gushed Lady Gunnor. "The image of His Lordship."

"Aye, she is," Melyssan said as she studied the dark curl drooping over Jenny's forehead, the same midnight shade as Jaufre's, the large round eyes that had deepened to the earl's rich shade of brown.

Gunnor's plump face grew wistful, and her eyes misted. "And to think that dark night you helped us to escape, my own Tom was just such a babe. Who would ever have thought you and I would meet again under such happy circumstances?"

"'Tis wonderful, Gunnor," Melyssan said. "I am so pleased that you could come home to Penhurst at last."

At the sound of male laughter ringing from the hearthside of the hall, Jenny wrenched her body around trying to see, nearly upsetting Melyssan's balance. Faith, but the child was an armful. It required both hands to keep hold of Jenny, which left none for the support of her cane.

Jenny craned her neck, her joyful crow telling Melyssan she had singled out Jaufre's voice even in the room full of men. It was amazing how the babe would perk up when her father was near, although Jaufre never paid her the least attention.

"I understand, little one," Melyssan whispered close to the child's ear. "'Tis the same for me." She often thought she could bear his present indifference better if only she had never known what it was like to be touched by him, feel his kiss burn upon her lips, be enfolded in the demanding strength of his arms. Some nights her longing for him grew so keen, she spent the hours until dawn gripping her arms tight against her body in restraint lest she throw herself at his feet and beg him to love her.

The same desire nigh overwhelmed her as she spotted him now, listening to Lord Oswin expound at length. Jaufre's dark hair brushed against the neckline of his long-sleeved tunic of rose-hued sendal, stretched taut over his broad shoulders. A long-tongued belt of silver hugged his waist, accenting the narrow leanness of his hips, where rested one heavily ringed hand. He stood taller than most of the men, wearing that moody look of detachment she had come to know all too well of late.

He watched unsmiling as the pages dragged forth the yule log, a giant section from the trunk of an ash tree, whose end was fitted into the hearth and ignited.

"'Twill be good luck if they keep it burning throughout the twelve days of Christmas," Gunnor said. "Your Ladyship must then take care the ashes are not thrown out. They have magical properties of fertility."

"I'll wager the earl has magical properties of his own without needing any old ash," said one of the men, setting up a roar of ribald laughter.

Gunnor blustered, "I was speaking of the earth, not my lady."

Not my lady indeed, Melyssan thought, her cheeks burning as her eyes suddenly locked with Jaufre's. How could a woman be fertile when she was so infrequently touched by her husband? Even when Jaufre did reach for her in the darkness, he pulled her close roughly, his lovemaking swift, unwilling, as though he sought to confine a desire that had escaped the bounds of reason. When done, he would quickly draw away to his side of the bed, silent, staring up at the canopy overhead. Was his mind filled with regret, or was she of so little importance that other thoughts immediately crowded her out?

Her speculations ended as she saw Jaufre start to cross the room with slow, measured tread. But he appeared to have great difficulty in escaping the talkative Lord Oswin, who trailed after him.

Melyssan froze, her hands tightening on Jenny as snatches of the baron's words drifted to her above the hubbub of the crowd.

"King John...need to revive the old charter. Danger of...following him to war in France...only way to preserve our...lives."

Were they speaking of the letter that had so absorbed Jaufre earlier that afternoon? The letter whose contents he had refused to divulge? Melyssan tried to fight it, but the same feeling of dread that had been stalking her all day seized her in its chilling grip.

Jaufre shrugged aside whatever Lord Oswin told him with such vehement gestures. He continued forward, planting himself in front of Melyssan.

"My lady, I am pleased you deigned to join us for the feast."

His words mocked her, but the hand that stroked her cheek was gentle. He did not spare Jenny so much as a glance, but the babe was determined not to be ignored. Before Melyssan could prevent it, Jenny lunged forward. Growling like a playful bear cub, she seized two large handfuls of Jaufre's beard. His eyes watering with pain, Jaufre swore, trying to pry open the babe's grasping fingers.

"No, no, Jenny. Naughty," Melyssan said, pulling the child back.

The onlooking guests howled with delight. "By the rood," Lord Oswin called out, "this soft domestic life has undone the Dark Knight when he can be brought to his knees by a mere babe."

"No swaddling," said one of the women. "No wonder the child acts so wild. Heaven knows what she will be when she is grown."

Tugging his head free, Jaufre glared first at the portly dame who had spoken, then at Melyssan. "Why isn't the child abed? Take her there at once."

"I—I am sorry, my lord," Melyssan stammered. "Please. I only brought her down to see the yule log." Melyssan soothed back the curl from Jenny's brow. The babe's tiny face puckered, looking stunned by her father's angry tone.

"Well, now she has seen it." Jaufre rubbed his chin. "Take her back to her nurse. She has no place at this feast."

"But...aye, my lord." Melyssan curtsied, swallowing any further attempts to reason with her husband. Holding her head up as best she might, she exited from the hall, deeply conscious of the sympathetic glances cast her way from many of the ladies. It helped matters not at all when Jenny set up a loud wail.

Suppressing her own desire to join the child, Melyssan carried her daughter back to the chamber the babe shared with Canice. But when the young woman bustled forward, Melyssan waved her aside. She rocked Jenny herself, crooning snatches of old songs until the babe quieted; then she lowered her into the carved oak cradle draped with a canopy of white sarcenet.

"My poor little one," she murmured, tucking a fur coverlet around Jenny, whose long dark lashes began to droop against the curve of her cheeks. Never had Jaufre shown his dislike for the babe so strongly. Melyssan's shoulders sagged. She knew too well what it was like to grow up in the shadow of a parent's hatred. She would give much to spare Jenny such pain.

By the time she returned to the great hall, the guests were taking their places at the tables. Jaufre was offering Sir Hugh and Lady Gunnor a place above the salt. The earl quirked an eyebrow at the couple, who squirmed guiltily in his presence. "Come, my friends. This time have a place of honor at my board. Unless you prefer sitting amongst the pilgrims?"

"N-nay, my lord, I thank you," Sir Hugh said with a sheepish smile as he led Gunnor to their seats.

Jaufre glanced in Melyssan's direction and beckoned her imperiously to his side, making no further comment upon her tardiness. He could sense the tension in her as she settled into her chair. Was she distressed because of the incident with Jenny?

Now that his anger had faded, it was all he could do to suppress a smile, although the roots of his beard still tingled. He could see now the dangers inherent in that little game he had taught his daughter. Oft when the nurse presumed Jenny to be napping, he would slip in, bending over the babe's cradle to play with her. Growling fiercely, he pretended to nip at Jenny's flailing fists. It had amused him greatly when the babe had begun to imitate his growl, latching on to his beard. But by St. George, the child waxed too strong for such sport. When she grew older, she might...

When she grew older, he might no longer be alive. Jaufre's thoughts turned involuntarily to the summons he had received from the king. His eyes rested upon Melyssan's honey-brown hair bound up so demurely within a net of pearls. He was seized by a sudden longing to take her out of this crowd of chattering fools. The blue silk he had selected with such care became her well, clinging to the soft swell of her breasts. Motherhood had ripened her, softened her curves, turning a lovely young girl into a most desirable woman. Leaving for France would be so much easier if his need for her were not so strong. No matter how he fought the feeling, he wanted nothing more than to pass the night lost in her gentle embrace, praying the morrow would never come.

When Melyssan risked a peek at Jaufre, she half expected to find his face dark with annoyance. She surprised a look in his eyes of such brooding melancholy as shattered the calm demeanor she sought to maintain.

"My lord. What—what is it?" She pressed his hand under the table, but at that moment four pages entered bearing aloft a huge boar's head upon a silver platter. Jaufre composed his features into a polite mask, withdrawing his hand as the feast began.

Venison, partridges, hares, lampreys, swans,

peacocks, dried fruit pudding...As the succession of dishes was paraded before the guests in the banquet hall, Melyssan complimented herself that she had done well in planning the feast. Neither lord nor villein would rise from the table complaining of the earl of Winterbourne's parsimony. Although she had little appetite for the quantity of food Jaufre heaped upon her trencher, she gaped in astonishment at the amount Jaufre consumed. He appeared to have little relish for any of the dishes, but he partook heartily of everything...like a man devouring his last meal.

The crowd grew more boisterous as the bowl of hot mulled cider passed from hand to hand. Cries of "Wassail!" were answered with the lusty shout of "Drink hale!" More than one face appeared flushed with conviviality as the guests rose from the table. Jaufre gave the signal for the pages to clear away the trestle benches so that the dancing might begin. In paraded the musicians garbed in red cloaks of sendal, playing trumpets, sackbutts, cornets, and reed pipes.

As the couples formed a line down the length of the hall, Melyssan slipped off to one side. She saw that she was not the only one seeking to avoid the dance. Roland leaned up against one of the arches, his arms folded across the front of his new golden surcoat trimmed with sable.

He straightened up with a courteous bow as Melyssan approached him. "Roland, why do you linger here? I vow you look so handsome tonight, there will be many a maiden with broken heart if you do not join in the dancing."

His lips twitched into the semblance of a smile. "Better a broken heart than a broken ankle. Dancing is the one area where I do not excel. As to my handsomeness, I fear Your Ladyship is dazzled by the clothing your husband has seen fit to place upon my back."

"The surcoat was a gift from Lord Jaufre?"

"Only one of many. I have been favored beyond belief this Christmas. A surcoat, a sword, iron boots, a coat of double-woven mail..."

Melyssan gave a shaky laugh. "My faith! 'Twould seem he expected you to march off to do battle tomorrow."

"Doubtless he wishes that I would." The young man hunched a shoulder, affecting a careless attitude as if to show it mattered naught to him.

She captured one of his hands, taking it gently between her own. "Nay, Roland. My lord is pleased to have you at Winterbourne. He would not give you such costly gifts if he had no pride in you."

Roland's haughty expression wavered, allowing an unaccustomed look of wistfulness to creep into his eyes. "I—I would be satisfied with much less. Fewer gifts given with more affection other than a sense of duty."

She opened her mouth to reassure him but found she could not speak. Each rustle of the silk gown whispered to her, reminding her that she felt the same.

"You are the only one who cares about me," he continued in a rush of emotion. He raised her hand to his lips. "I will serve you all the days of my life, Lady Melyssan."

A hand clamped down on Roland's shoulder. Melyssan looked up into Jaufre's stony brown eyes. She wondered how long he had stood listening to them.

"Since you are so eager to serve," he said to Roland, "you may begin by leading Lord Oswin's daughter into the dance."

Roland's nose wrinkled in distaste as he looked at the damsel to whom the earl gestured. The pert blonde gave him a toothy smile, furiously batting her eyelashes.

"Well, mayhap I will," Roland said grimly. "Any wench who grins like that at a man deserves to have her toes trampled. ...My lady." Ignoring the earl, Roland swept Melyssan a deep bow before departing.

"The whelp is still full of disrespect," Jaufre said. "But at least he is obedient, which is more than I can say for you, my lady."

Melyssan's eyes widened. "How have I defied you, my lord?"

He slipped his arm about her waist, his lips twitching into a half smile, a smile that did nothing to lighten the sadness in his eyes. "I told you not to worry. Yet too oft tonight have I seen that lovely face pinched with apprehension."

"'Tis difficult," she said in a small voice, "when I fear there is something you are keeping from me."

"Then I shall give it to you now. I fear I have sadly neglected you of late." A light glinted in his eyes, his expression far warmer than any he had worn of late. Her heart began to pound faster.

He pulled her into the shadow of the archway, his mouth claiming hers in rough embrace. The noise of the crowd faded as she responded to his passion, both stirred and frightened by the quality of desperation in his kiss. Suddenly, she knew.

She tipped her head back, her face inches from his own. "You're going to leave me," she whispered. "The letter—"

He nodded, pressing kisses upon her brow, her cheeks.

"How—how soon?"

"We shall have Christmas," he murmured against her ear. "Then, the day after..."

"Jaufre!" She flung her arms about his neck, burrowing her face into his shoulder.

He held her close, patted her back. "I have already sent for Tristan to return from Ashlar. He will look after Winterbourne in my absence. You and the child will be safe."

She drew away from him, wiping at the wetness on her cheeks. "And what of you?"

He chucked her under the chin, attempting a teasing laugh. "I shall do fine. What, Lyssa? Where has your faith in romance gone? You would have me be Sir Launcelot, yet keep me on a leash at your side, never let me loose to slay the dragons."

"I liked it better when the dragons were imaginary." She caught her lip between her teeth. "You go to fight with King John, but I trust him not. He once swore to see you dead. I would not put it beyond him to—"

The rest of her fear was silenced by a loud blast from a horn. The music stopped, a great roar of laughter erupting from the company. Jaufre linked his arm through Melyssan's, pulling her forward until she could see the cause of the mirth.

Father Christmas, garbed in a red robe open to the chest, cavorted into the center of the hall, a troop of mummers marching behind. The burly figure swooped upon the crowd, stealing kisses from the blushing ladies. As he planted a smacking buss upon her cheek, Melyssan saw that it was Sir Dreyfan, the face beneath his grizzled beard flushed from too much wassailing, a crown of holly tipped over his brow.

He doubled over in an attempted bow for Jaufre, then wove on his feet. Laughing, Arric rushed forward to straighten him.

Dreyfan nearly knocked the squire over as he flung wide his arms. "Gather round, my lords, my ladies. These mummers come for your pleasure to present the wondrous tale of how St. George did battle with that scurvy knave, the Bold Slasher."

Melyssan held back, but Jaufre placed his arm about her shoulder, whispering in her ear, "Nay, Lyssa, we will have time for the sadness of parting later. Forget King John and the war tonight. Enjoy the Christmas play. Let me see you smile."

She tried to comply, but her lips felt numb. Even the mummers, whose antics had delighted her ever since she was a child, took on sinister overtones, their painted masks and fringed tunics appearing garish, threatening, under the wax torchlights.

She watched the buffoonery of the Quack Doctor, unable to join in the chuckles of her guests. Applause broke out when St. George strode onto the scene, preparing to do battle with the evil Turkish knight, Bold Slasher. The mock duel with blunted swords caused Melyssan to shudder. Something in the movements of the tall, thin mummer playing St. George disturbed her, an elusive memory hovering just out of reach. She wondered which of the castle household he was, but she would never know. It was considered bad luck to unmask.

St. George took much the worst of the battle, nearly dropping his weapon. Melyssan saw Jaufre lean forward and heard him comment to Lord Oswin, "If the true St. George had handled his weapon so ineptly, England would still be beset with dragons."

Lord Oswin guffawed, spraying out drops of the wine he had just tasted.

St. George went down, slain by a mighty blow from the Bold Slasher, to the accompaniment of hisses from the crowd. But as the story had gone, year after year, the Quack Doctor bent over the fallen knight, pressing between his lips the magic pill. Up sprang St. George, bowing as the company cheered wildly. The triumph of life over death. Melyssan's hands moved together in wooden clapping. If only it were that easy. What if Jaufre should...She closed her eyes, refusing to let the thought enter her mind.

When she opened them, she saw most of the mummers dancing off to receive their portion of mead. Only St. George lingered, his white hand moving toward his mask.

"Look!" Nelda shrieked. "He's going to show his face."

A hush fell over the gathering as the mummer broke the age-old custom of concealment. Slipping off his mask, he raised his head to stare defiantly at the crowd.

"Whitney!" Melyssan cried. Her exclamation was not very loud, but her brother appeared to have heard it, his green eyes scanning the assembled faces until he found hers.

Still reeling from the shock, she felt Father Andrew take her by the elbow, leading her gently until she stood under the archway with the mistletoe.

"Remember, my lady," he said, "your words to me this morning. Reconciliation, all past grievances forgiven."

Then he stepped back. All eyes turned on her brother as Whitney walked slowly to where she stood. Over a year it had been since she had seen him ride away from Winterbourne, vowing she would be his sister no more. He had not deigned to see her again, angry when she had wed Lord Jaufre, sending her a letter filled with unforgivable insults against her husband.

Now he looked so much older. There was something in his eyes, a look of resignation, bitter wisdom, the sensitive set of his mouth a little harder than she remembered.

They stared at each other for long moments before Whitney spoke. "I—I have come to see if you can...forgive me, Lyssa."

Her throat constricted too much for her to speak. She flung wide her arms. Whitney swooped her up, lifting her off her feet as he hugged her close. Through the mist of her tears, she saw Father Andrew dabbing at his own eyes.

When Whitney at last released her, she kissed the priest's gaunt cheek. "Thank you, Father. 'Twas the most beautiful Christmas gift I could have received."

She heard the guests murmuring, some with approval, others still complaining about Whitney's unmasking. Clasping his hand, she gazed fondly at her brother. "Aye, you foolish fellow. Now ill fortune may befall you. Were you so unsure of your welcome within my walls that you crept in disguised?"

"Well..." Whitney hesitated. "Not yours so much as..."

"As mine, mayhap?" rumbled a familiar deep voice.

The joy Melyssan felt over the reunion with her brother fled before Jaufre's unsmiling eyes. She felt the shade of Jaufre's dead brother pass between them. Godric, whose treachery Whitney brought to mind.

Whitney stiffened, but she kept hold of his hand, leading him forward. "My—my lord, will you not welcome my brother?"

Jaufre's arms folded across his chest, his face as expressionless as granite. Then he relented enough to slowly extend his hand.

Whitney made no move to clasp it. "Before you offer me your hand, my lord, you should know that I seek more than a welcome for Christmas. I would undertake to serve with you, acknowledge you as my liege lord."

Jaufre's eyes narrowed with suspicion. "'Tis well known that your family owes fealty to the baron de Scoville."

"No longer." Whitney's jaw tightened. "The baron died a fortnight ago. The king has taken possession of his lands."

The crowd buzzed with the news. "How can that be?" Sir Dreyfan roared out. "The baron had a son, had he not?"

"A son only nine years of age. The king has taken the boy from his mother. He will act as his guardian."

"And we all know what that means." Lord Oswin's red mustache bristled with indignation. "Estates bled white so that by his majority, the lad will have little to inherit...if he lives that long."

Whitney's gaze returned to Melyssan. "It also means the king has taken control of the baron's fiefs. He has reapportioned Wydevale Manor to one of his courtiers."

At Melyssan's dismayed gasp, he gave her hand a reassuring squeeze. "'Tis all right,

Lyssa. Our parents are safe. They have gone to live with Enid."

Wydevale Manor gone. Taken by the king. Melyssan tried to summon up some feeling of regret for the home of her childhood, but she could not. She remembered few happy days there. But she grieved for Whitney's sake. All his prospects of inheritance whisked away at a tyrant's pleasure.

The guests muttered angrily, sympathy veering toward Whitney. Jaufre said nothing, his eyes hooded, concealing whatever he thought of the dire tidings.

"The king has no regard for the rules of fealty," one knight shouted. "Whose land is safe, I'd like to know?"

Sir Hugh plucked nervously at the ends of his beard. "Master Whitney could appeal to the courts of law. Mayhap the king misunderstood the circumstances. I am sure His Majesty is just."

"Just?" Lord Oswin sneered. "How just did you think it when you were driven from your castle for a year, simply because some monk from Boarshead decided to defy the king—"

"Swineshead," Lady Gunnor piped up indignantly. "My brother is with the Cistercian order at Swineshead."

Lord Oswin's heavy brows drew together as he scowled at her. "What is the difference? The thrust of the matter is you were unjustly exiled through no fault of your own."

"Nay." Sir Hugh mopped his sweating

brow, glancing about as if he expected to find the king's spies lurking beneath the rushes. "Our family had offended the king. But we don't mean to get ourselves exiled to the wilds of Ireland ever again. Neither Gunnor nor I will do or say anything to cause His Majesty displeasure."

Gunnor blushed, looking slightly ashamed of her husband's pronouncement.

"And do all the rest of you feel the same?" Lord Oswin leapt upon one of the stools, commanding the attention of the room. "Will you all bow and scrape yourselves into the ground, trying not to offend the king?"

"Step down, my lord," Jaufre said dryly. "The mummers provided enough entertainment."

"Nay, de Macy." Oswin straightened his tunic, puffing out his chest. "There are things that must be said. How much longer will we endure this tyranny, my friends? England was not always thus. There was a time, in our great-grandfathers' day, when men had liberties, the charter of good King Henry, laws to protect the widowed and orphaned."

"Oh, God's feet!" Jaufre groaned. Whatever had possessed him to mention the Great Charter to a madman like Oswin? During the course of his visit, Oswin had talked of nothing else but the fabled document which he had never seen before. Like a fool, Jaufre had confessed to owning a copy. He had played the good host, permitting the baron to read it, much to his present sorrow. Jaufre elbowed his way through the guests, who were spellbound by Oswin's rhetoric.

"I tell you, my friends, this charter holds the wisdom of the ages. Rights and liberties which would restore England to the glorious days of Henry the First, of Alfred the Great, of—of..."

"Of Camelot?" Melyssan breathed, her eyes shining.

Jaufre glared at her as he pulled Lord Oswin from the stool. "My lord, you have had too much wine. Be calm, lest you do yourself grave harm."

"What harm, sir? I am trying to help you and all these good folk. There is a movement afoot, even now, to bring back that charter, force King John to renew those pledges, insure our rights."

"There are only two ways for a man to have rights in this world," Jaufre said, aware that Melyssan regarded him intently. "By this." He fingered the purse attached to his belt. "Or this." He unsheathed his sword.

He watched Melyssan's eyes cloud with disappointment, and a flush of anger surged up his neck. Would the woman never give over her notion that he was some sort of knight-errant, a champion who could right the wrongs of the world?

"The sword of the Dark Knight is well respected," Oswin said. "If you would but pledge it to the cause of the charter."

"My sword is already pledged to another cause," Jaufre snarled. "In two days' time, I leave to join the king's army in London."

Silence descended over the hall at Jaufre's announcement. Lord Oswin scowled. "So you are determined to participate in that folly, the king's pathetic attempt to retake Normandy, waste your money and men serving this tyrant—"

"That is correct." Jaufre slid his sword back into its sheath. "And I would take it as the greatest of courtesies if you would cease inciting my tenants to rebellion."

He turned a mocking eye upon Melyssan's brother. "Now, Whitney, are you still so eager to enter my service?"

Whitney paled. He swallowed hard, but when he replied his voice was steady. "Aye, my lord. I will follow wheresoever you command."

Jaufre's gaze swept over his assembled knights and squires. "And the rest of you?"

"Aye, my lord," chorused the masculine voices, not enthusiastic but firm. Lord Oswin stroked his mustache, shaking his head.

To Melyssan, it seemed as if Jaufre's announcement cast a pall over the rest of the evening. She rubbed her arms, shivering. It was as if the dread phantom she could feel lurking in the shadows now stepped into the open, doffing his shrouded hood to reveal the death's-head grin of war.

If only Jaufre had not dismissed Lord Oswin's words so lightly. That men should no longer have to walk in fear of the king's cruelty, suffer the sting of injustice! It was such a noble cause, one for which she would be proud to see her husband arm himself. Her young Sir Jaufre might have done so, she reflected sadly. But the earl of Winterbourne would ride cynically by the side of a monarch he despised, fight for lands he cared nothing about, to keep an oath all but he had forgotten.

The subdued guests gathered about the hearth, passing the ale and chestnuts, listening to Father Andrew tell legends of long ago. A holy beauty illuminated the age-lined face as he recounted how the beasts of the field bowed down in homage at the exact hour of the Christ child's birth.

But Melyssan's mind was consumed with other tales she had heard, bleak prophecies of death. She stared at the bearded faces around the hearth; their eyes were soft with a childlike wonder at the priest's tales, but the firelight bathed their faces in a red glow, the angry color of blood and battle.

Behind them, their shadows flickered on Winterbourne's dark walls, looming like black armed specters, waiting to claim the souls of the unwary. Melyssan's breath caught in her throat as one of the shadows bobbed down, appearing headless. Her old nurse had oft told her the superstition that on Christmas Eve, a headless shadow foretold of death in the coming year.

She tried to still her nervous qualms, telling herself the phenomenon had been caused by one of the men bending over. It was folly to tremble over such gloomy legends. Yet she could not forbear studying the faces, trying to ascertain who had cast that eerie shadow. Only three men occupied that side of the hall. Whitney, Roland, and…Jaufre.

Chapter 16

THE PALE SUN pierced the gray sky and sparkled on the choppy waves of the Channel just enough to dye it that strange shade of blue green. Just enough to remind Jaufre de Macy of her eyes as he leaned against the rail of the great single-masted ship bearing him away from England. Just enough. It did not take much to send his thoughts spinning back to Melyssan.

He remembered the last time he'd held her in his arms, how her golden-brown head had nestled against his naked shoulder. She'd slept at last, her face pale and streaked with the tracks of her tears after he had made love to her. Made love in silence because his heart had been too heavy for words. He'd been too much of a coward to bid her final farewell, so he'd eased her away from him and slipped out of their bed in the shadowy hours of dawn. She'd looked so small, fragile, lying alone on the large mattress, her knees curling in toward her stomach as she shivered when deprived of his warmth. He'd tucked the furs around her, brushing a kiss across her brow.

Never had leaving anyone come so hard to him. If he had not persuaded Tristan to remain and take command at Winterbourne...Jaufre could still see the angry dismay on his friend's face when he had issued the order as they'd prepared to mount their horses in the courtyard....

"I did not summon you to follow me to France, Tristan. I want you to remain here at Winterbourne."

"So you have suggested several times before," Tristan said, checking his saddle girth. "Now, as then, I mean to ignore you."

"It's not a suggestion. It's a command."

Tristan's lips tightened. "Dreyfan is here. He will command the garrison. You have left the defense of Winterbourne to him before." He prepared to vault into the saddle, but Jaufre's hand clamped down on his wrist, gripping the flesh to the bone.

"I was not thinking of Winterbourne, Tristan. I trust no one as I do you. But Lyssa, Jenny...Without you looking after them, I do not think I can leave."

He shrank from the probing stare Tristan turned in his direction. Releasing his friend's wrist, he peered through the early dawn haze at the white stone wall behind which he knew Melyssan slept.

"So now you see." Jaufre scuffed the toe of his boot in the dirt. "I've once more permitted a woman to make half a man of me."

"Nay, my lord. This woman has made you whole again."

Had she? Jaufre wondered. Then why did he feel as if he were being torn asunder?

"My friend, all I ask of you," he said, "is to give me the peace of mind to concentrate upon what I must do in France. If I should fall in battle or be captured—I must know Melyssan and Jenny are in safe hands here at Winterbourne. Safe from the king." And then, setting aside his pride in a way foreign to him, he made his command a plea. "Please."

He knew he had won when Tristan's shoulders slumped.

"Arric!" called the knight. "Summon one of the grooms to unsaddle my horse. I won't be needing him." He turned back to Jaufre and nodded, assuring his friend without words that Melyssan and Jenny would be protected while life remained in him.

Jaufre clasped Tristan roughly in his arms, then vaulted into the saddle, leading his entourage through the gates of Winterbourne without looking back....

Without looking back, as he would be wise to do now, he thought. He braced himself against the roll of the ship, tugging his sable-lined mantle of red Irish cloth closer for protection against the bite of the icy winter wind. But try as he would, his eyes were drawn toward Portsmouth harbor, lost in the fog; the entire English shoreline was shrouded in mist, ethereal, like one of those imaginary lands in the ballads Lyssa sang to Jenny.

He had never before been disturbed by such feelings of melancholy upon leaving a place.

Strange, these emotions of pride and sadness that stirred inside of him, as if he were no longer simply the earl of Winterbourne, but belonged to all of England. The distant shores of France, Normandy, and Clairemont seemed more and more alien.

Was this all Melyssan's doing, caused by the knowledge that he left her behind on this misty island world? Without half realizing it, he mumbled aloud the words to an old poem, "Whoever becomes too deeply in love and cannot tear himself away, loses his soul."

"I don't believe that," piped up a voice beside him.

Too late Jaufre realized that his son had come to join him in leaning over the deck rail. "And what is your version of love, halfling?"

Roland's silver eyes took on a dreamy quality as he stared out at the whitecaps on the water. "Why, 'tis an ennobling emotion. A knight is incomplete without it. Love of a lady is what gives a man courage."

Jaufre's mouth curved in a smile. "Ah, the gilded eyes of youth."

"Sometimes they see clearer than those of ancient graybeards."

"Mayhap you are right." Self-consciously Jaufre fingered the ends of his own black beard, then laughed and clapped Roland on the back.

Roland put a hand to his shoulder, his eyes widening. "I—I think that is the first time you ever touched me when you were not seeking to restrain me or box my ears."

Jaufre shrugged. "I seem to be in a strangely mellow humor this morning."

They stood some while in silence, watching the shore recede, until Roland cleared his throat. "I trust you do not mind my company. Whitney is on yon opposite side doubled over the rail. If I had to watch him being sick one more time, I swear I would be tempted to join him."

"Spare me the details." Jaufre grimaced. He had never believed Whitney would have come this far. He had flung out the invitation to follow him as a challenge and had expected to be refused. But the man had come, and to his great aggravation, Jaufre felt responsible for him. Melyssan was apt not to forgive him if he allowed something to happen to her weak-willed brother.

Roland shaded his eyes with his hand and gazed into the distance at the other billowing masts of the English armada. "My lord, since you are disposed to be *mellow*, mayhap I might ask you a question."

"You might, although I cannot promise I will be able to answer it."

"What think you of this army the king has assembled?"

Jaufre frowned. Very few nobles besides himself had responded to the king's muster. Most of the troops consisted of low-born soldiers, mercenaries, and freemen. But what were such without knights and great lords to lead them?

"We are many in number," he hedged.

"Enough to win? Think you that we shall win?" Roland's brow wrinkled in anxiety.

Win? thought Jaufre. That indeed was the question of a youth about to face his first battle. How did one begin to explain to this fresh-faced lad that there was no such thing as winning where war was concerned? A castle might be taken one day and lost the next week. Men died or were maimed for life, and the most that could be wished for was to survive and hang on to what was rightfully yours in the greedy press of grasping men. Jaufre blinked at his own cynicism. At one time he had lived for the excitement of battle, thought there was no more noble and fitting occupation for a knight. Just as Roland did now. Jaufre de Macy, earl of Winterbourne, knight of the realm, had not yet seen thirty-five years...but Lord, how old this son of his was making him feel.

"When the time comes," he said, "you will fight and do the best you can. Beyond that..." He sighed. "Beyond that, who knows what the outcome will be?"

In the early days of the campaign, the outcome was better than Jaufre dared expect. King John showed a cunningness and determination that the earl had never seen in him before. The army made a series of swift, daring raids, deceptive changes that kept the French king in confusion as to where the English would strike next. The strongholds began to fall,

Mervant and Milecu, which covered the seaport of La Rochelle, Vouvant in La Marche, and the garrison at Nantes, until their entry in Angers was unopposed. The barons of Poitou rushed to John's side, swelling the English army with their numbers, but Jaufre trusted them no more than he did this new spurt of energy in the king. Poitou was not Normandy, and that was where Clairemont lay.

Jaufre waxed impatient when the king lingered overlong at the siege of Roches Aux Moines, an isolated enemy fortress whose conquest would do naught to augment the English position. It was already June. He had spent five months in this foreign land and marched nowhere near his objective in coming. Back at Winterbourne, Jenny would have marked off the first year of her life. Was she walking now? He pictured Melyssan's delight when their daughter took her first toddling steps, and he longed to be present to see it. Perhaps she would finally pardon him for opposing her over the swaddling.

Lyssa. The thought of her brought that familiar ache in his heart that was like a sickness with him these days. Other men found solace in the peasant wenches from the local villages, but even that release was denied him. He was like a man dying of thirst, surrounded by water but whose life depended upon a rare sweet elixir, which prevented him from sipping at any other well.

They had been a fortnight outside the walls of Roches Aux Moines. Jaufre stood watching the catapults shelling the walls with huge rocks at infrequent intervals. The tall siege towers covered with hides stood idly to one side, awaiting men to clamber inside and be wheeled toward the castle when it would please the king to make serious assault.

The earl was swinging his sword in vigorous arcs through the air, chafing at the torpor that seemed to have settled over the army, when he heard someone call his name.

"My lord Earl!" Arric called as he raced to Jaufre's side. He half collapsed, panting, "We took...Sir Whitney to your tent. He's taken...an arrow in the...shoulder."

"An arrow!" Jaufre shoved his weapon back into its sheath. "Now how in the devil did he manage that? There is so little fighting going on here, one could take a nap under the walls and come away unmolested."

Arric hunched up his shoulders and spread wide his hands. With a curt gesture, Jaufre indicated for the squire to precede him, taking refuge in exasperation to hide his concern. If Whitney were badly injured, should die, how would he ever face Melyssan or bear witnessing her grief?

The earl followed Arric back to his tent, clenching his teeth when they passed by the large silken apartments that housed the king. The sound of feminine laughter drifted toward him. In his complacency, John had had the queen and royal children brought to join him along with the coffers containing the royal jewels and treasure.

Jaufre's lip curled scornfully. He did not envy Queen Isabella if the army were ever obliged to flee. He had no doubts as to what the king would seek to save first.

When he reached his tent, he shoved Arric aside and stepped impatiently under the canvas. Whitney lay white-faced upon a straw pallet stained with blood. But he was not so weakened that he did not glare at Jaufre. "The arrow has been removed. There is naught for you to trouble yourself with, my lord."

"I'll judge that for myself." Jaufre knelt down beside him, reaching for the bandaged arm.

Whitney attempted to resist, then lapsed back against the straw, closing his eyes. He winced as Jaufre peeled back the blood-soaked linen.

"The wound looks clean enough," said the earl. "I think the only danger would be if some of the links of your mail got driven deep into the flesh and mortified."

Whitney started to shrug, then gasped. Taking several deep breaths, he replied curtly, "Good. Now you will be able to send my sister another message. *A miracle. Your nithling brother has not yet managed to get himself killed.*"

Jaufre flushed and stood up. It would seem his clerk had a loose tongue about what was dictated to him in the form of letters. The man would learn to be more discreet or have his tongue ripped out. "I do not mean to send word to your sister again until I am in possession of Clairemont."

"We'll all be dead long before that," Whitney muttered.

"Mayhap some of us. How did you—"

"How did I come to be shot when there is scarce any fighting going on?" His eyes blazed with the intensity of a man who has kept feelings locked inside himself for too long and now intends to let them loose. "I went past the catapults and got too close to the castle walls. I was so sick of the endless jests of your men about how I am forever in the vanguard of any action."

"So you got yourself wounded." Jaufre placed his hands on his hips, making no attempt to mask the contempt he felt. "What is that supposed to prove?"

"Nothing." Tears coursed a path down Whitney's dirt-streaked cheeks; impatiently, he dashed them aside with the back of his hand. "I am weary of trying to prove anything. I am a coward. My knees shake and my palms sweat every time I take the field. I confess it freely. Now you may all go and make merry at my expense."

"You think you're the first man ever to feel that way? Only a fool or an idiot knows no fear when facing the prospect of death."

"So which are you, my lord?"

"Neither. Simply because I don't parade my fear for all the world to see doesn't mean I am any more courageous than you are. You've done well enough on this campaign, better than I— I've had no complaints to make of your behavior—until now."

He had no way of knowing if his words had any effect on Whitney, for the young man turned his face aside. After regarding him for some little while in silence, Jaufre strode out of the tent. Faith, why should he be annoyed with Whitney? The man's foolishly gallant gesture in flinging himself to the front of the line was no more futile than this entire campaign was turning out to be, no more futile than the oath he had made his grandfather.

Once outside the tent, however, Jaufre noticed a change in the camp. Men-at-arms no longer idled on the grass but had begun sharpening their weapons, their stances alert.

"My lord," Arric said, his eyes shining with excitement, "they are saying a scout has returned with great news. Prince Louis and a large French army approach from Chinon, assembling to do battle."

Jaufre's lips set into a grim line as his hand stroked the sheath of his sword. Battle! Some decisive action might be forced upon the king at last. One way or another, they would see an end to this business. He hastened his steps toward the king's tent, where the other leaders of the army gathered around John in heated debate.

The barons from Poitou clustered together nervously. Their leader, Amery of Thouars, shouted at the king, "This is more than we bargained for, I assure you. Besieging and defending castles is one thing, but a pitched battle in an open field! We are noblemen, not a pack of demented mercenaries."

The king slumped down in his chair, his eyes as dark and sulky as a thwarted child's. "Bah, you have heard our scout's report. This is the chance we have been waiting for, to strike directly at Philip Augustus—through the person of his son. We are equal in strength to this French army. We can destroy them."

"You *were* equal," said Amery, beckoning to the other Poitevins. "Now if you fight, you will do so without us."

He stalked away, followed by the other barons.

John leapt to his feet. "Cowards! Traitors! You pledged me new oaths of loyalty. Return at once or I will slay you all."

He started to run after Amery, his face purpled with fury, but Jaufre blocked his path. He placed his hand on the king's shoulder. "Nay, my liege. Let them go. What would it avail you to have men at your side who might desert you at any moment? We will do better without them."

"Without them, we shall be overwhelmed." John's eyes darted wildly. "All my hopes. My plans! Curse all traitors to hell. Why must I forever be surrounded by such treachery?"

He looked at Jaufre's hand and struck it off as if it were an adder crawling along his skin. Before the earl could say anything more, he ran back into his tent.

Jaufre shook his head. There was no reasoning with John. In short order, the panic spread through the ranks of the entire army. The king headed a disorganized retreat back across the Loire River, fleeing as if the demons of hell pursued. Siege engines, tents, and baggage were abandoned as the army marched south.

The earl had no choice but to amass his men-at-arms and follow. And with every mile he covered, he sickened with the shame and folly of it. Never had he run from a fight before. If the king kept going, they would soon be all the way back to La Rochelle, from whence they had begun. Five months wasted! From La Rochelle it was only a step to slinking back home across the Channel.

Jaufre prodded his black stallion forward, making one last effort to reason with the king.

"If Your Majesty does not feel it prudent to confront Prince Louis, then at least let us ride to find the rest of the English army under the earl of Salisbury. He will be joining soon with Otto of Germany and the rest of your allies."

"Nay, we must to Rochelle." The king's eyes fixed upon the road ahead, a glazed look in them. "There we will be safe. We will wait, send messengers. More of my English barons must come."

"No more help is coming." Jaufre resisted the urge to grab the king's bridle and slap some sense into the man. "Your Majesty, my grandfather died, drained his life out, helping you to assemble this coalition against France. Will you now turn your back on your last chance to win what was yours?"

"Curse you to hell, de Macy. I turn my back on nothing. I say we go to La Rochelle.

We wait. Any who obey not my commands are as much my enemies as the French." John spurred his tired horse into a run, his stumpy frame seeming to shrink into the saddle as he rode away.

Jaufre held back his own mount, allowing the king's men to gallop around him. So the moment had come. His temporary alliance with the king was at an end. He rode back to his followers and signaled a halt. After giving the order to his knights that they were turning around, he sought out Whitney.

The young man had refused to be carried on a litter and now sat perched, tight-lipped and precarious, on his saddle. Jaufre saw that he was going to have to impart secret instructions to one of the squires to see that the fool got safely home.

"You and your men stay with the king," he told Whitney. "I am taking a small group of my knights and riding to join up with Salisbury."

"But I thought the king's orders were that none of us were to leave him."

"I came here to accomplish one thing, and I cannot go back to England until I have or I am—" He broke off and then added, "You return to Winterbourne. Warn Tristan the king's anger may be directed against me. Tell Lyssa..."

Tell Lyssa what? All the things he had never been able to say when he held her in his arms. Did he now think he could consign such a tender message to the care of her hostile brother? On impulse, Jaufre stripped off his leather gauntlet and removed his seal ring—the same ring he had claimed from Melyssan so long ago. He could remember as if it were yesterday how it had dangled from the chain, glittering in the creamy-white hollow between her breasts.

"Give this to Lyssa," he said hoarsely, thrusting the ring at Whitney. The young man's lips parted in surprise. Jaufre could feel Whitney studying his face, although he knew not how much of his emotions were written there for all to see. "Tell her I want her to have it, keep it safe for me if—when I return."

He pushed the ring into Whitney's hand without giving him a chance to reply. As he was riding away, he heard Whitney call his name. He turned, but Whitney did not, presenting Jaufre with the rigid line of his back. The earl was about to slap down on the reins when Whitney's words came to him like an echo borne on the wind.

"Good fortune attend you, my lord, and—Godspeed."

It was near noon on July 27, 1214. The sun broiled down upon Jaufre's back, scorching through his blue tunic to the links of the chain-mail hauberk beneath. The heat penetrated the final protective layer of his thick-quilted gambeson, bathing his body in sweat. He wiped at the beads of perspiration dotting his beard, staring longingly at the sparkling blue thread that was the river Marque.

But between himself and that river, along the grassy slopes of the plateau, stood the king of France himself. Philip Augustus was mounted upon a white charger amidst a sea of men, a mighty army of foot soldiers brandishing spears, tall warriors restraining their restive steeds, their bright-colored pennons hanging limp, without so much as a breath of air to unfurl them. By dusk, the river's sparkle would be dulled with the red of blood. Even now a column of black smoke stained the bright azure sky as the French burned the only bridge. Philip Augustus was taking no chances on his soldiers fleeing back to Paris. They would stand or die.

And the coalition army? Jaufre glanced around at the odd assortment of men by whose side he would fight. Germans, Flemish, and Dutch; contingents from Boulogne and Brabant; and English like himself led by the king's half brother, William of Salisbury. A shaky network of alliances soon to face the ultimate test.

Roland pressed his horse forward until it brushed against the flanks of Jaufre's black stallion. The earl watched as his son anxiously smoothed out the two-headed swans gracing the front of his golden tunic. The boy stubbornly clung to the heraldic device of Clairemont that had been on the medallion Jaufre had confiscated from him. For the first time, the earl noticed his son's shoulders appeared to have grown broader, the arms longer, more sinewy than he recalled. Roland double-checked the belt holding his sword as if to assure himself it was still there before raising his eyes to meet his father's.

Jaufre detected no fear in his son's eyes, only a certain reluctance. "The other nobles seem not so keen for this battle, my lord. I think if the mercenary Hugh of Bove had not shamed them, we would all have fled again as John Softs—I mean, King John—did a month ago."

Jaufre hesitated a moment, then said, "I will not lie to you, boy. They have reason to be afraid. This will be different from sieging a castle. Many more will die."

Roland squinted into the sun as he studied the lines of men, most of them silent, waiting for the signal that would begin the fray. "I think I have never seen such a large host. There must be—what think you—some twenty, twenty-five thousand? And the weapons! What are those ugly things the Germans carry?"

Jaufre followed his pointing finger to the troops of stalwart men flocked in the center of the coalition line, gathered under the insignia of the dragon and eagle.

"Those are halberds fitted with hooks. The infantry use them to drag the knights from their horses."

"A most unchivalrous sort of weapon, surely."

"Forget your notions of chivalry, boy. They will not apply today. There is something savage about a melee like this. All codes of honor and courtesy get set aside in favor of survival. Nobles, even kings will be fair sport."

Roland's eyes turned anxiously toward the middle of the French line, where could be discerned the royal banner with the golden fleur-de-lis. Philip's white charger was now hemmed in by a bodyguard of French chevaliers.

"By God, at least they have a king of courage." Roland sighed, his shoulders slumping. He passed his tongue over his lips before risking a quick glance at Jaufre. "My—my lord, you have been generous to me, and though I—I never said so, I am grateful. I will serve you as best as I am able, but 'twere less than honest if I did not tell you." He looked wistfully across the field at the French army with Philip Augustus in their midst. "My heart is not in this."

Jaufre, too, stared at the French army. He thought of England, of the white towers of Winterbourne set against the backdrop of the craggy Welsh hills, of Jenny with her dusky curls, of Melyssan. His lady Melyssan, with her soft smile and gentle touch. He weighed all that against Clairemont, a pile of rocks about which he no longer gave a damn.

"Forgive me, Grandfather," he murmured. "But neither is my heart in this. Neither is mine."

At that instant a shout arose from the right flank as the French army made their move, a cavalry assault against the Flemish light horse. Jaufre's squire handed him his kettle helmet, which he donned. He then took up his heart-shaped shield. The earl's standard-bearer rode forward, shaking out the folds of Jaufre's blue banner with its gold falcon crest. Unsheathing his sword and waving it aloft, the Dark Knight plunged himself and his men into a blinding world of dust and naked steel.

As from a great distance, he heard the thunder of hooves and braced himself for the shock of the first blow struck upon his shield. Through the narrow slit of his visor, he saw a helmet pointed like the beak of a large metal bird before his sword sliced down, clubbing his adversary from his horse. After that his opponents came and went in sprays of dirt from the parched ground, one faceless mask of armor succeeding another.

The sun climbed higher in the sky, beating down upon the top of his helm until it became an effort of will to draw breath. He pulled back from the melee to blink the grit from his eyes, trying to make some sense of the way the battle was going, but found himself being swept toward the center of the hollow. The German footmen rushed forward like a solid battering ram, smashing their way through the French infantry. For a moment the line held; then it scattered, leaving a clear path to the tall man on the white horse. The next instant one of the Germans had hooked the French monarch and dragged him out of the saddle. Even above the din of shrieking horses and shouting men, Jaufre heard the cry.

"No!"

Roland's horse plunged forward, his shield deflecting the pike before it pierced Philip's back. To his horror, Jaufre watched as the

French men-at-arms closed around his son, re-forming to protect their fallen king. As Jaufre struggled toward Roland, three French chevaliers beat him back. He cried out as a sword blade skimmed the side of his calf. Hammering a blow that dented his opponent's helmet, Jaufre sent the middle knight reeling to the ground. The other two were knocked aside as a blood-smeared horse plunged against their mounts and collapsed. The animal's legs pawed the air, and the creature emitted a death cry before the long neck sank down, the head falling still. Jaufre stared down at the sapphire-studded caparison he had presented his son at Christmas. With a savage cry, he flung himself at the nearest enemy, dealing death on all sides.

The sun trailed lower across the sky, and the fighting grew fiercer still. Jaufre's black stallion jerked his head, screaming as the quarrel from a crossbow penetrated its eye. The horse reared violently, flinging Jaufre from its back before bolting into the crowd. The earl's body slammed into dry earth now slick with blood. He felt as if his lungs were crushed as the air *whoosh*ed out of them. His men-at-arms gathered around him, buying him time to recover and get to his feet.

The press was so great, Jaufre could scarce find room to swing his sword. Arric fought his way forward, bringing the earl a fresh horse. When remounted, he realized their ranks were thinning. The Flemish had fled early in the battle. Now his horse stumbled over remnants of the dragon and eagle standard as the Germans and men of Brabant deserted the field.

The sun was setting, and few but the English fought on. The earl of Salisbury galloped up to Jaufre, his voice cracking as he shouted, "The day is lost, de Macy. Save yourself while there is still time."

Jaufre's reply died on his lips. Salisbury fell, his head bludgeoned by a heavy club. Whirling his horse around, the Dark Knight tried to round up what remained of his men-at-arms and signal retreat. As he thundered through the hollow, his weary arm still laying about him, a bloodstained patch of gold caught his eye. A badge of two swans streaked with red writhed along the ground. Roland. His son was still alive.

Jaufre dug in his knees, preparing to lunge forward. An infantryman leapt in his path, stabbing his spear into Jaufre's sword arm. Cursing, the earl dropped his weapon, losing control of his horse. For the second time that day, he tumbled to the hard ground, his helmet flying loose from his shoulders.

Groaning, he rolled over. Arric raced to bring him another sword, but the young man was ridden down from behind. An axe sliced through the air, cleaving his skull in twain.

Jaufre averted his gaze, then began crawling toward his son. Pain-glazed eyes regarded him through the visor slits. Jaufre eased the helmet from Roland's head.

"What—what are you doing?" the boy

gasped. "Could still…get away. Save yourself."

"Think you I would leave my son as carrion for these vultures? Be quiet. Save your strength." He hooked his good arm under Roland's shoulders, attempting to drag the boy to his feet. But when he raised his head, he found himself staring straight into the steel tip of a sword's blade.

Night had fallen. They were prisoners of the French.

Chapter 17

MELYSSAN PRESSED THE cup of horehound and honey to her daughter's clamped lips. "Come, Jenny. Open up and take one tiny sip for Mother. 'Twill make your throat feel ever so much better."

Large brown eyes flashed in the small round face before Genevieve screamed out the one word she could pronounce to perfection. "Nay!" Her chubby hand shot out and dashed the cup from Melyssan's hand.

"Genevieve!" Melyssan took a deep breath to curtail her exasperation, then retrieved the cup from where it had rolled under the stool by the hearthside. As she refilled it, she called out to Jenny's nurse, "You shall have to hold her down again, Canice, while I force her to drink it."

Canice grimaced, shoving the large flowing

sleeves of her kirtle above her elbows before tipping Jenny over backward. The child howled lustily, her plump feet flailing the air. She writhed and spluttered, choking on the medicine, flinging half of it over Canice before the cup was empty. Her cries of outrage did not stop then, nor with her release. Flinging herself facedown into the rushes, she pounded the floor with her tiny fists. Melyssan cast a despairing eye at the nurse.

"Heaven defend us, my lady," Canice said. "The girl has the strength of ten demons, and her not quite two. I must go change again, and I am running short of gowns."

With a disgusted shake of her head, Canice quit the room, leaving Melyssan to cope with her daughter's tantrum. Only when Jenny had exhausted her fury did she permit Melyssan to raise her from the floor. Melyssan perched on the edge of her bed, cuddling her small daughter, who hiccuped her remaining sobs into her mother's bosom.

"Jenny, Jenny," she crooned, rocking the child to and fro. " 'Twill never do. You are a lady, my love, and a very little one at that. You were never meant to possess a temper the size of your father's. What shall my lord say to you when he returns?

"And he will return," she whispered fiercely as she buried her face against the dusky tangle of baby-soft curls. "He will." She fought the urge to join Jenny's bout of weeping. It was a temptation she had succumbed to far too often since the news had reached Winterbourne last summer.

She had been hearing mass with the rest of the castle household. The messenger had burst into the chapel just as Father Andrew had raised the Eucharist aloft.

"Lady Melyssan. God forgive me for disturbing you thus," the servant had gasped. "But there has been a terrible battle at Bouvines. I—I fear Lord Jaufre and his son were captured by the French."

Tristan's strong arm saved Melyssan from sinking to the chapel floor, his calm words of reassurance all that sustained her. "'Tis not as dreadful as it sounds, my lady. Jaufre is a nobleman. He will be treated well. Meantime, we must summon the earl's tenants, collect money to meet the ransom Philip will demand."

But September fled, and no ransom demand came. Word reached Winterbourne of a truce with France. The other English captives were released, but not Jaufre. King John sailed home with the armada in October. Whitney and the earl's surviving men-at-arms returned home. Still no Jaufre.

Some said the king had left him a prisoner in France out of spite. Some said the earl had died in captivity. She received several messages from John to that effect, demanding payment of death duties in impossible amounts, threatening to make Jenny his ward, snatch her away from Melyssan. All that saved her daughter was the outbreak of rebellion amongst the northern barons. Led by one Robert Fitzwalter, they named themselves the Army of God and called for a return to the days of the Charter, the restoration of justice to England. Melyssan hoped Fitzwalter's army might succeed or at least buy her and Jenny enough time until Jaufre returned.

She prayed and waited. Long winter days, nights of cold, black despair, and still no word of Jaufre. Melyssan had huddled alone in the great bed, clutching his pillow in her arms, the terrifying thought creeping unbidden into her mind: This is what it would be like to be a widow, a numbing round of endless hours broken by sharp, painful stabs of remembrance.

"Nay." Melyssan shook aside the gloom-filled memories, hugging her daughter so tightly that Jenny squeaked a protest. "We won't think of those things anymore. 'Tis spring now, a season of new hope. The buds are beginning to show on the trees, the lambs will soon be born. And Tristan has taken all the pretty silver we collected and gone searching for my lord."

She wiped away the last traces of moisture from Jenny's round cheeks. "Sir Tristan will bring Father home. Soon. Very soon. So you must be a very, very good girl, my love."

With one of those charming reversals of mood that was so typical of Jenny, the child's lips parted in a sunny smile before puckering up to proffer her mother a kiss.

Melyssan hugged the child again before consigning her to the care of her nurse, instructing Canice to see that the little girl was kept warm and rested, knowing even as she gave them that the orders were impossible to carry out.

Before descending to the great hall, Melyssan had to spend several minutes trying to discover what Jenny had done with her cane. It was a favorite plaything of the child's whenever she could get her hands on it. This time she found it tangled up amongst the bed linens.

Belowstairs the household hummed with activity preparing for the feast at Easter. All the sacrifices of Lent would be set behind them, and Jaufre's tenants would expect a well-laden table in exchange for their gifts of eggs. In truth, Melyssan had no heart for the holiday rejoicing, but she was determined nothing should seem any different while Jaufre was away. She would have no one, not even the lowliest menial at Winterbourne, believing he was dead.

She passed her brother in the great hall. He was munching on a roll, readying himself to ride out with the men-at-arms on the morning's patrol over the earl's lands. By Tristan's orders, they had increased their vigilance because of the growing unrest that had engulfed the country since King John's failure in France.

"Good morrow, sister," Whitney said. "Have you emerged victorious in your latest skirmish with my niece?"

Melyssan wrinkled her brow in dismay. "Surely her screams could not be heard all the way down here."

"Nay, but you bear the scars of battle." He pointed to a spattering of honey across the bodice of her gown.

Sighing, she dabbed at the stains with her kerchief, pushing aside Jaufre's ring, which hung from a chain about her neck. Jaufre's ring. She paused, allowing its weight to brush against her hand. Wherever she turned, she was haunted with memories of her long-absent husband. How many times had she made Whitney rehearse the tale of how Jaufre had sent the ring to her, how he had looked, what he had said....

"I think he knew, Lyssa," Whitney had said at the time. "Somehow he knew he was not coming back." Angrily she had denied it, and her brother had said no more.

But now he surprised her by caressing her hand, an earnest look in his green eyes. "Do not worry, Lyssa. My lord will return to claim that ring. I do not doubt he will come back to you, if there is any earthly way."

She gave him a grateful smile. As he turned to walk away, he emitted a brief laugh and looked back over his shoulder. "Mind you, I do not believe I will ever be able to like the man. But it helps somewhat knowing that he loves you."

Knowing that he loved her? How could Whitney profess to know such a thing when she did not even know it herself? She thought of the last time Jaufre had held her in his arms, the night before he'd left for France. His mask of indifference had melted before the blazing heat of his desire. The memory of that passionate loving had been all that warmed her over the past year. She'd begun to hope that perhaps when Jaufre returned...

She closed her eyes, murmuring a brief prayer. "No, dear Lord. He does not have to say he loves me. Only send him safely home."

The sun was at its zenith when the riders approached Winterbourne. Melyssan heard the guards on the walls heralding their arrival as they prepared to open the gates. Surely it was too soon for her brother and the patrol to be returning. She caught her breath in apprehension, fearful that it might be soldiers of the king, come to seize her daughter.

"Look lively there," Master Galvan bellowed to the other men. "Raise that portcullis. And someone go tell Her Ladyship Sir Tristan is returning."

Tristan! Her heart's pace increased to a wild hammering as she hurried to the courtyard, dread and hope warring within her breast. What news would he have of her husband? Why had the knight returned without Jaufre? It was a question she scarce dared ask.

Pushing past the gathered servants, she made her way to the front of the line, watching as the great iron gate creaked upward. Her mind flew back to another day, so long ago, when she had stood waiting in the bailey, her hands shaking with trepidation, as Jaufre's great black warhorse galloped into the courtyard....

Wild cheering from the men on the walls snapped Melyssan back to the present. "My lord! My lord! Lord Jaufre's come home."

The horses stormed through the gate, became a thundering tangle of haunches and striking hooves as Melyssan's vision blurred. She stumbled forward, looking frantically for the familiar black destrier; but there was none. She saw Tristan dismount, followed by a knight who slid off the back of a sleek brown gelding. Blinking away the mist of her tears, she recognized the dark beard, the broad set of shoulders.

"Jaufre!"

With a strangled cry, she flung herself against his dust-covered tunic. His arms closed around her, his lips crushing hers in a kiss that consumed her, so hard it was almost painful. Warmth sparked along her veins like a fire new kindled in an empty hearth, reality blending with the dreams of him that had tormented her through months of anxious waiting.

All too soon he eased her away from him, stepping back. She raised her eyes, her hungry gaze devouring his beloved features. His face was paler, leaner than she remembered, and strands of silver threaded here and there through his shaggy mane of midnight black.

What most disturbed her were his eyes. The rich brown pools that had once teemed with anger, pride, passion...were empty, drained.

Trembling, she reached up to touch his face, her fingers grazing the rough beard. "My lord, you—you are not a dream? You are truly here?"

"Aye, my lady. I have come home." His voice sounded distant, inexpressibly weary.

Tristan, who had hung back discreetly, now stepped forward. "I do not wonder you should doubt his existence, my lady. From the look of him, you will think I have brought you a ghost. Why not give his beard a good tug and see how real he is?"

She waited, hoping Jaufre's lips would quirk into a smile as he flung a retort to Tristan's teasing. But the earl stared past them at the great white tower of the donjon as though the knight had not even spoken.

Sir Dreyfan rushed up and attempted a bow, but the doughty knight could not contain himself. He seized the unresponsive Jaufre in a bear hug, shouting his exuberance. "Hah! Welcome home, my lord. I told my lady you'd find some way to outwit those French poltroons."

Jaufre jerked himself free of the old knight's embrace. "Tristan bought my freedom with the ransom money. That is how I came to be freed, not through any cleverness of my own."

He grabbed his horse's bridle as though preparing to lead the animal to the stables himself.

"Get one of those lazy squires up here," Dreyfan bellowed. He craned his neck, appearing to seek someone among the ranks of men who had ridden in with Jaufre. "Where is that young fool Arric?"

The earl's jaw hardened. "Arric is...he did not return with me."

Dreyfan's face fell. "Ah, 'tis a pity. He was a saucy young pup, but had the makings of a good knight for all that." His head bent in sorrow, he took charge of Jaufre's horse, leading the animal away.

Melyssan reached for Jaufre's hand, but he stiffened. "I am sorry, my lord," she said. "We heard no news of the boy. We all assumed Arric must have shared your captivity." She swallowed, remembering the lad's eager face that Christmas he had hung the mistletoe for her, boasting to Roland of the number of Frenchmen he would kill.

Roland! She had been so overwhelmed by Jaufre's arrival, she had forgotten to look for the young man. A quick glance told her he had not ridden into the courtyard. Although Tristan's eyes warned her not to trouble Jaufre with further questions, she could not forbear asking:

"And your son, my lord?"

"Roland remained in Paris," Jaufre said, his words coming slow, strained. "From what I heard, he has become quite a favorite at the French court. He saved the life of their king at Bouvines. The boy always admired Philip Augustus above any other man, so I suppose Roland is at last content."

"I shall miss him," Melyssan whispered, remembering the solemn look on the young man's face when he had sworn to be her champion forever.

Jaufre shrugged, his mouth set in a bitter line.

"Well!" Tristan clapped his hands together with false heartiness. "Let us not stand here in the yard all day. My lady, I trust, despite the Lenten fast, you can offer a starving man some morsel to eat."

"A-aye," she stammered.

As they walked toward the donjon, she linked her arm through Jaufre's. Although he did not shake her off, his arm remained limp, offering her no encouragement. His gait, once so long and striding she had been hard put to keep pace with him, was now halting, hesitant.

The servants assembled to greet Jaufre fell back. Even they seemed to sense the changes in the earl, and their bright smiles of welcome vanished.

To cover Jaufre's unnerving silence, Melyssan began to chatter. "All has been well here at Winterbourne. The spring crops are sowed, the oats, beans, barley. And you cannot begin to imagine how happy we all are to be able to hear mass again. I had my churching in February at the Feast of Purification of the Virgin. Of course, since Jenny will be two this summer, 'twas a trifle late, but—but better late than never."

She paused, hoping he would make some inquiry after their daughter, but instead he froze outside the covered stairway leading inside the donjon. His face wore not the anticipation of a man about to see his home after a year's absence, but the bleak look of a prisoner being led to a narrow cell.

"I have no appetite. I believe I will—will walk down to the mews to see how my falcons have fared." He turned, waving her aside when she would have accompanied him. His falcons! And he had not even asked to see Jenny.

Melyssan bit her lip, watching until he was out of sight. She saw that Tristan had done the same, a troubled expression on his face.

"Tristan, what ails him? He—he is like a stranger. What dreadful things did they do to him in France?" Her voice shook. "You do not think he was tortured?"

"No, my lady," Tristan said gently. "But you must understand. Losing the battle, being captured. His pride has suffered a terrible blow. And despite how much he complained about it, I believe he is sick at heart that he did not retake Clairemont as he promised his grandfather."

He slipped an arm around her comfortingly. "Be patient with him, Melyssan. Time will restore to you the Jaufre you once knew. You must perforce wait a little longer."

She burst into tears. "But I have waited so long already. Since—since I was nine years old!"

She fled inside the donjon, leaving Tristan with his brow knotted in a frown, puzzled over her parting words.

During the ensuing days, Melyssan felt as though Jaufre had not returned to Winterbourne. It was his ghost that slunk along the curving stairs, a silent shadow that shrank from the company of other men. He spent many hours pacing the castle walls, pacing until Melyssan thought he must collapse from exhaustion.

Her bed remained as empty as when he had

been a prisoner in France. It was worse now, having him close enough to touch yet seeing no answering spark of desire in his eyes. She oft stepped out of her way, stumbled, just to brush up against him. He never seemed to see her, any more than he did Jenny. Although the child was never forthcoming with those unfamiliar to her, she had conceived a positive fascination for the tall, quiet stranger who was her father. She toddled after him at every available opportunity.

Storm clouds hovered over Winterbourne the Sunday after Jaufre's arrival. The rumble of thunder and gray sheets of rain did little to raise Melyssan's depressed spirits. She arranged a special mass to be said in the chapel, celebrating the earl's safe return. But Jaufre startled everyone by refusing to attend.

"I fear, after all those years of the interdict, I have little stomach for this sort of ceremony," he said. "The rest of you may go pray and bless yourselves, just as you wish."

"But—but my lord," Father Andrew faltered. "Do I understand you to say that you never mean to attend mass?"

"Aye, you've a keen understanding, Father."

The priest regarded Jaufre sternly. "You cannot have thought this matter through, my lord. Regardless of your personal feelings, you must be aware that you set the tone for the rest of the household. Your knights look to you for spiritual example."

"I provide an example for no man," Jaufre said. "Let them find their own road to hell."

He retreated to the solar, as oblivious to Father Andrew's shocked disapproval as he was to Melyssan's beseeching look.

She half feared the storm would not keep him from his endless tread along the battlements, but later that afternoon, when she adjourned to the solar, she found him there, staring out the croslet at the drenching rain. Tristan and Whitney sat playing checkers at the trestle table. But from the remote expression on Jaufre's face, he might well have been alone.

Melyssan gathered up her needlework, pulling her stool as near to Jaufre as she dared without disturbing him. Her stitching lay idle in her lap while she stole glances at Jaufre's silent profile. She noticed that Tristan and Whitney did the same. Every few minutes, Jaufre would take a restless turn about the room as if the walls constricted him.

The tension grew so heavy even the snap of the logs on the fire resounded through the quiet room like cracks of lightning. Tristan shifted his legs, cleared his throat. "I heard that whilst on patrol, you met some of Sir Hugh's men out hunting yesterday," he said to Whitney.

"Aye." Whitney shoved one of his red pieces forward. "They had some black tidings to pass along. The king..." He paused to look at Melyssan. "Mayhap I should tell you later."

"Do not hold back on my account," she said. "I do not believe there is anything more the king could do which would shock me."

She gazed up at her husband, wondering if

in his present frame of mind he would be distressed by more tales of the king. John was a subject Jaufre had avoided since his return. But he continued to stare out the window, his face expressionless.

Oh, my love, she longed to call to him. *You are no longer in a French prison. Forget those terrible days, the lost war. Come back to me, Jaufre. Come back.*

Whitney jumped one of Tristan's checkers, then, as though unable to keep still, went on with his story. "Sir Hugh's huntsman said the king hanged three knights from Bristol last week. No warning, no trial, no reason! Except mayhap the king coveted the wife of one."

Melyssan shuddered. "Poor woman."

"Such tales are so commonplace these days," said Tristan. "I think the king's temper has grown worse since his failure in France."

"We would not have to be at the mercy of the king's temper if we had the Great Charter." Whitney nearly knocked the checkerboard to the floor in his vehemence. "They say Fitzwalter's army means to march on London soon. I loathe fighting, but by God, I wish I were with them. If it ever pleased my lord to join the rebellion, I would follow him willingly."

"Well, it does not please my lord." Jaufre's deep voice caused Melyssan to jump. He spun around, looking like a man who had just been startled awake. "I have no intention of being involved in a skirmish which is none of my affair."

"None of your affair?" Whitney croaked.

"People robbed of their lands, wrongfully slain, even women and children such as Matilda de Briouse and her son—"

"These people are nothing to me. I shall consider myself fortunate to protect what is my own from the king. Others must do the same."

Tristan's mouth opened as if to speak, then closed. But Melyssan could no longer remain silent. "My lord, I thought as a knight, you are pledged to...would wish to..." She faltered, her eyes flicking to the mural, where Sir Launcelot charged, his lance aimed at a black-armored knight. "Not everyone is as strong, as invincible, as you are, Jaufre."

He followed the direction of her gaze, and Melyssan saw a flash of anger return to the mahogany eyes.

"Invincible?" He gave a mirthless laugh. "Aye, so invincible I rode to Paris chained to an ox cart like one of those pathetic bears dragged from town to town, performing for the rabble."

Melyssan felt the color drain from her cheeks. "Oh, Jaufre. I am so sorry. I—I never imagined..."

"What did you think? That I pranced along the streets like some sort of conqueror? Nay, my dear, defeated knights are treated like the cattle they are."

When she rose, stepping toward him, he held up one hand to ward her off. "Stay where you are. I do not need your pity." He shifted his gaze to glare at Tristan and Whitney.

"Any more than I need to hear this endless blathering about that charter. Christ's blood! The talk has been of nothing else since I set foot on English soil. I don't intend to risk my life, or imprisonment, for a worthless scrap of paper."

He strode out of the solar, slamming the door behind him. Melyssan turned slowly, her eyes locking with Tristan's. The knight lowered his head, seeming no longer able to give her the reassurance she sought.

She tried to stifle the surge of disappointment that welled inside her. Jaufre was home. Safe. She should be grateful. What more did she expect? She had always known that her husband had abandoned the ideals of his youth.

But she sensed he had abandoned other things as well. Somewhere at Bouvines, the dungeon in Paris, he had left behind the aura of strength and confidence that had once emanated from him. The confidence that had enveloped her like a warm mantle, making her feel safe, secure. Jaufre was home, but she still felt afraid.

Chapter 18

THE RAINS PASSED. By the next afternoon the sun broke through the clouds, burning away all traces of the storm. Jaufre watched as the servants erected a silk tent behind the apple tree in the garden. They dragged a large tub inside, carting buckets of water to fill the wooden vessel. Then he dismissed the servants, refusing all help with disrobing for his bath.

Alone, he removed his boots, mud-caked from a morning of tromping across the fields to settle a dispute between two of his tenants over a parcel of land. He stripped off his sword belt and sweat-stained surcoat. It was unusually warm for this early in spring. Breathing in the scent of the apple blossoms, he lifted his eyes to the tiny white petals fluttering from the tree. Above him loomed the great donjon, the sun glinting off the white arcading the masons had sculpted with such care nigh sixty years ago. Familiar scents and sights. Winterbourne was as ever unchanged. Why did it seem so foreign to him?

Because he had changed. He no longer felt worthy to be the master of these lands, not worthy to be the grandson of Comte Raoul de Macy of Clairemont. He had failed to keep his oath, returned home beaten. A knight who had lost his shield, his sword, his horse...his honor. He had crept back into England, a year of his life wasted languishing in a French fortress.

He could not complain he had been ill-treated while a prisoner. The food had been adequate, his cot comfortable, the chamber large enough to walk about. But his sleep had been tormented with dreams of Winterbourne, of Lyssa with her honey-brown hair and green eyes. Longing for her became an unbearable ache, his desire a fiery torture worse than if they had racked his body over live coals.

And now that he was back, he could hardly bear for her to look at him. Had he seen disappointment lurking in her eyes at having her husband return thus? Skulking back home like some vagabond? She, who had always cherished such a shining vision of him. Sir Launcelot.

Jaufre snorted. She must learn sooner or later he was naught but an ordinary man. There was no way he could live up to the chivalric fantasies she harbored in her soul. He even doubted his strength to hold what was his, defend his wife and daughter from a tyrant's madness. What would King John do when he discovered the earl who had defied him in France was still very much alive and back in England? Perhaps he should send Lyssa and Jenny away, hide them....

He shucked off his tunic and shirt until he stood clad only in his woolen breeches. Trailing his fingers through the chill water, he shuddered. How much would it take to cleanse himself of the shame of his failure?

A movement outside the tent caught his eye. He whistled low, half expecting it to be one of the greyhounds. A pair of dark curls appeared at the tent opening, followed by wide brown eyes that peered at him.

"What's this?" he said, starting forward. "Have pixies invaded Winterbourne in my absence?" At his approach, the babe backed away, nearly stumbling onto her rump. He stepped out of the tent, following her.

Babe. She was scarce that any longer, but more of a little girl. Her cheeks had lost some of that babelike roundness, her dusky hair brushing against the neckline of her linen shirt, which did not quite reach her knees.

"Jenny," he whispered, lowering himself on one knee to her level, stretching out his arms. Although he had been home over a week, she was still shy with him. It pained him to think she had no memory of him.

"Come, child. I will not hurt you." He spoke gently, withdrawing a pace. He longed to lift her into his arms but dreaded that he would frighten her. After studying him for several minutes, the child moved closer without a trace of fear in her eyes. He soon discovered it was not himself she had come to inspect. She swooped past him, pouncing upon his discarded clothing.

With a crow of delight, she lifted the jeweled sheath that contained his dagger, her stubby fingers attempting to pluck free the shining rubies embedded in the leather.

"No, Jenny." He snatched the weapon from her grasp. "'Tis naught for little girls to play with."

Shocked indignation swirled in her velvet-brown eyes. She plunked herself onto the ground, her lower lip thrust out before she let loose an ear-shattering wail.

He gaped at her in astonishment before

sternly commanding, "Genevieve. Stop that racket at once." He swiped ineffectually at the large tears trickling down her face. She ignored his soothing attempts at placation, stiffening her spine when he lifted her onto his lap. Despite himself, his irritation gave way to a twinge of amusement at the killing look his daughter directed at him. Faith, if the child were a queen, she would be screaming, "Off with his head!"

"Oh, here." He returned the sheathed weapon to her. "I do not suppose you are strong enough to draw forth the blade in any case."

Jenny gave several more wounded sniffs before she would accept the offering. Then she began to examine the jewels once more, her woebegone face splitting into a dazzling smile. Jaufre expelled a great sigh of relief.

"Such a temper! I'll wager someday you will make your husband tremble in his boots."

She peered up at him through long dark lashes, coy dimples quivering in her cheeks as though she understood his words. Jaufre tangled his fingers in the silken strands of her curls.

"Ah, Jenny. Do you have any notion at all who I am?"

A look of keen intelligence crossed the child's face. She poked one pudgy finger against his stomach. "Darnigh. Darnigh," she said.

"Darnigh?" he repeated, his brow furrowing in confusion. Then his face cleared, and he smiled at her. "Oh. Dark Knight."

Jenny bobbed her head vigorously. "Aye, darnigh."

"I can see your mother has been stuffing that wee head with too many foolish tales." He flicked his fingers under her plump chin. "Dark Knight is not my name, Jenny. I am your father. Fa-ther," he said, emphasizing each syllable.

Her small nose crinkled. She patted her warm, moist palm against his chest. "Fah-ver," she pronounced solemnly, then surprised him by bouncing upward to plant a wet kiss on his cheek. She hugged the dagger sheath, regarding him with large, innocent eyes, eyes that held no knowledge of lost battles, broken oaths, defeat....

The child's look of open adoration touched some chord deep inside him. For the first time in many months, Jaufre discovered he still knew how to smile.

It was sometime later when Melyssan realized the nurse had misplaced her daughter. Canice was full of apology. She had looked away for but a moment. Melyssan curtly ordered her to check the stable yard. Jenny wandered in that direction whenever she got the chance, and none of the men would possess the sense to send her back.

Melyssan turned her own footsteps to the garden, another of her daughter's favorite hiding places. As she neared the large apple tree she paused, listening in alarm. A deep growling issued from the bushes, followed by Jenny's high-pitched giggle. Surely the child could not be teasing one of the hounds again. She had been bitten a fortnight ago.

Hefting her cane like a club, Melyssan hurried forward—only to stop, frozen in her tracks. She blinked, rubbing her eyes to make sure she was not imagining the scene before her.

Jaufre scrambled on all fours, pursuing Jenny until he cornered her by the apple tree. The child squealed with delight, her small fist swiping at her father's nose. He rolled over, his arms and legs twitching in the air while he emitted some of the strangest gurgling sounds Melyssan had ever heard. When he finally lay still, Jenny leapt on top of him, shouting with triumph. Jaufre swooped the child up. Jumping to his feet, he spun her around, a light of tender pride in his eye. "Aye, you win again, my ferocious princess. Now give your poor beastie a kiss."

Melyssan took a quick breath as she watched Jaufre hug the child she had thought he despised. Her heart caught in her throat at the sight of them together, the tall, battle-scarred man and the fresh-faced child, so much alike Melyssan thought she could almost see the invisible bond forge itself between them. Somehow Jenny had accomplished what no one else could: she had breached Jaufre's wall of despair.

Loath to disrupt the magic surrounding them, she tried to retreat unseen, but a twig snapped beneath her foot, alerting Jaufre of her presence. His leathered face flushed the brightest shade of red she'd ever seen. With a sheepish expression, he set Jenny down, raking his hand back through the hair that had tumbled into his eyes.

"Well, what are you gawking at?" he blustered. "Someone has to see to the child if her nurse is going to let her run wild."

He folded his arms, trying to look stern and aloof, but Jenny would not permit it. She wrapped both arms around his leg, her bare toes pushing against his as if she would scale him like a tree.

"Fahver," she repeated in a demanding voice until he relented and lifted her back into his arms.

"Well?" he snapped. "Have you nothing to say about this neglect?"

Melyssan placed her hand across her lips to stifle her smile. "I crave your pardon, my lord, but she has always been permitted to play in the garden. We—we have never had bears here before."

Jaufre glared at her. "I was not a bear. I was a wolf. We—" He broke off, a peculiar expression crossing his face as if he had just taken a dose of very bitter medicine. "Summon this child's nurse at once."

"Oh, nay, my lord. Jenny is safe. Surely there is no reason to dismiss the woman."

"I said nothing of dismissing her. I merely want her to come and take the babe. She—she has great need of a dry tailclout."

Flinching, he thrust Jenny into Melyssan's arms. She realized that not only was the child soaked through, but a large wet stain was spreading across Jaufre's drawers. Unable to restrain herself any longer, she burst into peals of laughter right in the face of her outraged husband. Faith, but it felt good to laugh again; it had been so long. Jaufre stalked away in high dudgeon, but Melyssan sensed that his anger was feigned.

After she had returned Jenny to Canice, she followed him into the tent, feeling almost giddy from her discovery, as if a heavy weight had lifted from her heart. He stood by the large wooden tub, swearing and tugging at the cord of his drawers, the dampened material of which now molded to his powerful thighs, outlining the shape of his maleness.

"May I assist you with your bath, my lord?" she asked.

He hunched one shoulder, affecting indifference, but when she eased her fingers inside the waistline of his remaining garment, he did naught to prevent her.

She peeled away the wet wool, crouching down before him as she slid the breeches to his ankles. As he stepped out of them, she glanced up, her pulse quickening. He towered over her like some bronzed god out of the old pagan legends the villagers whispered of despite the disapproval of the priests.

Jaufre's eyes met hers, and she thought she detected a flicker of some stronger emotion before he averted his gaze as if embarrassed.

He eased himself into the large wooden tub, doubling up his knees so that the water lapped to a level just below his stomach.

Melyssan scooped up the soap. Slowly, sensually, she began to lather the broad plane of his back, her fingertips skimming the faint pink ridges, all that remained of the scars left by the whip. She began to talk to divert her thoughts from the desire that stirred inside her when her fingers made contact with the warmth of his flesh. "So what think you of our daughter, my lord? Has she not grown?"

He didn't answer as her hands trailed the soap across the dark curling hairs of his chest, gently washing the mark Yseult's treachery had left upon him. She felt him tense.

"Yes, she has grown." He spoke as if the words were wrung from him. "She promises— to be as beautiful—as her mother one day."

"Thank you, my lord." She flushed at the unexpected compliment. Or was it another kind of heat that flooded the color into her cheeks, the heat that grew inside of her as she soaped the sinewy lengths of Jaufre's arms down to the back of his hands, the strong, supple fingers that had always appeared so dark against the whiteness of her own skin, teasing, caressing, seeking out all those mysterious places only he seemed to know would render her weak with pleasure.

She hesitated an instant when she touched a fresh scar that streaked down Jaufre's forearm to his wrist.

"A memento from Bouvines" was all he would tell her as he drew the arm away.

He stared with fixed interest at the tent pole as she began to wash the flat surface of his stomach, the muscles tensing beneath her hand. He wet his lips and began to talk of Jenny again. "I suppose I shall be plagued with the task of finding her a husband one day. I do not know where we shall find a knight worthy of her."

"If we could find her a man like her father..." Melyssan's hand slipped below the surface of the water, leaving a trail of soap bubbles behind.

Jaufre squirmed, gripping the side of the tub. "Nay, she—she must do better. I'll not have her given short shrift in the matter of—" He sucked in his breath. Melyssan had closed her hand around his hardened shaft.

"I have never felt the lack of anything, my lord," she murmured, astonished at her own boldness.

Jaufre pulled her hand away, perspiration beading on his brow despite the coolness of the water. "I—I will wash my own—legs. You—you tend to my hair."

Her mouth went dry with disappointment. She had felt the evidence of his arousal. Why did he behave as though he wished to deny it?

Ducking his head in the water between his knees, he wet his hair so that she could apply the soap. Her hands began to tremble with the force of her rising passion so that she clumsily spattered soap in his eyes. When she tried to rinse him, the bucket slipped from her hands, banging the side of his temple and sending a cascade of water into his mouth that choked him.

As soon as he could draw breath, he flicked the soap out of his face and squinted at her. "Damn it, Lyssa. What are you trying to do? If I'd wanted to drown, I could have managed it myself." Scowling, he bent forward to rinse his own hair.

Her frustration boiled over. "Nay, let me help you," she said, shoving his head under. He came up sputtering, shaking back his thick mane like a sleek wet greyhound and seizing her by the wrist at the same time.

"No, Jaufre. Stop!" she cried in dismay as he tugged her down.

"Did you think to attempt such a deed and escape without tasting my vengeance, madam?" With a sharp heave, he toppled her over into the tub.

She gasped, feeling the cold water soak into the back of her skirts as she came to rest between Jaufre's slickened thighs. He splashed great handfuls of water up over her bodice until the layers of kirtle and chemise clung to her, revealing the swelling shape of her breasts and hardened nipples.

"Stop. Stop," she begged, blinking away the droplets that clouded her eyes, feeling the tendrils of her hair cling to her cheeks.

She felt the heat of Jaufre's hand pressing against her back as he pulled her forward, crushing her to his chest so that she could feel the erratic beat of his heart.

"There is only one way to purchase mercy from the Dark Knight," he said huskily, the anger in his eyes flaming into passion.

"Indeed? Then name your price." She slid her arms around his neck as his mouth claimed hers, the cool taste of the water replaced by the sweet fire of his lips. He hooked his arm beneath her knees, lifting her out of the tub, staggering beneath the weight of her dripping gown. Easing her down upon the grass, he murmured, "We shall have to get rid of these wet things, lest you drown me yet."

She helped him pull the gown and chemise over her head, her hands trembling with eagerness to be free of them. He spread his surcoat along the grass and placed her upon it, his eyes drinking in the beauty of her nakedness. How oft he had imagined her thus during those endless days in France, until he had become terrified his imagination waxed too keen, conjuring up visions of a beauty that did not exist, only to discover now his memory had been faulty. His dreams did not do her justice. He stroked back the wet strands of nutmeg from her brow, felt himself being drawn into the tumultuous sea of her green eyes.

"Lyssa," he groaned. "It has been so long." He seized her against him, molding the soft curves of her hips to the hard length of his manhood. "No matter how I fight it, I am nigh consumed with my desire for you."

"Then don't fight it, my lord. Don't. Am I not your wife?"

"Aye, mine."

He gave himself over to a pull too strong to resist, the call of all that was woman in her to the man in him. He spread her thighs, thrusting forward into the soft core of her desire, watched her head tip back, her pink lips parting, her eyes closing at the painful ecstasy of their union. He needed her too much to hold back, the passion that he had denied for so long clamored for release. But she did not ask for tenderness. The shy acceptance of his desire that he remembered was gone. She clutched his shoulders, arching against him with a fury that bespoke a need as raw and primal as his own.

Burying his face against her shoulder, he gave himself up to the fire, allowing it to devour them both, until he exploded inside of her, felt the shudders of her body as she, too, reached the apex of desire.

He collapsed on top of her, his heart steadying to a more normal beat as he remained joined with her. He felt her warm breath against his ear as she murmured his name over and over again. Then he became aware she was telling him how much she loved him. He wrenched away from her, his hands reaching out to cradle the softness of her passion-flushed face.

"Lyssa, I..." He shut his eyes, releasing her. Sitting up, he turned his back to her.

He felt her stir behind him, her arms sliding around his waist as she pressed her forehead to his back. At last she burst out, "Why? Why, my lord, do I no longer please you? Why do you always feel this regret after...?"

He placed his hand on top of hers, could feel it quiver. He sought to put into words what he scarce understood himself.

"I do not regret...'tis only that sometimes you frighten me, Lyssa."

He felt her raise her head, heard the surprise and disbelief in her voice. "I—frighten you?"

"You—you have become too much a part of me. No other woman has ever been so ingrained into my being. When I left here to go to France, I left with half a heart."

"Is it so terrible a thing to care that much for someone, Jaufre? You took all of my heart away with you, and I never complained."

"But I failed, Lyssa. I failed."

"Nay, 'twas not your doing. 'Twas the king. He—"

"I was not strong enough! My—my feelings for you weaken me." He broke off, rubbing his hand over his eyes.

"Not strong enough!" He heard the sudden intake of her breath. When he turned to look at her, he was surprised to see the anger rising in her face.

"Are you conceited enough to think you could have turned the tide of battle all by yourself? God's wounds!" She struggled to her feet, groping for her chemise.

"Lyssa." He tried to pull her down beside him, but she jerked away from him, tugging her kirtle back over her head.

"Nay, my patience has come to an end. I have waited too long to hear you say you loved me to listen to you ruin it once more. 'Tis not my love that weakens you, but the self-pity you have been wallowing in since your return. Nay, don't touch me. I don't want you. I want the man who left here for France a year ago."

He stood up, wrapping a towel about his lean hips, his face darkening with an anger to match hers. "Oh, no, that's not the man you want, Lyssa. You want the one who knelt at your feet when you were a child. Sir Launcelot ready to ride out on some damned fool quest, slay your dragons, sing love songs to you. Well, he's dead, Lyssa. He died many years ago."

"And you killed him! Not Yseult, not Godric! 'Twas you with your own miserable cynicism and bitterness." With a choked sob, she turned and stumbled from the tent.

Jaufre whirled, smashing his fist into the tub. How dare she speak thus to him? It only fueled his rage when a voice deep inside him persisted in taunting him, telling him her words were true.

Curse her! If she was not satisfied with what he was, let her go from Winterbourne, retire to a nunnery. She would have to beg on her hands and knees before he ever made love to her again.

He grabbed for his fresh clothing, savagely yanking on the drawers. What did he care if he had lost his wife's respect? It mattered not a whit. 'Twas no different than...

His shoulders sagged, the fury draining from him as suddenly as it had come. 'Twas no different than if the sun had gone out of the world.

Jaufre did not speak to Melyssan of their quarrel. It was as if nothing had passed between them, neither the lovemaking nor the anger, and yet the expression on his face became harder with each passing day, the light coming to his eyes only when they chanced to rest on Jenny.

He spent more time alone in the solar going through the contents of the trunk that contained his books, poring over old documents. Oft she caught him not reading at all, the parchment sprawled across the desk while his dark, brooding eyes fixed on the painting of Sir Launcelot. When he acknowledged her with the curtest of nods, she thought her heart would break.

But to her surprise, she found new reserves of strength within herself. She could no longer yield, accepting Jaufre on any terms while the man she had loved slowly disappeared before her eyes to be replaced by a cold, shallow stranger.

It was a sennight after their quarrel in the garden that the messenger arrived. A nobleman from court, Nelda whispered in Melyssan's ear, so scented with lavender and bedecked with gemstones he more resembled a lady's jewel chest than a man.

Her heart pounding with dread, Melyssan slipped down the stairs to the great hall, pausing in the shadows to listen. The short, blond courtier stood facing Jaufre, who slouched in his high-backed chair, propping one foot on the trestle table, his expression inscrutable as he listened.

"...and the number of rebels grows each day. His Majesty was pleased to hear of your safe return, but of course, his first concern is for the security of his realm. 'Tis not unusual for the king to request hostages in these instances. Already he has many from the noblest families in England."

Hostages? Melyssan gripped the top of her cane.

The man continued, nervously rubbing his hands. "She would be well cared for. The king swears no harm would ever come to her."

Melyssan's hand flew to her throat. She looked to Jaufre for his reaction. He cocked one skeptical eyebrow at the nobleman.

"And—and she would receive many privileges as the daughter of such an eminent lord as yourself. 'Twould actually be of benefit to her to be raised at court."

Daughter! Dear God, they were speaking of Jenny. Melyssan stifled her urge to cry out, to beg Jaufre to get rid of this stranger who had come to steal away their child.

But all the earl said was "Aye, 'tis well known how John treats those placed in his care."

How could Jaufre sit there so calmly and bandy words with this knave? He could not be considering this vile proposal.

She clenched her fists. No one—no one

was going to take her child. They would have to kill her first. She whirled around, falling and cracking her knee against the worn stonework of the stairs. Ignoring the shooting pain, she scrambled to her feet again.

She burst into Jenny's chamber, startling Canice, who was smoothing the child's shirt over her head. Melyssan snatched Jenny away from the astonished nurse, carrying the little girl to her own bedchamber.

"Nay," Jenny said, her brow puckering into a frown as she fought against being held so tightly. When she could not effect a release, she began to cry.

"Hush, love, hush," Melyssan said as they reached the safety of her room. Safe? Where was safe? Where could she hide her daughter to protect her from the king? Jenny kicked, trying to get away.

"Nay, sweetheart, don't. Mother must hide you. There is a bad man who is coming to take you away."

She was not sure how much Jenny understood, or if her own panic communicated itself to the child, but Jenny began to howl with fright.

The door to the room swung open. Jaufre's tall frame loomed across the threshold. He stared at the child clasped in her arms, his eyes cold. Melyssan backed away, her hand tangled in Jenny's curling hair, pressing the child to her breast.

"So 'twas you on the stairs," he said. "You heard what we spoke of?"

She regarded him through angry, tear-filled eyes. "Aye, I did. But I tell you no one, not God himself, could persuade me to surrender my child to that monster."

He stepped closer, his breath coming out in a furious hiss. "Damn you! You think I would? 'Fore God, Lyssa, is that what you think of me?"

She winced at the flash of raw pain that crossed his face. "I—I am sorry, my lord. But when I heard that man, I was so afraid."

"Put the child down, Lyssa," he said more gently. "No one is going to take her. You are frightening her half to death."

Reluctantly, her arms shaking, she set Jenny on her feet. Her heart ached when she saw how the little girl ran from her, seeking the shelter of her father's arms.

He scooped her up and deposited a kiss upon the tip of her nose. "There now, little one. Don't cry. There is no bad man. Father has already sent him away."

"He'll be back—with soldiers," Melyssan whispered. "You cannot refuse the king and go unpunished. Matilda de Briouse..." Her voice choked off at the horrible memory.

"I will deal with the king," he said as Jenny curled her arms around his neck, burying her face against his shoulder.

A sharp pang of envy pierced Melyssan. She wished that she, too, was still capable of finding strength in Jaufre's arms. "How will you deal with him?" she cried. "How? What will you give him this time?"

"That is not your concern, madam." He

turned and strode out of the room. Outside she heard the sound of heavy boots trampling up the steps.

"Jaufre, I heard the news." Tristan's breathless voice carried to her. "You are going to London. This time you shall not leave me behind."

It took little time for the earl to ready himself to leave. Melyssan lingered outside their bedchamber as he packed, leaning against the cool stone of the oriel. So soon he was going away again. She felt too drained for tears. Was he taking with him the large silver chest? Jaufre, who believed money could buy anything. Perhaps he was right.

When he emerged from the chamber he paused, staring at her so hard she wondered if he were trying to memorize her face. He said, "I hate to leave you thus alone with no proper person to command the garrison. Dreyfan grows old...." He frowned, his voice trailing off.

She thrust out her chin. "You forget, my brother is here."

Jaufre said nothing, the wry twist of his mouth expressing what he felt on that score.

"In any case, you will not be gone long. I would imagine it will not take much time to see the king—and—and buy his goodwill." The words all but stuck in her throat.

"Aye." He lowered his gaze. "Fare you well, then, my lady."

She thought he meant to brush past her without touching when he whirled about and caught her up in his arms. With a muffled sob, she melted in his embrace, her lips clinging to his, until he had to thrust her away. His eyes gleamed strangely as he brushed the hair back from her brow.

"Lyssa, I—" he said hoarsely. "I love you." He kissed her fiercely one last time and was gone.

She thought of following him down to the courtyard, but her knees felt so weak. She staggered back into the bedchamber and closed the door, his parting words echoing in her ears. Her dazed senses tried to absorb the meaning of them.

She had waited so long. Why should he fling those words at her now? She almost did not believe she had heard them. As she made her way to the bed, her eyes blinded with tears, she stumbled over a trunk. Jaufre's small chest. Had he meant to take it with him and forgot? She thought of hastening after him, but it was only the trunk of his manuscripts. He had no need of those on his journey to placate the king.

The lid lay half-open. She bent down to close it, but a piece of parchment blocked the hinge. She threw the chest open to rearrange the contents. Something about the manuscript on top caught her eye. It was not illuminated as the others were. The yellow parchment crinkled, proclaiming its great age, as if it were likely to crumple apart in her hands.

Her heart thudded as she focused on one of the words: *Charter*. She unfurled the corner, her hands shaking so badly she could scarce read. *This is the Charter of Henry I by means of which the barons sought their liberties.*

Was this what Jaufre had studied so intently for the past week? The paper nearly dropped from her grasp. As she clutched at the document something that had been rolled inside fell to the floor. She bent to retrieve it.

A child's garment. Her own linen sleeve! Melyssan's eyes misted over with a mixture of fear and pride. Jaufre was not going to placate the king this time. He rode to join the rebellion.

Chapter 19

THE LOCAL VILLAGERS called the meadow Runnymeade, its verdant pastures stretching down to be lapped by the waters of the Thames, halfway between the king's mighty fortress at Windsor and the rebel stronghold now based in London. Jaufre stared across the expanse of greenery at the distant billowing silk. The canopy formed the king's tents set beneath the brilliant azure of the June sky.

"Your sword, m'lord." His squire handed him the length of gleaming steel. Jaufre slid the weapon into its sheath as Lord Oswin emerged from his tent, likewise armed, with two daggers buckled to his belt besides.

He stretched his long arms overhead and

yawned before lapsing into a complacent smile behind his bristling mustache. "Good morrow, Lord Jaufre. This is the day, the end to our long struggle against tyranny."

Jaufre merely shot him a skeptical glance. Tristan strode up to join them. After greeting Lord Oswin, the knight looked Jaufre over and frowned.

"Did you not sleep again last night, Jaufre? You look exhausted."

"I am, but not from lack of sleep. I am tired of this whole business."

"I am sure that today will see the end of it, m'lord," Tristan said quietly. "The king will approve the new charter. Then we may all return to Winterbourne in peace."

Jaufre compressed his lips. Could Tristan truly be as naive as the rest of these fools, believing that King John's seal on a piece of paper would put an end to hostilities and grudges conceived over a lifetime?

"Aye, we will give each other the kiss of concord and clasp hands." Jaufre sneered, flicking his fingers against Tristan's own sword. "We are all wearing these merely for adornment."

Tristan's face flushed, but before he could speak, Lord Oswin chimed in, "Better safe than dead, m'lord. That's my motto. We're encamped less than a mile from the king's own followers. What few he has left, that is."

"Ah, but you do concede that the king is capable of sealing that worthless charter with one hand whilst signaling for an ambush with the other?"

"Well I—I..." Sir Oswin was saved from answering as the leader of the rebel army, Robert Fitzwalter, raised his banner, indicating they were to start their march across the field toward John's encampment. The knights surged forward, trampling the tiny yellow buttercups beneath their booted feet. Runnymeade blazed with a dashing array of silken tunics marked with the heraldic symbols of many of the most powerful houses in England.

As they joined the ranks of the other barons and nobles, Tristan fell into step beside Jaufre. "So tell me, my lord, if you feel this is all a waste of time, why did you come? You could have approached the king, bribed him with silver again. Friends are a scarce commodity for him these days. He probably would have forgot the past, received you with open arms."

Jaufre's lips twisted into a wry smile. "Ah, but I am on a quest, my friend."

"A—a quest?"

"To please a lady," the earl said lightly, then lengthened his stride to escape Tristan's discomfiting stare. Faith, but his friend asked the damnedest questions. Jaufre was not sure himself why he had gotten mixed up in this business, though he greatly feared it had too much to do with a wistful pair of green eyes, eyes that clouded with disappointment when he cynically pricked her visions of himself as some noble knight fighting for chivalric ideals. What was he trying to prove? That he could resurrect her shining Sir Jaufre for her? Bring back to life some part of him that had died long ago?

He still tasted their parting kiss on his lips, heard his own unbelievable words echoing on the wind. "Lyssa, I love you." How could he, who did not believe in such an emotion, have ever said such a thing? Was it not as amusing as the position he was in now, a man of no faith marching behind a rebel leader who styled himself "the Marshal of God"? Jaufre threw back his head and laughed.

At that moment, he caught up to Fitzwalter. "I am glad to see you in such spirits, my lord. Is this not a glorious day, an important day, whose fame will ring throughout the ages?"

"Aye, so 'tis," Jaufre said, a smile quivering upon his lips. "'Tis the second anniversary of my daughter's birth." With that he trudged forward, leaving Fitzwalter's jaw hanging in astonishment.

When they reached the royal tent, the king was prepared for them. He sat behind a small table, surrounded by those few nobles who had remained loyal to his cause. His costly satin robes did little to disguise his expanding waistline. The golden crown looked as if it weighed down the graying head. He sparkled with gemstones beringing his fingers, festooning his neck, as if he had worn every jewel he owned to enhance the stature he lacked.

His smile glittered when he greeted the rebel barons in turn by name. Jaufre eyed the king warily as John wrung his hand with false heartiness.

"Ah, my lord Jaufre. I am glad to see you took no ill effects from your sojourn in France. As hearty as ever. And how was your daughter when you last saw her? My messenger reports she is a taking little thing, pretty and straight of limb, nothing like her mother."

Jaufre withdrew his hand, his jaw clenching. He thought John's smile a shade too wolfish as the king settled himself behind the table once more. John stared down at the document spread out before him, his jeweled fingers drumming nervously.

"Well, then, shall we make an end...I mean, shall we commence the proceedings?"

One of the king's clerics stepped forward and began reading aloud the articles of the agreement that had been reached after a week of endless haggling.

"John, by Grace of God, King of England...by Divine intuition and the salvation of our soul...have granted by this our present Charter, confirmed on behalf of ourselves and our heirs forever..."

As Jaufre listened to the king's affirmation of the ancient laws of their land, something stirred inside him.

"The English Church shall be free, liberties unimpaired. ...To no one will we sell, deny, or delay right of justice. ...No free man shall be taken, imprisoned, or exiled except by legal judgment of his peers...no fines to financially ruin a man, not even the lowliest serf...the restoration of all hostages, lands, castles wrongfully dispossessed..."

Laws, ancient liberties, confirmed and set down for all time in that fragile parchment lying

450

beneath the king's hand. John's eyes roved over the barons, settling upon their swords. Grudgingly he reached for his seal.

For a moment, Jaufre forgot he had joined the rebellion to restore himself in Melyssan's eyes. He almost believed in the power of the Great Charter, almost believed that he had participated in an undertaking that was something fine and noble, that would outlive this day, the tyrant king himself, live as long as the old rolling Thames, whose bright waters he could see sparkling through the opening in the tent.

"Liberties unimpaired...for ourselves and our heirs forever."

Jaufre's eyes locked on the king's face, and his brief moment of hope vanished. For one instant John dropped his mask of good cheer. His wide-set eyes darkened with hate, studying the face of every rebel present, coming to rest upon Jaufre, encompassing him in their stygian blackness. Then John smiled.

"We will all ride back to Winterbourne in peace." Jaufre mimicked Tristan's voice five months later as his boots crunched against the cobbled pavement of London's streets. He hugged his sable-lined mantle tight against his body to shut out the chill November fog.

"You could well have done so," Tristan said, blowing against the raw red skin of his exposed hands. "No one constrained you to become involved with the committee of twenty-five."

"Did you truly expect John to uphold that damned charter without some body of men to compel him?" Jaufre snorted. "I might have known it would come down to a question of force in the end. I only hope Melyssan will be satisfied by the effects of this charming little crusade. I wish her much joy of her empty bed this winter."

Tristan grimaced. "More joy than I've had sharing a pallet with you. The way you toss and groan of nights, I think you need a cold plunge in the Thames."

Jaufre glared at him as they mounted the creaking wooden stairs leading to the house of the wealthy merchant whose hospitality they shared during their enforced stay in London. As they passed into the hall, the merchant's wife greeted them with sour looks. Aye, the rebel army had been hailed with great enthusiasm when it first marched into London, but now no one was pleased with the Great Charter.

The merchants were dissatisfied because the charter did not place restraints upon foreigners importing goods. The more radical northern rebels felt John had not conceded enough and were already busily devastating royal manors and forests. The king had only waited until the end of summer before reverting to his customary behavior. Even now he was importing mercenaries from overseas and laying siege to Rochester Castle, the stronghold that commanded the road south from London.

For the life of him, Jaufre could not understand what made him cling so stubbornly, lingering in London, trying to make the new laws work. The Great Charter was dead. A year from now, who would even remember its existence? Why could he not simply return to Winterbourne and worry only about protecting what was his, as he had always done? Let some other fool slay the dragon.

It did naught to improve his exacerbated temper when he found Lord Oswin and some of his cronies gathered by the fire, their feet propped up, red noses deep in cups of ale.

"Lord Jaufre. Sir Tristan." Oswin saluted them with his goblet. "What! Abroad so early on a Sunday? You weren't trying to sneak into a church, I trust."

He wagged his finger at Jaufre. "Tch. Tch. You know the pope has excommunicated all of us for rebelling against our good and pious King John, just when His Majesty took the pledge to recapture the holy lands. We dastardly knaves are all that stopped him from going."

Oswin and his companions guffawed heartily over the tale John had passed along to the pope. Jaufre and Tristan retreated to seats in the opposite corner of the room. Jaufre was surprised at himself. At one time, he would have joined in their mirth, greatly appreciating the jest that the irreverent John, after defying the pope for years, should now be among His Holiness's favorite sons. But he found himself wondering what Lyssa would think of her husband being excommunicate, his lands at Winterbourne once more under the interdict. She had been so happy, so at peace, to have the faith restored to her home.

"What's amiss, de Macy?" Lord Oswin called out. "Have we suddenly become not good enough to drink with you?"

"His Lordship is in no humor for such revelry," Tristan replied, making little effort to disguise his dislike for the baron.

"Eh, why so glum, man? Even if the king doesn't mean to keep faith with us, we have worsted him. Here we sit, entrenched in a position of strength."

"Position of strength?" Jaufre snarled, pushing to his feet. "Has it never occurred to you we are virtual prisoners here in London, skulking behind the city walls while John is free to attack any of our castles he chooses?"

Oswin dismissed the threat with a wave of his hand. "John is too busy trying to take over the castle at Rochester. With a soldier like William of Albini commanding our garrison, His Majesty and his Flemish mercenaries will be there forever."

But Jaufre was not so sure. Of late he had begun to worry more and more about Winterbourne. Most of the rebel barons flocked to London from the north and east. He was one of the few who came from the Welsh marches. In time, might not Lyssa find herself surrounded by enemies, with only Dreyfan and that foolish brother of hers to advise her? Whitney had showed some improvement during the war in France, but Jaufre feared the man might hand Winterbourne over to John at the first sign of trouble. What then would be the fate of Lyssa and Jenny at the hands of a monarch bent on leveling all of England to exact vengeance for his humiliation at Runnymeade?

"We have naught to worry about." Sir Oswin's booming voice penetrated Jaufre's thoughts. "For the French will soon arrive to reinforce us."

One of Oswin's companions tried to silence him, but it was too late. Jaufre had heard the remark. He leaned over Oswin, demanding with deadly quiet, "What did you say?"

Lord Oswin squirmed in his chair for a moment, then glowered defiantly. "'Tis well known, my lord, you have steadfastly opposed any schemes for appealing to France for aid in restoring order. But you are only one man. Fitzwalter thought it an excellent notion. He sent a delegation to Philip Augustus. The young Prince Louis will arrive in February—"

"You fools!" Jaufre seized the man and dragged him up by the front of his surcoat. "You bloody fools. Do you know what you've done? We've scarce dealt with one tyrant and you would set loose upon us another."

Oswin wriggled from Jaufre's grasp. "Nay, we've asked Prince Louis to be our king, our true king, who will help us preserve our ancient liberties."

Jaufre lunged forward but was restrained by Tristan. "Liberties. I'm sick to death of hearing you whine about your liberties when you only mean your petty self-interests. That charter meant no more to most of you than it did the king."

Lord Oswin puffed out his chest. "What! What! Do you think I shall listen to many more of these lies, these calumnies?"

While he blustered, Jaufre drew forth his sword. "Any man of you that says I lie is welcome to try my steel."

A silence settled over the room until one by one the other knights shuffled out the door. Oswin eyed the sword for one moment longer before storming after them.

Jaufre sheathed his weapon, then turned to face his grave-eyed friend. "So now this farce is completed. What do I do now, Tristan? Drag myself home to my wife, once more a failure? And a fool, this time, a fool, trying to be some sort of idealistic crusader I am not."

"I do not think you could ever be a failure in Melyssan's eyes," Tristan said. "She loves you, Jaufre."

Jaufre gazed into the fire, imagining a reflection of honey-brown hair framing the sweetest face he'd ever seen. His shoulders slumped as he leaned one arm against the wall, resting his head upon it. "I wish I thought I was worthy of that love. I wish I could still be that young knight she once saw on a long-ago summer's day."

He started up when a young page burst into the room, breathless with news. "My lord. You must come at once. Baron Fitz-walter is assembling all the nobles. There is dire news."

Tristan placed his hands on the boy's shoulders. "Get your breath, lad. Slow down and tell us what has happened."

"Rochester. Rochester Castle has fallen into the hands of the king. All the rebels there including William of Albini are His Majesty's prisoners."

Tristan and Jaufre looked at one another over the boy's head. So now the siege was ended, and King John controlled the road south from London. Even more important, John's mercenaries were now freed to carry the war to another part of England. Where would the king strike next?

A cold wave of apprehension rushed up Jaufre's spine. He closed his eyes, a vision of piercing clarity rising before him. Towers...white towers gleaming bright against the green Welsh hills. Winterbourne!

Chapter 20

DARK SMOKE BILLOWED into the gray sky, black curls of it whisked on the wind as far as the battlements at Winterbourne. Melyssan peered through the embrasure, tears stinging her eyes at the sight of the wattle and daub cottages dissolving in the roaring midst of red flame. Screams rent the air of those unfortunates who had not been able to flee the village fast enough to reach the safety of the castle gates. Flemish soldiers pierced the stragglers with their pikes. A horse and rider thundered after a young girl, who ran shrieking with a babe bundled in her arms. Melyssan turned away, covering her face.

"We cannot just stand here," she cried. "We must do something to help them."

"We shall be lucky to help ourselves," Whitney mumbled.

"Whitney. I am the mistress here. Open those gates and send some of our knights out. I command you."

He shook his head. "Nay, we will need every man. Unless you want that to be yourself out there running away, running away with Jenny."

She bit her lip as he hit upon her one weak spot. Willingly would she have risked her own life in an attempt to save those people. But not her child. Defeated, she drew back behind the merlon and waited, tears sliding down her cheeks. Waited until the screams came no more, until the only sound was the distant hiss of the flames, the rumble of marching feet, horses' hooves as the king's army marched on Winterbourne Castle.

Sir Dreyfan clambered up to the walkway. His grizzled face scowled when he saw Melyssan. "Are you mad, boy?" he shouted at Whitney. "Get my lady down from here."

She felt Whitney tense beside her. "You'd best get to the safety of the donjon, Lyssa. They—they are bringing up the catapults."

"Whitney, I—"

"Go on," he said, giving her a rough shove. "You'll only be in the way up here. You'd best go down below and begin making preparations to tend—in case anyone is wounded."

Her heart thudding, she did as he bade her. As she wound her way down the stone stair through the gate tower, she passed many of the castle guard, their friendly faces looking grim beneath their steel helms, the cross-bows in their hands aimed and ready.

There seemed to be so few of them, the king's soldiers so many. But she was forget-ting Jaufre. She doubted not that when news of the siege at Winterbourne reached his ears, he would rally his knights and ride to their rescue. If the news reached his ears...She was no longer sure exactly where her hus-band was. The last she had heard of him was when the messenger brought the news saying the Great Charter was accepted. How they had all cheered and celebrated! Tyranny and injustice vanquished forever! She was so proud that her husband should have played a part in it.

As she entered the great hall of the donjon, she found all her ladies-in-waiting gathered together by the chapel. Their faces reflected their fear, but Jenny bounded forward into Melyssan's arms, her brown eyes shining with excitement.

"Milady, milady." She hugged Melyssan around the neck, her smile expectant, hopeful. "Fahver has come home?"

"Nay, Jenny. 'Tis not Fahver." She watched

the child's face cloud with disappointment, marveling at how Jenny carried such a strong image of Jaufre. She had been so young when the earl left last spring, yet she retained a great impression of him in her heart.

As Melyssan cradled the child close in her arms, she thought it was not so hard to understand. Was not Jaufre forever impressed upon her own heart?

She looked over the child's head, speaking with courage and conviction. "The king's army has come. Nay, Nelda, don't weep. There is naught to fear. Winterbourne is a strong fortress."

"But—but," Canice faltered. "I've heard tales of the siege at Rochester. Shan't we all starve in here?"

"Of course not, you foolish woman. We are well stocked. And soon my lord Jaufre will come and drive them from our gates."

She noticed Father Andrew standing quietly in the shadows. Her voice sharpened with irritation when she saw the doubt register in his eyes.

"In the meantime, we must prepare linen and herbs for bandages. Stay inside the donjon and keep out of the men's way. Now, off with you and be about your tasks."

The women reluctantly dispersed, except for Canice, who waited quietly for Melyssan to release the child. Shamed she was to admit it, but the child's warm arms about her neck gave her courage. Jenny regarded her mother, her lively eyes unusually wide and serious in her small face.

"Is the bad king's army coming inside?"

"Nay, my love. Our castle is very strong." But even as she said so, Melyssan recalled snatches of things she had heard Jaufre say. How oft had he complained the castle lacked proper defense measures. "Unsafe," the earl had groused. "Unsafe."

"It doesn't matter in any case," Melyssan said, shifting Jenny in her arms. Faith, the child grew so heavy, soon she would be unable to lift her. "My lord will come and rescue us." Once again she noticed Father Andrew's lips tighten as he crossed himself.

Jenny nodded her approval. "Aye, Muvver. My lord will come and kill all those bad men." Her small brows knit together in an expression so fiercely reminiscent of Jaufre, Melyssan laughed, at the same time fighting back her tears.

She set Jenny on her feet, giving her a pat. "Mayhap you'd best run along with Canice. Mother has many things to do."

"Me, too. I'm going to go get a sword so I will be ready to help Fahver," she called over her shoulder as the nurse led her away.

"Mistress Genevieve, ladies do not wield swords," Canice scolded.

"This one does." Jenny left the hall staring truculently up at her nurse.

Melyssan followed Father Andrew where he had slipped into the chapel. He knelt before the altar, fingering his rosary. She knew she should leave, ignoring the disapproval she sensed from the priest ever since news had

461

reached them of Jaufre's excommunication. But her nerves were on edge. Outside the castle, the walls were too quiet. The battle had not yet begun. What were they waiting for?

"'Tis Sunday, Father," she said, her voice echoing loudly in the small chamber.

"And so?" he whispered.

"I want you to say mass."

He rose to his feet and faced her, his black robes brushing the altar. "You know I cannot do that, milady. Your husband is excommunicate. That places his lands under the interdict as well."

She flushed hotly. "I have been thinking about that. The pope's ruling is unjust. We shall ignore it. Lord Jaufre is master here. I want prayers said for his safe return."

"My first responsibility is to the Holy Church, to God," the priest said sternly. "I cannot pray for a man who offends both."

"Jaufre has offended no one but that tyrant king. He marched to London to try for peace, seeking only to secure the liberties that—"

"He marched as all the others did, to protect their own selfish interests. Do not try to make something noble out of his behavior, Melyssan. 'Twill only break your heart. There is no difference between Lord Jaufre and his barons and that marauding army outside."

"Don't speak of my husband that way. I'll no longer endure it. Too long have I tolerated your silent disapproval. You do not know him. You never have. He will come riding from London to help us."

"Aye, I suppose he will. He will want to save Winterbourne."

Her breath caught in her throat, but she refused to give way to tears, refused to let the old priest dim her image of Jaufre, cast aspersions upon the nobility of his actions. "Mayhap I cannot force you to pray for my husband. But—but I love him. I care naught for what the pope says or you. Nay, even if he should be condemned by God himself, I would follow him to hell."

A shudder tore through the old priest's frame as he bowed his head. "I have seen too much of the pain this man has brought into your life. And now you are driven to blaspheme God himself. Lord Jaufre has poisoned you at last."

She could bear to hear no more and fled from the chapel only to find Jenny romping in the great hall. Somehow she had eluded her nurse. Horror tore through Melyssan when she realized the child held a large dagger, which she now withdrew from its ruby-encrusted sheath.

"Jenny, give me that thing," she gasped, snatching it away.

Jenny's lower lip jutted out. "Give that back. I need it to kill King John."

Melyssan raised the weapon far above the child's grasping fingers. "Nay, 'tis not a plaything. Wherever did you get it?"

"From Fahver's chest. He always let me hold it."

"Did he indeed?" Melyssan's lips set in a taut line. "Well, Mother shall have a long talk with Father when he gets home."

When he gets home... The thought pounded through her brain. *Oh, Jaufre, my love, please come home. Put an end to this nightmare of uncertainty.*

Whitney strode into the great hall, the grim cast of his countenance telling her there was more bad news.

"Have they commenced—the assault?" she asked, ignoring Jenny, who stamped her foot and demanded the return of the dagger.

"They sent a messenger forward to parley. They—they would leave us in peace if their terms were met."

"What terms?" Melyssan asked, her suspicions aroused.

"If we surrender the castle to them, without resisting, the king pledges no one will be harmed. You may retire to the convent at St. Clare."

She studied her brother's uneasy expression. "Whitney, there is something more you are not telling me."

Whitney stared at the floor, not meeting her eyes. "The king wants Jenny."

The dagger clattered to the ground and Jenny dove for it, but Melyssan's arms had already closed around her despite her angry squeals of protest.

"Never!" she cried. "May he rot in hell first."

"He swears he will not hurt her, Lyssa. He wants her for a hostage."

"Aye, a hostage to use against Jaufre. You give the king his answer, Whitney. Have the men commence firing their arrows from the wall."

Whitney hesitated, his eyes lingering wistfully on Jenny's flushed face, triumphant as her fingers closed around the end of the dagger.

Melyssan's arms tightened on the child as she studied her brother's expression. She could not help remembering Jaufre's opinion of her brother. *Weak like Godric...he will betray you one day, Lyssa.*

"No!" she said aloud. She would allow no one to poison her mind against her husband or her brother. "We shall survive, Whitney. Jaufre will be here soon. You and Dreyfan muster the men to defend the walls, and—and do the best you can."

Whitney bit his lip and nodded. He tousled Jenny's curls. "Just remember, Lyssa. I love her as I do you. And I know how much she means to you."

With one final glance back, he strode away to hurl Melyssan's defiance at the king. The siege of Winterbourne had begun.

Chapter 21

THE CHEERS OF the crowd dinned in Jaufre's ears as the populace of London surged forward into the street to greet the French soldiers. The Frenchmen nodded and waved, carefully guiding their mounts around the women, who hiked up their skirts and rushed too close to the horses' hooves. Men clapped each other on the back and danced jigs along the cobblestones as if their deliverance were at hand. Although Prince Louis had yet to arrive, the French had marched to London unopposed by King John's army. At last report, it was rumored that John had fled north. To hide in Scotland, said his gleeful detractors.

Jaufre's lips curled in scorn as he and Tristan watched the proceedings from the doorway. Tristan's eyes were grave.

"It seems history would repeat itself. Only this time the conquerors come not from Normandy. The prospect of a French king is a strange one. I am not so sure it agrees with me."

"They have not conquered anything yet." Jaufre turned, preparing to reenter the house. "As to French king, English king, I am sick to death of either. Sometimes I feel as if I would like to retire from the world to a quiet monastery."

A cultured voice spoke up behind him. "Somehow I cannot envision you as a monk, my lord."

Jaufre whirled around to confront a tall young Frenchman who had dismounted. The earl's eyes traveled in disbelief up the lean hips to the broad shoulders until he reached the face. Silver-gray eyes glinted at him, a half smile twisting the thin lips.

Tristan found his voice long before Jaufre was able to speak. "Roland! God's blood, lad, I scarce recognized you." The young man returned Tristan's hearty embrace, but his eyes never left Jaufre.

Tristan drew back, laughing. "Just look at the young longshanks. You are as tall as your father now, and you quite dwarf me."

"That has never been so difficult to do. How are you, boy?" Jaufre clasped Roland's hand briefly, his gruff voice concealing the mixture of emotions that churned inside of him. "So you've come over to invade my lands?"

"Scarcely that, my lord," Roland said. "Upon finding you amongst the rebels, I assumed you were one of those who had invited the help of King Philip."

"Then you don't know me very well, do you?"

Roland arched one brow. "Mayhap I do not."

"Let us not stand around in the midst of this mob," Tristan said. "Come inside, lad, and tell us what mischief you've been up to over there in Paris."

Roland consigned his horse to the care of a young page and followed Tristan into the house. As Jaufre brought up the rear, he studied the boy's frame. Aye, Tristan was right, the lad had grown. He was a boy no longer. Jaufre also noted that the gold spurs of a knight adorned Roland's boots. The young man appeared to put an extra spring in his step to make them jangle more loudly.

Up in the small chamber where Jaufre and Tristan shared a pallet, the three men settled down to goblets of burgundy wine. Roland showed little inclination to talk about himself but made eager inquiries after the people at Winterbourne, especially Jenny and Melyssan.

"They are all well," Jaufre said, though his brow furrowed. The last messenger he had sent seeking news of Winterbourne had as yet failed to return. He felt the return of his earlier fear that John might attack his castle next. But by all reports, the king was headed for Yorkshire.

After teasing the young man about the fringe of hair sprouting on his upper lip, Tristan glanced from Roland to Jaufre, then abruptly excused himself. When he had left the room, an awkward silence descended.

Jaufre was first to speak. "'Tis a most handsome sword you've got strapped to your side. I see Philip has treated you well, Roland."

"'Tis Sir Roland now." The young man puffed out his chest, then looked slightly ashamed of his boastful manner. "That is— I am not sure I was worthy of the honor, but the king knighted me last Christmas."

"You saved his life. 'Twas the least he could do." Jaufre looked away, his spine stiffening as the words came out with great difficulty. " 'Twould seem I also am in your debt. I doubt that Philip would have released me so soon, even after Tristan paid the ransom, if you had not pleaded on my behalf."

Roland shrugged. "You would never have been captured if you had not tried to come back for me." He looked Jaufre directly in the eye. "Why did you?"

"I see you have not outgrown your habit of asking stupid questions," Jaufre said gruffly.

Roland's face split into a broad grin, which wavered after a moment. "There is one more honor the king would bestow upon me—which I am loath to tell you about." Roland drew in a deep breath. "He knew I was your son, but he—he did not quite understand the circumstances of my birth. He offered me Clairemont."

Clairemont. The name of that place had become the bane of Jaufre's existence. He could scarce bear hearing it. "Congratulations, *Sir* Roland," he said dryly. "A handsome estate for a man of your years."

Roland flushed a bright red. "Do you think I would keep it? I accepted the lands only to return them to you. To do otherwise would be the same as stealing. Especially now. Now that Prince Louis will become the king of England, it will be possible for you to be the lord of Clairemont without dividing your loyalties."

"I have no desire to be the lord of Clairemont. I never had, except for that damned oath." Jaufre's eyes bored into Roland as if seeing him for the first time. The young man fidgeted uncomfortably beneath the intensity of his gaze. "The solution to the problem has been under my nose all the time, and I too blind to see it."

He strode to the chests containing his clothing, tossing garments aside until he found the silver swan medallion. Next he snatched up his grandfather's sword and began tugging the Clairemont seal ring off his finger. He thrust all three in Roland's startled face. "Here. Take them."

"B-but, my lord! I do not understand. 'Tis the seal ring of—of the comte of Clairemont."

"Good. You recognize your own crest. You will make a most wise and sagacious comte." Impatiently, he seized Roland's finger and shoved the ring into place. "Don't lose this."

"But—but..."

Feeling almost light-headed as the burden he had carried since the night of his grandfather's death dropped from his shoulders, Jaufre yanked Roland's own sword from his sheath and flung it across the room. He began to slide his grandfather's sword into its place, but Roland's hand closed over his wrist.

"Nay, you cannot mean this, my lord. What of your oath?"

"My oath is fulfilled. All I ever promised my grandfather was that someday one of his blood would again be the lord of Clairemont."

"But I am a bastard!"

"You are Sir Roland or Roland Fitzmacy. But whatever you choose to call yourself, you are the great-grandson of Raoul de Macy, the son of Jaufre, earl of Winterbourne. Never forget that, boy."

"I never have yet, my lord," Roland whispered, his eyes misting. He released Jaufre's arm, permitting him to gird the sword to his side.

"Take care of it, boy. This sword has knighted the back of every de Macy male within my memory."

He started to throw the medallion over Roland's head, then stopped. "Nay, if you will pardon me, monsieur le Comte. This did belong to me, and I will keep it this time." Jaufre's lips tugged into a half smile as he placed the medallion about his own neck.

Now, Grandfather, he thought as he watched his son reverently examining the sword at his side, your wishes have been filled. May you rest in peace, and I at last may do the same.

Aloud he said, "Do not look the sword over too closely. It is not quite as bright and shining as your gift from the king."

"'Tis magnificent," Roland breathed, drawing the weapon forth to study it. "It bears the scars of many battles. I believe you said that you—you were knighted by this sword."

"Aye, boy. A lifetime ago."

Roland regarded him shyly. "I know I have already been through the ceremony with the king of France. But I was wondering if you—if you could...Nay, you would think it ridiculous." His words trailed off as he hung his head in embarrassment.

Jaufre swallowed the sudden constriction in his throat. "Give me the sword," he said. "Kneel down."

The heavy weight passed back into Jaufre's hands as Roland bent his knee, placing himself upon the floor before the earl. The young man dashed his hand quickly across his eyes before gazing up at Jaufre. His youthful face shone with such solemn purpose, such dreams of chivalry and valor yet untried, that Jaufre had to look away for a moment before he could proceed. The sword trembled slightly as he gripped the hilt between his hands and raised it above Roland's head.

"Go, fair son. Be a true knight and courageous in the face of enemies." He brought the flat of the sword down upon each of Roland's shoulders in turn.

"So shall I, with God's help." He rose and replaced the sword at his side, stepping forward to accept the ceremonial embrace. But instead Jaufre clasped his son hard against him.

When he released him, Roland's face was lit with joy. "Thank you, Father. I—I must leave you. The prince will be looking for me. I have responsibilities now."

Aye, son, more than you know, Jaufre thought as he granted the young man permission to leave.

Roland bounded out of the room, his steps bursting with exuberance. The earl knew it had likely never occurred to the young man his dreams of a French conquest could fail. Jaufre was convinced that England was now an entity unto itself, would never be ruled by a power from across the seas. Likewise he was sure that it had never occurred to Roland that one day he and his father might well find themselves as enemies again.

Tristan entered the chamber, shaking his head. "What did you say to Roland? His face blazes as bright as the firewheels on Midsummer Night's Eve."

"I surrendered to him my rights to Clairemont, along with my grandfather's sword." When Tristan merely smiled, Jaufre added, "You do not seem all that surprised."

"I thought that might be a solution to your problem a long time ago, but matters seemed so strained between you and the boy, I hesitated to offer my opinion."

" 'Twould be the first time you ever hesitated."

Tristan stared with an expression of great modesty at the floor. "'Tis difficult when one is always right." He grinned and backed off when Jaufre took a menacing step in his direction. "In any event, you may be sure Roland will make good use of that sword. I watched him ride off, and he was not halfway down the street before he came perilously near to involving himself in a quarrel with some English knight."

Jaufre scowled. "The boy has grown, but there is much ahead that I doubt his ability to handle. Tristan, I am about to request a great favor of you."

"I suppose I should bow and say, 'Command me what you will,' but knowing you I think I'd better ask what it is first."

"I want you to stay close to Roland, keep an eye on him. He can be damnably impulsive and hot-tempered—"

"Gets that from his mother, I suppose."

Jaufre fixed Tristan with a haughty stare, but it had no effect upon his incorrigible friend. Sighing, he gave it up. "There will be some difficult days for Roland. The English heartily welcome the French now, but I foresee a time when the tide will turn. When that day comes, I want you to make sure Roland flows with it, safely back to France."

"Where will you be, my lord?"

"I am going home, Tristan, home to Mel— to Winterbourne. The Great Charter is dead for the present. There is no more I can do here. I like not this being in the dark as regards the king's whereabouts and our last messenger— I think 'tis time I went home."

"I see. And while I am looking after your bear cub, who is to keep you out of trouble?"

"You will have to trust Lyssa for that." As Jaufre reached for his mantle, he glanced back, saying gruffly, "The day I left I—I told her I loved her. Think you she believed me after all this time?"

"I don't know. But I am sure when you get back to Winterbourne, you will find some way to convince her."

Jaufre returned his friend's grin. Their hands interlocked for a moment in a crushing grip that communicated so much that they could not say, so much they did not need to say.

"Godspeed, my lord."

"Farewell, my friend."

Jaufre raced down the stairs, summoning his knights to ride for Winterbourne.

The hail of stones barraging Winterbourne's walls stopped. Melyssan had become so accustomed to the periodic crashing that when the silence descended it took her a moment to realize what had happened. Such an unnatural calm. She had been penned up within the donjon for days upon days. Heedless of Whitney's warning, she slipped up the outer stairs to the top of the castle walls.

"Lyssa!" Her brother's tired, begrimed face registered his disapproval, but he appeared far too weary to remonstrate with her.

"Whitney, what has happened? Why have they stopped?"

She risked one peek through the embrasure, hoping to see the distant figure of a rider mounted on a great black stallion. ...No, she had forgotten. The black stallion was dead, slain at Bouvines. And Jaufre?

Whitney pulled her back before she obtained more than a glimpse of the king's army, the sun glinting off their suspended swords.

"What are they waiting for?"

"I think they finished shoring up the mine under the north tower," Whitney said. "We've tried to stop their digging, tried and tried. But they brought up that siege tower, held us back. It has been impossible to get clear shots at them around that corner."

His shoulders slumped. "'Tis not too late, even now, Lyssa. The king himself is no longer with them. He rode out this morning with a small party of men. His captain sent another messenger, wanting to know if we would surrender."

Her face drained white as she shook her head. The next instant, she heard a strange squealing in the distance. Despite Whitney's restraining hand, she peeked out again. To her amazement, she saw a soldier herding forward a cluster of large pigs.

"They must be running out of provisions," she said hopefully.

But Dreyfan, who strode forward to man the wall near them, shook his head and snorted. "Grease."

"I—I beg your pardon?"

"Grease, my lady." The old knight spat over the wall. "Grease for firing the mine."

Whitney's face paled. "They shored up the mine under the tower with timber logs. When they burn the logs, the mine will cave in, and the tower—" He took a deep, shuddering breath.

Dreyfan said, "I think you'd best get back down below, my lady."

Melyssan hastened back to the bailey, where the women prepared kettles of boiling water to fling upon the attackers. She checked on those who had been wounded, struck by arrows. So far they had been lucky, only six men had died. But if the tower wall did not hold...if Jaufre did not arrive soon...She sickened with fear. Jaufre must not know what danger they risked. He would never have abandoned them.

She retreated to the great chamber they had shared together, sinking down upon the bed where they had loved, fought, where she had given birth to his child. When he left, he had said he loved her. Would she ever hear him say it again? They said the king's mercenaries were ruthless, vicious men, who cared naught for the land and the people they destroyed. If they stormed Winterbourne, no one would be spared.

Jaufre, Jaufre. The tears slid down her cheeks. *I have tried so hard to be brave, to save Winterbourne for you. To save our child. But I need your strength. My love, come to me.*

Rising, she peered through the arrow loop and saw the sinister smoke darkening the sky as a hail of stones and arrows rained upon the castle. Then a terrible rumbling sound drowned all other noise, the earth itself groaning, writhing in pain at the fire belching from its womb. As if by some mighty wizard's spell, the old stone tower crumbled in upon itself, thundering to the ground in a thick cloud of earth and mortar. The dust had not yet cleared when she could hear the shouts, see the metal helms of faceless men pouring over the walls. With a frightened cry, she rushed down to the great hall.

The chamber teemed with Winterbourne's soldiers storming inside, slamming the outer gate as the last defense was manned. Outside came the screams of the dying trapped beyond the walls. Whitney's voice pitched above the turmoil, urging the men up onto the inner walkway. They poised before the arrow slits to aim their bows as Melyssan shoved her wailing ladies inside the relative safety of the chapel. Jenny clung to Melyssan's skirts, and she had to grab the child to avoid being struck by something plummeting to the earth...one of the defenders, pierced through the head by an arrow. Burying the child's frightened eyes against her shoulder, she hurried into the chapel.

Father Andrew remained calm, exhorting the women to pray. They all did, although their terror at the noise without was great, many of them breaking into sobs. Jenny huddled on Melyssan's lap, clutching Jaufre's sheathed dagger, which the child had carried like a talisman all the long days.

"Fahver. I want Fahver."

Melyssan held her daughter close, unable to breathe the familiar assurance any longer. Father Andrew gently stroked the child's head. "Child, you must pray to your Father in heaven."

"Nay. I want *my fahver*. He'll make these bad men go away!"

The door to the chapel crashed open. The women screamed, scattering to hide behind the altar. Melyssan crouched down, thrusting Jenny behind her, her nails bared like claws.

Master Galvan loomed in the doorway, his reddened eyes wild as he brandished his sword. "Where is the bratling? I'll not be killed for the likes of her. Hand her over and we'll all be saved."

"No!" Melyssan shrieked, her arms closing around Jenny as the burly man's seeking gaze lighted upon the child. He stepped closer, but Father Andrew flung himself in the path.

"Get back, coward. How will you ever face your Creator knowing you sacrificed an innocent—"

The priest's words broke off into a muffled groan as Master Galvan smashed the flat of his sword upon the old man's head. Father Andrew fell, struggled to raise himself up, then lay still, the blood trickling across the familiar peaceful features.

"Father!" Melyssan cried. But she had no chance to mourn for her old friend. Galvan roughly knocked her down, snatching Jenny from her arms. The other women tried to hold him back, but he kicked them aside.

Melyssan staggered to her feet, a red haze swirling before her eyes. All fear left her. In its place surged the fierce anger of a mother wolf whose cub is threatened. Her fingers found the dagger Jenny had dropped, unsheathed it, curled around the handle. The death cry burned in her throat as she launched herself at the broad back, burying the blade to the hilt.

Galvan dropped the child to the ground, losing his sword as his hands clawed the air wildly, trying to reach the knife. He slumped to the floor, writhing, his eyes rolling in their sockets.

Melyssan scooped up the sobbing child

and limped out of the chapel. Acrid smoke scorched her nostrils. She fell back, gasping at the intensity of the blaze.

"They've set the hall afire!" Nelda screamed. Soldiers tumbled from the walkway above, screaming as their bodies fell into the flames licking the rushes.

Whitney dashed to her side, taking Jenny from her arms. "We've got to get down below. To the waterway."

She tried to follow him, but his long strides left her far behind. She choked, her lungs aching from the smoke as she fell the remainder of the steps to the bottom floor of the donjon. She felt Nelda helping her to her feet and looked around wildly for Whitney and her child.

Nelda glanced fearfully overhead. "My lady, the fire. 'Twill eat through the floor and bring it down upon our heads."

But Melyssan's eyes were riveted on the distant figure of her brother. Dear God, what was he doing? Some of the men had raised the gateway far enough for him to get through.

"Whitney!" She shrieked his name as he leapt into the water, taking Jenny with him. He could not! He would not try to save himself by turning Jenny over to the king.

She hobbled after him, her feet slipping on the slick surface of the wall, plunging her into the cold water. Her skirts dragged her down beneath the surface, and she gasped in mouthfuls of water that burned her lungs worse than the fire. Then she felt hands pulling her up. Dreyfan! As she flailed in the water, his strong arm clung to her, both of them sweeping out into the stream.

Puffing, the old knight paddled toward shore, tossing her up onto the bank. She choked, straining to catch her breath. Whitney was some yards farther on, running toward one of the Flemish mercenaries.

"No! Jenny!" Her voice came out in a pathetic croak. "Whitney, *don't*!" But even as she cried, her brother's sword sang through the air, cutting the man out of the saddle. He threw Jenny up onto the horse and vaulted after her. Melyssan watched in horror as two more riders bore down upon him. An arrow from the walls cut down one, and Whitney laid into the other with a ferocity and strength that stunned her. As the second rider went down, Whitney whirled his frightened mount and looked back toward the castle.

"No, no, Whitney," she wept. "Don't try to come back for me. Ride out. Save Jenny."

He could not hear her, but as other Flemish soldiers came racing up, he had no choice. He spurred his horse and galloped off, clutching Jenny in front of him. The foot soldiers attempted a futile pursuit. There were no horsemen close enough to catch him.

"Dreyfan! They got away!" Laughing hysterically, she turned back to the old knight. He sprawled upon the bank, his sightless eyes raised toward the sun, a crossbolt protruding from his neck.

Melyssan backed away, sobbing. All the

fight had been taken out of her once she saw her daughter borne to safety. She waited, commending her soul to God as a horseman thundered at her, his sword drawn to strike.

He paused, pointing his blade down at her exposed foot. "Look, 'tis the crippled whore. Lord Jaufre's wife. By God, we may have lost the bratling, but mayhap the king will pay handsomely to get this wench."

Rough hands seized her, bound her, threw her across the back of a horse. She watched the death throes of Winterbourne in a daze, wishing blackness would claim her. After an eternity, a mighty roar, smoke pouring into the sky told her the fire had gutted the interior.

The mercenaries' captain barked, "Put everyone to the sword. Let there be none left alive. Level this place. The king wants not a stone of this rebel's hell left standing."

She was taken back to their encampment, where she spent her next day and night drifting in and out of blessed darkness, choking down the food they forced between her lips. Mercifully, the screams of the slaughtered were hushed, but the cloying stench of smoke hung in the air. She heard the smashing of stone as Jaufre's beloved Winterbourne was razed to the ground. With each crash, she felt something die inside her, the memory of their happy days together, the voices, the faces of the people who had shared those walls— Nelda, Canice, Dreyfan, Father Andrew... Camelot dying.

She scarce knew when they flung her onto

the back of a horse again. The only thing strengthening her in the long ride was her knowledge that Whitney and Jenny had escaped, that somewhere out there was Jaufre...her Dark Knight, who would yet ride down upon these murderers, showing no mercy.

By noon of the second day, they approached the walls of a nearby castle, Penhurst. Sir Hugh and Lady Gunnor's castle. Her heart soared with sudden hope. Old friends. Yet it was the king's banner that flew from Penhurst, not Sir Hugh's. When the tall, scrawny knight came forward in the courtyard to lift her out of the saddle, he was cold, distant, would not meet her eyes.

She sank against him at first, glad of a familiar face, but then drew back.

"His Majesty awaits you, my lady."

"You, Sir Hugh? You would give me up to the king?"

"I have no choice." His eyes traveled to the Flemish soldiers surrounding them. "I am the king's man now. I have my own wife and babes to think of."

He led her past Gunnor, who wept, cuddling her children against her skirts. Melyssan wanted to reach out and reassure the woman. "Don't cry, Gunnor. I understand." She knew well the urges of a mother to protect her children at any cost.

The king's cruel laughter rang in Melyssan's ears as he strode into the bailey. Even now the tyrant had one of Gunnor's children clutched in his arms. The little girl wriggled, wailing, "Muvver...Muvver."

Jenny! With a strangled cry, Melyssan flung herself at the king. The soldiers dragged her back. Jenny's tearful eyes pleaded, her small arms straining toward her mother. The wind shifted, and for the first time Melyssan heard the creak of rope overhead, saw the sinister black shadow pass back and forth over the king's gloating features. John nodded affably, indicating she should look overhead.

Slowly she did, and the sound of her screams pierced her own ears. A man weaved in the wind, his head lolling over the fibers of the rope from which he dangled, his features distorted in death.

Whitney.

Chapter 22

JAUFRE KICKED HIS horse in the sides, all weariness forgotten as he galloped the brown destrier up the rise of the hill. Heading for home, he eagerly motioned for his contingent of knights to pick up their pace. Yet it was not thoughts of Winterbourne that filled his head, but gentle green eyes, silken nutmeg waves of hair, and lips, honey sweet, sweeter than any stream to quench his thirst in this summer heat.

Images of her fragile beauty chased through his mind like the white wispy clouds scudding across the azure sky, disappearing behind the tall line of trees. He threw back his head, basking in the warmth of the sun, delighting in delicious fantasies raised by one cloud pattern in particular. Lyssa in a gown of gossamer white, so sheer it was transparent. But as the puff of vapor shifted, so did the daydreams that obscured his vision. The first pricklings of uneasiness stirred inside him.

He reined in his horse so abruptly, the animal's head lashed to one side. Nothing but clouds and sky. What should there be in that to brew this nameless fear? He sucked in his breath. Nothing but clouds and sky where he should have seen patches of stone. Winterbourne!

One of his knights, Sir Eldred, pressed forward as the rest of the troupe drew to a halt. "My lord. Mayhap we have taken the wrong road. Should we not be able to sight the donjon tower by now?"

"Do you think I know not where my own castle lies?" Jaufre snapped, but his voice sounded uncertain even to his own ears. He stared at the empty sky.

"What witchery is this?" he whispered, then dug in his knees, sending his horse forward at a cautious pace, trying to deny the sensation of dread creeping into his soul. His mount cantered around the bend, cresting the hill, until he reined it in to peer into the valley below.

The verdant pastureland ended abruptly, the soft shades of green transformed into blackened stumps, the fields scorched as if it had been decreed by the lord of death that summer should reign here no more. Piles of ash and charred frames bore silent testimony to where the village had stood outside the gates of Winterbourne.

Jaufre closed his eyes, wanting never to open them again; but against his will he looked toward the gates of Winterbourne. Gates, whose only barrier now a child might climb. Piles of rock, rubble, the dust appearing as if it had remained undisturbed for generations. The only wall that remained was a portion of the donjon, the arrow loops and thick-set windows glaring at him like the empty sockets of a corpse ravaged by vultures. Vacant windows where the shadow of Lyssa's face should have been, her pearl-white neck craning forward in eagerness as she watched him ride over the hill.

A wave of nausea churned deep in his gut, as if he could still smell the pallor of death befouling the air. Who? Who had done this? Welsh raiders had ever been a threat to Winterbourne, but some deep-rooted intuition told Jaufre this was not their work.

"God damn you to hell, John Plantagenet." He unsheathed his sword. "Death! Death to the king!" The bewildered faces of his men flashed before his eyes as they followed suit. He led them in a thundering charge down the hill, not checking his speed even as his horse began slipping on the loose rocks that had been the heart of Winterbourne.

He raced at the fire-scorched timber frames. All that was left of stables, barns, mews, danced before his fury-blurred vision like the bared bones of skeletons.

"Come out, you cowards! Come out and fight." The silence mocked him. Wheeling around, he circled the crumbling remains of the donjon, his sword whistling through the air. "Show yourselves, damn you!" His shout reverberated off the dark, scorched stone walls roofed by an indifferent blue sky.

Sir Eldred hedged uncertainly to his side. "This must have happened days ago. My lord, there is no enemy here."

Jaufre shifted in his saddle, glowering at the man, the sword gripped in his fist burning to taste of vengeance. Sir Eldred reined in his mount, backing away, moistening his lips. The silence thickened around them until Jaufre heard naught but the distant call of birds, the restless snorting of horses.

The sword became too heavy to hold aloft any longer. The earl's arm fell limp to his side, accompanied by Sir Eldred's sigh of relief.

"Aye," Jaufre muttered. "Too late. Mayhap years too late." He looked about him, trying to comprehend the nightmare ruins of all that he had cherished. It was as if Winterbourne had never been but a pile of ash and broken mortar, the castle with its four strong turrets and towering donjon but a dream conjured by some sorcerer. He had walked the walls of a place that did not exist, his lady Melyssan and her kisses but another part of the enchantment that had deceived him.

"No!" Jaufre shook his head to clear it. "She was no dream. All the rest of my life may have been a lie, but not she."

Sir Eldred swallowed. "The sun waxes hot here. Mayhap my lord would wish to ride down by the river, bathe his face in the cooling water. This—this has been a dreadful blow."

Jaufre sheathed his sword, taking one last look of fierce pleasure at the keenness of the blade. "Nay, we will keep riding. We must follow the king's army. 'Tis obvious he has taken my wife and babe as his prisoners."

The fear rose in him, to be swept away by the tide of his fury. "He shall rue the day if he harms either of them. I'll wash the ash from these walls with his blood."

"We will follow you anywhere, my lord," Sir Eldred said, mopping at his sweating brow. "But—but they say the king has imported many fearsome mercenaries. Mayhap we should return to London for Sir Tristan, seek the help of the French."

"There is no time. I was too late once to save my lady. I will not fail her again."

Sir Eldred's further pleas stilled as another of the knights came riding up. "My lord, we have found one of the peasants from your land. He is preparing to bury someone at the edge of the field."

"Take me to him," Jaufre said. "Mayhap he can tell me which direction the king took and what prisoners were with him."

He rode after the knight, impatient to question the man and be gone. Each hour more of delay, who knew what it might mean by way of misery for Melyssan and Jenny? He cursed himself over and over again for his folly in not leaving London sooner, his carelessness in not making sure they were safe.

Two of his men dragged forth the quaking peasant to meet him, shoving the ragged man to his knees. Dull-witted eyes risked a terrified glance at the earl.

"Well, sirrah, do you not know who I am?"

"Aye," the voice quavered. "You are my dread lord, the Dark Knight. But I did nothing wrong. I only seek to dig a grave for the dying."

"First I want answers. Were you here when the king's soldiers came?"

The man nodded, great tears coursing down his dirt-encrusted cheeks. "I ran from the swords, hid down by the edge of the river, pretending I was slain. But for the others, no place to hide. All dead, my lord, all dead. They pulled the walls down around them."

Jaufre's eyes narrowed. "But the prisoners. What did they with their prisoners?"

Sobs shook the thin frame crouched before him. "No prisoners. None. All dead. The captain cried, 'Slay them all. Leave not a stone standing.'"

Terror constricted Jaufre's chest, making it difficult for him to breathe. Terror of the one enemy he knew he could not fight, the enemy that had defeated him the night he'd watched the old comte slip away.

"You fool!" he roared. "The women. What of the women?"

"Trapped inside the donjon, my lord. Their screams. Ah, their screams." The peasant clutched his arms above his ears as if he could still hear them. "They buried them there. Pulled the stones over their scarred bodies."

"Liar!"

With a terrified howl, the man flattened himself to the earth as Jaufre plunged his horse forward. "Seize him. I'll have the truth whipped from his lying mouth."

At that instant a low groan sounded in Jaufre's ears, strange, unearthly because it did not issue from the man cowering below him.

"My lord," Sir Eldred called out. "This dolt was about to bury a man still alive."

Jaufre maneuvered his horse over to where Eldred knelt by a familiar black-robed figure. Father Andrew sprawled upon the ground, the upper portion of his head swathed in a filthy makeshift bandage. His blood-drained lips moved, whispering something.

As Jaufre flung himself out of the saddle, the peasant whimpered, "He be dying. I was just readying the grave. 'Twas a miracle he lived this long, crawling out of the donjon to the river. Like me, they thought him dead. But they didn't bury those outside the walls. They just left us, so I—"

"Be quiet, you fool." Jaufre bent over the near lifeless form of the priest and roughly pried open one eye. He thought he saw a spark of recognition. "Father Andrew. Where is Melyssan? My babe?" He repeated the demand several times without getting any response.

At last the lips moved, so faintly that he had to bend his head forward to hear. But when the whisper came, it was sharp enough to slice through his soul. "Dead. Soldier came. Sword in chapel."

"Chapel's gone," the peasant intoned. "They pulled down the walls. Pulled them on—"

His words choked off as Jaufre shoved him to the earth. The earl staggered past the man, past the bowed heads of his knights, and leapt upon his horse. He headed the animal back across the blackened bailey to the donjon, the ruins of which he had ridden across all unknowing, all unknowing that it was her tomb.

"No!" He leapt his horse over the heaping stones into the midst of the ruins. The animal lost its footing in the ash, going down upon its knees with a terrified whinny and flinging Jaufre out of the saddle. It struggled to its feet before bolting wild-eyed from the ruins.

Jaufre scrambled up, stumbling toward where the chapel once stood. "Lyssa! Jenny!" He clawed at the ashes, fighting with all his strength to move the heavy stones. He strained until he felt his muscles would snap, the sweat pouring down his shuddering body. The shards of rock shifted and settled back into place.

"Curse you!" Jaufre roared at the insensible rock. "Will you hold now when you wouldn't before—wouldn't keep that whoreson's sword away from my babes?"

Staggering back, he flung himself in a fit of

blind rage on the remaining wall, pounding at the blackened mortar with his fists, howling epithets at the worthless stone that had not sheltered Melyssan, worthless and weak as his own two arms, which had not been there to defend her, could not now draw her back from the crushing weight of this grave.

His flesh scraped raw but stung him no more keenly than the agonizing loss that pierced his heart. He drove his bleeding fists against the unyielding rock again and again until he sank to his knees. A dry sob burned his throat as he buried his lacerated hands deep into the ashes.

"Damn you, Lyssa. Damn you. You see what comes of love—of dreams?" He grabbed a handful of blackened soot and flung it into the wind before collapsing facedown onto the broken rock, willing himself to become part of it, as lifeless and unfeeling as the shattered stones of Winterbourne.

He was uncertain how long he lay there, but when he moved again, the sun was setting behind the trees. He heard whispers coming from behind the walls.

"He's gone mad, I tell you."

"Oh, that Sir Tristan were here."

"Well, he is not. Eldred, we cannot leave the earl thus. We must take him by force to some shelter and seek help."

"Nay, look, he stirs. Wait a few moments longer. Dost think you have the skill to capture him? I promise you I am in no hurry to attempt it."

Jaufre sat up, rubbing the grit from his eyes with a soot-streaked hand that only made matters worse. He tasted of his own blood but felt no pain. He was as gutted and empty as the ruined walls whose shadows loomed over him in the fleeting light of day. Staggering to his feet, he leaned against the stonework for support.

"My lord?" Sir Eldred's voice called timidly. When Jaufre did not reply, he stepped cautiously closer. "My lord, night approaches. I—we were wondering if—if you have done here."

"Aye. I am done."

"Then mayhap we should find some other place to camp."

Jaufre nodded, brushing past the man. "Get me my horse." He was more than ready to leave Winterbourne, lands that once had been beyond price. Now the castle, too, had betrayed him, surrendering all that he loved to the savagery of a tyrant's army. He wished to set eyes upon this desolation no more. Too many ghosts trod these grounds, threatening him with the return of memory, and with memory would come...pain.

Despite his resolve, his steps faltered, forcing him to linger outside the charred remains of the garden. Instead of the scorched tree trunk, he saw the old apple tree blossoming white as Jenny scrambled into its shade, her deep brown eyes alight with joy as he pursued her, giggling when he caught her up in his arms; he saw Lyssa watching them from a distance, her sea-green eyes going all misty. A piece farther back had stood the tent. He remembered the soft sheen of Lyssa's hair brushing against his skin as her hands trailed through the water...the day Melyssan had bathed him, the last time they had made love.

No! He crushed the memories. Let them lie forever amongst the ruins of Winterbourne. To remember brought such searing pain as would bring him to his knees, such agony as he could not survive.

But why cling to this wretchedness? whispered a voice inside him. What purpose was there to existence without her?

He became aware that Sir Eldred had retrieved his horse and was leading it forward. "My lord, from what the peasant said, I believe it most likely His Majesty's army headed north. If you would still follow King John, we should also head in that direction."

King John! Jaufre's slumped shoulders snapped back, the name acting upon him like some evil talisman. "Aye, the king," he whispered. "I had almost forgot."

"Mayhap now that you know your lady..." Sir Eldred's voice faded. He stared fixedly at the ground. "There seems no longer any need to confront the king thus unprepared. We would stand little chance against his army."

"Aye, little chance." Jaufre would have to find another way. "I believe you are right, Sir Eldred. You and the rest of the men may ride out. I no longer have any need of you."

"My lord?" The knight's eyes widened with incomprehension.

"You may return to your own manors, back to London, wherever you choose. I care not." Jaufre swung into the saddle. He could scarce bend his swollen hands to grip the reins, but he forced his fingers to do so, heedless of the pain that seemed so unimportant. He had a purpose again, something to fill the emptiness inside him, the cold venom of hatred, vengeance.

Still Eldred hesitated. "You would ride alone, my lord?"

"Are you hard of hearing or merely stupid? Have I not told you twice to be gone?"

"Aye, my lord. I—I shall tell the others of your command." He backed away. "But what of the priest, my lord? That half-witted peasant has run off, and the good father yet lives."

"I shall see to him. Be off with you."

Sir Eldred nodded, then scurried for his own horse.

Jaufre could see that the knight and the other men-at-arms spent some time discussing the situation, with many glances in his direction. One by one, they gradually dissolved into the twilight, the echoes of their coursers' hooves fading to silence, leaving him alone amongst the ruins of his castle. He turned his horse in the opposite direction, coming to a standstill beside Father Andrew where he lay beside the partially dug grave.

The old man would be dead before morning. Jaufre stared down through the gathering gloom at the black-robed figure, his heart twisting with bitterness. How had this miserable creature survived, whilst Lyssa and Jenny...

The earl prepared to urge his horse forward when a low moan escaped from the old man. So let him die here alone in the darkness where the devil might chance upon his soul. Had he or his God lifted one finger to save Melyssan? To save the woman he loved? Yet try as he would to suppress it, he could not forget the glow in Lyssa's face when she had asked if Father Andrew could marry them. Father Andrew, her comforter, her spiritual adviser, her friend ...If Lyssa could see him now, dumped upon the hard ground, dying...Jaufre clenched his jaw as if somehow he carried Melyssan inside himself, could feel the overwhelming intensity of her grief.

"Damn you, you old fool!" he cried. He dismounted and hoisted the priest's inert body over his saddle. "There, Lyssa. Let that satisfy you. I'll take him to where he can die with a roof over his head.

"But then," he muttered, leading his horse forward down the road, "then, my love, I have more important matters to attend." Aye, more important than life itself...

The death of a king.

Melyssan followed Gunnor down the curving stone stairs, clutching Jenny in her arms as if she would never let her go, clutching her as she had from the first moment King John had restored the child to her, a mocking smile upon his lips.

The lower they descended, the darker it became, until Melyssan lost her footing. She would have tumbled forward but for Sir Hugh's restraining arm. He eased her down the last step, and her eyes gradually accustomed themselves to the darkness. Jenny whimpered, tunneling her face against Melyssan's shoulder. "Let's go home, milady. Dark. Don't like this place."

Melyssan patted her back reassuringly, her throat too constricted for words. Gunnor paused before a stout oak door, stepping back to allow Sir Hugh to move aside the heavy bar before swinging it wide.

"In here, my lady," said Gunnor. "I have tried to make all as comfortable as possible for you during your—your stay with us."

As Melyssan stepped inside the small dank chamber, Gunnor averted her head. The room was empty except for a straw pallet and some plates of food arranged before a hearth that was devoid of any fire. The sole light came from a narrow slit set high above their heads.

"At least I am relieved you have not seen fit to put us in chains," Melyssan said. She tried to ease Jenny down from her aching arms, but the child clung to her neck.

Gunnor broke at last. "Oh, milady..." As she looked up at Melyssan, tears coursed down her face. "We cannot help it. If there were aught else we could do..."

"Gunnor!" Sir Hugh said sharply. "That's enough. Return upstairs at once."

With one final beseeching look at her grim-visaged husband, Gunnor covered her face and fled the room. Melyssan could hear her deep-throated sobs receding up the steps.

Left alone with Melyssan, Sir Hugh shifted from foot to foot, his gangly arms dangling awkwardly before him. He cleared his throat. "There's food. Wine. You and the child should eat." He made as if to go, then paused in the doorway, a perceptible softening in his stern eyes. "I am sorry, my lady. About your brother. My men tried to wave him off, warn him to go back. But he would keep coming."

" 'Twas because he thought he rode to the castle of a friend."

The red flushed from Sir Hugh's thin neck up to his brow. Glancing over his shoulder, he said loudly, "Then he was mistaken. I told you all long ago I was no rebel. I am the king's man."

"Well said, Sir Hugh," purred a voice from the shadows behind the knight.

Melyssan felt Jenny's grip tighten as King John glided into the small chamber. One dark brown eye peered at him from the safety of her shoulder. The king's thin lips twisted into a complacent smile. "Methought I should like to see what arrangements you have made for Lady Melyssan and her daughter. 'Tis well she should be accorded the respect owed the wife of such a redoubtable warrior as the Dark Knight."

John gave a mock sigh. "Ah, by St. Michael, I didst quake with terror while my army besieged Winterbourne, fearing Lord Jaufre would swoop down from the hills at any moment to wreak his vengeance." He paused a moment, twisting the great sapphire on his fourth finger, admiring the setting. "But then I suppose His Lordship could not tear himself away from the pleasures of London. They say our bawds there are more skilled than any in the world, even Paris. Do you not agree, Sir Hugh?" He poked the knight in the ribs, laughing raucously. Sir Hugh joined him weakly.

Although she knew it unwise, Melyssan could not restrain her anger. "How dare you mock my lord! No one has ever said of Lord Jaufre that he lay abed when there was fighting to be done." The king's dark eyes flashed dangerously, but she could not seem to stop herself. All the tension, the grief for those she had lost, poured out of her.

"Take care, madam," John growled. "Remember 'tis your king you address."

"My king. You are fit to be no one's king. You are even a poor excuse for a man."

"Lady Melyssan!" Sir Hugh admonished, his face going white with fear. Even Jenny raised her head, her brown eyes widening at the unaccustomed sharpness in her mother's tone.

But Melyssan rushed on, ignoring the knight's attempts to intervene. "You attacked our castle deliberately while my husband was away. Cravenly, making war on women and children because you have not the stomach to fight a man like Jaufre."

"Take care! Take care," John repeated,

purple veins beginning to stand out along his neck. "You are my prisoner. I will—"

"Will what? Hide behind my skirts when Jaufre comes after you?"

"Nay, I need neither you nor your bratling as hostages. I will crush the earl when the time comes." He seized Melyssan by the throat, gouging it painfully. "Crush him and all the rebels just like this."

Before Melyssan could make a move to free herself, she felt Jenny stiffen. "Don't touch my muvver. I'll kill you." The child lunged forward, sinking her teeth into John's wrist.

"Owww!" The king snatched his hand back. "You little shewolf." His eyes glazed over. Melyssan staggered back, half dropping her daughter in an attempt to shield her as the king drew back his fist.

"Nay, wait!" Although his knees shook, Sir Hugh stepped between them. "Please, Your Majesty. When we undertook to keep these prisoners for you, you pledged your word no harm should come to them."

For a moment Melyssan thought the king would strike Sir Hugh aside. She glanced wildly about for a weapon, anything to defend her daughter. If only she still had her cane...But then John took a steadying breath and drew back, turning away to compose himself. When he faced them again, it was with his customary expression of sly good humor.

"Why, so I did. You do well to remind me, Sir Hugh." He clapped the knight roughly on the back. "I would not wish to be guilty of breaking my word."

John's gaze settled on Melyssan and Jenny, his eyes narrowed to gleaming slits as he rubbed his hands together. "Aye, we shall not harm them, but we will not help them, either." He waved Sir Hugh out of the room, the sudden mirth he struggled to contain exploding on the other side of the door. Melyssan heard the heavy bar slam into place.

As she lowered Jenny onto the pallet, rubbing her exhausted arms, she tried to tell herself she was relieved the men had gone. She and Jenny were safe for the present. Yet it was as if the king had left behind some lingering trace of evil that swirled like a deadly mist around herself and Jenny.

That deep laughter, his strange parting words, triggered a memory. Suddenly she was back at Winterbourne, listening to the fat Father Hubert recount a jest to the company. *King said wouldn't harm...but wouldn't help, either.* She could still see *Le Gros* holding his shaking sides, guffawing at something only he found amusing. He'd been speaking of Matilda de Briouse and her son—starving to death in the king's dungeon!

A wave of horror assailed her, the calm that had sustained her throughout the siege of Winterbourne deserting her. She hurled herself at the heavy oak door, pounding it with her fists. "No, Sir Hugh—I beg you. Come back! Don't let him do this to us!"

Her cries were answered with silence. She sank down sobbing by the door. "Ah, sweet Mother in heaven. Nay, not that. Not that."

She rocked herself back and forth, giving way to the tears that had been penned up inside her for so long, tears over her longing for Jaufre and anxiety on his behalf, tears for the horrors of Winterbourne, tears for Whitney....

She'd almost forgotten she was not alone when she felt the small hand patting her hair. "Don't cry, Muvver. I taked care of you. I made that bad man go away." Through the haze of her tears, she looked up to see Jenny peering at her, her small chest swelled out with pride.

She reached out to envelop the child in a large hug. "Oh, aye, so you did, sweetheart. So you did. My lord would be so proud of you."

She held her daughter close, drawing strength from her, burying kisses along the top of her head as long as the little girl would permit it. Finally Jenny squirmed free. "I'm hundry. Let's eat now."

She scooted over to where Gunnor had left the plates, and Melyssan followed, wiping the last of her tears upon her sleeve. She watched her daughter stuffing a chunk of wheat bread into her mouth and felt the panic rise in her again. She fought the urge to stop Jenny. They should ration the food, try to make it last as long as possible. Yet most of the things Gunnor had left—the bread, the stew, the roast pigeons—would spoil if not eaten soon. How could she deprive Jenny if this were to be the child's last meal?

Melyssan gave herself a shake. Nay, she could not think that way. Even if the king gave such a command, Sir Hugh and Lady Gunnor could not be so cruel as to carry it out for him. News of the downfall of Winterbourne was bound to reach London. Then Jaufre would come. She had to believe that. This time Jaufre would come.

But it was difficult to keep her optimism, especially when it had to endure Jenny's repeated questionings. Her appetite replete, the child snuggled down beside her mother on the pallet. She refused to be lulled to sleep by any of the tunes Melyssan hummed, and she felt far too drained to regale Jenny with the usual tales of Camelot.

Suddenly Jenny sat bolt upright beside her. "Why doesn't Uncle Whitney come let us out?"

"He—he cannot, my love." Melyssan struggled to keep her voice steady. She did not want to think of Whitney now. Later, when she was safe in Jaufre's arms, she would deal with the grief of losing her brother.

But Jenny persisted. "Can't he get out of that rope those bad men put on him?"

"Please, Jenny, go to sleep. Uncle Whitney cannot come because—because he is dead."

Jenny's mouth turned down, and she frowned uncertainly. "The bad king killed him?"

"Aye, my love." She smoothed a stray curl back from the child's brow. How much Jenny was coming to understand at so tender an age. It was difficult to remember that her daughter had only seen three years of life. But

503

the next moment, Jenny disconcerted her by asking, "When will Uncle Whitney be alive again?"

"On this earth, never," she explained gently. "But in the world to come—"

"Fahver always came alive again. When he played wolf and I slew him, he always did."

Melyssan gave a laugh, half of frustration, half of wonder, at Jenny's words. Her daughter forever surprised her with accounts of things she and *Fahver* had done together. She suspected Jaufre had showered far more attention upon the child than she ever dreamt of, although she was never sure what had taken place and what was the product of Jenny's fertile imagination. She knew she had been wrong to believe that Jaufre did not love their child. She hugged that knowledge to herself in the darkness even as she hugged Jenny close and allowed the child to spin tales of her adventures with Lord Jaufre de Macy, the terrible, wonderful Dark Knight Without Mercy.

"Aye, he loved you, Jenny," she whispered when the child slept beside her at last. "And he loved me." The thought of his parting words comforted her through a restless night.

But in the morning, the door to the chamber did not open. No shamefaced Gunnor appeared bringing more food in defiance of the king. When Melyssan put her ear to the door, she heard nothing, as if the rest of the castle had ceased to exist. She fed Jenny some more of the bread, doling it out in smaller portions along with what remained of the stew. Her own stomach growled. By the end of the day she felt light-headed but resisted the urge to eat. The king would leave soon. He never stayed long in any one place. Tomorrow Gunnor would come to relieve them. She hushed Jenny's cries and rocked her to sleep.

But the second day passed, along with the next and the next, until eventually Melyssan lost all track of time. She paced the confines of the cell, staring at the closed door as if she could will it open with her mind. Jenny's whining rasped at her nerves, and her stomach began to feel as if her flesh caved in upon itself. She fed the bread to Jenny even though it had begun to molder. Still, she could not bring herself to believe Sir Hugh and Lady Gunnor would allow them to starve. But for the first time, as she watched Jenny fall asleep exhausted from weeping, she cursed Jaufre in her heart. Damn him! How could he not realize they needed him?

On days that it rained, she doubled the straw pallet in half so that she could stand upon it and reach the narrow window opening. By holding out the empty goblets, she could catch the precious droplets to ease their thirst. Although it pained her, she threw out what remained of the pigeon breasts, fearing they would be driven to gnaw on the bones and be poisoned with the stale meat. Jenny spent most of the time clutching her stomach, sobbing that it hurt.

Melyssan could scarce find the patience to

think up games and tales to distract her. They shared the last of the bread.

Her dreams were tormented by visions of Matilda de Briouse, the woman's flesh stretched taut against her skull, her teeth large and hideous, gnawing at the bones of her son...but the son became a girl child—Jenny—and Melyssan awoke screaming.

She pushed herself off the pallet, a new resolve strengthening her. She was not Matilda de Briouse. She and Jenny were not chained to the wall. They still had water. She would find some way to escape. Using the blunt end of one of the heavy silver goblets, Melyssan began driving it like a hammer against the door. Perhaps she could splinter the wood.

But the door was of oak. After an hour her hands were bruised and raw, the door barely scratched. Fighting back her tears, she paused to rub her aching wrist.

"I'm hundry, Muvver," Jenny wailed.

"I heard you the first time, Genevieve. Please be quiet for a little while."

"But I'm hundry!"

Melyssan flung the cup across the room. It was hopeless. Hopeless. There was no escaping this place. Damn all of them. How could they do this to her child? She covered her ears with her hands, unable to endure Jenny's cries any longer. To think that only a few months earlier there was little in the world she could not have given her child, and now she could not fulfill her most basic need.

Jenny pressed her pale face within inches of

her mother, so that Melyssan stared into her daughter's shadow-rimmed eyes. "I'm *hundry!*" the child screamed.

Involuntarily, Melyssan's hand shot out, striking the child to the ground. As she recoiled in horror of what she'd done, Jenny slowly sat up, stunned to silence. It was the first blow the child had ever received in her life. That it should have come from her broke Melyssan as nothing else had. She pulled Jenny hard against her, her body racked with great dry sobs. She had no tears left.

The days stretched on. Sometimes the gnawing pain in her middle grew so intense she could not even rise from the pallet. But the physical pain was no worse than the one in her heart when she gazed at Jenny. The once round, shining face was now drawn, pale, the sparkling brown eyes dull, listless. She slept longer and longer, scarce making a sound, not even a whimper. Her child was dying before her eyes, and she was helpless to prevent it.

Jaufre. She could not summon the strength to call his name. He must be dead, or he would have come. As she lay beside her daughter, her only thought was to join him wherever he might be. If in death, she prayed that it might come soon for her and Jenny. She drifted into a restless sleep in which she dreamed again, dreamed that Jaufre's black stallion thundered up the road to the castle. So clearly could she see him brandishing his sword, racing across the drawbridge. He was flinging open the door to the cell, tenderly brushing the hair back from her brow. "Melyssan, I've come for you and the little one. Make not a sound and follow me."

But the dream was so strange. Jaufre's voice—it was not the rich timbre she remembered. As she watched, the rugged planes of his face dissolved, the beard disappearing to become the broad, honest face of Lady Gunnor bending over her. The candlelight glistened upon the moisture in her eyes.

With a startled cry, Melyssan sat up, only to have Gunnor's thick hand cover her mouth. "Hush, my lady. The king is long gone, but many of his soldiers remain."

Melyssan sank back against the straw mattress, trying to clear her befuddled senses. "Gunnor! What—what are you doing?"

"I could bear it no more, my lady. I nigh went mad thinking of you and your little one down here. Even if we did not owe you what we do, I could not leave you here to die."

"You've come to help us?" Melyssan's eyes traveled past Gunnor to the outline of the doorway beyond. The heavy oak door was thrown back, the shadows of the outer world beckoned. "You've come to help us escape!"

Chapter 23

RAIN PELTED THE thatch covering of the hovel where Jaufre dragged the old priest, seeking shelter from the storm. Water dripped through the roof, splattering into the clay-lined hole in the center of the room, threatening to douse the fire that burned there. The flames hissed, sending forth an acrid stream of smoke that made breathing even more difficult in the dank confines of the cottage; the only ventilation came from one window cut through the thick mixture of dung and straw. Crouching to avoid brushing his head against the low roof, Jaufre kicked open the door, heedless of the wind-driven rain.

"Better we drown than suffocate," he said to the peasant woman who huddled in one corner, her arms wrapped around a small, half-naked child. The woman didn't answer, shrinking as a crack of lightning split the air. Her youthful face reflected the same bewildered terror that had been there ever since Jaufre had first burst in upon her, with Father Andrew slung over his shoulder.

Oblivious to the woman's fear, Jaufre left the door propped open. He bent down on the mud-caked earthen floor, kneeling beside the bag of dried ferns upon which he had laid Father Andrew. The priest looked so pale and cold. Jaufre drew a worn woolen blanket around him, pressing his hand against the thin chest. The heartbeat was faint, but steady. Damn, but the old man was tenacious. He should have died two days ago. In all that time, Jaufre had not found a roof to shelter him until now. He remembered his annoyance when he awoke that first morning and found the priest still alive, knew that he had no choice but to attempt to care for him. He had tromped the countryside, finding yarrow herbs, trying to recall all that he had ever seen Melyssan do when tending a wound. The gash on the old man's head was encrusted with dirt. He'd had to clean it, rebind it. As the peasant had remarked that day when Jaufre had found Winterbourne a ruin—had it been only two days or two centuries ago?—'twas nothing short of a miracle the priest had survived the siege.

Why was God so sparing with his miracles? Jaufre flopped down beside the old man. Mayhap tonight the old man's good fortune would wear out. Then he would be free to pick up his pace, before the king got too many miles out of reach.

He closed his eyes, praying for sleep without dreams. But as always, the dream came, Lyssa bending over him, whispering, "Nay, my love, 'twas only an evil spell cast by the king. Hold me, touch me. I'm alive, Jaufre, alive." Her lips were upon his, so warm, so real, he thought he could reach out his arms and draw her close. Her kiss was so vivid, he could feel the warmth of it—only to awake more bereft than ever when he found the lovely vision had fled and himself lying upon the damp earth of the cottage.

The fury of the summer storm had ended, but the chill morning mist seeped into the cottage, causing him to shiver. He noted the peasant woman struggling to relight the fire as he sat up to check upon the priest. Father Andrew's eyes were open, but he had experienced brief phases of consciousness before. Something was different this time. There was a lucidity in his gaze that had been absent. He studied the cottage, his pale blue eyes coming to rest upon Jaufre before he closed them again.

Jaufre's heart sang with savage exultation. The old man was getting well enough to be left behind.

"Lyssa," he whispered. "I have done my best. I saved him. Now let me go. Let me go and do what I must do."

"Sir Knight?" The soft voice startled him. He became aware the peasant woman pushed two wooden bowls toward him. The child hid behind her skirts, peering at him as he accepted the humble offering. He gulped down the lentil soup without tasting it, then propped up the old man and tried to feed him.

"Here. Eat this and get your strength back. I have to leave you soon. Do you understand?"

During the moments when he was weakest, the priest had permitted Jaufre to pour wine down his throat, swallowing obediently, but now that he was lucid, he struggled, averting his head.

"Too old. Too tired. Leave me alone."

"Open your mouth, you fool. You're hanging to life by a thread now. Don't tempt your fate. Even your God must have a limit to his patience."

"Ready to die. Why will you—not let me?"

Jaufre shoved him back down onto the floor. "Die, then. It matters naught to me. The choice is yours."

But as he backed away, he felt a rush of anger. He had already wasted two days caring for the old man. He should have kicked him into the grave at Winterbourne and been done with it. He could have been two days farther on the road to plunging a knife through John's black heart.

"Damn you! The choice is not yours. You'll live whether you wish it or not." He propped the priest up, this time forcing some of the liquid down his throat. The old man coughed, tried to pull away. Jaufre could sense him using what little reserves of strength he possessed to will himself into the grave.

"Why you—do this? Let me go—to God. You don't care."

"I don't, but *she* would have. You're going to live because she would have wished it so." He was uncertain if the sense of his words penetrated the priest's mind, but the old man went limp, allowing Jaufre to feed him like a child.

He no longer showed any resistance, but the earl still did not trust him. Forcing the priest to live became an obsession with him as great as his desire to kill the king. Despite his resolve to move on, he lingered at the cottage, obliging Father Andrew to eat what meager food the widowed peasant could provide for him.

While the old man rested, Jaufre spent his time poaching rabbits and small game from the woods nearby, long hours that provided more substantial meals and helped him grow familiar with the crossbow, a weapon that he had scarce ever touched before.

The delay gave him time to think. He would never get near John in the guise of the earl of Winterbourne before being captured. To encompass the death of the king would require much cold calculation and a new skill. Jaufre sent the quarrel flying from the crossbow, dead through the heart of a partridge as it fluttered beneath the underbrush.

Later that day, as he plucked the bird and roasted it upon a spit over the fire, he noted with satisfaction that the priest was sitting up. Father Andrew spoke so little, Jaufre wondered if the blow had addled his wits. But there was yet a keen intelligence that lurked in the faded, ancient eyes. He caught them turned upon himself as if to probe the secrets of his soul. He presented his back to the priest, pretending to be absorbed in his cooking.

The peasant woman was out grubbing in the meager patch of land that passed for a garden, leaving her child unattended. As he toddled too near the fire, Jaufre caught him by the tail of his smock and hauled him roughly back. But his voice was gentle as he said, "Stay away from the fire, little one."

He brushed the thick mat of hair aside from the child's face, the yellow-streaked brown nothing like Jenny's dusky curls. But the expression in the eyes was the same, the dancing light of curiosity.

"I know the flames look beautiful," Jaufre said. "So bright and warm, as if tiny faeries danced inside them. But you must remember, sometimes even that which is beautiful can hurt you."

How many times had he explained the same thing to Jenny? The hand he had placed upon the boy's head began to tremble, then he noticed Father Andrew's stare. "Off with you," he said sharply to the child. "Go out and find your mother." Frightened by the earl's abrupt change of tone, the boy scurried through the door.

Jaufre hunkered down by the fire, cursing when he burned his thumb removing the bird from the spit. "Will you assay some of this partridge, Father? It looks as if it were a tough old bird, but I'll wager 'tis tender enough upon the inside."

To his astonishment, the priest's lips parted in the vague semblance of a smile. "You are probably right. I begin to fear I am a very poor judge of—of birds."

When Jaufre scowled at him suspiciously, the priest said, "In any case, you will gag it down my throat if I refuse."

Taking that for consent, Jaufre tore off a portion of the fowl and plunked it into one of the wooden bowls. As the priest accepted it, he regarded Jaufre with another of those piercing stares the earl was coming to dislike heartily.

"I have never thanked you thus far for saving my life."

Jaufre shrugged, resuming his place by the fire, picking at his own portion of the bird.

"You saved me from a grave sin. I tried to impose my own will upon God, seeking death when 'twas clearly His design that I should survive."

"Spare me this confession, Father. You know why I helped you. I would have never given two shillings for your life. But Melyssan...She—" He broke off, unable to continue, reaching for his cup of bitter ale that the peasant woman brewed.

"I understand this." The priest's voice continued, soft but inexorable. "It only increases my gratitude to you threefold. I have been guilty of another sin. I presumed to look into your heart and judge you. But I was wrong. I see now that you loved her—"

"Be silent! Will you leave off speaking of this?" Jaufre flung down his bowl and stormed out of the cottage, fearing what the priest might say next, what other chords of emotion he might stir to life. Night would fall shortly. He needed no more dreams.

For the rest of the evening he avoided the old man, preferring to curl up on the grass outside than listen to that quiet voice again, raising gentle spirits to torment his empty heart. Shortly after the moon rose in the sky, he heard a rustling near him. He was about to leap up, to spring for his sword, when he felt someone fling a blanket over him.

He gazed up into the face of the peasant woman as if seeing her for the first time. Till then she had been naught but a silent shadow, doing his bidding, not questioning his presence there. Now he noticed how her face was lined with age. She must have been comely once, her bright yellow braids falling past ruddy cheeks. The hands that tucked the wool covering over him were callused with hard labor. It had been so long since a woman had touched him. He wondered how she had lost her husband. Then their eyes locked, and he saw in their depths a reflection of his own emptiness, his hunger. Without thinking, he began to draw her down beside him, the wind-chapped lips bare inches from his own.

Aye, she shared his hunger, but his longing was for that which he could never know again. Melyssan. He groaned and pushed the woman away from him. Binding the blanket around his body, he rolled on his side, scarce moving until he heard the woman retreat, weeping, back into the cottage. He would leave this place in the morning.

He was up at dawn, readying his horse, when Father Andrew limped out of the cottage, his wobbling steps braced with a large staff of wood.

Jaufre refused to look at him, feigning to check the tightness of his saddle. "Have you come to bid me farewell? You need not have put yourself to such difficulty. I would have forgiven you the courtesy in this instance."

"No, I am going with you."

"What!" Jaufre whirled around. Damn, why did the man always look so serene, even with his head bound up in a dirty linen bandage?

"I, too, owe my lady Melyssan a debt. I shall keep it by remaining with you."

"The devil you will. Unless you mean to limp after me clear across England."

The priest bowed his head. "If God wills it so."

With another impatient oath, Jaufre vaulted into the saddle. He noticed the woman and her child lingering in the shadows of the doorway. "Here," he said gruffly, tossing her a handful of coins. "Set this aside for a dowry—to get yourself another husband."

He dug in his heels and cantered away without another word, but he could not resist looking back. To his annoyance, he could make out a small figure tottering slowly but steadily down the road.

"Christ's blood. Am I to be haunted by one act of kindness for the rest of my life?"

Slapping down on the reins, he thundered back to where Father Andrew stopped, awaiting him. Cursing fluently for several minutes, he consigned the priest to hell, assuring him that was where he would end if he kept following. Father Andrew stood quietly, his hands folded, until Jaufre's tongue wore itself out.

Finally the earl thrust down one hand. "Damn you, grab hold and mount up behind me."

"Will your horse bear the load?" Father Andrew asked even as he vaulted up behind Jaufre.

"No worse than carrying along a bag of bones." Jaufre set the horse into a gallop before calling back, "I warn you, I won't tolerate you rattling all the way to our destination."

But Father Andrew said little in the days that followed as Jaufre tracked King John's progress through England. It was not difficult. The king's mercenary army left a trail of destruction behind it, charred villages, scorched fields painfully reminiscent of the scene at Winterbourne.

Jaufre slipped to the manor house of Sir Eldred to procure a horse for the priest, but most of the time he and Father Andrew shunned the company of other men, even to the point of risking ambush by sleeping in the open at night, within the shelter of forestlands.

Although the priest never asked questions, Jaufre could feel him watching as he made his final preparations, securing a coarse leather tunic such as any field laborer might wear and practicing, practicing with the crossbow at every opportunity.

"Tomorrow," Jaufre announced, "I will escort you to an abbey. There's a Cistercian order not far from here at Swineshead." Jaufre remembered hearing the place mentioned, although he could not recall where. He believed the old priest would be safe there.

Before Father Andrew could protest, he

added, "And do not even think to try coming after me. I will not tolerate it."

"So at last you are ready to kill the king."

Jaufre started, the crossbow nearly dropping from his hand. What sort of uncanny eyes did this old man possess that he could read intentions Jaufre had never spoken aloud?

"Do not look so astonished. Your hatred lies naked upon your face for all the world to see every time you lift that thing to your shoulder." Father Andrew grimaced as he gestured toward the crossbow.

Jaufre shrugged. "'Tis of no consequence. I intend to make no secret of the deed."

"You do not care if you are captured and executed?"

The earl smiled grimly. "I invite John's minions to try."

"And you truly believe you are capable of doing this deed?"

For reply, Jaufre raised the crossbow and drove one of the bolts deep into the trunk of a distant tree.

"'Tis not the same as killing a man in battle, my lord. 'Twill be outright murder."

"Aye, even as my wife and babe were slain."

"By men of no honor! But you—you are of a different breed." The priest placed one hand gently upon Jaufre's shoulder. "Do not turn away. This time you must hear me, my lord. Even when I thought the worst of you, I recognized that you had your own code. Oft I overheard you lecture your young son upon what a man's honor should be. A knight does not slay his enemy from behind, skulking in the trees, afraid to show his face."

"By God, if John would fight me as a man, do you not think that I would?" Jaufre burst out. "But he is a cowardly knave, and I will slay him the only way I can."

The priest's grip tightened, his pale blue eyes fixing Jaufre until he felt drawn into their peaceful depths. "You were never meant to be an assassin, my lord," the earnest voice pleaded. "Even if you escape, you taint yourself with the crime of murder. Can you live without your honor, Jaufre de Macy, or will it destroy your very soul?"

Jaufre wrenched free of the old man. "You want my soul? Go look for it amongst the rubble at Winterbourne. Any soul I had, Lyssa took with her when she died."

He strode away, pausing to fling over his shoulder, "Trouble yourself no more with my salvation, Father. 'Tis a bootless quest. We go our separate ways tomorrow."

Despite Jaufre's command, when the time came to leave Father Andrew outside the gates of the abbey, the priest seized the earl's bridle, venting one last plea.

"My lord, you saved my life, reminding me Lady Melyssan would have wished it so. Now I put the same question to you. How think you she would have felt knowing you are about to destroy yourself?"

Jaufre closed his eyes, wanting only to be gone; but he could see Melyssan's face swim before him, gazing at him with that wistful expression of hope, of admiration. Her noble Sir Launcelot. What would she think seeing him garbed in his role of lowly assassin? He began to waver, but Father Andrew's next ill-chosen words broke the spell.

"Come inside the abbey and pray with me, my son. Leave this vengeance against the king in God's hands, where it belongs."

Jaufre gave a bitter laugh and pulled his reins clear. "Do you think either of us would live that long? Your God is almighty slow when it comes to meting out punishment to a knave such as the king, far quicker to visit his wrath upon an innocent babe.

"I shall make a bargain with you, Father. I shall give God time until I have the king within my sights. If He chooses to strike down John before then, not only will I stay my hand, but I will ride back to you, make my confession, and accept whatever penance you give."

Jaufre whirled his mount around. "But don't stand there until the snow flies in hell, waiting for me."

The curving stone stair stretched forward into darkness. Melyssan summoned all her will to follow Gunnor, who carried Jenny's inert form up the steps. 'Twas so far to the top, she thought. She would be content to sink down here, content to know that at least her child would live. But somehow she found the will to keep going.

"Stay close," Gunnor hissed when they

arrived at the top. "I dare not light a candle for fear— Oh!" She screamed as a lighted torch was thrust into her face. Highlighted by the eerie glow, the sallow face of a Flemish soldier leered at them.

"Aye, the king be right to leave me behind," he said to Gunnor. "He feared you getting soft afore the deed was done."

The brief flicker of hope died in Melyssan's breast. With a low moan, she sank to the floor, softly crying her daughter's name.

The child did not stir. Gunnor backed away, turning tearful eyes upon the guard. "Oh, please. Please." Then she gasped, "Hugh!"

The scraggly bearded knight slunk out from the shadows.

"Yer wife has been about some mischief this night." The guard sneered. "See that you beat her well. For thirty pieces of gold, I will tell the king nothing of this. Now give me the bratling, woman. I will secure the prisoners below."

"No!" Gunnor squirmed away, preventing the man from taking Jenny. She fled to her husband's side. "Please, Hugh."

As if in a fog, Melyssan watched the woman clutch at his tunic, pleading, saw him turn away. "Then kill them!" Gunnor shrieked. "Just take your sword and kill them. 'Twill be the same as if you had."

Sir Hugh's face crumpled, the torchlight revealing the myriad emotions chasing through his haunted eyes. He nodded, slowly drawing forth his sword. Melyssan tried to draw herself up, crawl forward in one last desperate effort to save Jenny. But her weakened limbs refused to move.

"Here, now!" protested the guard. "I'd just as soon dispatch them myself and be done with it. But it's agin the king's orders. You—"

The man's eyes bulged in their sockets as Sir Hugh raised his weapon and plunged the steel into his stomach. Gunnor cowered back against the wall, sobbing, hiding her eyes against Jenny.

Melyssan watched it all as in a dream. The soldier wobbled, dropping the torch. He tumbled past her, falling headlong down the steps, the torch rolling after him. The light became naught but a spark that flickered, plunging them into darkness once more.

Voices whispered from a great distance. "But where shall we take them? To Lady Enid?"

"Nay, that is the first place the king would look. They must go to my brother."

Melyssan felt lanky arms banding around her, experienced a sensation of weightlessness as she was lifted. Her head lolled against a bony shoulder.

Taking a deep breath, she gave herself over to the feeling of exhaustion. Vaguely, she sensed a change in the air. It was fresh, sweet, like...like newly mown hay.

Then she was being lowered, her body nestled against prickly wisps of straw. The world lurched abruptly beneath her. She banged into a wooden board, heard a rumble of wheels. Panic assailed her, a sudden terror of having lost something very precious. Her hands groped through the hay, encountering a small warm body, silken curls of hair. She sighed, drifting into unconsciousness.

Time blurred into a haze of impressions: the rough jolting of the tumbril...steaming brewis of chicken being forced past her lips, gagging her, burning her stomach...Jenny choking as Lady Gunnor fed her with a spoon....

But the morning finally came when Melyssan opened her eyes, focused on the blue sky above, Jenny's wan smile. They were free! Alive! Melyssan's lips moved in a prayer of thanks.

She gripped the side of the cart, dragging herself to a sitting position. For the first time, she realized the perpetual jolting had stopped.

Below her, Sir Hugh gave a relieved smile as he reached up to lift Jenny from the cart. Other arms stretched out to her, arms garbed in a flowing white robe. She looked down into the face of a man with Gunnor's broad, honest features. But the monk's eyes held more of a serenity in them. Beyond him, she could see the massive bell tower of a church and cloisters.

"This is my brother, Adelard, my lady," Gunnor said. "He will take care of you and the child."

The monk smiled but said nothing as he carried her from the cart. She and Jenny were taken inside a low-roofed pilgrim's hostelry. The whitewashed chamber was austere, containing only a small pallet with a crucifix hanging above it. But the walls radiated a peace that comforted Melyssan like a father's loving embrace.

Gunnor blinked back her tears. "You will be safe here. We shall send you word of Lord Jaufre as soon as we hear anything." She bent down to where Melyssan sat on the pallet and gave her a quick hug, crying, "Ah, my lady, will the world ever come right again?"

"Aye, Gunnor. I know it will." Melyssan's voice was weak, but her heart beat strong with renewed faith. She and Jenny had survived. She could not believe that Jaufre would do otherwise.

Sir Hugh hung back, shamefaced. "Well, my lady, Gunnor and I must be going now. I hope—hope that someday you find it in your heart to forgive..."

Melyssan reached for the large hand hanging limp at the knight's side and gave it a squeeze. "I already have, Sir Hugh," she said softly.

The knight bowed, raising his fingers to her lips, his mouth compressed into a firm line. But when he and Gunnor quit the room, Melyssan heard him emit a loud sniff and blow his nose.

Although not as talkative as his sister, Brother Adelard had a full measure of Gunnor's kindliness. He saw to Melyssan and Jenny's needs in the days that followed. Melyssan's appetite returned much more slowly than Jenny's. The little girl remained a trifle thin, but with the resilience of childhood, she seemed to have put all the horrors of their captivity behind her. But when they sat down to dine, Melyssan noticed Jenny would grab for her dish and spoon. She huddled them close, her brown eyes darting fearfully as if expecting someone to snatch her food away. It nigh broke Melyssan's heart to watch her.

It was a fortnight after Sir Hugh and Lady Gunnor had brought her to Swineshead Abbey before Melyssan felt well enough to walk in the outer court. Sighing with relief, she sat on a bench by the almonry and watched Jenny romp with a kitten. The child had finally ceased plaguing her to go through the inner gate back into the cloistered area where women were forbidden.

"My lady?"

Melyssan broke off her contemplation of the child and turned to face the gentle-eyed Brother Adelard.

"I believe your prayers have been answered. I have discovered someone who has news of your husband."

She jumped up, her knees trembling so hard Brother Adelard had to steady her. "There is a priest come here today. He said he is a survivor of the siege at Winterbourne."

"But Brother Adelard," she said, "'tis not possible. All were slain except myself and my daughter. The only priest—" She broke off, suppressing the painful memory of Father Andrew lying bleeding upon the chapel floor.

"You must see for yourself, my lady." Brother Adelard gestured toward the gate, where stood a black-gowned figure, looking strangely out of place amongst the white-robed monks. The heavy ironwork clanked open as the gray-haired priest glided into the outer courtyard.

Any doubts Melyssan had were swept aside when she saw how Jenny ran to the old man, flinging her arms about his neck. As Melyssan stumbled forward, the child's face turned to her, flushed with triumph.

"See, milady? 'Tis Fahver Andrew. I told you people could come back alive!"

The priest eased Jenny to the ground, his pale blue eyes shining with tears as he looked at Melyssan. She threw herself against his thin chest.

"Ah, my dear child," he quavered. "This is the most joyous day of my life, finding you here when I thought..."

"But how is this possible?" she asked when she was able to speak.

"Your husband. He saved my life after Winterbourne, brought me here."

She pulled away from him, her eyes darting to the cloisters beyond, her heart pounding with sudden hope.

"Jaufre brought you? Then he is here, unharmed? Oh, Father, you must tell me, where is he?"

She watched in dismay as the joyous expression faded from the age-lined face. He fumbled with his rosary beads. "Mayhap we should go into the chapel now and—and pray."

"Father, where is he?" Fear welled inside her as she seized the thin black-robed shoulders.

"He's gone...he's gone to..." The priest faltered, unable to get out the words, his face contorting with anguish. "Oh, heed me, my lady. Get you hence into the chapel and pray for the earl. Pray for him as you have never done before. Only God can help him now."

Chapter 24

THE OCTOBER MIST draped Jaufre like a heavy cloak, obscuring his vision as his leather-shod feet sank into the muddy soil of the Nene estuary. Cautiously he led his horse forward, prodding the ground ahead of him with a long pole lest he be sucked down by a patch of treacherous quicksand.

Most travelers to Lincolnshire avoided this dangerous route. At low tide, the Nene River flowed to meet the North Sea over a broad bank of sand, unsure footing that disappeared altogether when the mighty surge of ocean returned. It was far safer to take the longer inland route. But Jaufre was not looking for safety.

He'd come too far to turn back now—today, he would rid the world of a tyrant, the murderer who had destroyed his love, his life...Lyssa...Jenny. Chance had favored him. He had encountered the king's baggage train outside Norfolk. For the price of a drink, he had loosened one of the driver's tongues, discovered that while the king and his army took the safer road around Wisbech, the slower-moving baggage train was to gain time by crossing the Nene. The king would join them, anxiously awaiting the precious treasure that accompanied him everywhere.

Jaufre's lips twitched with derision. He could well imagine what a restless night the king must have spent, being parted from his money for even a short time. So Jaufre would do him a great favor. He would give His Majesty an eternity to recover that lost sleep.

The earl regained the more solid footing of the opposite shore and drew his horse deeper into the line of trees. A frown furrowed his brow as he secured the animal to a low branch, gently stroking the velvet-brown nose. If he should chance not to come back...Nay, when the mist lifted, someone would find the courser, be grateful to care for it. 'Twas a magnificent beast and had served him well on his grim quest.

Untying the crossbow from its place upon the saddle, Jaufre hefted the weapon, slipping back down to the shoreline to begin his impatient vigil. As the morning wore on, the fog lifted but little. As yet there was no sign of the baggage train. He paced along the sandy bank, for the first time questioning the information he had received. If the train were to cross, it must do it soon or risk the incoming tide.

Just when he was certain they had chosen another route or put off the crossing to another day, the mist parted and he saw the first ghostly outlines of laden horses trekking across the sands, the shadowy guides preceding them with their prodding poles.

Jaufre slunk back into the trees. Where was the king? He should have come riding up to meet them. As if in answer to his question, he heard the thunder of approaching hooves. The fog confused his sense of direction, and before he could ascertain from whence the noise came, the riders were almost upon him. He crouched low, his heart thudding with anticipation. The standard-bearer galloped past, the royal banner unfurled, snapping in the wind. As other horses cantered past, Jaufre picked out the rider he sought. John's stumpy figure was nigh swallowed up in the midst of the tall soldiers. But his mantle swept back, revealing the flash of jewels adorning his person.

The king reined to a halt less than a hundred yards from where Jaufre lay hidden. Many of the soldiers dismounted, but the king remained in the saddle, his hand shading his eyes as he squinted in the direction of the approaching horses and wagons.

Using the tree for cover, Jaufre slowly stood up, his grip tightening on the crossbow. Drawing forth a bolt from his pouch, he pointed the bow downward, hooking the bowstring to his belt. Engaging the stirrup with his foot, he cocked the weapon. In the fog-hushed world, even the creak of the bow sounded loud to his ears. He looked anxiously toward the horsemen on the shore, but like the king, their attention was riveted upon the baggage train.

"Majesty," shouted one of the soldiers, "mayhap the baggage train should go back. They waited too long to cross. See where the tide already waxes higher."

John's angry reply carried to Jaufre's ears. "Do you think I mean to wait that long for my treasure to arrive? Simply because my guards are afraid to get their ankles wet! Signal them to hasten."

Hasten? Jaufre's mouth set into a line of grim amusement. Aye, he would *hasten*. Hasten John on his road to hell. He raised the bow to his shoulder. He was so close, he could have reached out and touched one of the guards' horses. But if he retreated, he would be out of range with the weapon. He would never be able to escape, but if the quarrel aimed true, nothing else mattered. They would taste of his steel before he died.

"Majesty!" cried a soldier. "The tide comes in fast. 'Tis already up to the hubs of the wagon wheels."

"Tell those fools to lay on their whips. Hurry!" The king waved his arms, gesturing frantically toward the men fording the river. In another moment, he might ride forward.

Jaufre inched his finger toward the trigger, lining up the king in his sight. He would have only one chance; he must make it count. Through the heart or through the head? If John possessed such an organ as a heart, it was likely so small and shriveled that not even the best marksman in the world would be able to locate it. Through the head, then. His breath stilled, he tipped the bow slightly, taking aim...

The sudden roaring assaulted his ears like thunder.

What by all that was holy...? Jaufre's hand faltered. His gaze was torn from the king, torn away by the sight of the water. Foam-flecked waves and swirling eddies burst over the baggage train, spewing white death as surely as the Red Sea had surged to claim the pharaoh's army.

Screams of men and terrified horses were muted by the pounding of the water. The oncoming rush of tide overran the estuary, catching the baggage train in its pull before it was within reaching distance of the opposite bank.

Jaufre froze, scarce hearing the king's demented cry of "My treasure! My treasure!" John hurled himself into the water, and several of his guards plunged after him.

"Your Majesty! Come back—come back. There is naught to be done."

Jaufre tried to move, but his limbs felt rooted to the spot as the scene imprinted itself upon his mind forever. Hands clawed above the waves, faces contorted with terror, the necks of wild-eyed horses craning, wagons splintering...All were swept away as if two giant arms stretched out, dragging everything in their path out to sea. All that remained was the bubbling green surface of the water.

Stunned, Jaufre lowered his bow. A few lucky men hauled themselves ashore, among them a small bedraggled figure with sparse gray hair plastered to his head. Coughing, sputtering, the dripping form set up such an inhuman wail as chilled the earl's blood, before collapsing in a sodden heap.

Overhead the mist suddenly parted, the sun breaking through like a fierce bright eye glaring down upon the writhing form of the king. The crossbow slipped from Jaufre's fingers, and he stumbled back, shielding his eyes.

He followed the king's army for the next few days as if in a trance, always keeping his distance. Although the soldiers were well within his sight, he never obtained so much as a glimpse of the king.

The unstrung crossbow hung in its place upon his saddle. Jaufre touched it nervously from time to time, his mind trying to reconstruct all that he had seen, find some logical explanation. The baggage train had simply waited too long to cross the estuary. The tide...He closed his eyes. Never would he forget that rampaging fury of white water, swirling men, horses, treasure, to the bottom of the sea. And King John, clenching his heart in agony as if he had been struck down by some invisible hand.

As he trailed after the army through Swineshead, the earl saw that they were heading for the Cistercian abbey where he had left Father Andrew. The king was borne to the gates on a litter, which drew out scores of people from the villages, pressing inside the monastery courtyard to see what had happened.

Jaufre mingled with the crowd of peasants and soldiers, picking up snatches of the conversation around him.

"They say the king be dying, half drowned in the river he was."

"Nay, I heard 'twas poison."

"The shock of losing the royal treasure."

"A surfeit of peaches and new cider. His Majesty gripped with dysentery."

"Nay, you fools." One voice boomed out louder than the others. "He was smitten by the hand of God himself, punished for his wickedness at last."

As Jaufre was jostled by the crowd, he scarce noticed the age-lined hand coming to rest upon his shoulder until he looked down into the anxious blue eyes of Father Andrew.

"Lord Jaufre. God be praised! It is you! When I first heard of the king's arrival, his condition, I greatly feared..." The priest's eyes probed Jaufre's.

The earl replied with a slight shake of his head. He pressed into the old priest's hands the unfired bolt.

"Forgive me, Father," he whispered, "for I have sinned...."

Melyssan lifted the train of her gown, pushing her way through the crowd in the outer court.

Her heart beat so hard against the fabric of her chemise, she thought it must soon burst.

He had come. Come at last, and Father Andrew said she would find him in the part of the church reserved for laymen. She paused by the side door to catch her breath. The priest told her that Jaufre believed both she and Jenny were dead. Mayhap she should wait until Father Andrew had prepared him.

But she could contain herself no longer. With trembling hand, she shoved open the door and stepped inside the cool, dark transept, breathing in the sweet, smoky scent of the ancient incense that had seeped into the stones. The chamber echoed with the distant chants of the choir reciting prayers in Latin for the dying king. Dying, and not by Jaufre's hand. Melyssan murmured her own words of thanks as she stepped farther into the church, her eyes adjusting to the dim light.

The great nave was empty except for one tall knight at the back of the church, who knelt on the cold stone floor, his head bowed. He looked like some devout crusader returned from the holy lands, a gold cross affixed around his neck, his mighty sword laid before him like a sacrificial offering.

He raised his head to the stained-glass window beyond her. She gasped. Surely it could not be...

"Jaufre?"

The whisper was so soft he scarce heard it

above the drone of the chanting monks. Yet it startled him all the same as his eyes came to rest upon the woman standing in the pool of colored light cast by the stained-glass window. The candles on the altar behind her cast a glow around her waving honey-brown hair, half-hidden by the sheen of the gossmer, half-circle veil falling over her delicate shoulders. The pale oval of her face was lost in the shadows, but the slender white hands before her rested lightly on the rounded surface of a cane.

Jaufre blinked at the golden vision, but it did not disappear. He rose slowly to his feet and walked toward it. After what he had seen, it was no longer in him to doubt the presence of another miracle. He moved within touching distance of the shimmering image, spellbound by the shining green eyes, the rose-petal lips trembling with eagerness, the pink flush entering into cheeks sparkling with drops of crystal.

"Jaufre. Oh, my love."

When the vision tried to hurl herself against his chest, he held her back. Too many times had he invited these dreams into his arms only to have them disappear, leaving behind such desolation as would drive him mad. Let him be content to gaze upon this one until she fled as all the others had done before her.

But his hands grasped her shoulders, flesh that was solid, warm even beneath the layers of silk. His fingers grazed the satin texture of her neck, and he felt the pulse beat, strong, steady, alive...alive.

As Melyssan stared at the dazed expression on Jaufre's face, her heart constricted with fear. Father Andrew had warned her he had passed through a grave ordeal. She coaxed back a disorderly lock of raven hair from his brow. "Do not look at me thus, my lord. I am no spirit, I assure you. I am alive, and your daughter as well." Straining upward, she gently brushed his lips with a kiss.

It was as if she had released him from a spell. His entire body shook as he sank to his knees before her.

"Lyssa." His arms encircled her. He buried his face against her waist, great sobs racking his frame. "Lyssa..."

"I'm here, love. I'm here." She held his head close against her, her own tears flowing as she pressed her lips into the midnight strands of hair, her hands gently stroking the nape of his neck. She held him thus for a long time until he quieted, her heart too full to speak. She closed her eyes, reveling in the almost painful joy of having him restored to her.

At last she whispered, "My lord, please rise."

"Nay, I cannot."

She tried to see his face. "Jaufre, what is it? Are—are you ill?"

"Nay." His arms fell to his sides as he drew away from her, tipping his head back, the liquid depths of his rich brown eyes shining with a light she had never seen in them before. No, whispered a voice inside her. She had seen

537

him look thus, such a very long time ago. A tournament on a summer's day.

"I cannot rise, my lady, until you have given me some token of your favor."

"I—I could give you my veil, Sir Knight."

Jaufre's lips curved into a semblance of his old smile. "Only a veil, my lady? I do not think I could any longer be satisfied with just that."

Melyssan felt her pulse skip a beat. "Then what would you ask of me?"

"Your heart, my lady. I will take nothing less."

She took his hand and placed it over the region between her breasts. "It is yours, my lord. It always has been."

He stood, his strong arms drawing her close within their protective circle, his lips pausing inches from her own.

"As I swear that my heart belongs to you, my beautiful Lyssa. Until the day of my death. Aye, the day of my death and beyond."

Then he sealed the vow with all the reverent passion of his kiss.

The light of dawn had not yet filtered through the closed shutters of the small room in the hostelry when Melyssan awoke in her husband's arms. Nearly a week had passed since she had been reunited with Jaufre in the church. But sometimes she could still not believe he was truly restored to her.

She nestled her head against the warmth of

his chest, lightly touching the dark curling hairs, breathing quietly so as not to awaken him. Her face glowed with the memory of the passion they had shared the night before, a mating of their bodies without constraint, each giving freely to the other with no shadows lingering between them, the joining of their flesh as joyous and complete as the union of their hearts.

How deeply he slept, Melyssan thought, feeling the even rise and fall of her husband's chest beneath her hand. She pressed a small kiss against the rough satin of his beard. Peaceful as a babe. Her lips curved into a half smile, half pout. Jaufre seemed to have grown younger, the lines carved by painful memory well-nigh smoothed away until she vowed she would soon feel positively ancient beside him.

Yawning, she stretched out her feet and recoiled in fright when they encountered a solid lump at the end of the bed. Sitting up quickly, she clutched the sheets across her naked breasts. Down below her, something burrowed onto the pallet. She risked a timid touch and encountered a smooth round bottom, a bunched-up shirt, a curly head.

Jenny! Sometime in the night, the child must have slipped away from the kindly woman Melyssan had found to look after her daughter. It was as if, having found her father again, Jenny could scarce bear to let him out of her sight. Sighing, Melyssan tucked a blanket around the form of her sleeping daughter. Would they ever find a nurse capable of keeping pace with the child or, when she had grown, a husband able to tame her indomitable spirit?

Taking care not to wake either Jaufre or the little girl, Melyssan eased herself out of bed. Judging by the pale light seeping through the wooden slats, it must be almost sunrise. She was just drawing the chemise over her head when she was startled by the loud clamor of church bells. She had become accustomed to the deep peal, as it often sounded, marking off the portions of the monks' day. But this clanging was different, ceaseless, urgent.

Jaufre bolted upright in the bed, his expression disoriented at having been awakened so abruptly. He scrambled out of bed, pulling on drawers and tunic. By this time Jenny had wakened and whimpered, rubbing her eyes.

"Fahver. Are more bad soldiers coming?"

"Nay, sweetheart," Jaufre said. He lifted Jenny into his arms, giving her an affectionate hug. "There is naught for you to fear."

But even as he spoke, shouts erupted from the inner courtyard, rising above the thunder of hooves.

"Jaufre?" Melyssan faltered.

Depositing a quick kiss upon her brow, he pushed the shutter open. He slipped his arm about her waist, drawing her closer as the three of them stared out the window.

In the pale light, they could make out the white-robed forms of the monks scurrying from their cells. The pealing of the bells stopped, then a trumpet sounded. Silence descended upon the courtyard, then a loud voice proclaimed, "The king is dead!"

Another moment of silence passed before someone took up the cry. "The king is dead. Long live King Henry!"

"Long live the king!"

Melyssan's hand closed over Jaufre's at her side. Dead. So the nightmare, indeed, had ended. Their greatest enemy, King John, was dead. She glanced up at her husband to see how he received the news.

There was no exultation or even satisfaction in his face. He was not looking toward the court but out past the monastery walls, to the distant horizon. The sky tinted gold and rose as the sun topped the trees.

"We can leave this place now, Lyssa. We can go home again—to Winterbourne."

"But Winterbourne isn't there, Fahver," Jenny protested. "The bad men broke it."

"Then we'll build it again, little one. Stronger than before." He smiled at the child, but his gaze traveled past her to rest upon Melyssan.

"See, Lyssa, how the sun rises over the hills. Is it not beautiful?"

She stared up into the dark-fringed mahogany eyes, shining softly with the light of dreams.

"Aye, my lord. Beautiful."

She rested her head against his shoulder, feeling Jenny's small hand touch her cheek as it curled around Jaufre's neck. Together they watched the dawn of a new day heralding the reign of a new king. New beginnings for their love, for their life together, for England...